He Crushe...

Penelope returned ... on, the savage fire of her desire more heated with every intimate touch.

Never had his kisses been so urgent; never had she craved them more. Every fiber of her being was alive and tingling with pleasure; fire danced beneath her skin.

Sighing her pleasure, Penelope melted against Seth, surrendering to the delicious sensations. His kisses were everything she remembered and more. Her fierce womanly desires were never stronger.

"Come to me, Seth," she whispered. . . .

TOPAZ

Journeys of Passion and Desire

☐ **YESTERDAY'S ROSES by Heather Cullman.** Dr. Hallie Gardiner knows something is terribly wrong with the handsome, haunted-looking man in the great San Francisco mansion. The Civil War had wounded Jake "Young Midas" Parrish, just as it had left Serena, his once-beautiful bride, hopelessly lost in her private universe. But when Serena is found mysteriously dead, Hallie finds herself falling in love with Jake who is now a murder suspect. (405749—$4.99)

☐ **LOVE ME TONIGHT by Nan Ryan.** The war had robbed Helen Burke Courtney of her money and her husband. All she had left was her coastal Alabama farm. Captain Kurt Northway of the Union Army might be the answer to her prayers, or a way to get to hell a little faster. She needed a man's help to plant her crops; she didn't know if she could stand to have a damned handsome Yankee do it. (404831—$4.99)

☐ **FIRES OF HEAVEN by Chelley Kitzmiller.** Independence Taylor had not been raised to survive the rigors of the West, but she was determined to mend her relationship with her father—even if it meant journeying across dangerous frontier to the Arizona Territory. But nothing prepared her for the terrifying moment when her wagon train was attacked, and she was carried away from certain death by the mysterious Apache known only as Shatto. (404548—$4.99)

☐ **RAWHIDE AND LACE by Margaret Brownley.** Libby Summerhill couldn't wait to get out of Deadman's Gulch—a lawless mining town filled with gunfights, brawls, and uncivilized mountain men—men like Logan St. John. He knew his town was no place for a woman and the sooner LIbby and her precious baby left for Boston, the better. But how could he bare to lose this spirited woman who melted his heart of stone forever? (404610—$4.99)

*Prices slightly higher in Canada

Buy them at your local bookstore or use this convenient coupon for ordering.

PENGUIN USA
P.O. Box 999 — Dept. #17109
Bergenfield, New Jersey 07621

Please send me the books I have checked above.
I am enclosing $_____ (please add $2.00 to cover postage and handling). Send check or money order (no cash or C.O.D.'s) or charge by Mastercard or VISA (with a $15.00 minimum). Prices and numbers are subject to change without notice.

Card #_____ Exp. Date _____
Signature_____
Name_____
Address_____
City _____ State _____ Zip Code _____

For faster service when ordering by credit card call **1-800-253-6476**

Allow a minimum of 4-6 weeks for delivery. This offer is subject to change without notice.

Tomorrow's Dreams

Heather Cullman

A TOPAZ BOOK

TOPAZ
Published by the Penguin Group
Penguin Books USA Inc., 375 Hudson Street,
New York, New York 10014, U.S.A.
Penguin Books Ltd, 27 Wrights Lane,
London W8 5TZ, England
Penguin Books Australia Ltd, Ringwood,
Victoria, Australia
Penguin Books Canada Ltd, 10 Alcorn Avenue,
Toronto, Ontario, Canada M4V 3B2
Penguin Books (N.Z.) Ltd, 182-190 Wairau Road,
Auckland 10, New Zealand

Penguin Books Ltd, Registered Offices:
Harmondsworth, Middlesex, England

First Printing, June, 1996
10 9 8 7 6 5 4 3 2 1

 REGISTERED TRADEMARK—MARCA REGISTRADA

Printed in the United States of America

For Madeline Baker,
my RWA big sister and godmother
to my writing career. Because
I'll never be able to tell you in
spoken words just how much your
kindness and generosity
have meant to me.

Sacrifices of the Heart

Such a love can never be.
Better forget me, this cannot be.

—*La Traviata*

Chapter 1

He had to tell her.

Seth Tyler closed his eyes and rested his face against the hansom cab window, letting the rain-chilled glass cool his hot skin. Never had he felt so wretchedly alone, never had he been so afraid. And never had he known such crushing despair.

He choked as burning gall rose in his throat, strangling him with nausea. At that moment he'd have lost the contents of his stomach, had he been able to put anything in it in the first place. He'd been too heartsick to eat so much as a morsel since the Pinkerton agent had revealed the unspeakable truth about his parentage early that morning.

It was that truth he needed to tell Penelope.

But how could he tell her? How could he bear to see her face contort with revulsion when he made his hideous confession? How could he survive the crippling grief of losing her?

And lose her he would, he had no choice. For how could he marry her knowing what he was and what he was destined to become?

As Seth searched for the courage to face his coming ordeal, the wheel of the trundling cab struck a deep pothole at the corner of Seventeenth Street and Irving Place, the same hole hit by every other driver who had driven him to the theater that week. The impact of the sudden lurch caused Seth's cheek to slam painfully against the window glass, warning him of his imminent arrival at the Academy of Music.

Too weary to raise his hand and soothe the soreness from his cheek, he merely opened his eyes and gazed dully at the rain-spattered world outside. Halos of fog from his heated breath misted the glass until the passing structures resembled a gaslit landscape viewed through a gauze-draped stereograph.

The cab slowed to a crawl as it approached the corner of Fourteenth and Irving, the driver jockeying for a place in the long line of carriages and cabs picking up the departing theatergoers. With a lurch the cabby cut in between a coupé and a lagging brougham, drawing a flurry of obscenities from the brougham's driver. Now in line, the cab came to a standstill.

"Penelope Parrish was excellent tonight," Seth heard a shrill voice announce from a knot of passersby.

"Extraordinary, that gel," boomed the woman's companion. "A voice like an angel, a face and figure to match. A rarity for an opera singer. Most of them look like worn-out brood mares." That remark drew squeals of indignation from the women.

Chuckling, the man added, "Mark my words, that gel has a bright future ahead of her. And all I can say to that is a hearty—brava!" As the rain began anew, the group hurried past Seth's cab, their voices fading with distance as they rushed to secure the shelter of their own waiting carriages.

Penelope Parrish. Extraordinary. Beautiful. Talented. Seth smiled with gentle pride. *His Penelope.*

But not for long, his conscience warned him.

Something deep inside him snapped at that reminder, and if he hadn't been in such a public place, he would have raised his fist to the heavens and screamed his fury.

He didn't deserve to have his life destroyed like this! Damn it to hell! He'd earned the right to a good life! He'd worked long and fought hard for everything he had. In the process he'd tried to be a good man, and in his own mind he'd succeeded. So why . . . dear God! . . . tell him why now, when he'd finally reached the pinnacle of his success and had found a love such as he'd never dreamed possible, was he handed this verdict of damnation?

Seth buried his face into his gloved hands, a sob tearing from his throat. What was he going to do? Grief, raw and violent, bubbled up from deep within, threatening to break through the fragile barrier of his composure at any moment. The most devastating part of his curse was that he was going to lose Penelope. He had no choice . . . he had to let her go.

His stomach twisted into agonizing knots as Seth contemplated his dismal life without Penelope. She was everything to him. She was his joy in life, his reason to smile. Everything he did, his every financial success, his personal triumph, he did for her, all in his endless quest to be worthy of her. He'd die inside without the nourishment of her love. He'd shrivel up until he was little more than a shell of a man . . . just like his newly discovered father.

Dear God! Was he truly condemned to share his father's fate? Was he doomed to spend his days bound naked to an asylum wall, despised and ignored, left to die alone? Would his life become a madness-wracked hell on earth from which death would be his only release? This wasn't to be his fate, was it?

But how could he escape it? More damning, more disturbing than the fact that he had been spawned by a madman was the horrifying catalyst that had lead his father to be confined to the asylum: His father had forced himself on his own sister.

And Seth was the cursed offspring of that rape.

So now, knowing of his tainted blood, knowing what he was and what he was doomed to become, how could he, in good conscience, marry Penelope? She was so beautiful and talented; she had such a bright future ahead of her. She deserved a man who had a future as well. A husband who would be there to cheer her on, to share and encourage her in her success; one who would give her children to carry on the legacy of her dazzling gift.

"Sir?"

Seth dropped his hands from his face to stare blankly at the cabby, who was peering at him with an expression of concern.

"You gonna be sick, sir?"

Seth forced himself to smile at the man. "No. Why?"

"We've been sittin' here a long time. The other drivers are gettin' antsy for us to move on."

Seth glanced out the window, frowning. While he'd been locked in his private hell, the cab had made its way to the front of the line and was now directly in front of the theater doors.

For a long moment Seth watched the throng of departing theatergoers mill beneath the entry portico. Somehow he had to find the courage to cut through that smiling horde, make his way backstage, and tell Penelope the truth.

For one wild instant it was on the tip of his tongue to tell the driver to take him back to his hotel, to say to hell with honor and simply flee without a word of explanation.

But, of course, he couldn't do that. Penelope was waiting for him, expecting him to take her to dinner at Sherry's. She trusted him, and she had a right to hear the truth. She also deserved the privilege of being the one to break their engagement. At least that way she'd be able to salvage her pride.

After paying the driver his fare, Seth strode through the jostling crowd on the sidewalk, past the knots of gossiping theatergoers in the lobby and into the auditorium.

Aside from two musicians, who were at the far end of the orchestra pit packing up their instruments and music, the gaudily gilded theater was as deserted as a barroom on Sunday morning. The crimson plush stage curtains were open, probably to adjust the scenery, and Seth paused to stare up at the impressive setting.

This was the first night since he'd arrived in New York that he'd missed a performance. For a moment he wondered if Penelope had noted his absence . . . after all, his borrowed seat was in one of the coveted stage boxes, courtesy of his friend and business associate, William C. Schermerhorn. With a faint smile he dismissed the idea. When Penelope was wrapped up in her singing, the rest of the world, save that created by the magic of the opera, ceased to exist for her.

Leaning against the railing in front of him, Seth visualized Penelope on the stage. She was presently performing in Wagner's *The Flying Dutchman,* singing the role of the beautiful, yet doomed, heroine, Senta.

She was magnificent as Senta, but never more so than during those last dramatic moments when she stood on the cliff, her white gown whipping in the wind in the wake of *The Flying Dutchman*'s hell-spawned tempest, her voice soaring with heartrending emotion as she sang, *"Hier steh' ich treu dir bis zum Tod!* . . . Here I stand, faithful to you until death!"

Faithful to you until death? Seth's heart seemed to still in his chest. What if, like Senta, Penelope insisted on sacrificing her life for him? In his self-pitying preoccupation, he hadn't considered the possibility that she might insist on marrying him, despite the overwhelming odds against their future happiness.

That thought was enough to turn his blood to ice. Hell! It was more than just a possibility that she might refuse to break their engagement. Knowing that stubborn woman, it was damn likely. Despite the fact that she'd been rather preoccupied with her career of late, and rightfully so considering her brilliant success, he knew that she loved him. Hadn't she shown him in the most intimate possible way just last night?

So what was he to do? Just the idea of her witnessing his shameful spiral into madness humiliated him beyond all endurance.

Convulsively he grasped on to the pit railing. He had to break their engagement. Now while his pain was still raw and his resolution firm.

But what if she cried? A cold ball of dread lodged deep in his throat at that thought. How was he to hold firm if she grew soft and pleading? How could he say no to her now, when he'd never been able to do so in the past?

His shoulders sagged with defeat. He'd simply have to find a way. He had to do something . . . anything to end their relationship.

Forever.

Chapter 2

"Wh-what happened?" Penelope gasped, starting at the sight of the hovering angel.

There was a clomping of boots; then Julian Tibbett, who sang the role of Erik, her huntsman betrothed, appeared in her line of vision next to the angel. "Ah, so you've finally decided to rejoin the world of the living, have you? You had us worried."

Penelope cringed at his choice of words. "You were worried." She jerked her head in the direction of the angel.

Julian let out a whoop of laughter, while the angel simply looked confused. Then dawning lit her face, and she too laughed.

Smiling faintly, Penelope insisted, "It was a shock to wake up and see an angel hovering over me like a blue-and-gold-clad vulture. For a moment I thought I'd died and gone to heaven."

"A vulture, eh?" Julian stroked his sleek black mustache, his dark-eyed gaze sweeping the length of the angel as if comparing her appearance to that of the rapacious bird.

The angel released an indignant squawk and punched his arm.

Grinning broadly, he looped his arm around the girl's waist and pulled her close to his side. "Pen, let me introduce you to your guardian vulture, Elizabeth Hempal. She'll be replacing Mathilde Meisslinger as one of the angels in next week's production of *Faust*."

Penelope returned the girl's cordial nod, wincing as her neck spasmed with a crick. "What happened to Mattie?" she asked, reaching up to massage the sore area.

"She got a better offer from Samuel Pike. Since I knew Lizzie, here, happened to be available, I suggested that she be hired as a replacement. When our harpy wardrobe mistress heard of the change, she insisted that our new angel try on the costume this very evening, just in case it needs adjustments. Hence"—he made a sweeping motion down the length of Lizzie's body—"the getup." Casting an appreciative glance at the woman's impressive bosom, which looked ready to pop out of the too tight bodice at her next breath, he added, "As you can see, it's a perfect fit."

Lizzie released a musical giggle and playfully slapped his lean cheek. "You're an out-and-out bounder, Julian!"

"True," he returned, eyeing her as though she was a sheep and he was a wolf with mutton on his mind. "However, if you go change your clothes, I'll take you to the German Winter Garden and let you mend my wicked ways."

Lizzie hesitated, glancing uncertainly at Penelope. "It doesn't seem right to leave Miss Parrish alone."

"She won't be alone. I'll be here."

By the weight of Lizzie's frown, Julian's reassurance had done nothing to assuage her concern.

"Never fear, sweet Lizzie," he crooned in a dulcet tone. "I may be a bounder, but I'm no fool. Miss Parrish has a fiancé who looks capable of breaking me in half should I behave improperly. Now, seeing as how I like being in one piece"—he straightened up and clasped his hands in front of him—"I'll stand here pious as a praying saint until the doctor arrives."

Wringing her hands with indecision, Lizzie glanced down at Penelope, who smiled and nodded her approval. For all his rakish reputation, Penelope knew she'd be perfectly safe in Julian's company. Though he had expressed a less than brotherly interest in her when she'd first joined the company, he'd respected her rebuffs to his advances, and over time they had become friends.

Having gained Penelope's blessing, Lizzie practically flew from the room.

"She seems nice," Penelope commented, struggling to sit up. While pretty to look at, the rose damask chaise upon which she lay certainly left much to be desired when it came to comfort.

"Lie down!" Julian barked. When she didn't immediately comply, he threatened, "If you don't lie back down this second, I'll take that fiancé of yours aside and tell him what a stubborn wench you are."

Penelope laughed. "I'm afraid it's too late for that. He's well aware of my willful ways."

"And he still wants to marry you?" Julian released a dramatic sigh. "Ah, well. I can't say as I blame him. One glimpse of those dimples of yours would be enough to convince any man to overlook a number of faults far worse than mere obstinacy. *However*"—he crossed his arms and fixed her with a severe stare—"in this particular instance, I'm certain that your Mr. Tyler would insist on your obedience, as I am now."

"But all this tufting is lumpy." She poked at the knobby surface with a grimace. "My back feels as if I've been lying on a bed of rocks."

Julian seized a velvet pillow from the overstuffed chair opposite the chaise and held it up by its fringe trim. "Down-filled," he announced, lightly punching it with his free hand to demonstrate its softness. With that, he slipped it beneath her back and shoulders. "There. Now, no more arguments. Lie down."

Penelope shot him a mutinous look.

"Now!" That single word warned her quite succinctly that if she didn't obey, he'd make her.

"This is ridiculous," she groused, settling back against the cushion with a beleaguered sigh. "I'm perfectly fine."

"Fine?" He raised one black eyebrow. "You came backstage after the last curtain and"—he slapped his palms together with a loud *smack!*—"fainted. That's hardly what I call fine."

"But I've never fainted in my life," she protested softly.

"Well, there's a first time for everything."

But why now, she wondered, more unsettled by the episode than she cared to admit. She'd never been a delicate sort of female, and she'd certainly never been one for swooning. So what had happened? Her brow creased. Granted, the theater had been rather stuffy tonight, and she hadn't been feeling at her best the last few days. Still—

"Lizzie was waiting in the wings to show me her costume, and you practically fainted at her feet," Julian added, his voice cutting into her musings. "It was she who ordered me to carry you to your dressing room and sent the stage manager for a doctor."

Too uncomfortable to endure the torments of the bumpy chaise a second longer, Penelope pushed herself into a sitting position, murmuring, "I'll have to remember to thank her." To her mortification, gravity sent the bodice of her unhooked gown slipping down her arm, exposing an indecent amount of lacy chemise and embroidered corset. As she wrestled it back up onto her shoulder, she felt her loosened corset begin to slip as well.

Like the gentleman he normally wasn't, Julian turned and sauntered over to the dressing table, where he pretended to study the extravagant bouquet of white roses Seth had sent. "By the way," he said, without turning from the flowers, "Lizzie made me wait outside while she loosened your cors— uh— garments."

Smiling at Julian's uncharacteristically delicate reference to her underclothes, Penelope tied her corset strings and latched the top hook of her gown. Decent now, she sat on the edge of the chaise and flexed her stiff muscles, teasing, "You're going to wilt those flowers if you stare at them any harder."

With a blasé shrug, Julian turned to face her. "So? That fiancé of yours sends you a fresh bouquet every evening." Grimacing as if someone had stuck a pin into his backside, he muttered, "I'd hate to see the man's florist bill."

"Seth does spoil me," she conceded, starting to rise.

In the blink of an eye, Julian was by her side, pushing her back down again. "You really should lie down until after the doctor has examined you."

Penelope smiled up into her friend's face, touched by his expression of grave concern. "I feel fine. Really. It must have been the heat from the footlights that caused me to faint."

"Be that as it may, it would be wise to wait and make sure you're all right."

"Surely it can't hurt me to sit at my dressing table?" she argued. "Seth will be here soon, and I want to remove my greasepaint before he arrives.

After considering her request for a moment, he nodded with obvious reluctance. "All right. But don't even think of moving from that table."

As Penelope lurched unsteadily to her feet, eager to prepare herself for Seth's arrival, her foot tangled in the trailing hem of her costume. She would have fallen had Julian not caught her. As his arms whipped around her waist to steady her, the single hook holding the back of her gown together gave way, and again her bodice slid down over her shoulders.

At that moment, as Penelope half stood and half lay in Julian's arms with her sagging bodice exposing more than a glimpse of her bosom, there was a firm rapping on the door. Before she could think, much less respond, the door swung open.

On the threshold stood Seth.

Her heart leapt with pleasure at the sight of him. Smiling with all the love she felt inside, she pulled herself from Julian's grasp and opened her arms to welcome him into her embrace. "Seth! Darling!"

Seth didn't say a word, nor did he acknowledge her greeting with so much as a glance. His stare was burning into Julian. Without letting his gaze waver, he stepped into the room, slamming the door behind him.

Julian stumbled backward, blanching the color of ashes. "This isn't how it looks," he choked, visibly quailing.

Seth's stare grew more intense. "Oh?"

Penelope dropped her arms to her sides, taken aback by the implication of his monosyllabic utterance. "You don't think that Julian and I were . . ." She released a shaky laugh.

Seth's gaze cut from Julian to Penelope. "What the hell am I supposed to think when I find my fiancée half-naked and lounging in another man's arms?" He practically spat the words.

Penelope flinched, stung by his accusation. "I wasn't lounging," she retorted. "And I'm certainly not half-naked!"

With insulting thoroughness, Seth's glittering gaze raked the length of her body, taking in every incriminating detail of her disheveled appearance. Suddenly his eyes stilled, as if arrested, and a grim smile twisted his lips. "Really?"

Penelope followed his line of vision to her breasts, gasping as she noted the way her nipples were clearly visible through the sheer cambric of her chemise. In her joy at seeing Seth, she'd completely disregarded her state of undress, never once pausing to consider that he might think the worse of her admittedly compromising situation. After all, he knew that she loved him and that she'd never do anything to jeopardize their future together.

Or did he? With suddenly nerveless fingers, she yanked her bodice up. Of course Seth knew how she felt. Hadn't she shown him how much he meant to her? She'd bestowed upon him the greatest gifts a woman could give a man: her love, loyalty, trust, and devotion. She'd promised him her forever.

Most significant of all, she'd given him her innocence. Shouldn't that in itself be enough to prove the depth of her commitment to him and their upcoming nuptials? Shouldn't the mere fact that she'd been a virgin when he'd first taken her two months ago be proof that she was no woman of easy virtue?

As she ineffectually attempted to secure the hooks at the back of her costume, her indignation at Seth's jealous suspicion escalated into self-righteous outrage. How dare he have so little faith in her and her love! How dare he sully her character with his contemptible accusations!

As Penelope fumbled with the contrary fastenings, her cheeks burning with resentment, Julian moved to gallantly shield her from Seth's insolent stare. Holding out his open hands to Seth in a gesture of supplication, he entreated, "If you'll listen for a moment, I can explain everything."

"And what are you going to tell me?" Seth pinned the man with his disdainful gaze. "That my fiancée somehow just happened to fall into your arms?"

"Well, yes," Julian admitted, realizing how improbable his explanation was going to sound. "Miss Parrish did fall, and it was only by a stroke of luck that I was near enough to catch her."

Seth lifted one tawny eyebrow. "Let me guess. Miss Parrish, who I happen to know has the constitution of a pack mule, succumbed to a fit of vapors, and being the gentleman you are, you rushed to her rescue." His jaw hardened into an angry line. "Of course, as a good samaritan, you felt it was your Christian duty to undress her."

Julian stiffened. "How dare you imply that I'd take advantage of a helpless woman, or of any woman for that matter!"

"I don't have to imply anything," Seth countered, his voice laced with biting scorn. "One has only to look at the children one sees clinging to the skirts of half the women in the chorus to see the evidence of your satyric machinations."

Julian advanced toward his antagonist, his face darkening to the color of aged claret. "I ought to drag you out into the alley and throttle you within an inch of your life for casting such aspersions against my character," he hissed.

"Try it." By his aggressive stance, it was obvious that Seth was spoiling for a fight.

"Stop this nonsense immediately . . . both of you!" Penelope pushed past Julian's anger-stiffened form to stand between the two men, both of whom looked ready to burst into violence at any moment. Facing Seth squarely, she said, "Despite what you're thinking, nothing happened between Julian and me. The simple truth is that in spite of my, as you so vulgarly put it, pack-mule constitution, I fainted after the final curtain. Julian was kind enough to carry me in here. If you don't believe me, you can ask anyone in the cast or crew. Go ask Elizabeth Hempal. She was the one who loosened my garments and was with me up until about five minutes ago."

Seth broke free of his glaring match with Julian long enough to cast her an incredulous look. "Oh? And why did this Elizabeth do something as improper as leave you alone in a state of undress with Don Juan here?" He jerked his thumb at Julian.

Penelope grabbed Julian's arm as he lunged at Seth, halting him. "Julian, please. Let me handle this."

After what seemed like a lifetime . . . a very long, tense one . . . he nodded. Giving him a grateful look, Penelope dropped her hand from his arm and turned back to Seth. His cynical expression made her long to take a few punches at him herself.

Firmly ordering herself not to say or do anything to further inflame the explosive situation at hand, she pressed her fists into the folds of her skirt and explained, "Lizzie and Julian have plans to go to the German Winter Garden this evening, and I saw no harm in her leaving me with Julian while she readied herself. The stage manager has gone for the doctor, and they should be arriving any minute now. We wouldn't have been alone for long."

Seth's eyes narrowed slightly as he seemed to consider her words. "Let me get this straight. You fainted right after the final curtain call? Correct?"

Penelope nodded.

Seth returned her nod. "All right. I'll buy that."

Heaving a sigh of relief, Penelope unclenched her tense hands. "I knew you'd see reason after you heard—"

Seth cut her off with a commanding sweep of his hand. "You fainted and Julian carried you in here. Then what?"

"I already told you what happened." Despite her best efforts to maintain an even tone, a querulous note crept into her voice.

He shrugged one shoulder. "Tell me again."

Unable to mask her aggravation a second longer, Penelope rolled her eyes toward the heavens and recited in a purposely monotone voice, "Lizzie had Julian carried me to my dressing room. After I was feeling a bit better, I gave her permission to go change out of her costume. Julian stayed with me." She shot Seth a defiant look. "Believe it or not, that's God's own truth."

"I believe it."

"Good. Now that we've got that settled, you can apologize to Julian. Then we'll all forget this whole ridiculous incident. Agreed?" She glanced expectantly from Seth to Julian. When Julian didn't respond, she gave him a severe look.

"Oh, all right," he relented. "I'll agree to forget the whole episode if Mr. Tyler apologizes. But only because you and I are friends, and he happens to be your fiancé."

Penelope gave him an approving look before transferring her gaze to Seth. "Seth?" she prodded.

"No."

"No? What do you mean, no?" She braced her hands on her hips, meeting his scowl with one of her own. "Julian has agreed to excuse your appalling behavior if you'll apologize. Why can't you be gracious as well and give him the apology he deserves?"

"Who says he deserves an apology?"

Releasing an irate growl, Julian lurched forward, his fists up and ready to strike. Again Penelope foiled his attack, this time by grabbing his elbow. "Julian! I said I'd handle this!"

Without waiting for his response, she released his arm and took a couple of steps toward Seth. Titling her head back, she peered up into his stony face. "Whatever has gotten into you, Seth?" she chided. "You said that you believed my explanation."

"So?"

She let out an irritated snort. "So . . . with that admission you also concede to have wrongly accused Julian of ungentlemanly behavior. Surely you can see why you owe him an apology? Even the lowest gutter rat has that much honor."

Seth laughed, but in an awful, humorless way. "True enough, my love. True enough." His lips contorted into a bitter line. "Even a gutter rat such as myself knows that it is proper to tender an apology . . . when one is due."

"You're deliberately twisting my words!" she snapped. "You know I wasn't calling you a gutter rat. I was simply using the term to illustrate—"

He cut her off with another laugh. "Words uttered in haste are always more candid than their well-considered counterparts. Invariably they reflect the speaker's true thoughts."

"But—" she sputtered.

"But we're digressing," he interjected in a cool tone. "I was about to give you my reason for not rushing to apologize to your professedly blameless Mr. Tibbett. While I admit to believing your explanation as to what he is doing in your dressing room, there are still a few things that have yet to be clarified."

"Such as?"

"Such as what you were doing in his arms just now."

His baiting tone, not to mention his goading smirk, was enough to make Penelope's foot itch to kick him. "For your information, *Mr. Tyler,* I insisted on getting up and going to my dressing table to prepare myself for your arrival . . . *against* Julian's better judgment. When I stood up, I tripped over my hem, and as Julian explained, he caught me. You just happened to walk in before I'd had a chance to right myself."

"Getting up after what?" His voice was ladened with a wealth of lurid insinuation. "It seems to me that he'd have had to be mighty close to have been near enough to catch you like he did."

"For God's sake, man! Be reasonable!" Julian exploded.

"Reasonable would be to kill you for dallying with my fiancée," Seth shot back.

"We weren't dallying!" Penelope objected, while Julian narrowed his eyes and clenched his fists tighter.

Seth's face could have been carved from marble for all the warmth it possessed. "You have your definitions and I have mine. And in my book, engaging in the kind of amorous play I witnessed when I walked into this room qualifies as a dalliance."

Roaring his rage, Julian hurled himself at Seth, knocking Penelope to the floor in the process.

Years of street fighting had made Seth an expert at self-defense, and he easily caught the other man's fist before it—

connected with his jaw. In one fluid motion he wrestled his attacker's arm behind his back, wrenching it until the man yelped with pain.

Scrambling to her knees, Penelope cried, "Don't, Seth! Please don't hurt him!" When he continued to glare down at Julian, pointedly ignoring her pleas, she crawled over and frantically tugged at the hem of his evening cape. "Please, Seth."

The silence was thunderous as Seth slowly shifted his gaze from the grimacing man in his grasp to the woman kneeling at his feet. "Please let him go," she entreated, her fingers tightening around the bunched fabric in her palm. "For me?"

Making a disgusted sound deep in his throat, Seth looked away. Roughly seizing Julian by the hair with his free hand, he yanked his head back, forcing him to meet his gaze.

"Since Miss Parrish seems to harbor a fondness for you and pleads so prettily on your behalf, I'm going to give you one chance to exit this room on your own accord. You'll walk through that door and leave me and Miss Parrish to finish our business in private." He jerked the man's head back farther. "Understood?"

"If you think I'm going to leave Miss Parrish alone to face your abuse—"

In the blink of an eye, Seth released Julian's hair and savagely slammed his forearm against his windpipe, effectively silencing him. "Damn you, Tibbett. I ought to strangle you here and now for even implying that I'd strike a woman."

Julian clawed ineffectually at Seth's garroting arm, gurgling hideously. Terrified that she was about to witness murder, Penelope furiously pummeled Seth's legs. "Seth! No! You're killing him!"

Seth glared down at her, the steely command in his eyes directing her to cease her flailing attack. As if under some dark spell, her arms fell to her sides. Visibly easing his pressure on Julian's throat, he rasped, "Never fear, Princess. I won't kill your lover. Even I'm not heartless enough to leave you without solace in the wake of our broken engagement."

Penelope heard his words, and her mind registered their meaning, but she was too incensed to care.

With his arm still wrapped around Julian's throat, Seth marched him to the door and flung him out into the hall. There was a loud *thud* as his body bounced off the facing wall, a sound accompanied by the buzz of shocked voices. Apparently their argument had drawn attention.

Pausing briefly on the threshold, probably, Penelope thought sourly, to intimidate the crowd with his glower, Seth ordered, "Please relay the message that Miss Parrish and I don't wish to be disturbed." With that, he slammed the door and faced her.

Infuriated beyond all reason, Penelope sprang to her feet and stalked across the room, stopping directly in front of him. "How dare you!" she spat. "How dare you humiliate me like this!"

"You humiliate yourself by carrying on with a womanizing bastard like Julian Tibbett," he sneered.

Bristling like a cat with its fur ruffled the wrong way, she hissed, "You're the bastard, not Julian. And if you were half the man I thought you were, you would have listened to reason instead of jumping to sordid conclusions as you did."

His eyes flickering like twin flames, Seth slowly leaned forward until his face was just inches from hers. In a voice that was little more than a savage whisper, he replied, "Then, perhaps you don't really know what kind of man I am after all."

Penelope jerked her face away from his. "Apparently not. The Seth I know and love would never have made such vile accusations.

"And the Penelope I wanted to marry wouldn't have insulted me by whoring with a sorry excuse of a man like Julian Tibbett."

"Damn it, Seth! I wasn't doing anything illicit with Julian." It was all she could do not to stamp her foot in anger. "I can't understand why you're having such a hard time believing me. I've never given you any reason to doubt my loyalty."

"The little scene I witnessed between you and Julian just now gives me every reason to doubt it." He let his cool gaze slide from her face to focus on her waistline. "Though I was blinded by your false sweetness, I now see you for the faithless jade you are, and I'm not about to be cuckolded into giving my name to the evidence of your infidelity when it makes an appearance in say ... eight or nine months."

Never in her life had Penelope hated anyone as much as she hated Seth Tyler at that moment. Desperate to hurt him as badly as he had just hurt her, she lashed back, "If you think that I'd even consider marrying you after the way you treated me this evening, well ..." She shot him a look that should have knocked him dead on the spot. "I wouldn't marry you if marriage was my only salvation from eternal damnation and you were the last bachelor on earth. Your offensive behavior has proved that you're nothing but ... but ... a gutter rat trussed up like a gentleman!"

Seth eyed her with contempt. "Perhaps. But even this gutter rat has higher standards than to tie himself to a slut like you."

"Fine! Then, go! Take your so-called standards and return to whatever sewer you crawled from."

"Oh. I'm going, but not to the sewer. I wouldn't want to run the risk of encountering you and Tibbett's bastard down there."

Tears of impotent rage sprang to Penelope's eyes. "I'd rather live in the foulest of sewers than in a fine palace with a contemptible bastard like you." With that, she sank down on the bench before her dressing table, tears coursing hotly down her cheeks. For a long moment she wept in silence, wanting nothing more than to hear the door slam behind the exiting Seth so she could freely release the fury of her emotions.

When he didn't leave, she choked out, "Go, damn you! ... Get out and stay out! I never want to see your arrogant face again!"

"Princess ..."

So soft was the utterance that Penelope was uncertain whether or not she'd truly heard it. Puzzled, she began to turn to face him, then stopped herself. Considering the brutal nature of their exchange, it was unlikely that Seth would be whispering her nickname, and in such an anguished tone. Apparently she was more hysterical than she thought and was hearing things.

But what if he had spoken? What if, by some miracle, the enormity of what had passed between them was just now sinking in, and he'd regained enough of his sense to realize what his made fit of jealous rage had cost him? What if his whisper had been a tentative plea for a chance to mend the rift between them?

Logic told her that she was hearing things, while her savaged pride commanded her to stem the torrent of irrational hope flooding her heart. He'd given her every reason to hate him, and if she had even an ounce of self-respect she'd march to that door and have him tossed out on his impeccably tailored backside.

Yet deep in the core of her wounded heart she refused to accept that their love could be so easily destroyed by a misunderstanding. Surely after all they had shared, their bond was strong enough to withstand this test of faith?

Hoping, yet not truly believing, that Seth shared her feelings and now sought to make amends, Penelope stole a glance at his reflection in the silvery circle of her looking glass. He was standing by the door, simply watching her.

Her breath strangled in her throat as his reflected gaze touched hers. The crushing ache in his eyes perfectly mirrored her own, and in that wrenching moment she could have sworn that she saw a shadow of regret pass through their unguarded depths. As quickly as it appeared, it disappeared, leaving her wondering if it had been there at all. In the next instant the indifferent gleam was back, and she was certain that she'd only imagined it.

Bitter disappointment flooded through her, forcing her to face the appalling truth: Despite his lack of faith in her love, despite all the atrocious things he'd said and done this evening, she still loved Seth Tyler.

Hating herself for harboring such desires, and hating him even more for possessing the power to evoke them, she picked up the first thing that came under her hand and flung it across the room at him. Oddly enough, she took no satisfaction from his grunt of pain when her silver-handled hair brush slammed into his midsection. She felt only soul-shattering grief.

Unable to bear the sight of him and all the turbulent feelings it provoked within her, she shrieked, "Get out, damn you! Now! Before I have you thrown out like the trash you are!"

Without a word he turned on his heels and followed her command. As the door closed behind him, Penelope surrendered to her sorrow.

Chapter 3

Penelope was miserable, more miserable than she'd ever been in her life. Not only was she soul-sick and heartbroken; her back felt as if it were being wrenched on a rack, and her stomach roiled with unrelenting queasiness.

Something was dreadfully wrong with her, she was sure of it.

After performing a cursory examination the night before, Dr. Goodwin, the physician who had been fetched by the stage manager after she'd fainted, had sternly ordered her to come to his office first thing in the morning. Though his tone had been cheerful and his smile reassuring, he'd evaded all her questions regarding her condition by saying that he needed to examine her further before he could make a conclusive diagnosis.

But she hadn't been fooled. No, not for a second. She was certain she'd detected an underlying note of concern beneath the matter-of-fact calm of his voice.

Now, as she sat in his cozy office, waiting for him to report the findings from the embarrassingly thorough examination he'd just performed, Penelope wondered if perhaps she was dying. After all, how could she possibly feel this wretched and not have one foot in the grave?

Nervously she plucked at the beaded purse on her lap, considering the ghastly possibility. Then she released a choked sob. Yes, that had to be the case. She was dying. Dr. Goodwin had probably suspected as much last night and was simply stalling for time while he thought of a tactful way to tell her.

Sobbing again, she reached around and rubbed at her sore lower back. As she attempted to ease the dull ache through the thick barrier of her gown and corset, she mournfully wondered how Seth would react to the news of her death.

He would hear of it, that much was certain, even if their

paths never again crossed during the pitifully brief time she had left on the earth. After all, her older brother, Jake, was his best friend and business partner.

Heaving a dejected little sigh, she dropped her hand from her back. Would the heartless—and she knew for sure after last night that he had no heart—Mr. Tyler care that she'd died? Would he feel even a smidgen of guilt or regret over all the terrible things he'd said during their final moments together?

She released another sigh, this one heavier, and settled back into the tapestry-upholstered wing chair. She hoped he'd be devastated by the news. It would serve him right to suffer as badly as he was now making her suffer. If he wept a hundred times more tears than she'd shed during the previous night, it wouldn't be penitence enough in her mind.

Absently she fidgeted with the beaded strap handle of her purse, her spirits lifting slightly as she imagined a very remorseful Seth at her funeral.

She would look beautiful, of course, like an angel, dressed in her new ivory silk and lace Worth gown. Clutching her cold, lifeless hand in his, he would fervently whisper words of love and regret, his anguish increasing a tenfold as he reminded himself that his declarations came too late. And as he pressed kisses on her death-paled lips, keening his sorrow between his sobs, he would wish that he too were dead, for only death could end the torment of knowing that he had lost her forever. Just as she was envisioning a broken and wailing Seth being wrestled away from her casket by her brother, Dr. Goodwin entered the office.

Drawing her mind from her morbid, yet satisfying daydream, Penelope looked up at the doctor. There was a no-nonsense air of competence about the gray-haired man that had instantly instilled a sense of trust in her. Right now his face wore a troubled frown . . . not an expression she found particularly reassuring.

After setting himself into his leather desk chair, he sat in silence for several moments, peering at her through the thick lenses of his spectacles as if unsure how to begin. Harrumphing once, he finally spoke. "Miss Parrish—it is Miss, isn't it?"

Oddly enough, Penelope could have sworn that she saw a spark of hope flash in his eyes as he inquired as to her marital status. Giving him a questioning look, she nodded. "It's Miss."

"Ah . . . yes . . . I see . . ." He cleared his throat loudly, as if plagued with the world's most stubborn frog. When he continued to speak, his expression was every bit as disconcerted as if he'd indeed swallowed one of the web-footed creatures. "May I be so bold as to ask if you have any— *har-rumph!*—plans to be married in the near future?"

The day before yesterday, she could have joyfully and honestly replied, "Yes. I'm to be married on December twenty-third." But now . . .

Overwhelmed with a wrenching sense of loss, Penelope stared down at her purse strap, which she'd somehow managed to knot around her index finger, hiding the moisture in her eyes. "No. I have no wedding plans." Her voice trembled with unshed tears.

She heard him release a heavy sigh. "Then I'm afraid I have some very distressing news for you. It seems you're expecting a baby. Your delicate condition is why you fainted last night."

Penelope's gaze flew to his face, and she could feel her jaw drop. She couldn't have been more shocked if he'd told her that she was suffering from some hideous and exotic disease like leprosy or the bubonic plague. "A b-baby?" she stuttered. "How can I be expecting a baby?"

Dr. Goodwin looked nonplussed at that. "Surely you're not trying to tell me that you're ignorant of the facts of life?"

"Of course not. I know . . ." Penelope gave the knotted strap around her finger an agitated tug. "My sister-in-law is a doctor, and she explained the . . . uh . . . ways between men and women to me."

"A female doctor?" He stared at her, visibly taken aback by her revelation. "*Har-rumph!* Yes . . . er . . . in that case, I assume you know that your condition comes from having relations with a man?"

"Yes, but I didn't think . . ." She shook her head helplessly.

"It's apparent that you didn't think," he pointed out dryly. "If you had, you would have considered the consequences of such actions and restrained your . . . er . . . carnal impulses."

Penelope's cheeks burned at the condemnation in his tone. "What I don't understand is why I didn't realize"—she gestured toward her belly, unwilling to voice her shameful condition.

The doctor frowned, but more in an expression of perplexity than censure. "Surely you've noticed changes in your body?"

"Changes?"

"Such as a cessation of your menses. When was the last time you had your monthlies?"

"A couple of months ago"—she shrugged—"I think. I don't know. I've never been, well, regular."

He nodded thoughtfully. "And did you have intimate relations around two months ago?"

"Yes, but it was my first time. I was sure that it was impossible to get pregnant the first time."

"Is that what the female doctor told you?"

"No, of course not. But—"

"There are no 'buts' about it," he interjected firmly. "You got caught your first time—not an uncommon occurrence, I might add—and according to my calculations, your baby will be born mid-September."

Penelope's initial numbness gave way to a full-blown case of panic. "But I can't have a baby!" she blurted out wildly. "It's impossible!" She tugged the delicate purse strap so hard that it snapped, sending a smattering of beads flying every which way.

"You have no choice in the matter. Whether or not you want to, you're having a baby in the fall."

Dropping the broken strap to her lap, Penelope reached out and clutched at the edge of his desk. "Whatever am I going to do?" she asked in a strangled whisper, her gaze beseeching.

The doctor tapped his index finger against his chin as he seemed to consider her plight. "You could marry the baby's father," he counseled. Abruptly his finger stilled, and he shot her a censorious look. "The father isn't already married, is he?"

"No, he's not married," Penelope admitted miserably, letting her hands drop back to her lap with a defeated air. Nor was there any way, come hell or high water, that Seth would marry her.

"Then, I suggest you contact him immediately and demand that he do the decent thing."

Penelope stared at the doctor as aghast as if he'd told her

to buy a shotgun and force her groom to the altar. She could just imagine Seth's reaction if she were to give him this particular piece of news. After he got over his cynical amusement, he'd tell her, in the cruelest possible terms, that she'd gotten exactly what she deserved for carrying on like a whore. And no matter how fervently she swore that the child was his, which unquestionably it was, he would never believe her.

With dark hopelessness seeping into her soul, she murmured, "Marrying the father is out of the question. We've had differences that would make a marriage between us impossible."

"I see," he replied, although by his tone and expression it was obvious that he didn't see at all. Shaking his head in a resigned fashion, he said, "Since you refuse to marry your child's father, the only thing left for you to do is to throw yourself on the mercy of your family. I assume you do have a family?" He eyed her inquisitively from behind his thick lenses.

She nodded, a lump of tears swelling in her throat. *Her family. Jake and Hallie.* They, too, were an option she preferred not to consider. While Hallie would probably be sympathetic, the thought of facing her brother's pain and disappointment at this mess was every bit as intimidating as confessing her condition to Seth. Worse yet, knowing Jake, he wouldn't give her a moment's peace until she revealed the identity of the baby's father. Once he found out who it was, he'd confront Seth.

Penelope closed her eyes, humiliated by the very idea. When Seth told her brother his version of the events leading to their broken engagement, thus branding her the worse sort of a whore, Jake would feel obligated to defend her honor.

That prospect made her tremble. Knowing her overprotective brother, he would insist on challenging Seth to a duel, if he didn't simply shoot him dead on the spot. The thought of her adored brother being hurt or killed in a duel, or being hanged for murdering Seth, was more than she could bear . . . not to mention how irrationally devastated she'd be if something happened to the heartless Mr. Tyler.

Feeling as if someone had just pulled the earth out from beneath her feet, Penelope lifted her finger to her mouth and gnawed on her fingernail. No. No matter what happened, she simply couldn't involve her family in this problem.

Of course, she'd have to write them of her broken engagement, for they were even now planning a grand wedding in San Francisco. But she would have to do it in a manner that made it sound like both she and Seth had simply had a change of heart. With luck, her letter would reach San Francisco before Seth did.

Dropping her hand from her mouth, she slipped it beneath her purse and superstitiously crossed her fingers. If Lady Luck was truly on her side, Seth would corroborate her story if Jake broached the subject. As for the baby . . .

"Are you all right, Miss Parrish?" Dr. Goodwin was leaning across his desk, peering anxiously at her face. "You're very pale all of a sudden. You're not going to faint again, are you?"

She released a shaky laugh. "Of course not. Despite what happened last night, I'm not in the habit of swooning."

"Perhaps. But when a women is in a delicate—"

Just then, a small, pleasant-looking woman who had been introduced to Penelope as the doctor's wife burst into the room. "You must come right away, Tony! There is a child out here who was just hit by a dray wagon, and she's in a terrible way!"

The doctor bounded to his feet. "Have the child taken to my surgery immediately." As she dashed off to do his bidding, his gaze returned to Penelope. "I hope you'll consider my advice, Miss Parrish. This world is no place for a woman alone, much less a pregnant one."

"I will," she promised, crossing her fingers again, this time to cancel out her falsehood.

"Good." He gave her a nod of approval as he came around his desk to stand by her chair. "There are hundreds of unconscionable scoundrels in this city who prey on women in your condition. I would hate for someone as lovely and talented as you to fall into their clutches." He reached down and gave her shoulder a reassuring pat. "Now, if you'll excuse me?"

Clutching her ruined purse, Penelope rose to her feet. "Of course, Doctor, and thank you. You've been more than kind." She forced a tremulous smile on her lips as she held out her hand.

Dr. Goodwin took her proffered hand in his and gave it a warm squeeze. "Everything will be fine. Just you wait and see."

Penelope nodded, although she had a hunch that for her, things would never again be fine.

Giving her hand a final squeeze, he added, "Count your blessings that you're not alone in the world. So many of the women I see in your condition are not so fortunate."

As the doctor disappeared through the door, Penelope's false smile faded. She was more alone than he would ever know.

Trick of Fate

—⚶—

Oh, then, why if I was fated
From the height of joy to fall,
Must I still those happy moments
In my hour of pain recall?

—*Le Nozze di Figaro*

Chapter 4

S he was the woman he'd been dreaming of all his life. Now that he had found her, he intended to destroy her.

Louisa Vanderlyn. Seth's eyes narrowed, his gaze shrewdly appraising. She walked with a proud, almost military bearing, and even from his vantage point across the street, he got an impression of cool command. It ever there was a woman in control of her destiny, it was Louisa Vanderlyn.

Until now. Seth's belly tightened with anticipation as he watched her march down the walkway of the Vanderlyn Brewery and approach the waiting buggy. Perhaps she was going to be a worthy adversary after all. He hoped so. It would make his vengeance all the more sweet if she had a spirit worth crushing.

Without letting his gaze waver from the object of his speculation, he reached into his waistcoat pocket and pulled out his cigar case. Two years ago he'd been shown a portrait of Louisa, the only daughter of the all-powerful Willem Van Cortlandt, one painted in honor of her sixteenth birthday. She'd been breathtaking in her youth. Perfection itself.

She had also been cold-blooded enough to order her newborn bastard son murdered.

Tightening his lips into a bitter line, Seth snapped open the case and removed a thin cigar. What would he see if he were to move across the street and pull her face into the light of the buggy lamp? Had years of wickedness and corruption left their mark on her once angelic countenance? Had time stripped away her beguiling mask of innocence to reveal a visage as ugly as her sin-rotted soul? If fate were indeed just, she would be an abomination to the eye.

But as Seth knew all too well, there was no fairness in

fate . . . or in life itself. And somehow he knew, though distance and the shadows of the approaching night obscured her features, that Louisa was still beautiful.

Muttering an oath beneath his breath, Seth savagely bit the end off the cigar and spit it into the dust at his feet. Just the sight of her dredged up all the hurt he'd suffered as an unwanted child, all the futile longings of his lonely youth, making him ache to shed the tears he'd repressed for so many years.

God! How he hated these conflicting emotions; how he hated her. Stifling a sob, Seth forced his mind from his pain to focus on searching his pockets for his matches. Like taunting children long ignored, his feelings ceased their torment and drifted away. And by the time he pulled out his match safe, only the trembling of his hands betrayed his surge of emotion at finally seeing the woman whose love he had once so desperately craved.

Clenching the cigar tensely between his teeth, he struck a match against the brick wall behind him. Immediately a tiny flame danced in the shadows. Willing his trembling hands to be still, he lit the cigar. Feeling more in control now, he leaned against the darkened shop window and resumed his scrutiny of Louisa.

She stood at the edge of the boardwalk, murmuring to the man holding the reins of her buggy horse. Beneath her Tyrolean-shaped hat, Seth could see a thick braid of fair hair coiled at her neck; hair that appeared to be a hue very like his own leonine mane. Briefly he wondered if that hair was still a dark honey blond streaked with ribbons of pale gold, like his own, or if it was now liberally sprinkled with gray.

As if sensing his stare, Louisa abruptly ceased her conversation and looked straight at him.

With a nonchalance he didn't feel, Seth took a deep draw from the cigar. Promptly he succumbed to a fit of choking. Try though he might, he had never really developed a taste for tobacco. In truth, the stuff made him violently ill—if he actually tried to smoke it, which he usually didn't. Yet, of late, he'd begun to indulge in the charade of smoking simply because he found the motions of the act oddly comforting. Especially in situations like this when he desperately needed something to distract him from his suffocating anger.

From atop the Vanderlyn Brewery building the clock chimed seven. Seth dropped the cigar to the boardwalk and ground it out beneath his boot. Louisa, who was now being helped into her buggy, seemed to have lost all interest in the stranger across the street.

"Beware, Louisa *Van Cortlandt*," Seth hissed beneath his breath. "I won't be a stranger for long."

The time had come to implement the final phase of his plan; the one that would sound the death knell on Vanderlyn Brewery and destroy everything Louisa held dear. And as her life fell into ruins, while she was mired in her own hopeless despair, she would be forced to face the avenging spawn of her own evil: Seth Tyler—her long-dead son.

"Here you are, gentlemen, the ace of hearts! Ace of hearts is the winning card! Here you see it—" With an extravagant flourish, the dealer turned up a card that was indeed the ace of hearts and flashed it before the passersby.

"Keep your eyes on the ace while I shuffle; watch it closely now." After giving the cards one final shuffle, he laid them facedown on the table, then searched the crowd for an easy mark. He let his gaze skim past a small cluster of drunken bummers and two saloon girls before homing in on a stranger lounging against the wall a few feet away. Everything about him, from his diamond shirt studs to his heavy gold watch fob, reeked of Eastern money.

"Make a bet, sir?" The dealer smiled in his most ingratiating manner, beckoning like a wolf intent on luring a lamb away from its flock. Indeed, these Easterners who came west in search of adventure were like lambs—lambs for the fleecing.

The stranger pushed away from the wall and sauntered over. "Fifty dollars." He tossed several gold coins onto the table.

"Pick your card, then!" the dealer urged.

Instead of pondering the cards, the stranger narrowed his eyes and studied the dealer. After a long moment, one corner of his mouth curved up.

Something about that smile made the dealer long to squirm like a schoolboy caught dipping a little girl's braids into the ink pot. Up close, the tall stranger looked less like a swell-headed Easterner and more like a marauding pirate—an effect that was heightened by his flowing mane of leonine hair and the wicked slant of his brows.

Uncomfortably aware that it was too late in the game to turn back now, he inquired hoarsely, "Your selection?"

Never once letting his gaze waver from the dealer's face, the stranger raised one hand and laid it over the middle card.

The dealer almost sagged with relief. The man hadn't detected his cheating after all. "Fifty dollars on the pasteboard in the center," he announced, preparing to flip the card over.

With the speed of a striking rattler, the stranger grabbed his arm and pinned it to the table. "Fifty dollars . . . on the pasteboard up your sleeve," he rasped, extracting a card from the dealer's false cuff and tossing it faceup on the table.

"What's goin' on here?" Floyd Temple, the bull-like owner of the Shakespeare Saloon elbowed his way through the gathering crowd. His jaw dropped at the sight of the stranger. "Mr. Tyler!"

"And a good evening to you, too, Floyd," Seth drawled, tossing the saloon owner a lazy grin.

"This fella ain't givin' you trouble is he?"

"No trouble." Seth glanced at the dealer. "I was just having a rather interesting conversation with Mr.—?"

The man sputtered.

"Mr.—?" prompted Seth, this time more forcefully.

"Higginbottom, sir. Horace P. Higginbottom."

"Horace P. Higginbottom. I'll make a note of that." Seth gave the man a look that told him exactly what kind of note he was making.

Floyd stared at the dealer's flushed face for a second, then at Mr. Tyler's amused one. The whole situation smelled worse than a polecat in hundred-degree weather. He groaned inwardly. Something was going on here, and he had a hunch he wasn't going to be happy when he found out what it was. Especially if it ruined his chances to sell the Shakespeare to Mr. Tyler.

"Mr. Tyler—" he began.

"Seth."

"Seth. If there's some sorta problem—"

"No problem." Seth winked at the dealer, whose color deepened to an alarming shade of purple. "Horace, here, was just telling me how he had an itch to move to Cheyenne. Said something about leaving tonight. Right?"

Horace bobbed his head frantically.

Sensing that this was one of those situations best left

alone, Floyd pasted on his most jovial smile and changed the subject. "Ever heard of Mademoiselle Lorelei Leroux?"

Seth let his gaze waver from the dealer to the beefy saloon owner. "Can't say as I have."

"Then, you're in for a real treat. Got the voice of an angel, the face of a goddess, and her figger," he let out a long whistle and sketched an exaggerated set of female curves in the air.

Raising one eyebrow in wonder, Seth copied the man's sketch in the air. "You don't say?"

Floyd winked in confirmation. Looping one arm around Seth's shoulders, he said, "Got a front-row seat set aside for you in the variety hall. Just wait till you get a peek at Lorelei's ankles, trim as an Arab filly's. A real Thoroughbred, that one."

Seth grinned. "Did you check her teeth and withers as well?"

Floyd let out a raucous whoop. "Not me. The missus would whup me good if I so much as sniffed in that direction. Tell you what, though. I'll set up a private supper after the show, and you can check her points yourself."

Seth's grin turned wicked at that. A little female companionship might be just the thing to get his mind off Louisa.

His smile faded as he shifted his gaze to the dealer, who was secreting gold from the game table. "Those are my winnings," he pointed out, motioning to the coins in the man's hand.

Horace's eyes bulged in terror. "Just c-collecting 'em for you, Mr. Tyler."

"Seth," Seth amended, taking the gold from the man's outstretched hands. He paused to contemplate the money for a moment, then tossed several coins onto the table. "For your trip to Cheyenne." Without sparing the dealer so much as a parting glance, he turned and rejoined the saloon owner.

Floyd, deliberately blind to the interplay between Horace and Seth, guided Seth toward the variety hall, pointing out the wonders of the Shakespeare Saloon with the smoothness of a patent medicine salesman as they went.

"As classy as any establishment in St. Louie" was how Floyd described the Shakespeare. Though Seth knew St. Louis well enough to disagree, he had to admit that by Denver's standards, the Shakespeare was very grand indeed.

Gaudy red and yellow paper covered the walls, their vivid

tones rivaled only by the well-worn rugs placed at intervals on the hardwood floors. Over the men's heads hung three gilded wagon wheels that had been fitted with kerosene lamps to fashion makeshift chandeliers. There was a large potbellied stove in every corner, and along the frosted glass front window was a row of tall potted plants. Scattered throughout the room were tables offering chances to win on games ranging from faro to roulette.

Seth's stomach gave a painful lurch as he passed the gaily painted wheel of fortune. When he was seventeen, he'd lost his last coin to the game, a bit of stupidity that had resulted in him going hungry and sleeping in the bitterly cold streets.

"Betcha never seen a finer bar than this," Floyd boasted, giving the well-polished surface a proud pat. "Thirty-two feet of gen-u-ine mahogany. Came all the way from Chicago."

Swallowing hard, Seth forced his gaze away from the wheel of fortune to glance toward the bar. His gentlemanly reflection in the plate-glass mirror along the wall served as a powerful reminder he hadn't gone hungry or slept in the streets for over a decade now. Slowly the ache in his belly receded.

"And this here is Monty Dowd," introduced Floyd. "The finest mixologist west of the Mississippi. Monty, meet Mr. Tyler."

Monty, a lanky, sandy-haired man with a properly waxed mustache and a friendly smile, extended his hand. "Pleasure."

Seth took the proffered hand and returned the man's smile as Monty proceeded to pump his arm with enthusiastic vigor.

"Well, then," Monty said. "Now that we're on hand-shakin' terms, why don't you nominate your poison?"

"What would you suggest?"

"You look like a man with a healthy constitution. I'm guessin' some Red Dynamite would put a spin in your sombrero."

"No way, no how," Floyd bellowed, grabbing Seth's arm and pulling him from the bar. "Save your pizen for the bummers. Only the finest of the Shakespeare's li-bations for Mr. Tyler."

As Floyd guided Seth through the door leading into the variety hall, Seth tossed the bartender a look promising that he would be back later to sample the infamous Red Dynamite.

"Make way! Make way!" bawled Floyd, shoving his way through the crush. The variety hall was packed tonight. "You sit here, Seth," he said, snatching up and tossing aside a cowboy who had dared to sit at the front-center table. After plopping down in the opposite chair, he pulled out two fat cigars and handed one to his prospective buyer. "Finest bit of tobaccy in the world. Rolled between the bare, supple thighs of a Cuban virgin."

Carefully hiding his distaste, Seth pulled out his silver cigar cutter and expertly notched the end. That formality completed, he jammed the nasty thing between his lips and leaned back in his chair, hoping that no one would notice that he hadn't lit it. Nothing choked him quicker than the initial puff it took to make the tobacco catch the flame.

But someone had noticed. No sooner was he settled than he heard a faint hiss and caught a whiff of sulfur mixed with cheap perfume. "Light your cigar, mister?" A moon-faced saloon girl with hair an improbable shade of blond leaned over his shoulder, holding out a lit match.

Stifling his urge to groan aloud, Seth gave the girl his most charming grin and, against his better judgment, accepted the light. Manfully he inhaled, praying that he wouldn't disgrace himself by collapsing in a hacking heap on the floor. Luck was with him and, aside from succumbing to one discreet cough, he managed to have the cigar lit with minimal embarrassment.

Tucking a coin in the girl's hand, Seth drawled. "What's your name, sweetheart?"

She rubbed her breasts against his shoulder. "Desdemona."

"Desdemona?" He tossed Floyd a wry look.

Floyd shrugged. "All the girls are named after Shakespeare's ladies." Counting them off on his fingers, he recited, "We got Juliet, Ophelia, Miranda, Titania, Portia, Jessica, Katharina, Cleopatra, Beatrice, Cordelia, Helena, and Hermia." He looked puzzled and appeared to recount, his lips moving as he went over the names again. With a heavy sigh he added, "Oh, and Gladys."

"Gladys?" Seth laughed as he extinguished his cigar with practiced stealth. "Can't say as I've read that play."

"Tried to call her Cassandra, but she was too stupid to remember the name. Never came when she was called." Floyd took a drag off his cigar. "With her figger, she don't need a brain, so I kept her anyway."

Pouting at being ignored, Desdemona eased herself onto Seth's lap and blatantly ground her backside against his groin. He grinned down at her, noting that her golden hair was black at the roots. "So, Desdemona, have you an Othello?" he teased.

She stared up at him as if he'd lost his mind. "What would I want with a mangy black varmint like that? Nasty fella left a headless rat in front of my bedroom door this morning."

Seth looked back at her as if she were the crazy one.

"Othello is Monty Dowd's cat. Best mouser in town," supplied Floyd.

"Mangiest cat in town, more like it," mumbled Desdemona.

Capturing the girl's gaze with his, Seth asked gently, "Ever read Shakespeare?"

"Never read nothin', never learned how."

Seth felt a surge of pity for the girl. It wasn't so long ago that he, too, had been unable to read. Toying with the coarse lace trimming her neckline, he explained, "Othello was a noble blackamoor who married a beautiful girl named Desdemona."

"And they lived happily ever after?" she asked, dreamily.

"Not exactly. He strangled her."

Her eyes widened with horrified fascination. "How come?"

"Jealousy, of course."

"But if he loved her enough to marry her, why did he kill her over a little thing like jealousy?"

Seth chuckled, but in a way that voiced no amusement. "Love is a kind of madness, sweetheart. It possesses a man's soul and consumes his reason. When he's in its clutches, he does all sorts of crazy things."

Desdemona considered his words, then smiled flirtatiously. "You ever been possessed by crazy love?"

Seth stared into her dark eyes for a moment, remembering another pair of eyes: silvery-green ones, seductively tiptilted at the outer corners. Penelope's eyes. Like a pugilist striking his challenger, the memory slammed the breath out of him.

"Well, have you?" she demanded.

He drew in a hissing breath. "Only once."

Chapter 5

Even from where she stood waiting in the stage wings, Penelope could tell it was going to be another rough night at the Shakespeare Variety Hall. Uncouth men, drunk off cheap liquor and crude company, were already heckling Euphemia Hotchkiss, the actress who was onstage singing, venting their impatience for a glimpse of Lorelei Leroux. It was the same depressing scenario night after night, and Penelope knew that it was only a matter of minutes before the rest of the crowd joined in the badgering.

This evening the audience was right on schedule.

"Sounds like my ma-in-law after she got kicked in the head by our mule," jeered one man, his lampoon accompanied by the tinkle of breaking glass.

"Hell. Sounds jist like *my* mother-in-law when I told her to put a cork in it and mind her own business." That drew a roar of approval from the crowd.

As if by clockwork the rest of the men joined in, each taunt louder and more barbed than the last. Eventually they grew so thunderous that they all but drowned out Euphemia's admittedly grating voice. As she warbled the last note, Penelope heard Bertram McAllister, the dramatic actor, shout her cue:

"Here comes the stagecoach now!"

Self-conscious in her scanty costume, Penelope gave her peacock blue bodice a tug, though she knew that all the tugging in the world wouldn't render the neckline decent. After rubbing her lucky ribbon, which she'd tied around her throat, she strutted onto the stage, swinging her hips in a seductive manner.

As always the hisses and boos gave way to whistles and cheers, followed by clapping and foot-stamping. Somewhere in the back of the hall, she heard the chant: "Lorelei! Lorelei!"

When she lifted her skirts almost to her knees and swayed to the prelude of her solo, an appreciative roar shook the walls.

"Yank it higher, darlin'. Pull it up! Pull it up!" hooted a drunken bullwhacker in the front row.

Ignoring the man, Penelope began to sing, trilling sweetly at the entrance of Miles Prescott, the actor playing the hero in the piece. Spellbound by her voice, the rowdy crowd fell silent.

Tonight the company was performing *The Gregory Gulch Bride,* one of Denver's favorite operettas. It was the tale of a mail-order bride trying to win the love of her indifferent husband.

Swishing her skirts in a tantalizing manner, Penelope danced around Miles, tempting him with her amply displayed charms. The measures poor Molly Snow, the lovesick heroine, took to seduce her husband were nothing short of vulgar.

"Pull 'em up! Bend 'er over!"

From the corner of her eye, Penelope saw that the bullwacker had staggered to the edge of the stage and was now trying to look up her skirt, his face the picture of besotted lechery. Shuddering with disgust, she dropped her hem back to her ankles.

"Hell, we paid our money—show us some leg!" he shouted, pounding his fists against the stage floor in protest.

"Shut up and let the lady sing!" hollered a cowboy, seizing the bullwacker by the neck and attempting to pull him back to his seat. With a backhand swat the bullwacker sent the cowboy flying into the crowd, knocking over several onlookers and drawing a threatening rumble from the rest of the audience.

"I paid my money to see some leg, and I'm gonna git what I paid for," he snarled.

Before Penelope could think, much less react, the man jumped onto the stage and wrestled her into his arms. In one rending yank, he ripped her skirt open. One more jerk and the skirt fell to the floor, exposing her red flannel pantaloons.

Shrieking her indignation, she ground her boot heel into the man's instep. His grunt of surprise escalated into a howl of pain as she finished her performance by kicking him in the shins.

With an echoing roar the crowd surged forward. Some of the men were intent on rescuing the beauteous Lorelei, while others were eager to join the bullwacker in his molestation. Everyone was enjoying the ensuing brawl.

Panicked, Penelope hastily presented her bruising encore, an act accompanied by the ever-gallant Bertram. Executing their movements with the precision of an elaborately chore-ographed ballet, Bert thwacked the bullwacker over the head with a prop tree while Penelope hooked her foot behind the man's ankle and pulled his leg out from under him. The ac-tors' combined efforts were enough to send the drunk top-pling backward, a performance that brought down the curtain . . .

. . . Literally. In a wild attempt to break his fall, the bullwacker grabbed the curtains, wrenching them from their moorings. With a *whoosh!* of gold velvet the curtains bil-lowed downward, engulfing everyone onstage in their suffo-cating folds.

As Penelope grappled with the imprisoned cloth, she could hear her attacker cursing in the darkness . . . cursing that grew louder as the seconds ticked by. Alarmed by the man's nearness and terrified of being recaptured, she scram-bled toward a sliver of light. To her everlasting relief, the sliver broadened into a warm ribbon, and she easily found an opening in the curtains.

But her relief was short-lived. No sooner had she crawled from her velvet prison than she was pulled from the stage by another man, this one drunker and dirtier than the first.

Violently she struggled, gagging at the stench emanating from her new captor's filth-encrusted clothes.

"Hows 'bout a kiss, girlie?" he growled, smiling in a way that displayed the sum of his teeth—two rotten stumps. Pin-ning her against his body, he ground his lips against hers, trying to force his tongue between her clenched teeth.

Feeling as if she were living her worse nightmare, Penel-ope increased her struggles tenfold. But it was to no avail. Aside from grunting once when she managed to land a kick on his booted ankle, he easily ignored her frenzied efforts to escape.

Somebody else's efforts were harder to ignore. As the man groped at her bodice, Penelope heard a mighty *smack!*, which elicited an even mightier *yelp!* from her molester, im-mediately followed by a *thud!* and a breathless *oomph!* Bellowing like a wounded buffalo, the bullwacker thrust her aside and rounded on the man who was attacking him from behind.

Without pausing to spare her rescuer so much as a backward glance, Penelope raced toward the stairs leading up to the private rooms, swatting away the arms that sought to recapture her. With breakneck speed she vaulted up the stairs until a stitch in her side forced her to sink to the steps. It was then that she heard the pounding of footsteps hot on her trail.

On the verge of hysteria now, she tried to crawl the rest of the way up the stairs. But it was too late, and once again she was wrested into a steely grip.

Blind to everything except her desperation to free herself, Penelope fought, kicking and punching with mindless fury. Beneath her screams she could hear the man shouting, but she was too panicked to listen. A year and a half of playing the gold circuit had taught her that most men's intentions were less than honorable, especially where actresses were concerned. And she would have bet her lucky ribbon that this man was no exception.

With that certainty in mind, she jabbed her elbow into her attacker's belly with all her strength. To her relief, he uttered an agonized groan and released her. Feeling her freedom close at hand now, she gave him one final shove before turning to resume her flight. But before she could take a step, she heard him moan.

"That's a hell of a way to greet a man, Princess."

That stopped her short. Only two people ever called her Princess: her brother, Jake, and . . .

"Seth Tyler!" she gasped, finally looking at her latest captor. Even slumped on the stairs with his face shadowed by his veil of sun-kissed hair, the man's identity was unmistakable. Stunned, she slowly sank down next to him.

Damn! Of all the people in the world, why did it have to be Seth who had discovered her in such a disreputable place, performing in such a bawdy show? Too shocked by his presence to mask her dismay, she blurted out, "What are you doing here?"

"Shouldn't that be my line?" he drawled, shifting aside to allow a scantily-clad saloon girl and her eager client to pass.

"What I'm doing here should be obvious," she replied tautly.

"You're doing the obvious?" He stared after the pair with a significant lift of his brow.

It took all of Penelope's self-control not to do a repeat performance and jab him in the belly again. "Damn it, Seth! You know better than that!"

"Do I?" His gaze slowly and deliberately took in every tawdry detail of her appearance.

Bristling like a cat with its back up, she hissed, "How dare you insinuate that I'd—"

"I dare because I know you," he snapped, effectively silencing her protests. "Have you forgotten about the little scene I witnessed in New York?"

Penelope released an exasperated snort. Apparently the words *forgive* and *forget* weren't in Seth Tyler's vocabulary, just as it was equally apparent that he hadn't come to his senses about what had happened in New York. She snorted again. Well, to hell with the narrow-minded bastard! If he wanted to hold a grudge, then so be it. She'd gladly oblige his stupidity and do the same.

Calling forth all of her acting ability, she assumed an air of imperious cool and retorted, "You have no right to judge me on something that you're obviously incapable of understanding."

He eyed her with disdain. "I'm perfectly capable of understanding what's going on when I find a half-naked woman lolling in a man's arms. I'd venture to guess that the foregone conclusion would be the same no matter who was drawing it."

Abandoning all pretense of composure, she practically shouted, "I wasn't half-naked, and I certainly wasn't—lolling!"

He shrugged. "You have your definitions, and I have mine."

"And my definition of Seth Tyler is arrogant bastard."

"Is that listed before or after the term 'trash'?" he inquired cryptically. "I believe that was the word you used to describe my person the last time we met."

"Well, if the title fits . . ."

Seth laughed at that. "Touché. One point for the lady."

"One point for what?"

"One point for your frank response, of course."

She shrugged dismissively. "Who's keeping score?"

"I am. And I feel obligated to report that you're running woefully behind in the honesty column."

A thousand scathing retorts sprang to Penelope's lips, but she firmly refrained from voicing them. It would be a cold day in hell before she rose to Seth Tyler's bait. Pointedly ignoring his goading expression, she demanded, "What do you want? Surely you have better things to do than torment me."

"Better things? Yes. More entertaining? No."

Rankled by his arrogance, she opened her mouth to tell him exactly what he could do with his amusement, but again she stifled the urge. Instead she repeated, "What do you want?"

"I want to know why you lied to your brother."

"Why I . . . what?" she asked, genuinely taken aback by his words. "I didn't lie to Jake."

Seth raised one slashing eyebrow. "He showed me your last letter, the one where you were bragging about going abroad and singing for the crowned heads of Europe. You said that you'd be touring the Continent and therefore unable to write. So unless the Colorado Territory has been annexed by Europe and crowned a few heads in the process, I think it's safe to assume you lied."

Penelope groaned privately. Of course Jake had shown Seth her letter; she should have realized he would when she wrote it. He'd probably been so puffed up with pride at her fictitious success that he'd shown it to everyone in San Francisco.

With what she hoped was a nonchalant shrug, she gave him the same lie she'd given the opera company the night she'd announced her resignation, "I changed my plans a little, that's all."

"A little?" He made a derisive noise. "Now, there's the understatement of the century."

"Life in the theater can be very uncertain. Things happen, changes are made."

Seth folded his arms across his chest and fixed her with his flinty stare. "So tell me, Princess. What 'thing' happened that made you accept an engagement in this god-awful saloon?"

Blinking once, she looked away, knowing that it was hopeless to lie and impossible to tell the truth. Taking the only avenue left open, she replied, "I didn't write that letter to you. Therefore I don't owe you an explanation. As for

what I'm doing here, well, I don't see why that is any of
your concern."

"As your brother's best friend, I consider it my duty to
make it my concern." His lips flattened into a grim line.
"And regardless of your low opinion of me, I have too much
respect for Jake to allow his sister to carry on like a common
trollop."

Penelope flinched as if struck. "How dare you! Jake will
kill you when I tell him you called me a trollop!"

Seth emitted a bark of laughter. "Jake is a sensible man,
and as such, he's not likely to kill me for stating the obvious." He stared pointedly at her immodest attire. "No doubt
he'll thank me for calling your lapse of morals to his attention."

"You wouldn't dare risk his friendship by making such
vile accusations!"

"Watch me." Seth rose to his feet and stood looming over
her like a dark specter of doom. "I remember seeing a telegraph office down the block. By train, it shouldn't take him
more than a week to get here." He gave her a final warning
glance before turning to leave. "I'd hate to be in your shoes
when he arrives. Perhaps he'll give you the beating you so
richly deserve."

Penelope hated the thought of being in her own shoes if
her brother caught her within a hundred miles of a place like
the Shakespeare. Not that Jake would beat her; he'd never
laid a hand on her, though God knows her behavior had often merited it.

No. What made her sick with dread was the prospect of
facing his disappointment. Having raised her after the death
of their parents, she knew that he would blame himself as
much as her when he discovered what a mess she'd made of
her life. And she loved him too much to bring him such
pain.

As Seth began to descend the stairs, she jumped to her
feet and grasped his arm. "Wait."

He paused to stare at her hand on his arm, his expression
as revulsed as if it were rotted by gangrene. After a long moment, his gaze slid up to her face. With a grimace he looked
away.

Acutely aware of the sordid picture she made with her
heavily made-up face and garish attire, it took all her courage to say, "You once swore that you would do anything for

me. You said that all I had to do was ask you." Her expressive voice became soft, pleading. "Please, Seth. I'm asking now."

"Only the illustrious Penelope Parrish"—he paused to stab her with his contemptuous gaze—"or should I call you Lorelei Leroux?—would have the audacity to remind me of my lovesick promise at a time like this." His glare burned through her. "Sorry, Princess. You forfeited the right to that promise when you took a lover."

"You know Julian wasn't my lover! He was my friend, nothing more. You simply didn't choose to understand the situation."

"Nor do I care to now," he retorted, shaking himself free from her restraining grip. "So don't ask for understanding, because I have none to give . . . least of all to you."

Sharp, irrational pain gripped Penelope's heart at his words, and she was stunned to find tears in her eyes. "I guess I never realized just how much you loathe me," she whispered.

"You still don't."

Drawing her few remaining shreds of dignity around her like a tattered shawl, she made one final appeal. "Please, Seth. Can't you put your feelings for me aside for one moment and think of Jake? I know you care for him, and he you. Don't you see how it would devastate him to have to take sides against one of us?"

Lacking a skirt, she pleated the fabric of her full bloomers between her fingers, desperate to suppress her urge to latch on to his arm again. "And he would be forced to choose should you level such terrible accusations against me."

"Do you think it would devastate him any less if I were to leave you here and you were to come to harm?"

"Of course not," she admitted miserably.

"Then, it appears that I'm damned no matter what I do."

Penelope looked up from the red flannel bunched between her fingers, shaking her head. "But it doesn't have to be like that."

"Really?" He was looking down his nose at her in a way that told her that she, too, would be damned no matter what decision he should ultimately make.

Unnerved, she disentangled her fingers from her bloomers and raised her hand to her mouth to gnaw on one well-bitten nail. Between pacifying nibbles, she suggested, "You could

let me return to San Francisco quietly and resume my old
life. I promise I'll behave like a perfect lady. Nobody will
ever be the wiser."

"After all your experience, 'lady' is hardly a term I would
use to describe you," he commented sarcastically.

Penelope bit her cuticle hard enough to make it bleed.
"Damn it, Seth!" She dropped her hand to her lap to dab at
the wound with a handful of bloomer fabric. "I'm no more
experienced now than I was in New York. Back then, you
acted like a gentleman."

"Or like a gutter rat trussed up like a gentleman, as you
so eloquently put it," he shot back.

"You know I didn't mean that."

"Sure you did. But I can't fault you for telling the truth."

The tears stinging in Penelope's eyes gave way and cut
zigzagging paths down her cheeks. "I only said those things
because you were being such a bastard."

"I'm going to be an even bigger bastard if I decide to
agree to your proposal. And whether or not you like it,
you're going to answer my questions." Grasping her chin in
his palm, he forced her to meet his stony gaze. "You're going to be so firmly under my thumb that I'll know if you so
much as tremble. Understand?"

Penelope sniffled and nodded.

Tightening his grip on her chin, Seth pulled her face close
to his. He seemed to be judging her, weighing his options.
After a moment, he nodded. "I accept your proposition. But
only because I want to save Jake from being hurt by your
selfishness."

She gave him a watery smile.

Which he ignored. Seizing her arm, he commanded,
"We're going downstairs now, and you're going to tell the
company that you're leaving. Tonight."

"B-but I can't just up and l-leave," she stuttered, struggling to free her arm. "Not right now!"

His grip turned bruising. "You can and you will."

"But you don't understand!"

"We're back to that worn-out excuse, are we?" he growled
impatiently. "All right. Then, explain what I don't understand?"

She squirmed. "I c-can't."

"You mean you won't. Well, I hope you like trains, Princess. Because I intend to have your backside enthroned on

the next one back to San Francisco. There is one due the day after tomorrow."

His eyes took on an unholy gleam as he pinned her with his gaze. "Oh. And don't expect an open-armed reception from your brother. I intend to telegraph the news of your disgrace ahead."

Hating him with the same kind of impotent hatred a prisoner feels for his warden, Penelope at last admitted to herself that he had her trapped. Frantic to escape, with nowhere to turn and no way out, the threatening storm of her emotions burst.

"I'm not the type of man who dissolves at the sight of a weeping female, so you can stop your caterwauling," Seth snapped as her tempest of tears became punctuated by thunderous sobs.

She expelled a heartrending whimper.

Seth countered with an impatient grunt. "Damnit, Penelope. I told you I would accept your proposal."

She choked and gave her head a despairing shake.

Heaving a long-suffering sigh, he pulled out his handkerchief and handed it to her. "I don't see what the hell you're so hysterical about. Do you enjoy performing half-naked?"

"O-of c-course not! It's n-not that at all!"

"Then, what is it?"

Not what, she wanted to shout. *Who.* Instead, she gasped, "Y-y-you w-wouldn't—"

"Understand," he finished for her with a pained expression.

She blew her nose and nodded.

"Damn it to hell!" He looked ready to strangle her.

"I-I—" she wailed, before choking on her tears once again.

Cursing graphically, Seth sat down on the stairs and pulled her onto his lap. "Sit," he commanded when she gave a token sob of protest. Awkwardly patting her back, he mumbled, "I can't imagine anything being as bad as all that."

Feeling impossibly wretched, Penelope melted against the reassuring strength of his chest. Mindless of everything except her need for solace, she wrapped her arms around his neck and buried her face into the warm hollow at his throat.

His body turned stiffer than an undertaker's measuring

stick. "Penelope," he growled, seizing her arms and pulling her away. Scowling, he stared down into her tear-streaked face.

When she looked up, their gazes met. Hers was vulnerable and pleading for understanding; his was angry and confused.

Murmuring something about Jake never forgiving him if he let his troublesome sister drown in her own tears, Seth crushed her into his embrace. The feel of his breath softly ruffling her hair served as a potent reminder of the tenderness they had once shared. For a moment Penelope allowed herself the luxury of forgetting the terrible reality of her life and let herself revel in the soothing intimacy of his touch. Gradually her sobs eased.

When her tears were at last spent, Seth nestled his lips close to her ear and whispered, "Better?"

His unexpected kindness almost undid her. Ruthlessly harnessing her urge to burst into tears again, she nodded.

"Good." He actually smiled as he smoothed a damp curl from her cheek. "Now, why don't you tell me what we can do about your obvious, but as of yet nameless, dilemma?"

Penelope dabbed her eyes with the handkerchief. What she needed was time. "Three months," she replied after a quick calculation. "Give me three months to finish my engagement here. Then I swear I'll go home without so much as a word of protest."

Seth cocked his head to one side as he considered her words, unconsciously stroking the curve of her jaw. "One month," he finally decided. "I'll have completed my business here by then."

"Lorelei!" called a strident female voice, promptly echoed by a masculine one.

Oh, great! Penelope thought miserably, recognizing the voices as belonging to Adele du Charme, the owner of the company, and Miles Prescott, Adele's son and the company's leading man. Just what she needed, two more people railing at her. Crossing her fingers that it would be long enough, she countered, "Six weeks."

"Lorelei!" The voices were drawing nearer now.

Penelope cast a desperate glance toward the foot of the stairs. Adele had promised to deal harshly with her should she catch her being overly familiar with any man. And nestling in Seth's arms could definitely be construed as overly familiar. Alarmed, she tired to scramble from his embrace.

Ignoring the calls, and Penelope's efforts to squirm away, Seth began to deny her request. But as she looked up, her beseeching gaze captured his, and the words froze in his throat.

Damn those eyes. He groaned inwardly. Like winter frost glazing the branches of a Christmas fir, those eyes were still the silvery-green hue he had always found so captivating, and they were still seductively tip-tilted at the outer corners.

It was those eyes that made up his mind.

"Princess, you've got yourself a deal," he murmured as the man whom he recognized as being the hero from the operetta spotted his quarry and came bounding up the stairs.

Stopping three steps below where Seth and Penelope sat, the actor raised his fists and began bobbing around in a pathetic imitation of a pugilist. "Fiend! Unhand Lorelei this instant!"

Penelope rolled her eyes toward the heavens, exasperated. "For pity's sake, Miles! I'm fine!" she exclaimed, resuming her efforts to wiggle from Seth's arms.

Easily immobilizing her in his grip, Seth tilted his head to one side and contemplated the other man's performance. The actor's movements were as stiff and exaggerated as if he were rehearsing the fight scene from a poorly staged melodrama.

Eyeing the man critically, Seth pointed out, "I'd suggest that you either stick to your mealymouthed milksop roles or find someone to give you some acting lessons."

The actor gaped like a fool with his breeches on fire, the red of his flushed face visible beneath his white greasepaint. "Why, you—you—" he sputtered.

"Forgotten your lines, have you?" Seth arched one brow in amusement. "I believe you're supposed to look at Lorelei and bellow 'I'll save you, gentle maiden,' or some such absurdity."

The man's rouged lips began to quiver. "You bastard!" he shrieked, his voice coming out in an infuriated falsetto.

Seth heaved a sigh and shook his head. "A soprano? Hardly an effective delivery for that particular line. You need to deepen your voice and enunciate the word *bastard* more forcefully." He glanced down at Penelope, who was trying to pry his arm from around her waist. "Why don't you show him how it's done, Princess? Nobody growls the word *bastard* better than you do."

"Seth!" Penelope cast him an irate look.

"Right intonation, wrong word," Seth quipped, winking down into her scowling face.

With a growl the actor sprang forward, his dark eyes flashing with rage. "I ought to do Denver a favor and break your neck right here and now, you-um—" His face went blank as he tried to think up an appropriate denouncement. He stuttered several times before finally blurting out, "You—despoiler of innocence!"

"Shut up, Miles!" commanded a husky female voice.

All three heads snapped around to stare at the newcomer, a stunning blond woman standing at the foot of the stairs.

"M-mother . . ." Miles whined, retreating like a whipped cur.

Dismissing her son's sniveling with a frown, the woman turned her glacial gaze on Penelope. "As for you, Lorelei, we'll discuss your appalling lack of professionalism later. Right now, however, you have a performance to finish."

Penelope nodded, her mouth suddenly too dry with dread to speak. Adele was staring at her in a way that clearly boded ill, and the possible consequences of the woman's fury terrified her.

Desperate to obey her command, Penelope tried to slip from Seth's lap. But again he foiled her escape. "Please, Seth," she whispered in a suffocated voice. "You promised to give me six weeks to arrange everything. You promised."

Ignoring her struggles, and her frantic pleas, Seth focused his attention on the woman ascending the stairs.

Dressed in an evening gown of rich violet silk, she carried herself as regally as Queen Victoria, whom he'd once had the honor of meeting. Unlike plain Victoria, however, this woman was blessed with the kind of classic elegance that kept the tally of her years a carefully guarded secret; a secret that was betrayed the second her gaze bore into his. Pale as ice and twice as cold, her blue eyes glinted with malice that could only have come from years of bitter disillusionment and the futility of a hard life.

Feeling a shiver convulse Penelope's body, Seth crushed her protectively against his chest and announced, "Lorelei has had a nasty shock. I say she's finished performing for the evening."

The woman fixed him with a disdainful stare. "As her employer, I say she'll finish her performance."

"And as *your* employer, Adele, I say that Miss Leroux is excused for the rest of the evening." It was Floyd.

Adele glared at the saloon owner, her resentment of his intrusion abundantly clear. "Surely you don't want to disappoint the audience?" she asked through gritted teeth.

"What's left of the audience is either lying in the corral knocked out from the ruckus, or too corned up to care," Floyd replied reasonably. " 'Sides, I promised Mr. Tyler here a get-acquainted supper with our Lorelei."

Penelope groaned at that idea. The last thing she wanted to do was to resume her sparring match with Seth. But before she could voice her objections, Adele snapped, "As Mr. Tyler pointed out, Lorelei has had a nasty shock. In which case, she should be resting, not"—her mouth contorted as if she'd just taken a mouthful of cod-liver oil—*"entertaining."*

Turning a deaf ear to Adele's protests, Floyd gave Penelope a wink of conspiracy. "A glass of champagne should spruce her up right 'nough. Ain't that so, Miss Leroux?"

Hoping to escape Seth's imprisoning embrace, and Adele's obvious displeasure, Penelope made a sudden lunge forward. Unexpectedly Seth released his hold, and she would have gone diving headfirst down the stairs had Miles not caught her.

Pulling herself from Miles's too eager grasp, she murmured, "Adele is right. I am feeling out of sorts." To Penelope's relief, her remark drew a curt nod of approval from Adele.

"If Miss Leroux is feeling ill, she should be allowed to go home to her bed," Seth said, standing up and straightening to his full height. He didn't miss the look of alarm that swept across the actor's face, or the speculative gleam in the blond woman's eyes as she scrutinized him from head to toe. Coolly disregarding both parties, he stared at Penelope, adding, "I'll have plenty of time in the future to get acquainted with Miss Leroux."

Adele looked none too pleased at that prospect. "You intend to be a regular customer of the Shakespeare?"

"You can bet your bloomers on that!" trumpeted Floyd, giving Seth a hearty slap on the back. "Folks. Say hul-lo to the new owner of the Shakespeare—and your new boss—Mr. Seth Tyler."

Chapter 6

Seth leaned back in his chair, frowning as he watched Adele du Charme regally ascend the stage stairs. He was deranged, definitely deranged. How else could he explain the bargain he'd just made with the woman?

Emitting a snort of self-disgust, he lifted his glass of whiskey in a mock salute to her retreating form, then tossed down the entire contents in one fiery gulp. Not only was he as crazy as a bedlamite; he was an imbecile to boot.

After Adele had ordered Penelope to go change out of what was left of her costume, she had cordially invited Seth to join her for a drink in the now-deserted variety hall. Determined to get to the bottom of Penelope's mysterious presence at the Shakespeare, he'd readily agreed. More fool he.

The woman was shrewd, he'd give her that. So shrewd that he'd been duped into seriously underestimating her cunning, something that seldom happened these days. As a result, she'd not only expertly dodged his questions regarding Penelope, she'd used his obvious interest in the actress to her own advantage.

Muttering a self-denigrating profanity beneath his breath, he dug his cigar case out of his pocket and snapped it open. The interview had started out innocuous enough, with Madame du Charme graciously inquiring about his comfort at the American House and congratulating him on his purchase of the Shakespeare. Indeed, even their exchange over the agreement between the theatrical company and the variety hall couldn't have been more genial. Instead of whining or hedging as he'd expected, she merely shrugged and discussed it in a surprisingly philosophical manner.

Her son, Miles, it seemed, had a problem with gambling: he lost more than he won, and like most compulsive gamblers he truly believed that his next big win was only a card turn away. As a result of his weakness, he'd accrued an im-

mense faro debt during the company's original week-long
run at the Shakespeare.

To repay his debt, Adele had committed the company to
an additional twelve weeks at the variety hall, with the
Shakespeare keeping all the monies collected at the door. As
she'd so succinctly pointed out, the Shakespeare was coming
out on the winning end of the deal, since every performance
by Mademoiselle Leroux yielded a veritable gold mine.

Heaving a gusty sigh, Seth drew his last cigar from the
case. In all honesty, he'd been so overwrought at seeing Penelope again, that he'd only half listened to Adele's inane
pleasantries and rote explanations. Like most women he
knew, her chatter was agreeable but not particularly stimulating or interesting.

However, when she'd segued her dialogue from her deal
with the Shakespeare to an anecdote about how some man
had offered a small fortune for the privilege of dining
with—how had she phrased it? Oh, yes—Lorelei Leroux,
Toast of the West, she'd done more than stimulate his interest; she'd aroused his jealousy. To Seth's dismay, her narra-
tive had sent a startling rush of possessiveness through him
that he had no right or desire to feel for Penelope.

As if sensing his mood and correctly guessing its cause,
Adele had chosen that moment to deliver her coup de grâce:
she proposed that he accept the beauteous Lorelei as his evening companion—his *platonic* companion, she stipu-
lated—in exchange for reducing their performance
obligation from twelve weeks to six.

Like the fool she'd obviously and, it seemed, correctly
taken him for, he'd promptly agreed, never once stopping to
consider the havoc such a deal would play with his heart . . .
or his loins. With jealousy masquerading as gallantry, he'd
justified his actions by telling himself that he'd be better
able to protect Penelope if he kept her close during her hours
at the Shakespeare, which he figured was when she faced the
most peril.

Trouble was, he hadn't stopped to think of his own impetuous feelings or how he would protect himself from them.

Seth groaned aloud at his own folly. Whatever had possessed him to let himself be roped into this fiasco? Especially in light of his pathetically erratic behavior during his
earlier encounter with Penelope. Why, he was mad to have

thought he'd be able to endure her company and not let his emotions get the best of him.

Mad. Seth stared bleakly at the greenish-brown cigar in his fingers. After almost three agonizing years of waiting, it appeared his nightmares were becoming reality: his tainted blood was poisoning his mind. At long last the madness was upon him.

At long last? his conscience mocked him. *Since when have you ever acted the least bit sane in matters concerning Penelope?*

Smiling bitterly, he acknowledged that truth. From the very instant Penelope had looked at him as something more than just her brother's best friend, he'd lost not only his heart, but his self-control and good sense as well. For the first time in his life he'd been in love, and had found himself acting from raw emotion instead of his usual cool intellect. And because he'd let his illogical heart rule his sensible head, he'd made one inexcusable mistake after another. Take, for example, the ignominious way he'd treated her in New York.

Seth cringed inwardly, as he always did when he remembered that night. Like the misguided ass he was, he'd rationalized his boorish behavior by telling himself that he'd broken her heart for her own good. After all, how could he marry her knowing what he was and what he might become?

Like hell it was for her own good, his conscience scoffed. *It was for the good of your own insufferable pride.*

That admission sent a wave of self-condemnation crashing through him. It was true: he had been too proud to confess the humiliating truth about his parentage to Penelope. He still was. Except for his friend, Jake, whom he'd asked to be custodian of himself and his fortune when the worst happened, he hadn't confided his secret to anyone. His pride wouldn't allow it.

Not for the first time, Seth cursed his overweening pride. During rare moments like this, when he allowed himself to remember his disgraceful conduct in New York, he sometimes wondered if, like love and jealousy, pride, too, was a form of madness. For what, if not madness, had possessed him when he opened that door and found Penelope in Julian Tibbett's arms?

Guilt crushed at his chest as he remembered Penelope's face when he'd walked into her dressing room that night.

Even if she hadn't had a ready and admittedly plausible explanation for her compromising predicament, the expression on her face would have been enough to dispel any notions of wrongdoing. Hell. She'd practically glowed with happiness at the sight of him. And the way she'd held out her arms to him, her love burning like emerald fire in the depths of her beautiful eyes, was hardly the action of an unfaithful woman caught in a tryst with her lover.

But because of his damnable pride, he had ignored the truth in her eyes, just as he'd ignored his heart's prompting to have faith in her love. It had been far easier to play the wronged bridegroom than to confess his mortifying secret.

Making a sound of disgust deep in his throat, Seth shoved the cigar into his mouth. Tensely clenching it between his bared teeth, he searched his pocket for his cigar cutter. There was a name for what he had been that night, one more dishonorable than that of madman or bastard. That name was coward.

Being a coward might account for your demented conduct in New York, his mind jeered. *But what of your lunacy in agreeing to Adele du Charme's proposition? If you were in complete possession of your wits, you'd drag Penelope back to San Francisco and let her brother deal with whatever trouble has landed her here.*

Frustrated at his lack of self-control, Seth bit down so hard that his teeth punctured the tobacco-leaf cigar wrapping. Grimacing at the acrid taste, he pulled it from his lips and tossed it to the floor.

How the hell was he going to keep his emotions in check for the next six weeks? With a low, tormented moan, he buried his face into his hands. All this time he'd honestly believed that his love for Penelope was dead. He had wished it to be so. Yet, when he'd looked into her tear-filled eyes, he had once again experienced the desperate, almost obsessive, need he'd always felt for her. Dear God! What was he to do?

There was only one way to handle the situation: ignore his feelings and continue to provoke Penelope into thinking that he was the most black-hearted bastard to ever walk the earth.

Slowly Seth raised his face from his hands, a bleak smile contorting his lips. The latter part of the plan shouldn't prove too onerous a task. Penelope had made it bitingly clear that she still harbored ill feelings toward him for the way he'd treated her in New York. Not that he'd expected any differently, for her pride ranked only second to his. That being the case, there should be no danger of an unintentional reconciliation.

Are you so sure about her feelings? his devil's advocate of a conscience piped in. *It seems to me that if she truly despised you, she wouldn't have cried in your arms and clung to your chest like you were the last piece of flotsam on a sinking ship.*

The remembrance of Penelope crying in his arms made Seth do something he hadn't done in decades: he blushed. Despite his best efforts to remain aloof during their physical contact, the feel of her body against his had aroused him almost beyond endurance.

The heat in his face deepened to a slow burn. Had she noticed his inflamed state? He groaned. How could she not have noticed? She'd been sitting directly on top of his hardness.

Seth shook his head. Well, it didn't do any good to worry about it now. He'd just have to take care to exercise more control in the future. Perhaps he'd accept the offers made by several of the saloon girls, and spend his lust to the point where he wouldn't be able to get an erection even if he wanted one. At least then he could concentrate on the more difficult problem of grappling with his emotions.

He stroked the angle of his jaw, considering the idea. It had merit. In fact, it was downright brilliant. He'd get started on his plan this very evening. He'd invite one of the saloon girls to partake in the private dinner Penelope had declined earlier, and let her feed his carnal hunger.

For the first time since his encounter with Penelope, Seth's lips curved into a genuine smile. Come tomorrow night, Penelope Parrish could lounge in his lap buck naked, and he wouldn't feel so much as a twinge of desire.

Chapter 7

For the first time that evening, Penelope was alone. Slowly she raised her face from where it lay cradled in her hands and stared at her tear-soaked reflection in the mirror.

Inky runnels of eyelash black streaked through layers of greasepaint and rouge, etching war-paint-like stripes down her cheeks. Her carmine lip paste, so carefully applied earlier that evening, was now smeared across her chin, resembling blood oozing from an open wound.

It might have been blood if Seth hadn't come to my rescue, she reminded herself. Disturbed by the thought, she tore her gaze from the mirror and turned her attention to removing her makeup. After slathering her face with a thick layer of cold cream, she snatched up a crumpled bit of cloth and began her messy task.

She usually found the ritual calming, reassuring in its mundanity. But tonight, as she scrubbed her skin with hide-flaying fierceness, she found the cream's familiar scent oddly disturbing . . . subtly different.

Perplexed, she lifted the jar to her nose and sniffed.

Almonds and glycerin and . . . what?

Her brow furrowed. She'd smelled that provocative fragrance before; somewhere in a different life, a hundred years ago and a million miles away from the Shakespeare's dingy dressing room. Mystified, she closed her eyes and took another whiff. Like a balm to her battered spirit the warm, woodsy aroma coiled around her heart, soothing her with memories of happier times. *Boston . . .*

I don't want to remember Boston, her heart protested, all too familiar with the wrenching aftermath of such reminiscences. But Penelope's mind betrayed her heart and blissfully surrendered to the sweetness of yesterday.

Back in time her mind slipped, back almost three years to

the night she'd made her triumphant solo debut at the Boston Theater. Back to the unforgettable moment when Seth had proposed.

Beneath Penelope's hand the rough table shifted and changed shape, transforming itself into an exquisite dressing table. The walls, a tattered collage of newsprint and playbills, were magically overlaid with fine yellow silk. There were bouquets of hothouse flowers everywhere. And behind her, reflected in the mirror, his blond hair shining like sunshine silk against the Cimmerian darkness of his evening clothes, was Seth Tyler.

Penelope's heart thrilled at the sight of him; she was giddy with joy. With his quicksilver wit and indomitable spirit, he was everything she ever wanted, all she would ever need.

Standing close behind where she sat, he bent down and nuzzled his face to her ear. *Marry me,* he whispered passionately. Then he pressed a string of kisses down the side of her neck, fervently demonstrating the sincerity of his proposal.

A soft moan escaped Penelope as she arched against his lips. His breath was hot, scorching her with desire. And when he slowly trailed his tongue across her bare shoulder, the slippery warmth of his licking caress sent a flurry of sensation rushing to the pit of her stomach, melting her insides into liquid fire.

Seth . . . , she gasped, breathlessly protesting his amorous assault. But then his mouth slipped lower to nip at the swell of her breasts, and she surrendered to his seductive ministrations.

Say yes, Princess. Playfully he bit the delicate lace edging the neckline of her dressing gown. *Say you'll be mine forever.*

Her breath was coming in short, strangled gasps now, her body quivered out of control. Instinctively she curved her back against his belly, eagerly absorbing the heat of his passion, hungrily accepting his promise of rapture.

Moaning his name over and over again, she reached back and wrapped her arms around his lean waist, urging his body nearer. Like a submissive slave helplessly obeying his mistress's sensual command, he sobbed once and pressed his groin against her back.

The feel of his arousal, rock-hard and thrusting between her shoulder blades, maddened her beyond shame. Heedless of everything, save her own desire for Seth, she slipped her hands lower and wantonly clenched at his tight buttocks.

No, he growled, pulling away. *Not like this.*

Penelope whimpered, suddenly bereft without his touch. *Seth—*

Kneeling beside her chair, he pressed a finger to her lips, silencing her. His expression tender, he reached out and lightly sketched through the masklike coating of cold cream on her cheek.

Marry me, he wrote. Then he enclosed the words in a heart, branding her with his loving declaration. She could smell his scent now. Distinctively woodsy ... exotically sweet ... beguiling.

Slowly his lips curved into the crooked smile she always found so entrancing. As his gaze captured hers in the mirror, she saw his naked longing reflected in the topaz richness of his wonderful eyes. It was then that he whispered ...

"It was dreadful, my dear! Absolutely dreadful!"

Instantly Penelope's bittersweet dream shattered into a thousand razor-edged slivers of regret. "W-what?" she stuttered, completely disoriented.

"Why, the way those filthy cretins tried to ravish you, of course." Euphemia Hotchkiss plopped down onto the stool next to Penelope's and kicked off her slippers. "I shudder to think what might have happened if your brave knight hadn't rescued you." Resting her left foot on top of her right knee, she inspected where her big toe had poked a hole through her stocking.

Penelope stared stupidly at her companion's exposed toe for a moment, her mind still too foggy to grasp a coherent thought. *Knight? Rescue?* Then the fog cleared, and she grimaced as the events of the dismal evening came crashing back.

Too distracted by the sorry state of her stocking to notice her friend's discomfiture, Euphemia rattled on. "Fine figure of a man, your rescuer. Handsome as a prince. Gallant to a fault."

Penelope rolled her eyes heavenward. She was in no mood to listen to Effie's tiresome fluttering over members of the opposite sex. Especially when that member happened to be Seth Tyler. Snatching up her cleansing cloth, she grumbled, "Believe me, Effie. The man isn't gallant." As she resumed scrubbing her face, she was again surrounded by Seth's distinctive scent.

Frowning, Penelope held the cold-cream-stained square of fabric up by one corner. What in the world . . . ?

Abruptly she released the cloth, wrinkling her nose with distaste. No wonder she was daydreaming like a witless ninny. She was cleansing her face with Seth's handkerchief. The blasted thing smelled just like him.

"He didn't take . . . *liberties,* did he?" Effie dropped her foot to the floor, her blue eyes round as saucers. "Do tell!"

"Well?" Effie prompted, scooting her stool closer.

Which she undoubtedly has, Penelope thought sourly. Still glaring at the handkerchief, she snapped, "I know the unsavory man from San Francisco. His name is Seth Tyler, and he's considered to be the worst kind of rogue."

"Seth." Effie sighed like a schoolgirl with a crush. Penelope decided she'd nip Effie's romantic infatuation in the bud quickly enough.

Lowering her voice to a conspiratorial whisper, she confided, "Mr. Tyler has a terrible reputation where women are concerned. He's so lecherous that mothers shudder in horror and lock their daughters in their rooms when he comes to call. Why, the only reason polite society receives him at all is because he's so darn rich. The cad practically owns half the town."

Of course, except for the part about Seth being rich, the allegations were out-and-out lies. Not only was Seth respected by the men of the city; he was considered quite a catch by the unmarried girls and their matchmaking mamas. Not that she was about to tell Effie any of that.

Apparently she didn't have to. "A naughty rascal, eh?" Effie's face took on an expression of starry-eyed bliss. "Nothing like a touch of wickedness to make a man interesting. I remember being courted by a particularly handsome devil back in—" She stopped mid-sentence, squinting myopically at her friend's face. "Why, just look at your nose! It's redder than a piece of raw meat." She pointed at the offending feature, clearly appalled.

Penelope drew the cracked lantern closer to the tarnished mirror and peered at her reflection. Effie was right. Her skin looked dreadful. Not only did her nose look as if someone had dropped a cherry in the middle of her face; her skin was blotchy from her agitated rubbing and her eyes were red from crying.

Lovely. Not only had Seth Tyler destroyed her peace of mind, but he was ruining her looks as well.

Seeing her friend's morose expression, Effie crooned soothingly, "Never you mind, dear. I have just the thing to restore your complexion." After giving Penelope's cheek a fond pat, she turned to the bewildering array of toiletries on the table before her, her face as serious as that of a conjuring necromancer. After much muttering and frowning, she finally settled on and exotic-looking bottle with a mysterious label.

"This should do the trick. 'Persian secret skin beautifier.' The advertisement says it's guaranteed to whiten the complexion and instill a pearllike luster. It's *patented,* you know."

Suspicious of anything touted patented, Penelope shook her head. "Thanks, Effie. But I don't want to waste your beautifier."

"But, my dear! What if someone . . . especially one of the gentlemen . . . should see you looking like that!" Effie's face perfectly reflected her horror at such a happenstance.

"No one will see me. I intend to go straight back to the boardinghouse and climb right into bed."

Effie eyed her friend dubiously. "A girl can't be to careful, you know. It simply wouldn't do—"

"Lorelei!"

Both women jumped at the pistol-report sharp exclamation.

In a snakelike hiss of silk skirts, Adele stepped from the doorway and stalked across the narrow confines of the room.

Just the sight of the woman was enough to send a suffocating wave of fear crashing in on Penelope. She'd prayed that Adele would recognize that she had been an unwilling player in the scene on the stairs, but as the woman came to a stop just inches from her back, she sensed that her prayers had been in vain.

Reluctantly she raised her eyes to meet Adele's gaze in the mirror. Pure, unconscionable evil glared back at her. She had seen that expression in the awful woman's eyes once before; it'd been the day Adele had condemned her to a life of shame, and her newborn son, Thomas, to a future of terrifying uncertainty.

Tommy. Penelope's breath caught in her throat. *How she loved him.* His every smile was a miracle, his sweetness a gift from God. He was her heart, her very reason for living. And his fragile life was being held in the balance by a malevolent demon named Adele du Charme. Paralyzed by fear and panicked almost beyond reason, Penelope could only stare back with mute appeal.

"Madame du Charme," Effie began, her voice quavering as badly as Penelope knew her own would if she were to speak. "What happened this evening wasn't our fault. We—"

"Leave us, Madame Hotchkiss," Adele interrupted brusquely. "I want a word alone with Lorelei." Never once did she release Penelope's gaze from the punishing shackles of her own.

Not daring to countermand her employer, Effie gave Penelope's hand a reassuring squeeze and then complied.

As the door closed behind the elderly actress, Adele buried her hand in Penelope's curls and brutally yanked her head back. "You little fool! Didn't I warn you what would happen if I caught you cozying up to a man?" She gave Penelope's hair another scalp-rending jerk. "Are you really stupid enough to believe that I won't harm that half-witted brat of yours?"

Held immobile more by fear's merciless grip than by Adele's physical one, Penelope moved her mouth in soundless terror.

Adele's lips twisted into a cruel smirk. "Children have been known to die of exposure when left alone in the mountains. That is, if the animals don't get them first."

It took all of Penelope's control not to lose the contents of her stomach at the thought of her son's frail body being savaged by wild beasts. "Please . . . ," she managed to choke out.

Ignoring Penelope's strangled plea, Adele continued, "Not that anyone would mourn the loss of the little imbecile, mind you. After all, he's nothing but a dirty little secret . . . yours, mine, Miles's, and, of course, the Skolfields'. But unlike yourself, Minerva and Sam Skolfield are wise enough not to disobey me. They'll do as I say, when I say it."

With a sinking feeling, Penelope acknowledged the truth of Adele's words. While the Skolfields were genuinely fond of Tommy, caring for him as best they could under squalid conditions, they, too, were victims of Adele's treachery. And like herself, they had no choice but to follow the vile woman's dictates.

Desperation born of that terrible knowledge gave Penelope the courage to blurt out, "But I didn't disobey you! I swear it! That wretched Mr. Tyler forced his attentions on me."

"Indeed?" Adele's thinly arched brows rose in disbelief. "According to Miles, you weren't struggling any too hard to escape the man's embrace." She let out an unpleasant laugh. "Not that I blame you. That Tyler person is a virile-looking piece."

"I-I didn't n-notice."

"Then, you're either blind or a fool. Or could it be that you're lying?" She gave the ebony curls in her hand another vicious pull. This time Penelope cried out, a response that brought a smile of sadistic pleasure to Adele's lips. "Shall I guess which answer is correct?"

The woman's diamond-hard eyes narrowed as she pretended to mull over the question. "Since you don't carry a cane and wear spectacles, it's obvious that you're not blind. And considering your bastard's existence, I can assume that you're intelligent enough to recognize a man's more—shall we say—potent charms."

Her voice grew soft, dangerously so. "Therefore, you must be lying. My guess is that you know Seth Tyler, and that you know him well. He seemed entirely too possessive to be a stranger."

The pain in Penelope's scalp was excruciating now. Desperate to escape Adele's punishing grasp, she admitted, "Mr. Tyler is my brother's closest friend. He's known me since I was twelve and seems to think it's his duty to protect me." A film of tears welled up in her eyes, blurring her vision. "Please believe me. I'm trying to discourage him. I promise I'll get rid of him."

"Unfortunately it's not that simple." Adele released her hair abruptly. "I had a drink with this Tyler person to—well, let's just say I wanted to learn the lay of the land. You might be interested to know that Floyd included Miles's promissory note in the sale of the Shakespeare."

Penelope rubbed her sore scalp gingerly. "I'm not surprised. Seth Tyler drives a hard bargain."

"True. But I drive a harder one. And I was able to persuade him to reduce our theatrical commitment from twelve weeks to six. That means we'll be free of Miles's gambling debt in time to make our engagement in Tombstone. I hear it's possible for a pretty singer to make over two hundred dollars a night there."

Penelope refrained from informing Adele that Seth only intended to stay in town for six weeks. She also knew better than to mention that he meant to take her with him when he left. Instead she asked, "How did you manage to talk him around?"

Adele shrugged. "It was amazingly simple. Like most men, his brains are between his legs. When he expressed an interest in you, I pointed out that you could be persuaded to spend time with him if he agreed to a certain concession. That concession was that he reduce the duration of our performance obligation."

Penelope was as shocked as if Adele had slapped her, which would have been preferable to being forced into Seth's company. How dare Adele make such a promise! How dare Seth agree!

How dare she say no? Picking up her hairbrush, she asked with a sigh of resignation, "What do you expect me to do?"

"For a start, you'll surprise him with your company tonight. Floyd's had a private supper set up in Room Four."

"But I can't dine with him tonight. I didn't wear an appropriate frock." Penelope pointed the brush at a much mended walking suit hanging from a wall hook. The garment was at least three years out of style and could best be described as ratty.

Adele eyed the suit with distaste. "I can't understand why you insist on dressing like a washerwoman these days." She gave a derogatory sniff. "You used to have exquisite taste in clothing."

It was on the tip of Penelope's tongue to retort that she wouldn't be forced to dress like one out of ten neediest charity cases if Adele didn't take every cent she made. But, of course, she didn't dare. Plucking at the brush bristles, she explained:

"Tommy needed medicine last month. It took most of my savings, since everything costs twice as much out here. Perhaps I'll be able to afford a new gown in a few months."

"Well, that's not going to do us any good tonight, is it?" Crossing her arms over her chest, Adele considered the problem. Suddenly she snapped her fingers and uttered a triumphant, "Aha!"

After rummaging through several of the wardrobe trunks, she produced the ivory taffeta evening gown Penelope had worn in a recent production of *The Count's Courtship*. Though the material was cheap and the workmanship poor, it was still far more modish than anything in Penelope's hopelessly dated wardrobe.

Nodding her satisfaction, Adele straightened the crushed silk roses in the basque corsage. "Yes. This should do quite nicely." She held up the frothy creation for further inspection. "The cut is elegant, but the neckline is discreet enough so as not to give that Tyler person the wrong idea."

Lowering the gown a fraction, she fixed Penelope with a severe glare. "I won't have you giving the man any wrong ideas, either. You may dine, dance, or play cards with him, but you'll keep him at arm's length at all times. And you will only associate with him during working hours and under this roof. Understood?"

Penelope nodded. No problem there. The real problem was going to be keeping herself from wringing the infuriating man's neck during her stint as his reluctant companion.

Laying the gown across a closed steamer trunk, Adele continued, "I expect you to return the costume right after dinner. If I find any stains or damage, the cost of the repairs will be taken out of your wages."

Penelope stared down at her hairbrush, taking care to hide her resentment. Not only did Adele pay her less than the lowliest scullery maid; the greedy woman was always levying ridiculous fines. There was a fine if Penelope was a minute late for rehearsal, one for forgetting a line. If her voice wavered during a song? That blunder would cost her plenty. It was a wonder she wasn't fined for blowing her nose or using the outhouse.

She stole a glance over to where Adele was digging through a box of costume jewelry. Well, she'd be free of the she-devil and her fines soon enough. She had a plan; one that would regain her freedom and put Thomas back in her arms, where he belonged. She just needed to get her hands on five hundred dollars.

As Penelope began to pull the pins from her hair, still contemplating her scheme to reclaim her son, Adele draped a pearl bead necklace around her neck. "You'll wear your hair down, like in *The Mountain Sylph*," she commanded, snapping the necklace clasp closed. "The sight of all those curls seems to turn men into witless fools. Why, we swept up close to two hundred dollars worth of gold from the stage last time you wore it like that."

She paused a moment to critically examine Penelope's face, before adding, "And for God's sake, do something about your nose. It's redder than a boil on a bookkeeper's backside." With that, she pivoted on her heels and glided toward the door.

But before she got more than halfway across the room, she paused. "Oh. By the way." When she turned, Penelope could see cruelty gleaming in her eyes. "Sam was in town today. He says to tell you that your brat has the croup again."

"Tommy is nearby?" Penelope held her breath as she awaited the answer. During the past year and a half, Adele had had the Skolfields hold the baby in hiding places along the company's performing route. Having him near was an effective way to control Penelope, for it made Adele's threats terrifyingly possible.

It also made it possible for Penelope to see him regularly. It was those few hours with her son that made her life bearable.

As if reading her thoughts, Adele replied, "Yes. If you're wise, you'll remember that while you entertain Seth Tyler."

"I'll do anything you say. I promise," Penelope swore. "Just let me see him for a few hours on Sunday. It's his second birthday, and I want to take him some presents."

Adele let out a scornful grate of laughter. "As if the brainless little brat knows what day it is . . . or anything else for that matter. I've seen smarter children in idiot asylums."

Prudently curbing her impulse to protest Adele's cruel assessment of her son, Penelope implored, "I know what day it is, and it's important to me that I make it special for him. Won't you please just consider letting me go?"

Adele gave a noncommittal shrug. "I'll consider it . . . if all goes well this evening."

Chapter 8

"How come them Injuns didn't scalp you?" gasped the saloon girl, her red-rouged lips forming a wide O of horror.

Seth stuffed another bonbon into her mouth, grinning at the way she wiggled her backside against his groin as she chewed.

"I was rescued by a fellow stagecoach passenger, a traveling saleslady from Chicago," he explained, letting one finger meander from her lips to her thinly veiled breasts. "Seems she was set on making a killing peddling her extra-heavy cast-iron frying pans to Denver's wives. Claimed those pans were thick enough to fry a steak to perfection and heavy enough to persuade a roving husband to stay home at night."

With tantalizing slowness, the girl unfastened the tiny pearl buttons at the front of her camisole. "Nivver seen a travelin' saleslady before," she murmured, baring her plump breasts to her new boss's appreciative gaze. "Was she pretty?"

"Aside from the fact that she was six feet tall and almost bald—"

"Bald!" The girl's eyes bulged with disbelief.

"Curling tongs accident," Seth replied mournfully, though his expression was anything but mournful as he cupped the girl's soft breasts in his palms. "Burnt her hair off to the roots. What was left stood straight up on end, kind of like an irate porcupine."

"Poor saleslady." The girl practically purred as she arched her back in response to Seth's caresses.

"Poor me. Since the other passengers had gotten off the stage at Fort Lyon and the driver had headed back for help, the Indians were left with slim pickings as far as scalps went. Hers, of course, was rejected without a second glance, while it was decided that mine would make a fine trophy."

The girl raked her fingers through his hair, pulling it over his shoulders. "Can't say I blame 'em. You do have purty hair."

Seth chuckled and dropped a kiss on her vanilla-cream flavored lips. "Fortunately the saleslady liked it, too—on my head. So just as those two savages were all set to scalp me, she came bounding up behind them bellowing like a raging bull. Before they could say 'Ugh,' she whomped them over the head with her top-of-the-line frying pan and knocked them out cold."

The girl shrieked with laughter and threw her weight against him, sending him sprawling backward across the worn red velvet settee. "Yer funnin' me!"

"Want to see my top-of-the-line, extra-heavy cast-iron frying pans?" he countered, wrestling her down on top of him.

Still giggling, she snaked her hand between their closely pressed bodies and slipped it into his trousers to give his sex a naughty tweak. "You swear? There really was a saleslady?"

"Swear on Chief Left Hand's ghost," Seth murmured, arching up against her wantonly probing fingers.

"It don't count none to swear on a dead Injun. Everybody knows Injuns ain't honest." With that pronouncement, she began to rub up and down his length.

"Sure they are, sweetheart," he said, rolling his hips in rhythm with her hand. "Those two Indians honestly indicated that they were going to scalp me." Despite his best efforts to become aroused and her skillful ministrations, his sex barely stirred.

What the hell is wrong with me? he wondered, opening his legs as she cupped him. He held is breath, awaiting the shock of pleasure he knew he should feel.

Nothing. He felt nothing but a vaguely annoying prodding sensation in his nether regions. His breath escaped in a hiss. Why the hell wouldn't the damn thing behave? It wasn't as if he couldn't get an erection. He got them all the time . . . day . . . night. He awoke as hard as a rock every morning.

The answer, as disturbing as it was, was one he knew all too well. It was the reason he'd failed to find pleasure the single time he'd bedded a woman since his split with Penel-

ope; the same reason he hadn't accepted the numerous carnal
invitations he'd received during the past two years.

That reason was that he still loved Penelope. And the
thought, much less the act, of having sexual relations with
anyone else left him about as excited as attending a Temper-
ance Society meeting. He'd been a fool to think he could
spend his lust like this. Frustrated and more than a little
shamed by his dismal performance, he gently pulled the
girl's hand away.

"Mr. Tyler," she protested.

"Seth."

"Seth," she echoed, reaching for his trouser buttons.
"Don't you worry none. Titania'll have you hard in no time
at'll."

Before he could reply, there was a soft knock at the door.
"Seth?" queried a half-muffled voice.

"Who could that be?" he muttered, relieved by the interruption. As if in response to his question, the door swung
open and in strolled Penelope.

"Seth—" Penelope stopped in her tracks, taken aback by
the sight of the couple on the settee. Though Seth was fully
clothed and the girl was merely kneeling between his legs,
his flushed face and her glare confirmed her suspicion that
she'd interrupted something intimate. Stammering an apology, she turned to leave.

"Wait!" he barked.

She paused, wanting nothing more than to flee the oddly
painful sight of Seth with another woman. Yet, it had been
a long while since she'd had the freedom to do what she
wanted, and like everything else she'd done over the past
two years, her reason now for seeking Seth out had nothing
to do with her own wants. It was remembering that reason
that made her turn and face him.

"Have you met Titania, Princess?" he drawled.

Penelope nodded, discomforted by her irrational urge to
yank the hussy off him and boot her broad backside out the
door. As she watched, Seth drew the girl down on top of him
to whisper in her ear. The girl giggled and nodded at whatever he said, then stood up, blatantly flaunting her bare
breasts.

Penelope didn't miss the lazy look of admiration that
crossed Seth's face. For some inexplicable reason that look

made her temper rise a few degrees. "I see you found a willing *dinner* companion," she snapped.

Seth sat up and tossed his tousled hair back over his shoulders. "Plenty of hungry girls here at the Shakespeare."

His indifference made her temper hit the boiling point. "I can just imagine what those girls are hungry for," she muttered.

"I'm sure you can." His gaze never wavered from the near-naked form sauntering toward the door. "Titania?"

The girl paused.

"Thanks." He tossed a gold coin to her, which she caught with practiced ease.

"Believe me, honey. It was my pleasure."

Eyeing the exiting saloon girl with distaste, Penelope plastered herself against the doorjamb, scrupulously avoiding contact as she passed. As the woman disappeared down the hall, she let out a snort of disgust. "Really, Seth. Is that little trollop the best you could find?"

"I have no complaint. Her appetite was hearty enough," he said, sauntering to the sideboard to study the untouched dishes.

Penelope sniffed. "I imagine you'll complain loudly enough when you find yourself with the French pox. It's excruciating, I hear. Especially when your man's part turns black and rots off."

Seth laughed. "I'm sure you'd enjoy watching me suffer in such a manner."

She sniffed.

He laughed again. "Sorry to disappoint you, sweetheart. But I have it on good authority that Titania is as clean as a freshly laundered sheet. Speaking of ailments, I thought you were too ill to dine with me. Nobody informed me of your miraculous recovery."

Uncomfortable at having to add yet another lie to her already infinite list, Penelope reached down and fidgeted with the brass doorknob. "I decided that Floyd is"—*scr-e-e-ch!* the unoiled knob protested as she fitfully twisted it back and forth—"right. Perhaps what I need is a glass of champagne and some food. I haven't eaten"—*screech! grind!*— "anything since this morning, and not eating always gives me a headache."

Seth winced at the shrill sounds emanating from the doorknob. "Then, why don't you stop lurking in the doorway and come eat something?" He motioned to the white-clothed table in the center of the red and gold embellished room.

As happy as a martyr on the way to the stake, she complied. "For the record, I wasn't lurking," she grumbled, perching on the edge of a gilded "Fancy" chair.

"You have your definitions, and I have mine."

"So you've been kind enough to point out."

They lapsed into strained silence as Seth lifted the silver covers off the serving dishes. From where Penelope sat, she could see that there was antelope steak in mushroom sauce, wild goose liver in jelly, and what appeared to be some sort of fish, all accompanied by an eye-popping array of side dishes. When Seth pulled the cover off the last charger to reveal something she couldn't identify, she broke the silence. "What is that?"

He peered down at it for a moment, then smiled. "Lamb fries." Glancing across the table to where she sat listlessly toying with her silverware, he added, "If I remember correctly, lamb is a particular favorite of yours."

She nodded without enthusiasm.

Ignoring her marked lack of interest in the food, Seth picked up a plate, inquiring politely, "May I serve you?"

She sighed in resignation. "If you wish."

Starting with a heaping serving of the lamb, he quickly filled her plate. After setting the food in front of her, he poured them each a glass of champagne, then served himself. That task completed, he settled into the chair opposite hers and began to devour his meal with gastronomic delight.

Penelope, on the other hand, merely stared at her plate, restlessly spinning her knife like a top.

"Why so nervous, Princess?"

She glanced up, startled. "I'm not nervous," she lied.

"Sure you are." He nodded meaningfully at her hands.

She jerked her hand from the knife and flattened her palms against the tabletop, willing herself to stop fidgeting. "That's ridiculous," she muttered. "Why would I be nervous?"

"Good question. Why don't you answer it." Seth took another bite of antelope steak. Chewing rhythmically, he transferred his gaze from his plate to her hands, watching with the fascination of a ten-year-old seeing a freak show for the first time.

Penelope frowned and followed his line of vision. Damn!

Now she was wadding the tablecloth up beneath her palms. Stifling a frustrated groan, she balled her hands into fists and retorted, "I can't answer your asinine question, because I'm not nervous."

"Don't forget that I've known you since you were twelve. Even back then you had that annoying habit of picking at everything in sight when you were nervous or upset." He paused to take a sip of champagne. "So? Are you nervous or upset?"

"Neither! I'm merely bored with your questions."

"I distinctly remember you agreeing to answer my questions when we struck our bargain." Seth's gaze skewered her over the rim of his glass. "Of course, if you'd like, we could always renegotiate the terms"—his gaze traveled suggestively from her face to her breasts—"find a less *boring* way for you to fulfill your half of the deal."

She gasped at his leering insinuation. "How dare you! What would my brother say if he heard you make such a crude proposal?"

"Who do you think taught me how to bargain?" Seth put down his glass and leaned forward, his eyes glittering with challenge. "Now, if you're a true Parrish, if you've inherited even an iota of your father and brother's legendary business acumen, you'll come up with an appropriate counteroffer."

She sputtered with outrage. "I w-won't be your doxy!"

He made a clicking noise between his teeth. "Just as I suspected. You're a changeling child." He leaned back in his chair and crossed his arms over his chest. "Shall I assume that you'll stick to our original bargain and answer my questions?"

She jerked her head once in grudging assent. He wanted answers? Fine. He'd get them. Fictional ones. After all, he hadn't specified that she tell the truth, had he?

As if reading her mind, he added, "Oh, and don't think to fob me off with lies. I intend to verify each and every one of your answers. Madame du Charme should come in handy for that."

Penelope stared at him, horror-struck at what Adele might do if faced with his questions. If he pried too deeply into her business, and knowing Seth's propensity for thoroughness, he probably would, Adele might panic and take drastic steps to keep her crimes from being discovered. The results would be tragic.

Apparently her face reflected her thoughts, for Seth inquired, "What? Changed your mind again?" When she didn't reply, he snorted. "I'll take your silence for a yes. All right, then. If you won't answer my questions or be my doxy, how do you propose to uphold your end of the bargain?"

Penelope scrambled for something—anything—she could offer him. Money was out of the question, for even if Adele didn't demand every cent she made, she'd never have enough to buy his cooperation. The blasted man was richer than old Croesus himself.

"Surely you have something worth bartering. Some kind of skill or talent?" His gaze was unwavering as it bore into hers.

"Nothing that would interest you."

"You'd be amazed at what I find interesting."

"Well, let's see. I can sing and dance." She looked at him hopefully.

Without so much as blinking, he rasped, "What else?"

"I write a fine hand, and I'm good with numbers. Perhaps I could help with your accounts?" She crossed her fingers.

"My solicitor takes care of that. What else?"

Sighing, she uncrossed her fingers. "I can draw and paint, and I've learned simple sewing. Oh, and I play the pianoforte."

He yawned. "All admirable traits, I'm sure. What else?"

She was at a loss. When itemized, her skills did sound negligible. Feeling utterly useless, she murmured, "Effie says—"

"Effie?" he queried sharply.

"Euphemia Hotchkiss. She's the dramatic actress of our company. We share a room at the boardinghouse."

He nodded. "Do continue."

"Yes. Well. Effie says that I make the best face cream she's ever tried and that I'm particularly skilled at styling hair. Of course, you'd hardly be interested in such services."

A calculating gleam entered his eyes. "Ever tie a man's tie?"

"I've helped the men in the company with theirs."

"Ever shine boots or shave a man?"

"No to the former, and yes to the latter."

"You've shaved a man?" His eyes narrowed. "Who? A lover?"

"Must you drag everything down to your own filthy level?" she snapped, picking up her knife. "For your information, I shaved Jake when he first returned home from the war. He was too ill to do it himself, and I liked helping him." She stabbed a creamed artichoke heart with murderous intent.

"And I know for a fact that he actually survived your efforts. Excellent! We're finally getting somewhere."

She looked up from her skewered artichoke, incredulous. "Where exactly are we getting to?"

"We're getting to the point where we can strike a bargain."

"We are?"

He sighed. "It's a pity about your lack of Parrish business acuity. However, such skills aren't required by a valet."

"Valet!"—*Clunk!*—She dropped her knife, artichoke and all.

"Valet," he repeated. "Since my valet, Roper, has an inordinate fear of being scalped by what he terms 'red-skinned heathen devils' and refused to accompany me here, I've had the tiresome chore of tending to my own needs."

She sputtered wordlessly for a moment. "I-I hardly think it appropriate that I act as your valet!"

"Less appropriate than being my mistress?" He lifted one eyebrow tauntingly.

"Of course not. Being either is out of the question."

He gave a dismissive shrug. "Then, we're back to where we started. You'll answer all my questions, and do it to my satisfaction." Picking up his knife and fork, he sliced another piece off his antelope steak.

Penelope sucked in a shuddering breath. Whatever was she to do? Adele had warned her not to see Seth outside the Shakespeare, and being his valet would mean that she'd be seeing quite a bit of him . . . literally. But if she didn't . . .

"What do you expect me to do as your valet?" she hissed.

He seemed to consider her question while he finished chewing his meat. After swallowing, he murmured, "Don't look so worried, Princess. I promise not to make you shine my boots."

"You're too kind."

"A regular philanthropist, so I've been told."

She snorted. "It's amazing how a few million dollars can instantly endow a man with all sorts of virtues."

"Who said anything about virtue? But we're digressing." He made a chopping motion in the air. "As my valet, you'll arrive at my hotel room every morning at seven sharp."

"Seven!" she wailed. Why, most nights she didn't get out of the Shakespeare until almost two.

"Seven," he repeated, ignoring her outburst. "You'll select and lay out my clothes, and make certain that my linen is well pressed. Though you won't be required to shine my boots, it will be your job to make sure the bellboy does it. Of course, you'll be expected to shave me, assist me with my bath—"

"Your bath! You can't be serious! You'll be naked!" Penelope felt her face turn redder than her flannel pantaloons.

"Of course I'll be naked. I'm hardly a nun who bathes in a linen shift." He cocked his head to one side, viewing her with sardonic amusement. "Why the blushing and stammering, Princess? It's not as if you're not familiar with my naked body."

If looks could kill . . . "Be that as it may, I have no desire to see or touch it again. Ever!"

"Pity. I was looking forward to having you scrub my . . ." his gaze stripped her with lascivious thoroughness, ". . . back."

She gasped, outraged by his vulgar innuendo.

He merely laughed. "All right. If you won't bathe me, you'll have to agree to answer one simple question a day. *Every day* until the six weeks are up and we return to San Francisco."

"But that's not fair!"

"Whoever said that life is fair?"

"But—"

"Do you agree or not?"

Crossing her fingers again, she desperately tried a little negotiating of her own. "Only if you agree not to pester the company with your infernal questioning."

"Perhaps you're a Parrish after all." He chuckled. "All right, then. I won't consult anyone else in the company if you promise to answer my questions to the best of your ability."

She nodded. "I promise." Of course any question that might endanger Tommy would be beyond her ability to answer, so technically she wasn't perjuring herself by agreeing.

"Then, it's a deal. You can start your duties the day after tomorrow. I'm staying at the American House on Blake Street." He lifted his glass. "Now, shall we drink to our bargain?"

When she merely glared at him, he murmured, "If you don't have that glass in the air by the count of three, I'll assume that you've changed your mind again and invite the company to join us for dinner so I can begin my questioning. One."

Penelope raised her glass with such force that the champagne bubbled over the rim and foamed across her hand.

Seth nodded. "Here's to clean boots and a question a day." He touched his glass to hers with a bell-like ring of crystal, then drained the contents in one gulp.

Penelope angrily followed suit. The champagne was good. French. Expensive. But she refused to savor it. Slamming her empty glass down on the table, she snapped, "What now, master? Do you want me to grovel on my hands and knees and kiss your feet?"

Seth set down his own glass and leaned across the narrow table. Boldly and with provocative slowness, he traced the shape of her mouth with his thumb. "Oh, no, my sweet serving wench," he purred. "Those lips are meant for much higher places and more pleasurable purposes."

Penelope's breath caught in her throat, and her body went as limp as a poke bonnet in the driving rain. She wanted to pull away, she wanted to feel repulsion at his touch. But . . . damn him! As much as she hated him at that moment, she liked what his fingers were doing to her lips. And to her everlasting shame, she found herself wishing that he'd replace his thumb with his mouth and tongue. Hating herself for wanting him, yet powerless to deny her own desire, she sagged toward him.

Seth cupped his cool hand beneath her chin and tilted her face up to his. Their lips were scant inches apart. Trembling with expectation, her lips parted, wantonly begging for his kiss. As he captured her stunned gaze with his smoldering one, he murmured, "Such lovely lips. Such a sweet mouth. It should be . . . eating." With that, he pulled away and sat back in his chair, chuckling. "I thought you said you were hungry, Princess."

Penelope jerked back against her own chair, mortified. Oh, she was hungry all right, and by the way Seth was gloating, he knew exactly what she craved. Hating him for his arrogance and herself for her ninny-witted weakness, she picked up her fork, staring at her plate as she fought to regain her composure.

After a long moment, Seth leaned over and crooned, "Never fear, Princess. The food is the one thing Titania didn't touch."

That reminder was like salt being rubbed into her wounded pride: it stung. But she'd die before she let him see her hurt. Instead she fixed him with a disdainful stare and retorted, "Loss of appetite is the first symptom of the French pox."

He returned her haughty gaze with one of amusement. "You seem to have become quite an expert on the pox of late."

"Hallie told me all about the pox . . . and other things before I left San Francisco. She said that it wouldn't do for me to be ignorant about the ways of the world and men."

Seth guffawed. He'd like to have been a fly on the wall when Jake's wife, Hallie, who was not only a doctor, but a mission worker as well, lectured Penelope on the facts of life. Intrigued, he asked, "Oh? And what are the ways of the world?"

"Considering your reputation with women, I'd guess you know them well." She cut a dainty piece of lamb and tasted it. It was good. She took a bigger bite.

"I know them. I just wanted to make sure you do."

"I don't see how that is any of your concern." She swirled a piece of lamb in the accompanying brown sauce, wishing he'd drop the whole uncomfortable subject.

This time she got her wish. "How's the lamb?" he inquired, watching her stuff the sauce-drenched morsel into her mouth.

"Different . . . but good. Not at all like ordinary fried lamb."

"I didn't say it was fried lamb. I said it was lamb fries."

"Surely it's the same thing?"

"Well, both are lamb." Seth's expression was angelic as he explained the difference. "Fried lamb usually consists of lamb chops that have been fried. Lamb fries are sheep testicles. The locals claim it's food fit for royalty."

Penelope gagged. "Lamb . . ." She sputtered and choked.

". . . Testicles," he finished for her. Tilting his head to one side, he peered at her face, his eyes bright with interest. "I didn't realize it was possible for a live person to turn that shade of green." He bent nearer and touched her cheek. "Striking color. Lovely, really. It perfectly compliments your red nose."

Seth leaned against the Shakespeare's back door, sucking in the night air. It smelled fresh, with just a hint of the pungent-sweet scent he'd come to associate with the West. From the moment he'd smelled that prairie perfume, he'd loved it, but never had he appreciated it more than he did tonight after being cloistered in the vomit-stench permeated private room with Penelope.

Unbidden the vision of Penelope retching miserably into the chamber pot flashed through his mind. That picture was enough to make him exhale the fresh air guiltily. When in God's name had she become so weak-bellied? Three years ago she wouldn't have so much as batted an eyelash at the notion of eating sheep's testicles. Back then she'd had a cast-iron stomach and gastronomic valor to challenge his own.

Swearing beneath his breath, he yanked his cigar case from his pocket and cradled it between his palms. The worse part of his prank-gone-wrong was that he couldn't allow himself to comfort her. He couldn't hold her and soothe away her nausea. He couldn't playfully tease and distract her from her misery the way he'd done the time she'd been so wretchedly ill with influenza.

No. Because of his cursed lack of self-control, he didn't dare do more than express tepid concern. For he knew that if he were to bow to his emotions now, he might be powerless to deny them in the future. And that was a chance he couldn't take.

The object of his remorseful musings let out a misery-laced groan. "I th-think I'm going to be s-sick again."

Seth looked with alarm over to where Penelope stood clutching at an empty beer barrel. She was wavering back and forth like a green sailor on a roiling deck, retching dryly.

Muttering a self-denigrating oath, he dropped his cigar case back into his pocket and hastened to her side. Though his good sense warned him that he should maintain his pretense of icy indifference and keep his distance, his sense of honor argued that she was Jake's sister, and for his friend's sake he had an obligation to see to her welfare.

Or so he tried to tell himself as he pulled her trembling form into his embrace. "Breathe deeply," he murmured, stroking her back and hair. "The nausea will pass in a moment."

He could hear her gasping for air and feel her soft breasts heaving against his chest as she struggled to comply. "Good girl. Now take another one," he coaxed, resting his cheek against her silky hair. "Draw it in slowly and hold it for a count of five."

Nodding against his chest, she did as he directed.

They continued on like that for a long while, he crooning commands and she dutifully obeying. Eventually her dry heaves subsided into soft, hiccuping burps.

"Better?" he inquired, massaging the base of her neck.

Penelope nodded and emitted another burp.

For some odd reason, Seth found those unladylike sounds charming. Smiling at his own absurdity, he moved his hands lower to knead her tense shoulders. She melted against him with a sigh.

As he worked, his gaze returned again and again to the ivory taffeta beneath his palm. Being a man who adored women, he'd had more than a little experience in selecting feminine frippery. That experience told him that Penelope's gown was of third-rate material, sewn by a fourth-rate seamstress. Hardly the type of garment the Penelope he'd once known would have worn. The Penelope he remembered had been the epitome of elegance.

His eyes narrowed as he fingered the coarse lace of her Vandyke bertha collar. A couple of hours earlier he'd almost managed to convince himself that her Shakespeare escapade was simply a poor career decision. After all, she was adventurous by nature and touring the West was just the sort of thing that might appeal to her. He also knew that, like himself, she was full of stubborn pride and that she would suffer the consequences of her bad judgment rather than admit that she'd made a mistake.

At least that was how he'd rationalized her defensive behavior on the stairs. Pride and embarrassment. But now, seeing the normally impeccably garbed Penelope Parrish in this shoddy gown ... well, to his way of reasoning, this gown confirmed his initial suspicion that she was in trouble. And whatever sort of trouble she was in, he'd have laid ten to one odds that it was far more serious than she cared for him to know.

The thought of Penelope all alone and in trouble, too frightened or ashamed to seek help or comfort, sent a fierce flood of protectiveness washing through him. What he wouldn't give for the chance to be her modern-day Sir Galahad. He wanted to be the man she trusted above all others, the one she turned to in times of trouble. He wished—

Smothering his urge to curse a blue streak, Seth abruptly pushed Penelope away. He might as well wish for the moon for all the chance he had of attaining his heart's desire. Damn it to hell! He had to get a grip on his emotions before he did something disastrously stupid.

It didn't help his confused state of mind when Penelope took his hand in hers and whispered, "Thank you for being so kind, Seth. I'm sorry to be such a nuisance."

The humility of Penelope's unwarranted gratitude shamed Seth to the very core of his being. Feeling smaller than an ear mite and lower than a villain with a noose around his neck, he replied sincerely, "I'm the one who should be apologizing. Feeding you those fries was a nasty trick."

The light of a million stars and the full moon illuminated Penelope's features as she tilted her face up to meet his gaze. Seth's breath caught in his throat as he stared down at her.

Dear God! She was beautiful. Especially when she smiled the way she was smiling now, displaying the most irresistible pair of dimples this side of heaven. Seth had always loved those dimples, and it took all of his remaining willpower not to pull her back into his arms and kiss them.

Still smiling, Penelope shook her head. "It was silly of me not to remember what a prankster you are ... especially where food is concerned. I'll never forget the time you brought me a beribboned box of chocolate dipped snails." She reached up and tucked a tendril of his hair behind her ear, just like she used to do during their courtship. "You let me eat every last one before you told me what they were."

The sweet familiarity of her gesture took Seth's breath away. When he was finally able to reply, his voice was little more than a raw whisper. "The confectioner who sold me those bonbons assured me that they were all the vogue."

She laughed, and he couldn't resist grinning in return.

"Greedy girl. As I recall, you didn't bother to ask what they were before you attacked them like a starving street urchin."

He also recalled how she had shrieked with mock indignation when he'd confessed his little joke, and tickled every ticklish inch of him in retaliation. It made him ache with longing just remembering the closeness they had once shared.

"I'll make you a deal," she said. "You promise not to feed me any more of your exotic delicacies, and I'll forgive you for making me sick this evening."

It was Seth's turn to laugh. "Now you're sounding like a true Parrish. Perhaps there's hope for you yet."

"Perhaps." She grinned up at him. "Do you agree?"

He focused his warm gaze on her dimples. "How can I say no in the face of such charming persuasion?"

As they shook hands, sealing their bargain, the door creaked opened. Out piled Bertram, Effie, and Miles. Penelope dropped his hand and backed away, her face the color of bleached muslin.

Troubled and more than a little perplexed by her reaction, Seth turned to study the intruders through narrowed eyes.

"I've been looking all over for you, Lorelei," Miles scolded, roughly seizing Penelope's arm. "Mother says I'm to take you back to the boardinghouse now."

Seth moved protectively to Penelope's other side. "The lady is feeling ill. As her companion this evening, it's my duty to escort her home."

Clucking like a mother hen over her chicks, Effie shoved Miles aside. "Poor dear. She does look a bit green around the gills." She planted her palm against Penelope's forehead. "Hmm. She feels warm, too." Nodding knowingly, she concluded, "I think a dose of Flannigan's Patented Female Regulator is in order."

Penelope's stomach churned at the thought of one of Effie's nasty patented cures. Fighting her nausea, she groaned, "I'll be fine. I just want to go to the boardinghouse and lie down."

"Which is where I intend to take you," Seth replied, looping his arm through hers.

"Oh, no you don't!" Miles planted himself squarely in front of the couple. "We may be at your beck and call during working hours, but you have no say in what we do outside the Shakespeare. Mother told me to escort Lorelei, and I intend to do just that!"

Seth raised one eyebrow in sardonic amusement. "Do you always do what your mother tells you?"

Miles's face contorted with indignation. "My mother is the finest woman in the world," he declared defensively. "As such, it is my duty to obey her. I'd remember that if I were you."

"And I would remember who held my gambling voucher if I were you," Seth snapped back, his patience wearing dangerously thin.

Miles had the good grace to flush. "A *gentleman* would never bring up that subject in front of ladies."

"And a *man* would never allow those same ladies to degrade themselves in order to repay his gambling debts."

"Why, you—!" Miles sputtered with impotent rage. "Y-you—! I'll show you who's the m-man around here!"

"Oh, my!" Effie frantically fanned herself with her dog-eared script. "I do hope you gentlemen aren't going to come to fisticuffs!" She peered back and forth between the warring factions, her gleeful expression belying her anxious words.

Penelope hoped not, either. She shuddered to think of what Adele might do if she should be the cause of Miles getting his dainty nose bloodied. Determined to circumvent the impending row, she disengaged her arm from Seth's. "Miles always serves as my escort. Perhaps it would be best if he saw me home." She cast Seth a pleading look, praying that he would let the matter drop.

But Seth wasn't about to be put off. Tossing Miles a scathing look, he growled, "As your brother's friend and confidant, I consider it my duty to decide what is best for you. And allowing you to wander the streets of Denver in the middle of the night with this mewling mama's boy as your protector is definitely against my better judgment. You'll come with me."

Miles let out an infuriated screech and advanced toward the taller man, his fists poised to strike. Seth simply looked down his nose at the actor, amused.

"Harrumph!"

All gazes darted toward Bertram, who'd remained silent until now. Clearing his throat again, he announced, "I shall escort the lovely child home." Always the gentleman, he deferred to Penelope. "That is, if you have no objections, my dear?"

Penelope smiled gratefully at the bewhiskered old actor. "I would be honored."

"Let me assure you that the honor is all mine. It's been a long while since I've had the pleasure of such charming company." With a gallant flourish, he offered Penelope his arm. After nodding first to Seth, who inclined his head in consent, and then to the sulking Miles, Bert led her down the shallow back stairs.

When they reached the dusty alley below, the old actor glared up at Effie and barked, "Egad, woman! Will you stop dawdling and come along? We don't have all night you know."

Muttering something about pompous old goats, Effie scampered to join the couple. As for Miles, he shot his new employer a venomous look before stamping back into the saloon, undoubtedly intent on whining to his mama.

Seth shrugged. Narrowing his eyes in thought, he watched as the trio of actors vanished into the shadows of the night. There was something going on here. Something dark and dangerous if his senses served him right, which they usually did. And he fully intended to find out what it was. Question by probing question.

Chapter 9

It was a perfect day for revenge. Sullen black clouds hung thick and low, shrouding the rising sun in an amorphous pall. High above the rooftops lightning stabbed the storm-swept sky. Wind rattled at every window and door. In the distance, garbed in mist and jutting regally against the leaden sky, the Rocky Mountains presented a stunning still life in muted shades of purple and gray.

Snug within the elegant confines of the American House dining room, his palms flexed around a mug of steaming coffee, Seth studied the approaching storm through the plush-draped window. The weather suited his mood perfectly. Dark. Wrathful. For today would see the culmination of all his meticulously laid plans. Today was the day he would take the final, devastating step in his scheme to destroy Louisa Vanderlyn.

With savage exaltation swelling deep in his chest, he raised the mug to his lips and took a swallow of coffee, watching as his reflection in the polished window glass followed suit. Every contour, every line of the face in the glass bore the unmistakable stamp of the aristocratic Van Cortlandt family. So much so, that when he'd gone to the decaying Van Cortlandt Manor two years earlier seeking information about his birth, the ancient retainer had gasped and stumbled back, keening, "Get ye back to yer grave, Willem Van Cortlandt!" It was from that servant that Seth had learned of Louisa's treachery.

After poking and prodding his unexpected visitor to assure himself that he was a living, breathing mortal, the old man had invited Seth to the kitchen to warm himself by the hearth. The eerie echoing of their footsteps as they made their way through the long central hallway and down the steep back servant's stairs had made Seth pause more than once to peer uneasily over his shoulder. There was something chilling about the hollow emptiness of the house that had made him half expect to see Willem Van Cortlandt's ghost stalking them in the shadows.

Once they were in the kitchen, comfortably ensconced at a battered trestle table with a stein of home-brewed beer in hand, the servant had prattled with the unremitting zeal of a man long-starved for company. After an hour of answering questions and listening to small talk, ranging from local folklore to the latest harvest, Seth had cautiously broached the subject of his birth.

At first the retainer refused to dig up the long-buried tale, but when Seth told him his own story, starting with his abandonment at birth and ending with the Pinkerton report linking him to the Van Cortlandt family, the man reluctantly relented.

The servant prefaced his tale by explaining, rather boastfully, that he'd once occupied the position of Willem Van Cortlandt's valet, and it was only because of the familiar nature of his duties that he knew of the secrecy-shrouded birth.

According to the man's rambling account, Willem had just negotiated an advantageous marriage between his daughter, Louisa, and their wealthy neighbor, Cornelius De Windt, when Louisa's maid privately confided her suspicions that the bride-to-be was pregnant. When Willem confronted his daughter with the allegation, she'd tearfully blamed her older brother, Pieter, for her condition. From what the servant could ascertain from his eavesdropping, Pieter, who everyone but Willem agreed was quite mad, had violated his sister, and she'd been too humiliated to report the rape when it had happened two months earlier.

In a confidential tone the man added that Pieter had forced himself on three housemaids prior to his assault on his sister, but because the women were mere servants, Willem had ignored the crimes. The incestuous rape and resulting pregnancy of his own daughter, however, were things he couldn't overlook, especially in light of her upcoming nuptials.

Though Cornelius was forty years older than sixteen-year-old Louisa and the father of two grown sons, he was offering her an enviable position in clannish New York society, and Willem a long-coveted parcel of farmland adjoining the Van Cortlandt estate. Neither the land-greedy father or the society-conscious daughter was willing to let such a fine catch off the hook.

At this point the servant's tale began to falter. Scratching his balding pate, he vaguely recalled Willem telling Cornelius that Louisa's heart was set on buying her trousseau in Paris, and that she refused to be married in anything but a gown by Madame Delatour, dressmaker to Queen Marie-Amèlie. That piece of fiction had yielded the desired results, for De Windt had indulgently agreed to set the wedding date eight months in the future so as to allow his bride time to procure the trousseau of her dreams.

Where Louisa actually went for those months, the servant couldn't say. All he knew was that it couldn't have been more than a few miles from the manor, for seven months later Willem had clandestinely presented him with her hours-old babe.

The man's creased face perfectly reflected his horror as he related how Willem had ordered the newborn killed rather than fostered as was customary for bastards, claiming that it was Louisa's wish that all evidence of her shame be destroyed. As Willem's most trusted servant, the inhuman task had fallen to him. Being a God-fearing man, he hadn't had the heart to kill the babe, so he'd secreted him into the city, where he eventually abandoned him in the vestibule of St. John's Chapel.

It wasn't until seventeen years later, when Willem was on his deathbed, that he'd finally confessed his deception to his employer. That was in 1851, and according to the servant it was the last time he'd ever spoken of the lurid affair.

For a long while after the man's voice faded away, Seth had sat staring at the smoke-blackened hearth, too devastated to speak. That a mother could be so cold-blooded as to order her own son killed was evil almost beyond his comprehension.

The servant had finally broken the silence by offering to show him the family portrait gallery. When the man pointed to a picture of Willem, one painted when he was in his prime, Seth had been stunned by his uncanny resemblance to his grandfather.

From the wicked slant of his hazel eyes to the squareness of his jaw, his every feature perfectly mirrored those of the once mighty Van Cortlandt patriarch. Only their expressions differed. Where Seth tended to smile easily, Willem's lips were twisted into a cruel sneer, his face a mask of icy dignity.

Remembering that portrait now hardened Seth's mouth into a line as harsh as that of his grandfather. Idly tracing the rim of the mug with his thumb, he wondered what Louisa would do when she finally came face-to-face with the living image of her father. Would she guess his identity? And if she did, what would she say to the son she'd ordered murdered thirty-six years ago?

In a roaring blast of wind, the first splatters of rain pelted against the window glass, smearing diamond-like droplets of moisture down the cheeks of his ghostly image. Like the solitary tears of an unloved child, the raindrops fell in silence and rolled away undried. The sight wrenched at Seth's heart; sudden loneliness choked him. He remembered all too well the pain of shedding such tears; he remembered the anguish of being unwanted. Because of his mother's selfishness, he'd been left at the mercy of a world where orphans were despised as pariahs and subjected to hardship that no child should be forced to endure.

A cold ball of emotion lodged in Seth's throat, strangling his breath as he struggled to banish the ugly memories. He was a man now, a rich, powerful man. He was educated. Successful. Respected. He had friends who loved him, women who desired him, and associates who valued him. He was important . . . wanted.

Empowered by that knowledge, he ruthlessly shackled his childhood demons, muzzling their taunts with reminders of his own achievements. Gradually he was able to refocus his mind on the purpose of today's business meeting. That purpose was to make Louisa Vanderlyn suffer. She was about to find out for herself how it felt to be utterly and completely without hope. Today his mother would be the one shedding tears.

That thought was enough to make Seth smile. Finally meeting his solicitor's gaze across the table, he rasped, "Do it."

The young man paled. "Are you certain, sir? Mrs. Vanderlyn is only asking for a six-month extension on her loan. She's sure she'll have the money to buy back her vouchers by then."

Seth shrugged. "I don't intend to be in Denver in six months. Besides, I doubt if she'll be able to raise the money in six months, or six years, for that matter." He'd make sure of it.

A year earlier, shortly after the Pinkerton Agency traced Louisa to Denver, he'd had his solicitors conduct a discreet yet extensive investigation into the Vanderlyn affairs. Upon learning that the successful Vanderlyn Brewery was the family's sole financial support, he'd had his solicitor secretly purchase Vanderlyn's main competitor, the Queen City Brewery. Immediately he'd had the price per barrel of beer dropped so low that the Vanderlyns were unable to compete.

Within a short time, Queen City had stolen all the Vanderlyn accounts. All except the lucrative Shakespeare Saloon one. Floyd Temple proved to be stubbornly loyal to Louisa. But now Seth owned the Shakespeare, and he'd make damn sure that the patrons drank Queen City beer.

Holding out a sheaf of documents, the solicitor suggested, "Perhaps you should look over Mrs. Vanderlyn's proposal before you decide. The interest she's offering is more than generous."

Seth took another gulp of coffee before setting down his mug and taking the papers. Relaxing against the well-padded chair back, he reviewed the contents.

His most recent victory in the battle to destroy his mother was the acquisition of the Vanderlyn bank loan vouchers. Before his death two years earlier, Louisa's second husband, Martin, had borrowed thirty-seven thousand dollars for the expansion of the brewery. It was a sure bet. It had meant a handsome profit for everyone concerned. After all, Vanderlyn had been the reigning brewery in the Colorado Territory for almost a decade.

But that was before Seth learned of Louisa's treachery. That was before Queen City waged a price war. Once Seth set his vengeful plan into action, it had only taken a few months for the Vanderlyn's fortunes to take a drastic downward turn. And the bank, being familiar with the contrary nature of frontier trade, had been eager to sell the foundering Vanderlyn's loan vouchers.

Now it was payback time.

Satisfaction, fierce and sweet, raged through Seth. The pain of his mother's betrayal dulled a fraction. Louisa Vanderlyn was about to have a very bad day indeed. For not only was she going to receive the news that the Shakespeare was canceling its beer account, her bank loan was going to be called due. By the time he left Denver, his mother was going to be truly destitute, just as he'd been all those years ago.

"Sir?"

Seth's lips spread into a grim smile as he returned his attention to the solicitor. "Sorry, Mr. Penn. You were saying?"

Edward Penn fumbled nervously with his napkin. As a mere junior partner, he'd never been permitted to do business with the prominent Seth Tyler. It was only because Archibald Swain, the firm's senior partner, was tied up with one of Mr. Tyler's more important San Francisco transactions that he was allowed this opportunity at all. With that in mind, he proceeded cautiously.

"I was pointing out that it would be to your advantage to allow Mrs. Vanderlyn her six months. After all, her brewery is no longer a threat to Queen City, and it would make far better business sense to give her the opportunity to repay the debt rather than be saddled with a bankrupt brewery."

Seth snorted his impatience as he handed the papers back to Edward. "My time is far too valuable to waste on a trifling matter such as this." He nodded to a brown-and-gold uniformed waiter who indicated that he was ready to serve the men their breakfast. "Let's foreclose and be done with it."

"But, sir! Think of the money you'll lose!"

Seth waited until the waiter finished serving them before inquiring in a cool voice, "How much money do I have, Mr. Penn?"

"Just over five million dollars. Of course, we are expecting another half million on your European railroad investments, not to mention the income from your other interests."

Seth shrugged dismissively. "Then I think I can afford to lose the money." Picking up his fork, he said, "Now, if you don't mind, I'd like to see the new sugar refinery proposal." With that, he turned his attention to his breakfast.

After taking several bites of baked trout and devouring a ginger biscuit slathered with butter, he glanced expectantly at the solicitor. The young man was watching him eat, his expression as morose as if he'd just bankrupted his richest client.

Raising one eyebrow in question, Seth asked, "Is there something else you wanted to discuss?"

Edward ran his hand through his carrot-colored hair,

messing it into jagged peaks. "It's just that, well, Mrs. Vanderlyn is a mighty fine woman. She'll be ruined if you foreclose. Perhaps if you spoke with her yourself—"

"I distinctly remember specifying that I was to remain anonymous in all matters regarding the brewery," Seth interjected, leveling the solicitor with his most quelling look. "For your sake, I hope you haven't breached that confidence."

Visibly shaken, he stammered, "O-of course not M-Mr. Tyler. I thought, well, knowing your reputation for being understanding in matters such as these, well, I thought that if you s-spoke to her yourself that you might reconsider."

"Then, you thought wrong." Seth's eyes narrowed slightly. "Why all this sudden concern for the Vanderlyns?"

Edward met his gaze earnestly. "I just thought you might want to know the Vanderlyns' situation before you did anything hasty. I think you'd agree to give her the six months if you spoke with her yourself. She's a good woman. Smart, too."

"I have no desire to speak with Louisa Vanderlyn, no matter how good or smart she might be. And I could care less about her dire straits." Seth practically shouted the last few words, prompting several of the other diners to turn and stare. Ignoring their speculative glances, he smashed his fist against the table and barked, "You'll do as I say. If she doesn't have the money in thirty days, we'll foreclose. That's final!"

The bitterness behind his words stunned Edward speechless. Too shocked to do anything else, he sat gaping at his client, watching as he went through an elaborate ritual of selecting and lighting a cigar. Oddly enough, after the initial puff it took to light the expensive cigar, he never once took another draw. He merely cradled it between his index and forefinger, moodily watching the curls of blue-gray smoke spiral toward the ceiling.

After a long moment, he mustered up the courage to ask, "Excuse me, sir? Do you have reason to dislike Mrs. Vanderlyn?"

"Dislike her?" Seth snubbed out the cigar. "Hell. I've never even met her."

Chapter 10

By mid-afternoon there wasn't a cloud in the sky. The early morning squall had departed almost as quickly as it arrived, lingering only long enough to dampen the Denver streets.

Dirt-packed and generally bone-dry, the unpaved streets of the town were the bane of Penelope's fastidious existence. From early morning till late at night, horses and wagons barreled up and down the filthy roads, kicking tornado-like swirls of dust into the air. The gritty gray grime flew everywhere. It clogged her nose and irritated her eyes. It streaked her skirts. Why, she'd once found enough dirt in her bloomers to make a mud pie if she'd been so inclined. Dreadful!

But this afternoon was wonderfully different. The sky had released just enough moisture to keep the dust to the road, and as Penelope stood at the corner of Larimer and Fifteenth waiting for a wagon train to pass, she found herself actually enjoying the bustling activity.

Beside her, Effie stood clutching a dainty handkerchief to her nose, scowling fiercely at a horse who'd had the audacity to relieve itself in front of them. "Horrid beast," she muttered, thoroughly affronted. "Its owner should be required by law to buy it one of those diaper contraptions."

Penelope fixed her companion with an incredulous stare. "A horse diaper? They actually make such a thing?"

"It's patented, my dear. They manufacture any number of things to make the filthy animals more tolerate. Why, Dombittle has just patented a cologne, Eau de Equine, which is guaranteed to make a mare smell as sweet as her mistress."

Penelope laughed as she stepped off the boardwalk and crossed the slightly muddy street. She was about to question Effie further about the cologne when she suddenly caught sight of a crowd gathered in front of the City Drugstore. Curious as to what could be causing the stir, she joined the throng.

It was a circus poster, a colorful one depicting a scantily clad girl being shot from a smoking cannon. In the background a ringmaster cracked his whip, while a plump equestrienne in a scarlet gown balanced atop a plume-bedecked horse. Across the top, emblazoned in bold letters was the proclamation: BUCKLEY & WILDER'S AMERICAN CIRCUS! THE BEST SHOW AND MENAGERIE IN AMERICA!

Delighted, Penelope leaned over the shoulder of the man in front of her, eagerly reading the list of acts. As she thrilled at the prospect of seeing Vlado, the India rubber man, and Kongo, the dancing African elephant, she felt a frantic tug on her arm.

"Look!" Effie squealed, dragging her away to point excitedly at the display in the drugstore window.

Penelope cast a longing gaze toward the poster, before peering through the rain-streaked glass with a sigh.

Several jars and bottles of patented remedies were on display, as well as a harness-like contraption with numerous leather straps and buckles. To the right was an advertising board promoting the miraculous skin-preserving properties of something called Palmer Brothers Wrinkle Resister Cream.

Penelope bit the inside of her cheek to keep from giggling. The wrinkle cream was just the sort of thing Effie loved. Feeling mischievous, she teased, "Don't tell me you need Hendrick's Liver Prescription?" She pointed to a tall brown bottle on the left.

Effie let out an unladylike snort. "Of course not. I'm as fit as a fiddle." She jabbed her finger at the advertisement. "I was referring to the Palmer Brothers Wrinkle Resister Cream. I read about it in *Peterson's*. I've been dying to try it."

"I can't imagine why you'd be interested in such a cream," Penelope said, following her friend through the shop door. "Not with your lovely complexion." It was true. Effie might not look eighteen, or twenty-five, or even forty anymore, but she did have a remarkably smooth complexion for a woman her age.

Effie turned pick with pleasure at the genuine compliment. "It's a wrinkle *resister,* not a wrinkle *remover,*" she pointed out. "While it's true that I have no need for the latter, a girl is never too young for the former. We females must never surrender in our battle against the ravages of age." She imparted that last platitude with much the same air as a general disclosing his plan of action to his troops.

Inside, the store was as neatly fitted and well stocked as the pharmacies Penelope had patronized back East. There was a gleaming wood counter along the back of the shop, topped with an impressive display of pharmaceutical equipment. Lining the walls were numerous shelves, upon which sat rows of bottles, jars, and boxes, all arranged with military precision. Glass-topped cases and heavy wooden tables displayed goods ranging from perfume and combs to cutlery. A sign with an arrow pointed the way to the upper-story photographic rooms.

Effie immediately fluttered over to the wrinkle-resister display, while Penelope studied the infant remedies.

Adele had informed her earlier that she'd be allowed to see Tommy on Sunday, and she wanted to take him something for his croup. He'd had several terrifying episodes of the illness for which she'd spent a fortune on remedies, none of which helped.

Shaking her head, she picked up first one bottle, then another, reading the outrageous claims listed on the labels. If only Adele would allow her to take Tommy to see a real doctor. Not that she expected miracles, mind you. Even with her relative inexperience with children, she knew that he wasn't developing as he should. Still, there must be more she could do to help him.

Frowning, she shoved the bottle she was holding back on the shelf. If anyone could help Tommy, it was Hallie. Her sister-in-law took a special interest in treating women and children. She was the only doctor Penelope truly trusted.

Soon, she assured herself. She'd get the money she needed to execute her plan, even if she had to steal it. Once she had Tommy back, she'd go straight home and enlist Hallie's aid.

Dread clutched at Penelope's heart at the thought of facing her family and confessing the shameful events of the past two and a half years. The hardest part would be explaining to her brother why she hadn't turned to him first when she'd found herself in trouble. She knew her foolish lack of faith in his love was going to hurt him far more than all the rest of her sins combined. But she would do it. She'd explain until her face turned blue, if necessary. Anything for Tommy.

As she stood there, imagining herself groveling in front of her brother, she was approached by the pharmacist.

"Having a problem deciding?" he asked, his lips stretching into a congenial smile beneath his bristly mustache.

She stared at him blankly. "Excuse me?"

"I noticed that you seem to be having trouble selecting an infant remedy." He indicated the shelf in front of them. "If you tell me your baby's symptoms, I might be of some assistance."

"Yes ... uh ... croup," she murmured, turning her mind back to the task at hand. "The baby has croup."

The man nodded sympathetically. "Poor little thing. My third daughter was prone to croup. How old is your baby?"

"He'll be two on Sunday."

He nodded again. Stroking his mustache thoughtfully, he picked up a bottle of amber-colored syrup and studied the label. After a moment of deliberation, he handed it to her. "You might give this honey and tar expectorant a try. You also might try adding several drops of eucalyptus oil to a pan of steaming water and hold the baby's face over it. That particular remedy worked like a charm for my own little Sybil."

Penelope thanked the man and agreed to try his croup remedy. When he'd gone back to the counter to wrap her purchases, she joined Effie, who was standing by the window examining the strange leather contraption from the wrinkle-resister display.

"What have you got there?" she asked, eyeing the gadget warily. The device was suspiciously similar to one she'd seen in a picture depicting modes of medieval torture.

"It's a Keeley Gravity Defier. You strap it on while you sleep to hold your chin and facial muscles in place. It's supposed to prevent the sagging and wrinkles that come from sleeping with your face pressed against your pillows." Her brow furrowed as she studied the straps. "I wonder how it's worn?"

Penelope shrugged and picked up one of the ornate jars of wrinkle-resister cream for closer inspection. "I guess you'll have to try it to find out."

"But there's no mirror in here," Effie bemoaned. "However will I be able to judge its merits if I can't see how it fits? How can I—" She stopped midstream, her eyes aglow with inspiration. "Of course. How silly of me. I'll try it on you."

Just looking at the contraption made Penelope claustrophobic. "I'm not so certain that would be a good idea," she demurred, feeling uncomfortably breathless.

Effie stared up at her, her blue eyes pleading.

Penelope released a sigh of resignation. "All right. But only for a moment." Knowing that she was probably going to regret this adventure, she removed her bonnet. No sooner had Effie strapped her into the device, than she heard what sounded like a crazed woodpecker tapping at the window.

"Why, if it isn't that good-looking Mr. Tyler!" exclaimed Effie, waving enthusiastically.

Sure enough, Seth stood just outside the window, his lips twisted into an unholy grin as he gaily returned Effie's wave.

Penelope let out a muffled groan. The blasted man really did have the damnedest knack for showing up at the most inopportune moments. Wishing him to hell and herself anywhere else, she clawed at the immobilizing straps of the gravity defier, feeling as idiotic as she knew she must look. To her frustration, she succeeded only in tangling her hair in the buckles.

As Seth paused at the shop door, gallantly tipping his hat to an exiting lady, she gave Effie a furious poke in the back and hissed, "E-pfe! Re-lsth me no-o!" which was the best she could manage with the leather straps clamped around her jaw and cheeks.

But Effie had lost all interest in the gravity-defier experiment and now stood with her mouth ajar, visibly enthralled by the sight of Seth. Letting out a snort of disgust, Penelope transferred her glower to his rapidly approaching form.

Grudgingly she admitted that he was a splendid, if unwelcome, sight. Fashionably dressed as always, his skintight brown riding trousers hugged every muscular inch of his thighs and belly, molding to his groin in a manner that left little doubt as to his masculinity. His jacket, constructed of checkered wool in shades of brown, gold, and rust, emphasized the impressive breadth of his shoulders, while his showy bronze-shot silk vest drew the eye to his broad chest and tapered waist.

Just the sight of him, so perfectly turned out, was enough to make Penelope acutely aware that her red gros grain skirt

was worn shiny in places and that there were bald spots in
the black fringe trimming her jacket. Tossing him a disgruntled look, she jerked one of the gravity-defier straps
free, painfully ripping out a small clump of hair in the process.

The arrogant man was too handsome by half, she decided,
gingerly rubbing her abused scalp. By the way the other
women in the shop had fallen into an awed silence at his
presence, it was obvious that she wasn't the only one of that
opinion.

Seemingly oblivious to his stunning effect, Seth lifted
Effie's hand to his lips and suavely kissed her palm. "A
pleasure to see you again, sweetheart," he murmured, treating the older woman to the same brand of charm Penelope
had seen him use on sixteen-year-old debutantes.

Effie blushed every bit as pink as one of those debutantes.
"Mr. Tyler—" she murmured, batting her stubby eyelashes.

"I'd be honored if you would call me Seth," he interjected, flashing the crooked grin Penelope always found so
irresistible. "Unless a young girl like yourself thinks I'm too
old to be addressed in such a familiar manner?"

"Oh, no. You're not old at all. At least you don't look
old." She paused her simpering long enough to sweep him
with a calculating glance. "By the way, how old are you?"

"I turned thirty-six last month."

About twenty-five years younger than Effie. Penelope
glared at Seth, momentarily forgetting that she was trussed
up like a violent maniac at Bedlam. The man was a shame-
less flirt.

Effie twittered at his response and resumed her coquetry.
"Why, you're just entering your prime, Mr. Tyler."

"Seth."

Effie preened. "Seth. And you may call me Effie."

His expression blandly polite, Seth looked over Effie's
head at Penelope, inquiring, "Say, Miss Effie. Is that a
Brennan's Patented Wife Silencer Miss Leroux is wearing?"

"You're familiar with Mr. Brennan's invention?" Effie's
eyes brightened at the prospect of a discussion on patented
devices.

Seth walked around Penelope, circling like a vulture
around a particularly tasty carcass. "I've seen them advertised," he replied, pausing to examine the device's rigging.
Fixing her with a goading stare, he added, "Not that I have

need for such a device. My women never have reason to complain."

Penelope gasped at his audacity. Well, she was a woman, and she certainly had her share of complaints about the conceited scoundrel. However, when she tried to open her mouth to voice her displeasure, the gravity defier silenced her every bit as effectively as one of Mr. Brennan's patented devices.

Effie, on the other hand, completely missed Seth's sly innuendo. Shaking her head, she replied, "This particular device happens to be Mr. Keeley's Gravity Defier." When Seth lifted one eyebrow in question, she elaborated. "It's supposed to keep the skin from sagging and promote firmness of the facial muscles."

Seth's eyebrows shot up in amazement. "Certainly a youthful beauty like yourself has no need of such a thing!"

Penelope didn't miss the way he excluded her from his flattering assessment. Really! The man would try the patience of Job. Infuriated by his slight, she yanked the jaw strap so hard that it cut into the tender skin beneath her chin.

"Oh, no. We were just conducting a scientific experiment." Effie blinked twice, the embarrassment of Penelope's dilemma finally dawning on her. Flushing, she hurried to her aid.

Seth joined Effie in examining the gravity defier. Lightly touching one of the straps, he asked, "Have you drawn any conclusions as to the device's effectiveness?"

"I'd have to compare it to Eppington's Facial Firmer before I could say for certain." Effie pursed her lips as she gingerly disengaged a skein of Penelope's hair from one of the buckles. "And of course there is that ageless wonder contraption. What is that thing called?" She glanced up briefly.

Seth shrugged. "I'm afraid I'll have to plead ignorance on that particular invention.

Muttering several unflattering remarks as to the extent of his ignorance, Penelope gave the jaw strap another vicious tug.

"Do hold still, Lorelei," Effie chided, her face perfectly reflecting her dismay as she fidgeted with the buckle. "However did you manage to get your hair so tangled in the device?"

Penelope's only reply was a muffled, "Ouch!" as Effie inadvertently pulled out a few strands of hair.

With a defeated sigh, the elderly actress stepped back and surveyed the situation. "This is impossible. Aside from cutting the knotted hair, I don't see how we're going to get you loose."

Penelope gasped, appalled at Effie's suggestion.

Frowning, Seth tested one of the buckles. After a moment he concluded, "It's not so bad as all that. I think I can remove the device without cutting her hair." He leaned over Penelope's shoulder to peer at her face, his expression properly deferential. "That is, if Miss Lorelei has no objections?"

Penelope stared at him out of the corner of her eye, not a bit fooled by his obeisance. But before she could make a sound, Effie chimed in, "Such gallantry! Why, I'm sure Lorelei will be forever in your debt if you save her hair. After all, a woman's hair is her crowning glory."

As much as Penelope hated the idea of being further indebted to Seth, she didn't see how she had any choice in the matter. Not if she wanted to be released from the awful gravity defier with her "crowning glory" intact. Miserably, she nodded her agreement.

"Good decision," Seth whispered, keeping his voice low enough to be out of Effie's earshot. "We can't have the Toast of the West looking like a plucked hen."

Penelope let out an indignant squawk, a sound that came out comically resembling that of a chicken being relieved of its feathers. Chuckling, Seth began to free her hair.

His touch was gentle, and despite her anger, Penelope relaxed by degrees. Lulled by the low drone of Seth and Effie's conversation, she eventually closed her eyes and let herself lean against his chest.

He smelled good. His usual woodsy scent was underlaid with notes of sweat and tobacco, creating a bouquet as undeniably masculine as Seth himself. Instinctively drawn to his fragrance, she pressed closer. His body was hard, unyielding in its strength. Even through the layers of their clothes she could feel his powerful muscles ripple as he worked.

Just the thought of the sculpted perfection beneath his expensive jacket and crisp linen shirt sent an unwelcome surge of excitement racing through her body. To her discomfiture, the vision of Seth as he'd looked the first time she'd seen his bare chest popped into her mind.

It had been almost four years ago during a visit home to San Francisco. Unaware of Hallie and Penelope's plans to entertain friends in the rose garden, Seth and her brother had doffed their shirts and challenged each other to an impromptu boxing match. When the women had discovered them, they were half-naked and heckling each other in the crudest of terms.

Normally unflappable, Hallie had dissolved into helpless laughter, while their guests either squealed with shock or expressed self-righteous indignation at the men's ungentlemanly behavior. Penelope, who was leading the chattering group, stopped abruptly in her tracks, shamelessly gawking at Seth's bare chest.

He'd looked magnificent. Standing amid the colorful roses, his tawny skin slick with sweat and his honey-colored hair tumbling damply around his broad shoulders, he'd reminded her of a sun-drenched Viking raider bent on wrecking havoc.

He'd certainly wrecked havoc on her emotions. Captivated by the blatant masculinity of his body, she'd let her gaze slide from his powerful shoulders and chest, down the muscular planes of his stomach. There wasn't an ounce of fat anywhere. He had unbuttoned the top of his trousers, probably when he removed his shirt, and it was with unmaidenly interest that her gaze moved downward. Unable to look away, she'd wantonly wondered how he looked completely naked. Was the rest of his skin as smooth and silky as that of his chest? Was he golden everywhere? Lost in wonderment, she'd stared for the longest time.

It was Seth himself who had broken her trance. As he leaned over to retrieve his shirt, he'd looked her straight in the eye and given her a conspiratorial wink. True to form, he seemed to be enjoying the feminine attention. His expression was playful, almost mischievous . . . until he traced her line of vision.

In that instant, as he captured her startled gaze with his all-knowing one, she saw what other, more worldly women had seen in him. Finally she understood the covetous way those women looked at him; she knew the reason for their enamored whispers.

His appeal was magnetic. Irresistible. Seth Tyler exuded a dark, smoldering sensuality that made her mind reel with all sorts of improper thoughts. If Penelope lived to be a hundred, she'd never forget the way he'd looked at her, his gaze hungry and full of yearning, his lips curved with seductive promise. He'd made her feel like the most desirable woman in the world. And in that heated moment, Penelope knew she wanted Seth Tyler. She'd been overwhelmed by his virile appeal then . . .

. . . Just as she was now. She shuddered as Seth massaged a particularly sensitive place behind her ear. As she savored the feel of his fingers against her skin, she fleetingly wondered if he was as affected by their close proximity as she was.

Seth was. Embarrassingly so. He couldn't remember the last time he'd been so aroused. Well, actually he did remember. It was the last time he'd kissed Penelope.

Mumbling an inane response to Effie, who was excusing herself to go speak with a clerk at the far side of the shop, he released another strap. The stiff leather left an angry red mark across Penelope's cheek. Disturbed at seeing her beautiful face marred in such a careless fashion, he stroked the newly exposed skin, gently coaxing the blood back to the surface. To his supreme discomfort, she moaned softly in response and briefly pressed her backside against his sex.

The unconscious sensuality of her action made Seth's belly spasm with urgency, and it took all his control not to yank her against him and grind his groin against her rounded posterior. Never in his life had he wanted a woman as badly as he wanted Penelope. Never was there a woman he had less chance of having.

Stifling an oath, he jerked his hips away from her skirts, feeling perilously close to disgracing himself. Damnation! Why, after two years of telling himself that he no longer loved her, did he still desire her so?

By the time the last strap fell loose, Seth was seriously considering going back to the hotel and ordering a bath . . . one with ice. As he set aside the leather contraption, he noticed for the first time that three roughly dressed men had gathered at the window and were watching Penelope with avid interest. Apparently they recognized her from her performances as Lorelei Leroux.

Grinning down at Penelope, who lounged against him, head lolled forward and eyes closed, he quipped, "Curtain-call time. Take a bow, Lorelei Leroux."

"W-what?" She raised her head, blinking rapidly.

Seth pointed to the men. "Your audience awaits you."

She glanced vacantly toward the window and then back at

him. Abruptly she returned her gaze to the window. Her eyes flew open so wide that, for a moment, Seth thought her eyeballs would pop right out of her head.

"By the audience's smiles, I'd guess that this was one of your better performances," he drawled. Pressing his lips close to her ear, he added, "I personally liked the part where you lollygagged against me and moaned. Quite effective, as you can see." Cheating his back to the spectators, he glanced down at the bulge in his trousers with a significant lift of his brow.

Though Seth hadn't thought it possible, her eyes widened even more at the sight of his obvious arousal. "You're insufferable!" she hissed, jamming her bonnet over her matted hair. "And for the record, I wasn't lollygagging!"

He laughed. "You have your definitions, and I have mine. As for being insufferable, well, there is a certain part of me that feels that way at the moment."

Pointedly ignoring his jest and the men outside, Penelope marched toward the counter. The store was mercifully empty of customers, and the pharmacist, who was having an animated conversation with a clerk, seemed uninterested in the whole gravity-defier fiasco. Apparently mishaps with patented devices were a regular occurrence at the shop.

Just as she was about to request her purchases, Seth grabbed her elbow and pulled her aside. "Not so fast, Princess. As much as I enjoyed participating in your little experiment, it wasn't the reason I came into the shop."

"Really?" She sniffed. "I thought bedeviling me was one of your missions in life."

Seth's lips curved into a naughty grin. "I distinctly remember you doing all the bedeviling."

She fixed him with a glower, ignoring his banter. "Just tell me what you want and go away."

He removed something from his pocket, then lifted her hand and slipped it in her palm. "My hotel room key," he said in a low voice. "As my valet, it will be your job to wake me at seven."

Penelope opened her mouth to protest the impropriety of his demand, but he swiftly cut her off. "Unless you've changed your mind again and would prefer that I wire your brother?"

Her mouth clamped shut. If her brother came to Denver, he'd ask questions. He'd pry into her affairs and those of the company, something which would prove disastrous, for she knew, beyond all doubt, that Adele would dispose of the baby to avoid being exposed as the kidnapper and extortionist she was.

Having no choice, as usual, Penelope nodded. "Is that all?"

"Not quite. There is a matter of my question. A question a day keeps your brother away. Remember?"

How could she forget? Glancing around to make sure that Effie was occupied elsewhere, she hissed, "All right, then. Ask your blasted question."

With leisurely deliberation, Seth's gaze swept her length, pausing to focus on a particularly worn area of fabric at the elbow of her jacket. "What time to you leave for the theater?"

Self-conscious beneath his scrutiny, she pressed her arm close to her body to hide the flaw. "Around seven? Why?"

He nodded and refocused his gaze on the balding fringe at her shoulder. "I'll be at your boardinghouse at seven sharp. You can answer my question while I escort you to the Shakespeare."

It was going to be tricky enough sneaking in and out of his hotel room every morning without the added risk of arousing Adele's suspicions by accepting Seth's escort over Miles's. With that in mind, she demurred. "That's impossible. Miles always walks me to and from the theater."

"Not anymore. I don't trust that sniveling jackass any further than the stretch of his mama's apron strings."

Penelope inhaled sharply, infuriated by his high-handedness. "Our bargain didn't include me being at your beck and call at all hours," she retorted.

"That point is debatable." He shrugged. "However, since I have another engagement and don't have time to argue, I'll make a deal with you." The calculating gleam in his eyes sent a frisson of uneasiness snaking down her spine.

Without waiting for her response, he continued, "Since you're so set on having the mewling Mr. Prescott serve as your escort, I'll be a gentleman and bow to your desire. But only on one condition.

"Which is?" Penelope asked. His wily expression was definitely making her uncomfortable.

"If, for some reason, Miles should be unable to act as your escort, you'll promise to allow me the privilege. Agreed?"

Penelope let out a lông sigh of relief and nodded. Since Miles had never once failed to do his duty, there should be no problem agreeing to Seth's terms. That bit of business concluded, she signaled to the pharmacist.

When Seth made no move to leave, she made an impatient noise. "I thought you had business elsewhere," she pointed out, rudely. "Was there something else you wanted?"

He shrugged. "Not from you."

Before she could voice her tart retort, the pharmacist appeared at her side with her purchases. As he handed her the parcel, he instructed, "Give your baby a half teaspoon of the tar and honey preparation every two hours. If his croup doesn't ease a bit within a day, increase the dose to a full teaspoon."

Seth's eyebrows shot up at the man's words. "Baby?"

"One of the girls at the Shakespeare asked me to buy medicine for her baby," Penelope lied, hating herself for having to deny her son. Sure that her face perfectly reflected her guilt, she lowered her head and busied herself with her reticule. "How much do I owe you?" she asked the pharmacist.

"One dollar and forty-five cents."

As she reached out to pay the man, Seth stayed her arm. "If the woman's baby is ill, it should be tended by a doctor."

Penelope couldn't have agreed more. However, since that was impossible, she replied lightly, "It's just the croup. The baby isn't seriously ill."

Seth shook his head, unconvinced. "Be that as it may, it still wouldn't hurt for a doctor to examine the child."

"I'll relay your message to the mother." She tried to jerk her arm from his grip, but he held firm.

"And ask the mother to let me know if the child's condition worsens. Tell her I'll be glad to pay the doctor's fees." With that he dropped her arm and nodded to the pharmacist. "Please add the cost of the lady's purchases to my bill."

Penelope felt an unwilling surge of admiration for Seth. In a world full of people who gave little or no thought to the plight of needy women and their children, Seth showed he cared. Not that she should be surprised. Everyone in San

Francisco knew that he had a soft spot in his heart for children.

As she put away her coins, she heard the pharmacist reply, "My pleasure, sir. However, in order to add to one's bill, one must run up a bill. You haven't purchased anything."

"Yes. Well, I do have a problem I'd like to discuss."

Penelope glanced up in surprise. Seth was the healthiest person she knew. So much so, that her sister-in-law had often teased him that if all her patients had his constitution, she'd have to take up embroidery to fill her time.

"Of course." The pharmacist nodded, his expression serious. "What are your symptoms?"

"My—" Seth paused and glanced down at Penelope, his eyes gleaming with the devilry she knew all too well. Leaning nearer to the pharmacist, he replied in a loud whisper, "I've been riding too much, and my backside is all raw and chafed."

Embarrassed, Penelope dropped her open reticule, spilling the contents across the floor.

"A common problem to newcomers," clucked the pharmacist. "I have a salve that should fix you right up."

As the man went to get the salve, Seth crouched down to help Penelope retrieve her belongings.

"Really, Seth!" she scolded, fumbling with a coin. "Have you no decorum? Surely you know better than to discuss your backside in front of a lady!"

He stared at her from beneath his lowered lashes, fingering her lucky ribbon, which had landed on the toe of his boot. "I'd hardly call it decorous behavior to eavesdrop on a personal conversation between a man and his pharmacist."

"You know damn well I wasn't eavesdropping!" she shot back, grabbing the ribbon and stuffing it into her bag.

He chuckled and handed her her bottle of smelling salts. "You have your—"

"—definitions and I have mine," she cut in. "So you insist on reminding me."

Just as she was jerking her reticule shut, the pharmacist reappeared. Presenting Seth with a large blue jar, he instructed, "You'll need to massage a liberal amount of this salve into the sore area every morning and every evening. Perhaps your wife can help you, considering where you need it applied."

An unholy grin curved Seth's lips at the man's suggestion.
Tossing Penelope a meaningful glance, he drawled, "Oh. I'm
not married. However, I'm sure my valet will be more than
satisfactory at performing that duty."

Chapter 11

Seth was a man who was used to getting what he wanted. What he wanted now was to know what Penelope was doing in Denver.

It's my duty to find out, he told himself, urging his horse around the corner of Holladay Street and onto Fifteenth. *She's obviously in some sort of trouble, and as her brother's best friend, I'm obligated to see to her welfare.* Which was his reason for demanding that she act as his valet: to keep her close so he could see to her safety.

He snorted at his feeble excuse. *Right. And they'll be canonizing me any day now for my altruistic acts and pure thoughts.* He let out another snort. *Admit it, Saint Seth. You bullied her into being your valet to satisfy your own selfish need to be near her. You did it because you still love her.*

It was true, no matter how he tried to deny it. He loved Penelope. And as he knew too well, love was dangerous. It robbed a man of his senses and made him dare anything in its name.

If I'm smart, I'll jump on the first train out of town and get away from her before I do something stupid. His lips curled with self-contempt. As if running away would do any good. It hadn't worked before, and it wouldn't work now. Besides, after the shabby way he'd treated her in New York, he owed it to her to at least see to her safety. Unlike New York, this time he intended to do the honorable thing.

Ha! his mind jeered. *Let's see just how long your noble intentions last once Penelope starts her duties. You're mad as a March hare if you think you can remain impassive while she performs the intimate tasks required of a valet.*

Seth groaned as he guided his horse onto Blake Street. Sweet Jesus! He *was* mad! How else could he explain proposing a bargain that would thrust him in such close quarters with Penelope?

Love, he reminded himself. *Crazy, impetuous love.* Add that to the lust he felt every time he so much as heard her name, and it was no mystery why he'd made the crackbrained deal.

He clutched the reins so tight the leather cut into his palms. How the hell was he supposed to keep up his charade of disdain when his sex sprang to attention like a sergeant saluting a major every time the damn woman simply glanced at him? If he wasn't mad now, his unrelieved lust at being near her would quickly drive him to the brink. God! What was he going to do?

What you're going to do, Seth, my randy friend, he commanded himself, stopping in front of the Shakespeare and sliding from the saddle, *is get your mind from between your legs and back on business where it belongs ... before you forget your true purpose for coming to town. As for Penelope, your only concern with her is to deliver her to her brother safe and sound.*

And in order to do that, he'd have to make sure she didn't come to harm while in Denver, which brought him back to his initial question: what was she doing here? More perplexing yet: how was he going to find out?

Wincing with every step, Seth hobbled over to the hitching post, stoically resisting the urge to massage his saddlesore backside as he went. As he paused to stroke his palomino's muscular neck, he pondered his dilemma. Questioning the actors was out. He'd promised Penelope he wouldn't, and he'd keep his promise, just as he intended to make sure she kept hers.

Her promise. He absently transferred his soothing ministrations from his horse's neck to his abused buttock. She *had* promised to answer a question a day. Maybe he should simply ask her what she was doing here.

He dropped his hand from his backside, chuckling at the absurdity of the idea as he began hitching his horse to the post. He could just imagine the kind of response he'd get if he were to ask that particular question point-blank. Despite her promise, the evasive Miss Parrish would probably give him one of her vague, offhanded excuses, and then attempt to change the subject by provoking him into an argument. And her ploy would work.

He gave the reins a final tug to test his knot. After all, nobody provoked him more than Penelope Parrish did these days.

And in more ways than one, he added silently, unwillingly remembering his body's carnal response to her nearness as he had freed her from the ridiculous gravity defier.

Cursing himself for a lecherous fool, he stepped stiffly from the street and up onto the boardwalk, only to find himself in front of a playbill. Below the caption, LORELEI LEROUX, TOAST OF THE WEST, was a drawing of a plump woman wearing a vapid expression and little else. If Seth hadn't known better, the picture would have led him to believe that Penelope had had a significant increase in girth and a complete decrease of wits. Grinning, he pushed his way through the swinging saloon doors.

It was late afternoon, and the Shakespeare was almost deserted . . . the lull before the storm of miners, cowboys, and sodbusters blew into town for a whirlwind evening of merriment.

By the staircase a tight cluster of saloon girls whispered among themselves, occasionally emitting a flurry of high-pitched giggles. Sitting alone at a table along the far wall, his powerful body hunched over a bottle and his scarred face partially masked by the lengthening shadows, was a man whom Seth had heard Floyd refer to as One-eyed Caleb. At a gaming table in the right corner, four men sat smoking and playing cards. Standing behind one of the men was Adele du Charme.

After greeting a girl who sat at the square piano listlessly picking out the tune "Daisy Dean," Seth headed to where Monty was polishing the already gleaming mahogany bar.

When the bartender caught sight of him, he waved his grubby dust cloth in welcome. *"Buenos días,"* he greeted in badly accented Spanish, his smile wide beneath his waxed mustache.

Ignoring the pain radiating from the muscles in his thighs and buttocks, Seth gingerly hooked his heel on the brass boot rail and leaned against the counter. "How's business, Monty?"

"Dead as old Leroy over there." Monty jabbed his thumb to where a stuffed grizzly bear stood posed menacingly on its hind legs. In a fit of drunken whimsy, someone had put an empty whiskey bottle in old Leroy's paws and balanced a beaver hat gaily festooned with an Independence Day ribbon on his head.

Seth chuckled. "That bad, huh?"

Monty squinted at a smudge marring the otherwise immaculate wooden counter. "Seein' as how it's Saturday, I reckon it'll pick up. My guess is that you won't be able to get within a mile of this bar by nine o'clock." With that prediction, he rubbed at the offending spot with varnish-stripping fury.

"Then, I guess I'd better have my drink now," Seth said.

Monty glanced up, his blue eyes twinkling with devilry. "Eager for another snort of Red Dynamite, are you?"

Seth stifled a groan. "That stuff made me feel like I'd downed a lit kerosene lamp. I was up all night with a bellyache."

The bartender clicked his tongue between his teeth. "Sorry. Must've been one of my weaker batches."

"Weaker batches?" Seth felt the gall rise in his throat. "I'd hate to taste what you call a strong batch."

"I've got a fresh bottle if you wanna give it a try."

Seth's stomach rumbled ominously in reply. "I think I'll take a rain check. What else do you suggest?"

"Let's see, now." Monty rolled one pointy end of his mustache between his fingers as he considered the options. "Seein' as how you're havin' belly problems, you might wanna try some Grizzly Bear's Milk. My granny swears it cures her dyspepsia every time."

"Grizzly Bear's Milk?" Seth eyed the bartender suspiciously. "What's in it?"

"Half a glass of milk and a handful of sugar mixed with two fingers of raw whiskey."

Seth's stomach gurgled so loud, he was sure it could be heard all the way to Cheyenne. No wonder the mortality out here was so high! Resolved not to join the legions of unfortunates pushing up prairie grass, he asked, "Don't you have anything less—exotic? Say, some plain Kentucky whiskey, for example?"

Monty reached beneath the bar and produced an almost-full bottle of the requested beverage with a flourish. "Ask and ye shall receive," he quoted solemnly. "Mr. Prescott was havin' me save this for him"—he emitted a grunt as he wrestled the cork free—"but seein' as how he's taken a likin' to the Weddin' whiskey, I doubt he'll miss it."

As he set a glass in front of Seth and poured a healthy ration, he confided, "You might want to try the Weddin' whiskey yourself if you ever get a mind for some fun." He winked suggestively. "Makes a man go all night and into the mornin' . . . if you catch my drift. Mr. Prescott swears by it."

Seth's eyes narrowed with speculation at the bartender's casual reference to Miles Prescott. Having spent his fair share of time in saloons, he knew that men talked when they were in their cups. And the person they usually talked to was the bartender. That being the case, it was possible that Miles had said something to Monty about Penelope. With that odds-on chance in mind, he ventured, "Miles is a frequent customer?"

"Sure 'nough. Spends just about every afternoon cozied up to a bottle and babblin' his woes to anyone who'll listen."

"I take it you're none too impressed with Mr. Prescott?"

"Let's just say that I wouldn't trust him with the family fortune or my sister's virtue."

"Any particular reason why?" Seth sampled the whiskey, then gave the bartender a quick nod of approval.

Assured of his boss's satisfaction, Monty picked up a clean towel and began to dry a load of glasses soaking in a tub behind the bar. As he worked, he explained, "Never saw a man with a bigger weakness for gamblin' than Miles Prescott. Never heard of anyone with less luck at it, either. Can't decide if the fella is careless or just plumb stupid. Heard tell his wife—"

Towel still in hand, he reached across the bar and thumped Seth on the back. "Stuff burns like a son of a bitch when it goes down the wrong way, don't it?" he commiserated.

Between hacking and gasping for air, Seth managed to sputter, "M-Miles is m-married?"

"Yep. But you wouldn't know it the way he's always sniffin' around Lorelei. Jealous as a dog with a bone over that gal."

Seth cleared his throat several times. "So I've noticed."

"Everybody's noticed," Monty shot back, giving the glass in his hand a final rub and setting it aside. As he fished a tall tumbler from the water, he muttered, "Too bad his missus ain't around. Imagine she'd shorten his chain quick 'nough."

"And where is Mrs. Prescott?" Seth inquired.

"It's kind of a long story. But if you've got the time . . . ?" Monty looked at him hopefully.

"Sure. I've got the time." Seth bowed his head over his glass, hiding his satisfied smile. He had a hunch that once he got the bartender gossiping, it wouldn't take too much effort to steer the conversation back around to Penelope.

Thus encouraged, Monty tossed aside his towel and set down the tumbler. After looking around to assure himself that they were out of earshot of eavesdroppers, he prefaced, "Keep in mind that Mr. Prescott was mighty drunk when he told me this story. But seein' as how it's harder for a drunk man to tell a convincin' lie than a sober one, I'm inclined to believe him."

Seth made a wry face. "After observing Miles's acting, I doubt if he could tell a convincing lie, sober or drunk."

Monty snickered at that. "True 'nough, Mr. Tyler."

"Seth."

"Seth," the bartender parroted. "Sorry. I'm not used to callin' swanky gentlemen by their Christian names."

It was Seth's turn to snicker. "Swanky gentleman is hardly a term I'd use to describe myself."

"But—" protested Monty.

"But we're digressing," Seth interposed smoothly. "You were telling me about Miles's wife."

"Oh. Right." Monty scratched the bridge of his nose as he switched his mind back to his previous train of thought. "Mrs. Prescott, yes. Learned about her just last Sunday night. Bein' the Sabbath and all, business was slow so I had time to listen when Mr. Prescott got the hankerin' to talk. Felt kinda sorry for him. He'd just lost big at faro and was worried about breakin' the news to his mama. Seems he promised not to gamble until his debt to the Shakespeare is paid off." He paused to shoot his boss a questioning look. " 'Course, you already know about the debt?"

"It seems that everyone in town knows," Seth muttered, remembering all the people who'd made it their business to tell him about the debt in the last twenty-four hours.

" 'Course they do. It's a small town. Everyone knows everything about everybody else. Wait till I tell you what I heard about that uppity new schoolmarm, Miss Skyler, and what—"

"I'd rather hear about Mrs. Prescott," Seth cut in.

"Right. Sorry." Monty grinned sheepishly. "Bad habit of

mine, jumpin' on and off subjects like a leap frog on hot coals. Anyways ..." He stroked his mustache, frowning. "Where were we?"

"Miles lost big at faro and was afraid to tell his mama."

"Oh. Well, that's when he came over to the bar lookin' for a bit of fortification. After a few shots of Taos Lightnin', he took to spoutin' off about his wife. Said she's one of those overbred society gals with a pedigree longer than a twenty-mule-team freight wagon and a family fortune to match."

"A society girl?" Seth repeated, incredulous. "What the hell would a debutante see in a dolt like Miles Prescott?"

"Flabbergasted the heck outta me, too," Monty confided. "Accordin' to Mr. Prescott, the gal saw him in some play and fell head over heels in love with him. Says she showed up at the theater every night, just to get a look at him."

Seth snorted. "I can just imagine how much the poor chit's adoration must have appealed to Mr. Prescott's insufferable ego."

Monty shook his head. "Man's got an eye for a trim ankle and a pretty face. He says the gal ain't blessed with either. 'Course, her face looked a heap prettier and her ankles trimmer after he found out how much money her folks have."

"It's amazing how money can magically transform an undesirable woman—or man, for that matter—into a creature of infinite appeal," Seth observed sardonically.

"Amen to that," Monty concurred. "Seems that gal looked downright fetchin' after Mr. Prescott lost a thousand dollars to a less-than-patient pair of cardsharpers. Said the men threatened to cut up his pretty face if he didn't pay quick-like. To make a long story short, he saw the gal as his chance to save his face, so he bedded her and then convinced her to elope with him."

"I'm sure her family was thrilled to no end when they were introduced to their new son-in-law," Seth interjected.

"Accordin' to Mr. Prescott, her folks put up a heck of a fuss. 'Course, by then, it was too late to do anything about it, 'specially since the gal was expecting his baby."

Seth clicked his tongue between his teeth. "The whole thing sounds like a bad melodrama."

"Maybe," Monty intoned in a singsong voice. "But I betcha five bucks you can't guess how it all turned out."

Intrigued by the challenge, Seth pulled a gold piece from

his waistcoat pocket and tossed it to the counter. "You're on."

"Shoot."

After a moment's deliberation, Seth ventured, "I'll guess that the honorable Mr. Prescott took off with his bride's dowry, leaving the poor girl alone and pregnant."

"Good try, boss, but no dice," Monty chortled, snatching up the coin. "Mr. Prescott never got the dowry. Her folks wouldn't give it to him when they found out about the debt. Seems they were hopin' the cardsharpers would make their daughter a widow."

"Looks like the sharpers disappointed them," Seth commented, raising his glass to his lips.

Monty flipped the gold piece into the air and caught it in his palm, chuckling. "Only 'cause Mr. Prescott got outta there before they could get their hands on him. He's been hidin' out with his mama's theater company ever since. 'Course now that he wants to marry Lorelei, he'll have to go back to get a divorce."

That disclosure was enough to make Seth choke on his whiskey again. "L-L-orelei and Miles?"

Monty leaned over and thumped his back again. "You're havin' a heck of a time swallowin' your liquor today. Maybe you ought to lay off the whiskey and try some Grizzly Bear's Milk."

Ignoring the man's advice and his concerned expression, Seth demanded, "Lorelei hasn't encouraged that jackanape, has she?"

Monty dropped his hand from Seth's back with a sigh. "Naw. And that's another thing stickin' in his craw: Lorelei won't give him so much as the time of day." Absently he resumed tossing the coin into the air. " 'Course, she never pays much mind to any of the men. She don't flirt like the other gals."

Seth watched Monty toss and catch the coin several times in quick succession, fighting his impulse to grab the man by his starched shirtfront and ruthlessly grill him about Penelope.

Fortunately the grilling proved unnecessary. Unprompted, the bartender volunteered, "All except for One-eyed Caleb, that is. Seen Miss Leroux and him whisperin' up a storm a few times." With a suggestive wink, he sent the coin spinning high above his head.

Seth snatched the gold piece from the air and slammed it down on the counter. "Is that all Miss Leroux has been doing with this Caleb?" He cringed inwardly as soon as the words left his mouth. Damn if he didn't sound like a jealous lover. His mood darkened a shade as realization struck him: he was jealous.

Monty cackled and slanted him a sly look. "Got a hankerin' for Miss Lorelei yourself, do you?"

Seth leveled the bartender with a glower that clearly warned him to mind his own business.

A glower that the man blithely ignored. His smile broadening a hint, he mused, "Got your work cut out for you if you aim to turn that gal's head. 'Course"—he nodded at Seth's diamond and ruby watch fob—"seein' as how you're rich and not bad lookin', you might have a chance at that."

Seth laughed and slid the coin across the counter to the bartender. "And as we've already established, enough money could turn Quasimodo into Prince Charming."

Monty frowned as he slipped the coin into the pocket of his red silk vest. "Quazy—who? Don't think I've served the fella."

"Quasimodo. He was a hunchback who was in love with a beautiful girl in Victor Hugo's book *Notre-Dame de Paris*."

The bartender made a disdainful noise. "Ain't it just like a damn Frenchy to waste perfectly good paper writin' about a horny hunchback? Speakin' of horny . . ." His eyes took on an impish gleam. "It seems the saloon gals are all hot in the drawers for you. Overheard them gossipin' just this mornin'. They were chatterin' and sighin', sayin' how you're the most tantalizin' thing in trousers this side of the Mississippi. Seems you've got somethin' real interestin', and that somethin' ain't your money."

He nodded in the direction of the blowsy blonde Seth had met the night before. "Desdemona bet the other gals ten bucks that she'd have you in her bed before the end of the week." He tossed the woman a pitying look. "Guess she's gonna lose, seein' as how your heart's set on havin' Lorelei."

"Not if Lorelei's heart is set on Caleb," Seth ground out.

"Oh, I wouldn't give up on Lorelei just yet. She and Caleb don't seem to be on kissin' terms or anything like that . . . yet." He injected an ominous note into the word *yet*.

Seth exhaled in a hiss. He'd see that *yet* never came.

" 'Course, your big problem isn't gonna be winning Lorelei from One-eyed Caleb," Monty continued. "It's gonna be—*ouch!*" Quick as a coward in a barroom brawl, he ducked behind the bar, reappearing an instant later holding a squirming black cat. Unceremoniously dumping the now yowling animal onto the counter, he scolded, "You know better than to claw my leg like that, Othello. I oughtta toss you out for the evenin' and make you miss out on your beer drinkin'. Serve you right for bein' rascally."

Seth released a silent groan. Just when he'd finally gotten the conversation where he wanted it, Monty's attention was stolen by a beer-guzzling cat.

As if to confirm his suspicion, the bartender expounded, "Never seen a cat go for beer the way Othello does. Little fella spends every evenin' lappin' up spills from the bar." Smiling at the cat, who was pointedly ignoring him in favor of eyeing Seth's glass, he finished, "Don't need a mop with Othello around."

Almost out of patience, Seth reminded him, "You were about to list the difficulties in courting Lorelei. Remember?"

"Oh, right." With obvious reluctance, Monty drew his attention from his pet and back to the matter at hand. "Well, the way I see it, your biggest problem will be gettin' her away from Mr. Prescott and Madame du Charme long enough to pay your addresses. That pair are like sap on a tree when it comes to stickin' to Lorelei."

"Any ideas why they maintain such a close watch?"

Monty shrugged. "I imagine bein' in love with her is reason enough for Mr. Prescott. As for Madame ... hmm ... well, I suppose she's protectin' her bread and butter. Everyone knows that it's Miss Leroux's looks and talent that draws in the crowds. Company would be ruined if she ran off with some fella."

Having at last reached the point where he could broach the mystery of Penelope's presence in Denver, Seth said, "I can't understand why Miss Leroux joined up with that second-rate bunch of hams in the first place. With her beauty and talent, she would be welcome in any theatrical company in the world."

Monty stroked his mustache with his thumb thoughtfully. "Can't say as I ever considered the matter one way or another." He shrugged. "Guess you'll have to ask her yourself. Guess—" He pounded his fist against the bar abruptly.

"Othello! You take your paw outta Mr. Tyler's glass, pronto!"

Seth jumped, startled by the bartender's sudden outburst. *Clunk!* His forearm hit the glass.

Splash! Yowl! The glass tipped over, drenching Othello with whiskey. Emitting a furious *r-r-r!* the cat hurled from the bar and scrambled beneath the roulette table, where he sat washing his liquor-spiked fur, growling between slurping licks.

Armed with his trusty bar towel, Monty promptly mopped up the spill. "Sorry," he murmured. "Want me to pour you another?"

Seth looked up from his whiskey-drenched sleeve and shook his head. "What I want is to know how to get Lorelei alone."

"So I figured right," the bartender crowed. "You are set on courtin' Miss Leroux."

"Maybe."

"If that maybe means yes, then this is your lucky day." The man's smirk was enigmatic enough to rival that of the Mona Lisa.

"In what way?"

With a conspiratorial wink he confided, "I happen to know for a fact that Mr. Prescott is across the street at Goldie's Palace visitin' his favorite whore. Now seein' as how Madame du Charme is busy with her fancy man at the poker table, it would appear that Miss Leroux is all by her lonesome about now."

"She is at that," Seth acknowledged thoughtfully. "Question is, for how long? If she's as particular as you say, this courting business might take some time."

"As I said, it's your lucky day. It so happens that Madame du Charme and her fancy man have a private supper arranged for six o'clock. As for Mr. Prescott, well, I'd guess that for a nominal fee of say, twenty dollars, Goldie could be persuaded to see that he's kept busy. Now, seein' as it's"—he yanked a heavy gold watch out of his vest pocket and squinted down at it—"five-twenty, and how the show doesn't start until nine, I figure you have about two hours to plant some sugar in Miss Leroux's ear."

Seth tipped his hat in salute. "In that case I'd better get busy."

As he turned to go, Monty reminded him, "Don't forget to

tell Miss Leroux how pretty she looks. And make sure you mention how much you admire her singin'. It wouldn't hurt to say that she's just about the sweetest gal in the world and that you worship the ground she walks on."

"Don't you think that might be laying it on a little thick?"

"As my blessed granny always says: 'Nothin' like a heap of bull manure to fertilize a lady's regard and get her fondness growin'.' If anyone knows about courtin', it's Granny. She's had five husbands. Says every last one of them charmed her out of her calico by talkin' sweet and tellin' lies as tall as Pike's Peak."

Seth laughed. "I'll keep that in mind." Still chuckling, he strode toward the door.

"Well, Othello," Monty murmured, stroking the cat, which had jumped back up on the counter and was now sniffing at the whiskey-soaked towel in his hand. "Should be mighty interestin' to see how Miss Leroux takes to Mr. Tyler."

Monty wasn't the only one interested in Seth's effect on Penelope's heart. Adele du Charme had just spent the last half hour studying the new saloon owner from afar, and what she discovered shook her to her very core.

Seth Tyler had *it*. *It* was that indefinable aura of sensuality that few men possessed and all men coveted. *It* was a mysterious seductive allure that empowered its possessor to attract any woman he desired and mesmerize her with his charm.

Adele gritted her teeth in annoyance. Why the hell hadn't she noticed his special quality earlier? If she had, she certainly wouldn't have made a bargain that would make Penelope the constant target of all that raw sensuality. With his virile strength and inviting warmth, he was the kind of man a woman would naturally turn to in time of need. And the last person in the world she wanted Penelope turning to was Seth Tyler.

The sound of a boot tapping three times against the wooden floor intruded sharply into her thoughts. That was her signal it was time to make her move. Stretching and emitting a bored sigh, she strolled aimlessly around the table, surreptitiously glimpsing the cards in the other players' hands.

After determining that none of the men held a hand that rivaled Harley's four of a kind, she yawned and slapped her fan against her wrist, signaling her lover to call.

When he shifted his body to the right in acknowledgment of her clandestine communication, she sauntered back to her position at his shoulder and returned to the problem of Seth Tyler.

According to her calculations, at the rate Penelope was bringing in gold, it wouldn't take more than another nine months on the gold circuit to make the remainder of the money she needed to execute her plan. With what she made from the company, combined with what she had managed to save from her stint as an abortionist in New York, she would have adequate funds to go back to Boston and set herself up as a wealthy widow.

Adele smiled with greedy anticipation. Her plan was flawless. With the aid of a little blackmail, Miles's wife's family, the high and might Ellisons, should prove amenable to introducing her to a likely widower. And when she'd neatly trapped the man into marriage, she, Dorcas Grace Butler, who had once slaved in the kitchens of Boston's crème-de-la-crème and had endured the repulsive, fumbling advances from the heads of those same households, would be the queen of Beacon Hill. As its ruler, she would see to it that every man who had ever fondled her and every woman who had ever turned her out as a result of that fondling would get their well-deserved comeuppance.

But now Seth Tyler had entered into the equation.

A chill cut through her like a draft from an open window. If anyone had the power to free Penelope and her brat from her imprisoning blackmail, it was the mighty Mr. Tyler.

Suddenly Harley let out a barking cough, dropping a card in the process. On cue, Adele ducked down and retrieved the fallen card, covertly substituting the two of spades with the ace of hearts. As she handed the ace to Harley, inspiration struck.

Like a bad card spoiling a winning hand, Seth Tyler, too, could be eliminated. As Adele resumed her vigil at Harley's back, she found herself smiling. *Eliminate Seth Tyler.* Yes, that's exactly what she'd do if he proved to be troublesome. She'd come too far and worked too hard to have her dreams snatched away by a man who was too damn attractive for his own good.

After bribing the madame of Goldie's Palace to keep Miles occupied, Seth returned to his room for a quick bath and a change of clothes. As he stripped off his whiskey-stained suit and stepped into the tub of steaming water, he struggled to determine the best way to handle his coming encounter with Penelope.

She wasn't going to be pleased when she heard the news of Miles's delay, and that was a fact. Especially when he reminded her of their most recent bargain and insisted that she honor it.

Drawing in a hissing breath, Seth eased his stiff body down into the tub, only to shoot back up again as his raw backside made stinging contact with the hot water. Gritting his teeth with pain, he twisted and turned until he got a clear view of his derriere. What he saw made him groan aloud.

From the curve of his buttocks down to his upper thighs, his flesh was chafed a livid, angry red. Adding to his discomfort, his morning ride out to examine Denver's irrigation system, a ditch running from the South Platte Canyon down to Smith Lake, had yielded not only an understanding of water distribution, but several ugly blisters on his inner thighs as well.

Suddenly the idea of a hot bath seemed less tempting than it had only moments earlier. He toyed with the idea of skipping it altogether; then he sighed and cast the water at his feet a resigned look. It wouldn't do to show up at Penelope's door smelling like a saloon floor, not when he wanted to make a favorable impression. He'd just have to buck up and endure the discomfort like the man he prided himself on being.

Besides, he added sardonically, if this was the worst pain he suffered in his rear this evening, he'd count himself lucky. After all, he was about to cross Penelope and no one was a bigger pain in the ass than Miss Parrish when she was provoked.

As Seth stood calf-deep in water, waiting for it to cool a few degrees, he moodily envisioned the scene in store for him.

He could just see Penelope's face when she opened the door. Her expression would perfectly reflect her shock at finding him there, an expression that would promptly be replaced by one of displeasure when he conveyed the news of Miles's delay. When he reminded her of their latest bargain and insisted that she honor it, she would hem and haw and do her damnedest to renege.

But as Penelope Parrish would soon learn, her damnedest wasn't good enough. Not when it came to a battle of wills with him. And especially not after all the trouble he'd gone to to assure himself this opportunity to wage his assault on her seemingly impenetrable wall of secrets.

Which brought him around to another problem: considering her less than charitable opinion of him, how was he going to get her to honor their latest deal without alienating her in the process? In order for him to solve the mystery of her presence at the Shakespeare, he would first have to lull her into lowering her defenses enough for her to let slip a clue or two as to what had led her to her current situation. And he knew damn well that if he angered her by high-handedly demanding that she hold to their bargain, she would probably shut him out completely.

Gritting his teeth, as much out of frustration as in anticipation of pain, he sat back down. The burning in his abused flesh resumed with a fiery vengeance. Stoically ignoring his impulse to yelp and jump out of the water, he sat still, waiting for the unpleasant sensation to subside. When it had faded to a tolerable tingle, he picked up his bar of sandalwood soap.

As he rubbed it between his palms, working up a fragrant lather, he returned to the problem of Penelope and their bargain. So how was he going to get her to honor their deal without appearing arrogant or using coercive tactics?

Unbidden, Granny Dowd's crude colloquialism intruded into his thoughts: *Nothin' like a heap of bull manure to fertilize a lady's regard and get her fondness growin'.*

His hand stilled in the act of scrubbing his chest. Granny's advice just might be the key to unlock Penelope's Pandora's box of secrets. Absently he lifted his arm and scrubbed the area beneath it. He knew from experience that flattery and pretty phrases did go a long way toward winning a woman's trust.

But would it work? He transferred the slippery bar of soap from his right hand to his left. Would honeyed words be enough to soften Penelope's heart and melt her resistance?

Making a disgusted noise deep in his throat, he raised his right arm and washed his armpit. Perhaps under any other circumstances it might work. But considering the unqualified success of his ploy to make her hate and distrust him, he figured that he now had approximately as much chance as a snowman had in hell of winning her over that easily.

So what was he going to do? Growling a string of foul oaths, he flung the soap into the water. His dangerous infatuation aside, by virtue of his friendship with Jake he truly did have a responsibility to see to her welfare. And right now she bore all the earmarks of being in trouble. Big trouble. How else could you explain the way she dodged his questions and looked on the verge of tears every time she was pressed for an answer?

And what about her terror of Adele du Charme? He hadn't missed the way she had trembled when the woman discovered them on the stairs, nor had he been blind to the panic in her eyes when he'd threatened to include her in his questioning.

And then there was the fact that she, Penelope Parrish, one of opera's greatest singers, was performing at the Shakespeare and under an assumed name, no less. Add it all up, and it equaled trouble, trouble from which he felt bound to rescue her. Yet to do so, he had to make her trust him enough to turn to him for help. Which brought him back to where he had started.

Scowling at his dilemma, Seth fished the soap from the water and began scouring his legs. After several moments of drawing a blank, he reconsidered Granny's advice.

Granted, it wouldn't be easy. But perhaps with a little ingenuity and a lot of patience, he just might be able to pull it off. After all, didn't he know Penelope better than anyone else? Didn't he know what touched her heart and made her smile? Most important of all, hadn't he been the one to introduce her to the pleasures of womanhood? That alone gave them a special bond.

His hands stilled on his foamy leg as he considered the consequences of his actions. What if it actually worked? What if, by some misguided miracle, he was able to recapture her affection and trust to the extent that she took him into her confidence? What then? After rescuing her from whatever predicament had brought her here, would he simply tip his hat and walk out of her life, breaking her heart—and his—all over again?

Mulling over his new and troubling dilemma, he leaned back against the tub's backrest and bent his knee to his chest to wash his foot. Well, there was only one way to keep from hurting her again, and that was to make sure their new relationship didn't transcend beyond the bounds of platonic friendship.

His conscience guffawed at that notion. *Do you honestly think that you've got the strength to resist Penelope's charms? Why not just leave well enough alone? After all, she did promise to accompany you to San Francisco in six weeks' time.*

True. But if the nature of her trouble had an element of danger attached to it, then it was entirely possible that she might come to harm before the six weeks were up.

With that very real and frightening possibility in mind, Seth picked up the pitcher beside the tub and rose to his feet. His teeth chattering from chill, he poured the now-cool water over his shoulders and chest, rinsing away the last traces of soap.

By the time he stood on the too small floor cloth, drying himself with an even smaller towel, he'd made the only decision he could comfortably make: in a manner that would hopefully spare both their hearts, he'd charm Penelope into revealing her secrets and rescue her from her trouble.

Webs of Deception

And first atonement
Must be made
For unforgiven wrong—

—*Tristan und Isolde*

Chapter 12

Miles was late.

Penelope ceased her agitated pacing and plopped down on the faded sofa, sighing her exasperation as she dumped her bonnet onto her lap. She'd been waiting in the shabby boardinghouse parlor for almost a half hour, and her patience was at an end.

Muttering several unflattering adjectives as to the actor's parentage, she fretfully toyed with her bonnet. Blasted man! Where was he anyway? He knew she needed to arrive at the theater early on the evenings they performed *The Matchmaking Fairy.*

The Matchmaking Fairy, a rather risqué fantasy piece, necessitated that she don a complex series of harnesses, which were in turn rigged to a pulley that lifted her into the air and sent her flying across the stage, treating the audience to a tantalizing view of her ankles and calves. The preparation was not only time-consuming, but physically uncomfortable as well.

Restlessly Penelope twisted one of the forest green satin bonnet streamers around her index finger. If Miles didn't arrive soon, she'd never make the nine o'clock curtain. Not that she cared if the drunken louts in the audience had to wait to ogle her legs; if she had her way they'd wait forever.

No. What concerned her was the fine Adele would levy for her tardiness. There would be a fine, no doubt about it, even though the woman would know that the fault for her lateness lay entirely with Miles. Yet, as usual, she wouldn't dare protest out of fear that Adele would deny her her visit with Tommy tomorrow. And what was the loss of a few dollars compared to the priceless joy of spending time with her baby? Of course, if she was too late, the penalty might very well be the forefeiture of the visit altogether. And that was one punishment she wouldn't risk.

That thought was enough to make her glance nervously at the clock. It was ten after seven. If Miles didn't arrive within the next five minutes, she would be forced to walk the short distance to the theater by herself . . . not a thought she found comforting.

While calm enough during the day, by night the streets of Denver was overrun by scores of cowboys, sodbusters, miners, and farmers, all in town for a bacchanal evening of drinking, gambling, and female companionship. That being the case, any woman caught on the streets unescorted was likely to be perceived as fair game, and consequently treated as such. Especially if the woman happened to be an actress such as herself.

But what choice did she have? A tendril of dread snaked down Penelope's spine as she admitted that she had none. Bertram and Effie had left for the variety hall over an hour ago; Bertram being eager to get to the saloon for his customary preperformance shifter of brandy, and Effie needing the extra time to experiment with some new hair-enhancing treatment.

Heaving a sigh of defeat, she glanced down at the bonnet streamer, which in the course of her mindless fidgeting had become tangled around her index finger. As she attempted to right the mess, she mentally cursed Miles's unreliability. Though the actor was frequently late—for a promising poker hand, a fine bottle of liquor, or a particularly accommodating whore always took precedence over punctuality—this latest display of irresponsibility went beyond the bounds of tolerable behavior.

Mumbling an unladylike expletive, she gave the ribbon a vicious twist, smiling as she visualized Miles's neck in place of the streamer. She succeeded only in further tightening the knot.

As she sat clumsily trying to extract her finger from its satin snare, the clock announced a quarter after the hour. Snorting her frustration, she marched toward the front door, shaking her hand as she went in a frantic attempt to dislodge her still-trapped finger. As she paused in the tiny entry hall to claw at the recalcitrant streamer, there was a rap at the door.

Miles, at last. With the bonnet still dangling from her index finger, she yanked the door open, berating, "It's about time! Do you know how late—" The words died on her lips when she saw who it was. It was Seth Tyler. A resplendently garbed, impossibly handsome Seth, who was lounging against the doorjamb with one hand behind his back and his sensuous mouth tilted into the crooked grin she always found so disarming.

"Sorry, sweetheart," he murmured, seizing her right hand and lifting it to his lips. Gallantly refraining from commenting on the hat hanging cockeyed from her finger, he pressed a kiss to her palm. As he released her, he explained, "I would have been here at seven sharp, but I had a devil of a time finding these."

With a courtly flourish, he pulled a beribboned nosegay of pink roses, blue columbine, yellow marigolds, and white daisies from behind his back. Peering at her from beneath his thick sweep of lowered eyelashes, he pleaded, "Forgive me?" Then his lips curved into a repentant smile that she found every bit as endearing as his previous grin.

Staring at him and his bouquet with as much amazement as if he were wearing a ruffled skirt and dancing the cancan, Penelope sputtered, "W-what are you doing here?"

"You've forgotten?" He clasped the flowers to his heart and sighed with dramatic effect. "You wound me!"

She frowned at his flirtatious response. Whatever had gotten into him? If she didn't know better, she'd swear he was wooing her. She shot him a wary look.

He flashed her a very wide, very alluring smile.

Her heart missed a beat. He hadn't smiled at her like that since the night at Delmonico's two and a half years earlier when they had celebrated the three-month anniversary of their engagement. As it turned out, it had been their last romantic night together.

Seth had been at his most charming that evening, playfully challenging her to a contest to see who could eat the most oysters and drink the most champagne. After devouring thirty-nine oysters and drinking three bottles of fine champagne, they were both too full to move and completely—

"Seth Tyler! Are you drunk?" Penelope leaned forward and sniffed his breath suspiciously.

He exhaled, bathing her lips in the warmth of his breath. "Sure I am," he purred. "I'm drunk off your beauty . . . intoxicated by your sweetness, and"—his mouth was so close, she could feel his lips move against hers ever so slightly as he finished—"I'm tipsy with the pleasure from your company."

Their sudden intimacy caught Penelope completely off guard, leaving her powerless to do more than just stare into his eyes. She'd always heard that the eyes were the mirror to the soul, and Seth's beautiful, chameleonlike eyes were proof that the saying was more than just empty words.

For instance, when they were soft sage green, rimmed in chocolate brown with a sunburst-like star of gold surrounding his pupils, she knew he was happy. On those rare occasions when his irises were stormy-gray edged in charcoal and speckled with mossy green, she tread lightly, for experience had taught her that he was displeased. And when they were dark, as they were now, indeterminate in hue, yet burning with sultry topaz fire, they bespoke of simmering passion and promised ecstasy.

Passion? Ecstasy? She stumbled back in stunned disbelief, clumsily catching her heel in her hem. She swayed perilously and would have tumbled backward had Seth not whipped his arm around her to steady her.

Crushing her against his chest, he stared down into her flushed face, drawling, "Sure you're not the tipsy one? Your face is awfully red, and you seem a little unsteady."

"Don't be ridiculous!" she snapped, squirming from his embrace. "I tripped over my skirts, that's all." When she'd put several feet between them, she braced her hands on her hips and gritted out, "Now, why don't you stop babbling nonsense and tell me what you want. I'm terribly late for the theater." Tapping her foot impatiently, she folded her arms across her chest and stared at him with ill-concealed annoyance, an effect that was completely ruined by the frilly hat dangling from her finger.

Smiling faintly, he shifted his gaze from the bonnet to her glowering face. "I said I'd be here at seven to walk you to the variety hall, and"—he spread his arms wide—"here I am."

"I told you that Miles always escorts me." Without thinking, she shook her finger at him for emphasis . . . her right index finger to be exact . . . smacking him in the chest with the attached bonnet.

"But Miles didn't show, did he?" From his strained expression she could tell that he was struggling not to laugh.

Mortified, she dropped her gaze from his face to scowl

down at the bonnet. Giving the stubborn streamer a series of vicious but futile tugs, she admitted, "No, but I'm sure he'll be along any—" Her hands stilled suddenly, and she shot him a suspicious look. "How did you know?"

An enigmatic half smile curved his lips. "Call it a hunch."

"A hunch? Ha! I'd bet my lucky ribbon that you did something awful to Miles, like tie him up and toss him into the corral, just so you could ask your blasted question!"

"If we were wagering, I'd now own a lucky ribbon." Seth's half smile broadened into a full one. "By the way, thanks for reminding me about the question. It had slipped my mind."

Penelope clicked her tongue between her teeth and rolled her eyes in a gesture of disbelief. "I'll just bet you forgot!"

"In that case, you lose again. Maybe you'd better stop betting while you're ahead."

She graced him with a scowl. "Be that as it may, I still don't believe that Miles would willingly let you escort me."

"He was willing all right."

"Oh?"

Seth tipped his head to one side and studied her for a moment, then shrugged. "Since you're so worried about the harebrained jackanape's welfare, I guess I'll have to put aside all gentlemanly discretion and tell you the truth. Your escort was detained by an obliging young lady named Sweet-Lips Alice."

At Penelope's blush he observed, "I can see by your face that you know who I'm talking about."

"I've heard her mentioned," Penelope muttered, humiliated to feel her flush darken a shade. She'd heard more than a mere mention of the notorious Alice. Not a day passed since they had arrived in Denver that Miles hadn't regaled her with his exploits with the prostitute. Through his graphic descriptions, she was beginning to feel as if she knew the woman personally, a sensation she found disturbing. Strangely enough, she was even more disturbed by the thought of Seth patronizing Goldie's.

Not that I care what the blasted man does, she reminded herself sternly. Yet try as she might, she couldn't deny that she did care what he did. Worse yet, she was jealous of whomever he did it with. Her heart twisted with sudden misery. Just as undeniable as her feelings for Seth was the fact that he'd visited the brothel that very afternoon. How else would he know about Miles and Alice? His assignation at Goldie's was probably the pressing appointment he'd mentioned at the drugstore.

Unable to meet his gaze for fear that he'd see the hurt in her eyes, she busied herself with her bonnet, which was now beginning to look to be permanently affixed to her finger. "How is it that you know about Miles and Alice's—tryst?" she blurted out before she could stop herself.

Seth shrugged. "I stopped by the saloon awhile ago, and Monty happened to mention Miles's rendezvous. I put two and two together and knew you'd need someone to escort you to the theater." Correctly divining the purpose of her question, he leaned over and added, "Never fear, Princess. I wasn't at Goldie's sampling her girls' charms."

Penelope sniffed. "As if I care."

"Well, I do care," he replied softly. "Very much."

Penelope stared up at his face, completely caught off guard by his admission. His smile was gentle, and his eyes were shadowed with what? Regret? Flustered and confused, she murmured, "Why?"

Tucking the nosegay into the crook of his arm, Seth grasped her wrist and raised her hand to examine the tangled ribbon more closely. "Just because we argued doesn't mean I no longer care."

"But last night, you said—"

"Forget last night," he interjected, his hand tightening convulsively on her wrist. "I behaved like a fool. The shock of finding you at the Shakespeare made me say things I didn't mean." His grip tightened a degree as he remembered his vile behavior the evening before, drawing a soft whimper from Penelope.

Instantly he relaxed his grasp. "Sorry," he murmured.

"It's all right. You didn't hurt me."

Her eyes were glowing softly and were filled with such a wealth of tenderness, that Seth was struck speechless by the turbulence of his own answering emotion. When he was finally able to speak, his voice had dried to a whisper. "You're wrong. I did hurt you, and very badly I suspect."

"Oh, no." She nodded to where her wrist lay cradled in his hand. "See. My wrist isn't even the slightest bit red."

Staring down at her wrist, which looked so delicate resting against the obvious strength of his square palm, he replied, "I was referring to your heart . . . your soul . . . about New York. I—"

"Seth—" she interrupted in a broken voice.

"No." He shook his head sharply, suddenly desperate to say all the things he'd wished he could say a hundred times before. "Please . . . just hear me out?"

His gaze locked into hers, silently pleading for permission to continue. He longed to apologize for the terrible things he'd said and done in New York; he needed to seek her forgiveness. And no matter how long it took, no matter the personal price, he wanted to rebuild the collapsed bridges of trust between them.

When she didn't answer, he repeated in a breathless whisper, "Please, sweetheart?" All of a sudden regaining Penelope's regard seemed the most important thing in the world. Not for the reasons he'd given himself earlier: not for the sake of his friendship with Jake and certainly not out of some misguided sense of gallantry. But for the sake of his own peace of mind.

After a moment, Penelope nodded her consent.

He let out his breath in a forceful gust, stunned to discover that he'd been holding it. With a tiny smile of gratitude playing on his lips, he began, "I said a lot of hurtful things that night in New York, things said in the heat of anger that I didn't mean. I was a bastard, and I've never been able to forgive myself for treating you so shabbily. I needed—"

His voice faltered as he felt Penelope's wrist slide from his hand, and for a moment he was overcome with a crushing sense of defeat, certain that she was retreating from both him and his apology. But then he felt her soft, cool palm press against his, and when her fingers, ribbon and all, threaded through his, he found the strength to continue.

Staring at the bonnet dangling from between their entwined hands, and thinking that he'd never seen a more wonderful sight, Seth confessed, "I've said and done a lot of stupid things, but none that I regret more than hurting you. I always promised myself that if I ever had the chance to make things right with you, I would. So I'm asking you . . ." He gave his head a shake and clutched her hand tighter. "No. I'm *begging* you to forgive me, to give me a chance to make up for the terrible way I treated you."

When she opened her mouth, perhaps, Seth feared, to

deny his request, he rushed to clarify, "I'm not asking that we go back to being lovers, and I certainly don't expect you to care for me the way you once did. All I'm asking is to be your friend."

Penelope suddenly had difficulty drawing a breath, hardly daring to believe what she was hearing. How many times had she, too, prayed for a chance to right the wrong they'd done each other in New York . . . for her own sake as well as Tommy's?

She stared at their clasped hands reflectively, noting with a pang that he was caressing her thumb with his, just the way he had when they were in love. Filled with sudden grief for the love that once was and would never again be, she tore her gaze away from the wrenching sight and refocused on her swaying bonnet.

She had to remember that he was only offering her friendship, a far cry from the turbulent carousal of passion they had once shared. She sighed inwardly. *Friendship*. It would have to be enough. Perhaps nurturing that friendship would grow to where she could trust him enough to tell him about Tommy.

"Say yes, Princess," she heard him whisper urgently. When she looked up to reply, she was stunned into speechlessness. Never, not even during their most intimate moments, had he worn an expression of such naked vulnerability. Seeing him like this, he who was always so confident and seemingly invincible, looking so hopeful, yet so uncertain, made her long to pull him into her arms and croon away his fears the way she did Tommy when he was frightened. Aching with tenderness, she dragged in a ragged breath and exhaled, "Yes. I'd like to be friends."

It was all Seth could do not to pull Penelope into his arms and shout his joy between pressing kisses to her sweetly bowed lips. But, of course, they had only agreed to be friends, and since he intended to see that their relationship never again transcend those platonic bounds, he restrained his impulses.

Turning his attention back to the bonnet streamer, he whispered, "Thank you."

"You're welcome."

They fell silent while he untangled the ribbon, each lost in his own thoughts, both ignoring their hopeless longing to be more than just friends. After several minutes, Seth freed her finger.

"There now," he murmured, smoothing the crumbled streamer between his fingers. Smiling faintly, he set the bonnet atop her head and tied the ribbons just below her left ear. As he puffed the bow loops, the chimes from the parlor clock echoed through the hallway and out the front door, breaking the intimate spell.

"Blast! It's seven-thirty! I'll never be ready in time for the curtain." Penelope slammed the front door closed and gave Seth a tug toward the porch steps. "We've got to go. Now!"

Without budging so much as an inch, Seth removed the bouquet from where it was still wedged in the crook of his arm and pressed it into her free hand. "We're not going anywhere until you fetch a shawl," he informed her, nodding at her bare shoulders and arms. "I won't have you getting chilled."

When she looked to argue, he reminded her, "You promised to do my bidding while in Denver, and I'm bidding you to get a wrap." Laying his hand over hers, he closed her fingers around the ribbon-wrapped flower stems. "Besides, I seem to remember buying you a green cashmere shawl to match that gown."

"You still intend to hold me to our bargain?" she inquired, incredulously. "I mean, since we're friends and all, well, I thought we might forget about our deal."

Seth chuckled and shook his head. "Oh, no. There will be no worming out of our bargain. All our agreements stand, including your acting as my valet and my asking a question a day."

"But—"

"No 'buts,' no exceptions. Rule number one of friendship: Friends always honor their word, and as such I expect you to honor yours." Gently nudging her toward the door, he added, "Now, go get your wrap. We're late for the variety hall, remember?"

Scowling, she hurried to do as he commanded. When she returned a moment later with the shawl in question draped around her shoulders, Seth gallantly tipped his top hat and offered her his arm. Seizing it, she pulled him down the porch stairs and rushed him down the walkway toward the gate.

To Penelope's vexation, he was slow to fall into step and

soon lagged behind. "For pity's sake, Seth! It's going to take us all night to get to the variety hall if you don't hurry up." Tossing him an irritated glance, she scolded, "With your long legs I'd think that—oh, my!" She stopped abruptly in front of the gate, her annoyance transforming into dismay. "You're limping! Why didn't you tell me that you'd hurt your leg?"

"Because my leg isn't hurt," he informed her cryptically.

"Then, why are you limping like that?"

"Because my reluctant valet was unavailable to help me apply the salve I purchased this afternoon." He grinned wickedly as he unlatched the whitewashed gate. "Or have you already forgotten the conversation you were eavesdropping on this afternoon?"

Penelope certainly hadn't forgotten, and she had the good grace to flush. "I-I wasn't eavesdropping!" she protested.

"So you've said," he returned evenly, ushering her through the gate. "All right, then. For the sake of our newfound friendship, we'll strike a compromise. We'll say that you overheard my conversation." He extended his hand. "Agreed?"

"Oh. All right," she muttered ungraciously, giving his hand an unenthusiastic shake. "I agree. But only because I don't have time to argue the point right now." Dropping her hand from his, she grumbled, "Can we please go to the variety hall now?"

"Your wish is my command." With that, he whisked her down the street with as much speed as his sore backside would allow.

They walked in silence for several minutes; she, feigning interest in the shop windows along Blake Street; he, waiting for something to send a flicker of interest across her face, thus providing him the opportunity to resume their conversation.

They hadn't gone more than a block before he saw her eyes widen and felt her steps falter. As she tilted her head for a better view into the shop window, her lips parted and slowly curled up at the corners. So sweet, so rapturous was her smile, that it took all his willpower to tear his gaze away and look into the window to see what had prompted such a response.

There, hanging in the grimy butcher shop window, were a bloody side of beef and two dead chickens. His nostrils flared with repulsion as he quickly glanced back at Penelope. She was still smiling in that same moonstruck manner, only more so.

Seth frowned. Could it be that she was hungry? Was she envisioning the chicken braised in Madeira wine sauce, and the beef roasted and surrounded by a ring of fluffy puffed potatoes? Troubled that Penelope might be so ravenous as to gawk at meat in a butcher shop window the way most woman ogled a display of Paris fashions, he followed the direction of her gaze.

Then he, too, smiled. Braced in the lower right corner of the window was a poster announcing the arrival of a circus the following Saturday. He studied the colorfully lithographed placard for a moment before shifting his attention back to Penelope, who now looked barely able to contain her excitement.

Overwhelmed with tenderness, Seth gently laid his hand over her small one resting on his arm. "Are you fond of the circus, sweetheart?" he asked quietly, giving her hand a light squeeze.

"Yes. But it's been years since I've seen one."

Seth didn't miss the note of longing in her voice, nor was he blind to the shadow of wistfulness that flitted across her features. Wanting to nurture the unexpected intimacy of the moment, he encouraged, "What did you like best?"

"The elephants," she replied without hesitation. "I always thought they looked kind and wise."

Seth considered the picture of the elaborately bedecked elephant at the bottom of the poster. Rubbing his jaw thoughtfully, he mused, "He does appear to be a pleasant sort of beast, doesn't he?" He tipped his head to one side and narrowed his eyes. "You know something? With those big ears and wrinkly hide, he kind of reminds me of an old miner I once hooked up with. He was a nice old fellow with a fondness for butterscotch . . . and peanuts."

Penelope giggled and shot him a mischievous look. "My father always said that the elephants reminded him of the two old maids who lived next door, all gray and wrinkled with noses long enough to stick into everyone else's business." She grinned at Seth's hoot of laughter. "We had such fun looking at the animals and deciding which of our acquaintances each of them resembled. My mother would have swooned had she heard our wickedness."

"It sounds like you and your father were close," Seth commented as they resumed their trek to the Shakespeare.

"We were. By the time I was born, Jake was fourteen and our sister, Annie, was eighteen, both too old to be interested in the circus any longer. But my father never outgrew it. He adored clowns and aerial acts, so I was only four the first time he took me. I, too, fell in love with the color and excitement."

She paused as Seth handed her down from the boardwalk into the street. "From then on, until my parents died, my father and I always had a date together whenever the circus was in town."

Seth smiled gently down at her upturned face. "Your father sounds like a wonderful man. You must miss him a great deal."

"I do. After my parents died in the fire, I often comforted myself by remembering all the wonderful times we'd had at the circus." She bowed her head then and in a choked voice that barely rose above a whisper, confessed, "I felt so lost and uncertain as to where I belonged and to whom, that I pretended that the circus was my family and that the elephant was my special friend. I imagined myself all decked out in a scandalous purple and gold costume, riding atop my elephant down the streets of every town in America, waving to the adoring crowds."

Moved by her unexpected confidence, Seth murmured, "I think that that was a wonderful dream. Did you tell Jake about it?"

She shook her head. "He was living in San Francisco, and it took several months for him to travel to New York. By the time he arrived, I was so wretched living with my soberside aunt, and so grateful that he wanted me to live with him, that I was determined to put aside all my childish fancies and act like an adult. I wanted to make sure he never regretted my guardianship."

"Poor Princess. So you never again went to the circus?"

"Three months after we arrived in San Francisco, a small circus came to town. Jake insisted on taking me, saying that I was far too solemn for a child of ten and that I needed a few lessons in having fun. When I timidly mentioned how much I loved the elephants, he confessed that he too harbored a secret fondness for them." She paused to release a soft, bell-like peal of laughter. "Do know what he did then?"

"Knowing your brother, probably something outrageous."

"Look who's calling who outrageous," Penelope teased. "What he did was tell me a story how he once stole the stable boy's clothes and snuck down to where the circus was camped. He said he pretended to be a street urchin in desperate need of a meal and offered the elephant trainer his help in washing the elephants in exchange for food. It took a bit of pestering, but the trainer finally took pity on him. Jake said that it was the best afternoon he'd ever had, well worth the hiding he received for running off like that and frightening our mother half to death."

She glanced up, her expression pensive. "I knew then that it was all right for me to be a child and that he wouldn't send me back to live with my aunt, no matter how much I frolicked."

Seth gave her hand a squeeze. "Jake enjoyed having you around. Besides, I don't know anyone who likes a good frolic better than your brother."

"Except for you," she contradicted, tossing him an impudent look. "Nobody knows how to have fun like you do."

A grin tugged at his lips. "In that case, how about letting me show you how much fun I can be at the circus?"

Penelope's heartbeat tripled at his invitation. There was nothing she'd love more. She had a hunch that she'd never really seen a circus until she'd attended one with the high-spirited Seth Tyler. It was on the tip of her tongue to accept when he said, "We could go on a picnic and then attend the afternoon performance. I'll have you back at the variety hall in plenty of time to make the nine o'clock curtain."

The reminder of the variety hall—and Adele—deflated her buoyant spirits like a knife to a hot-air balloon. Of course she couldn't go. She'd been a fool to even consider it. Adele had specifically forbidden her to see Seth outside the theater. With that dispiriting thought in mind, she demurred.

"I can't. I have rehearsal. Besides, Adele doesn't allow her actresses to consort with men while on the road."

"But I'm not just any man," Seth persisted. "For the next few weeks, I happen to be yours and Adele's boss. I seriously doubt she'll object if I ask her permission to take you."

Penelope's chest tightened with anxiety at his suggestion. While Adele probably wouldn't voice her objections to Seth, she'd make damn sure that she felt the brunt of her displeasure. Not only might the dreadful woman dock her a whole week's pay; she might refuse to let her see Tommy.

Desperate to insure against such a happenstance, she countered, "As wonderful as the circus sounds, I really do need to rehearse. We're premiering a new play next Saturday."

Seth wasn't deaf to the pleading note in Penelope's voice, nor did he miss the way her breath had caught when he'd mentioned Adele. For a moment he considered asking her about her alliance with the company, then changed his mind. He didn't want to ruin their tentative, newfound intimacy by poking into what appeared to be a very sore subject. He also didn't want to start an argument by pointing out that, as the owner of the variety hall, he could easily order Adele to postpone the premiere, thus freeing her for the circus next Saturday. And since that didn't leave anything left to be said on the matter of the circus, he had no choice but to change the subject.

"Speaking of elephants and the company, I noticed the rather buxom manner in which the artist portrayed you on the playbill."

"Isn't it awful?" she exclaimed, quickly seizing upon the new topic. "Adele decided that it was too expensive to have the printer make a plate of a drawing of me, so she had him print the posters with one he had left over from a previous job. I believe the lady portrayed is Catarina Contortina, a contortionist whose claim to fame is playing "Dixie" on the harmonica with her feet."

Seth shouted with laughter at that. "Catarina Contortina! I'll bet that's her real name!" He guffawed again. "Speaking of names, how did you come up with Lorelei Leroux?"

Penelope looked at him hopefully. "Is that your question?"

He grinned. "Sure."

"Adele read that the men out West are particularly fond of female performers with foreign-sounding names, so she decided to change my last name to Leroux in keeping with the French name du Charme. As for Lorelei," she shrugged. "It goes with Leroux."

They were in front of the Shakespeare now. Eyeing the swinging doors with distaste, she asked, "Can I ask you a question as well?"

His grin broadened. "They say that turnabout is fair play, and I always like to play fair. Ask."

"Why did you buy the saloon? I mean," she gestured toward the building. "It's not what I'd call a great investment."

"No, but it's a great toy." He chuckled at her shocked expression. He'd known she'd eventually ask him about the purchase and was ready for the question. "I've always had a fascination for the West and got an itch to own a piece of it after reading a recent article on Denver in the *Saturday Evening Post*." He let his appreciative gaze sweep her from head to toe. "I took one look at the Shakespeare's entertainment and knew that the saloon was the piece for me."

Miles was late. Very late.

Cursing her delinquent son beneath her breath, Adele flashed a hastily scribbled cue card to the corseted and bewigged Bert, who was onstage valiantly muddling his way through the first act in Miles's usual role as the hero.

Bert, who had forgotten his line and was now improvising to the visibly confused Lorelei, stopped dead in his tracks to squint at the placard. After hemming and hawing several times, he followed Adele's prompting and pulled Lorelei into his arms, declaring his undying love in a thunderous voice more suited to a commanding general than a lovelorn lothario.

"Jist kiss the gal and be done with it!" hooted one man.

"Hey, Lorelei-honey! Why don't ya come down here 'n let me show ya how a real man smooches!" That catcall prompted a chorus of exaggerated kissing sounds.

Gritting her teeth with annoyance, Adele tossed the card to the floor. Where the hell was Miles? She mentally ran through the list of unsavory possibilities. The jackass! Due to his lamebrain irresponsibility, she'd been forced to cancel *The Matchmaking Fairy,* a piece involving five characters of which two were played by Bert, and substitute it with *The Ballad of Lucy Mae,* a humdrum musical written for three players.

Notorious for the way it shockingly exhibited Lorelei's ankles and calves, an announcement of a performance of *The Matchmaking Fairy* never failed to pack whatever theater the company was playing. And it was packed tonight ...

... Until Seth Tyler announced the change of program. In

response to the disappointed crowd's boos, he'd magnanimously offered a refund of admission and a free drink to any man not wishing to view the company's tamer exhibition, an offer that proved to be very popular. So popular that he'd threatened to add an extra day to their run to make up for the lost revenue. And an extra day's run would mean losing their Tombstone engagement.

Peeking out at the now-sparse audience, of which two were raucously arguing over a mule named Trixie Belle, and a handful of the others were asleep, Adele mentally redirected several of her more vituperate thoughts from Miles to Seth Tyler.

The man was becoming troublesome, and in more ways than one. It raised her ire just remembering the possessive manner in which his arm had been slung around Lorelei's waist as they waltzed into the Shakespeare that evening. Barely able to contain her rage, she'd ordered the little hussy to her dressing room, bent on punishing her for disobeying her rules. However, when she tried to follow, the saloon owner had ordered her to stay.

With galling arrogance he informed her of Miles's negligence, then had the nerve to chide her for her thoughtlessness in designating him the girl's protector. After astutely pointing out that the company would be ruined should its star performer come to harm, and thus be worthless in the repayment of Miles's debt, he had imperiously reappointed himself as Lorelei's escort. She hadn't been deaf to the underlying threat in his voice, nor blind to the predatory glint sparking his narrowed hazel eyes.

A babel of catcalls drew Adele's mind away from Seth Tyler and back to the action onstage. Bert was kneeling before Lorelei, awkwardly shoving his wig back over his bald pate. Apparently the false hair had come off when he removed his hat to propose to Lorelei's character, Lucy Mae.

As Adele hissed at Bert, trying to alert him to the fact that his wig was on sideways, she heard the scurry of feet behind her. Whipping around and dropping to a crouch, a life-preserving reflex bred from years of association with the seamy underworlds of Boston and New York, she snatched her derringer from a pocket discreetly sewn into her underskirt. When she saw who it was she relaxed, but only a hair.

"Where the hell have you been?" she whispered harshly as Miles came dashing harum-scarum into the stage wing.

Stumbling over a sandbag in his haste, he whined, "It wasn't my fault. I would have been on time if—"

"Silence, you fool!" Adele commanded, raking his unkempt appearance with her disdainful gaze.

Miles stuttered once, then did as he was told. Turning red beneath her relentless scrutiny, he self-consciously combed his fingers through his rumpled hair.

Adele's eyes narrowed as they came to rest on his misbuttoned waistcoat and dangling shirttail. "You've been whoring again, I see." She made a contemptuous noise in the back of her throat. "I'd have thought you'd have more sense after catching the clap from that slut in St. Louis."

"I haven't ridden a whore since St. Louis," he informed her in an indignant squeak. "That's why I'm seeing Sweet-Lips Alice. A man doesn't have to ride her to get his pleasure."

Adele expelled a short, nasty laugh as she shoved her gun back into its hiding place. "Well, just make sure you don't forget yourself and buy anything else she's selling. The next time, I won't be so eager to shell out twenty dollars to pay for the cure. Especially not after tonight."

Without warning, she lashed out and viciously boxed his ear. "Damn it, Miles!" she ranted. "We might lose the Tombstone engagement, and all because you couldn't bear to tear your precious cock away from some two-bit whore."

Miles stared at his mother, his mouth working soundlessly.

"Well?" she demanded. "Don't just stand there gaping at me like a dyspeptic toad. What do you have to say for yourself?"

By degrees Miles's dumbfounded expression faded, replaced by one of wounded resentment. Pressing his palm against the side of his head, he blubbered, "It wasn't my fault!"

Adele eyed him scornfully. "Oh?"

"It was that Seth Tyler!" he accused wildly. "If he hadn't paid Goldie twenty dollars to have Alice ply me with booze, I wouldn't have fallen asleep like I did."

"Let me make sure I understand what you're saying," she gritted out. "You're telling me that that Tyler person bribed Goldie and Alice to make you late?"

"That's what Goldie said. She laughed and acted like it was all a big joke." The corners of his mouth drooped petulantly. "I told her that I didn't think her prank was very funny."

Adele wasn't amused, either. Through his adversarial actions this evening, Seth Tyler had thrown down the gauntlet and challenged her for the right to possess Penelope Parrish; a challenge she intended neither to ignore ... or lose.

Not even if winning meant murder.

Chapter 13

It was just after seven the next morning when Penelope arrived at Seth's hotel. Dressed as she was, with her figure hidden beneath the shapeless brown wrapper she usually reserved for laundry day and her face shielded by the wide brim of a calico bonnet she'd borrowed from the company's costume trunk, she had managed to pass through the streets without drawing more than a cursory glance from the passersby.

As she stood beneath the wide entry portico adjusting the bonnet brim to better conceal her face, she silently implored God to let her pass through the lobby unnoticed as well. She knew that if she were seen at the hotel, the backwash of gossip might reach Adele's ears, and just imagining the consequences of such an occurrence was enough to turn her blood to ice.

Concluding her brief but fervent prayer with a murmured "Amen," she reached into her reticule and rubbed her lucky ribbon for good measure. Crossing her fingers as an added precaution, she pushed her way through the plate-glass door.

This morning both Lady Luck and God were in a merciful mood. Save the nattily attired clerk, who was too engrossed in the magazine he was reading to do more than nod as she entered, the lobby was completely empty. Sighing her relief, Penelope uncrossed her fingers, quietly giving thanks as she moved to the center of the well-appointed room.

The American House, completed only a year earlier, was said to provide the finest accommodations in Colorado, and the lobby bore sumptuous testimony to the truth of that boast.

Tastefully decorated in cream and coppery brown with splashes of scarlet and gold, the lobby contained furnishings as fine as many of the first-rate hotels Penelope had once patronized back East. Comfortable chairs and sofas upholstered in hues ranging from tawny gold to deep chocolate were clustered throughout the spacious room; the floor was covered with carpet that bore earmarks of having been loomed by Wilton. Adding a crowning touch to the room's air of regal refinement were the rows of tall windows, which were arrayed to perfection with extravagantly swagged draperies of rich brown velvet.

To Penelope, who counted herself lucky these days if her lodgings included a vermin-free bed, the stylish elegance of the hotel lobby was a bittersweet reminder of the privileged lifestyle she had once so easily taken for granted . . . and lost.

After pausing a moment to savor her surroundings, she moved to the wide staircase and began her ascent to Seth's second-floor room. With her palm lightly brushing the smooth surface of the handrail, she slowly mounted each step. Higher and higher she rose. When she was out of sight of the lobby, she reluctantly forced her mind from her safe thoughts of the fine furnishings below to the dangerous ones of the man awaiting her above.

Just the idea of going to the hotel room of a man who was not her husband and serving in the intimate capacity of his valet should have shocked her into a fit of well-bred vapors. According to society's tenet of propriety, of which she was well versed in each and every inflexible rule, a true lady would have swooned the second Seth made his scandalous proposition. Should the aforementioned lady have the strength to retain her sensibilities in the face of such an affront, she would never—ever!—consider, much less agree to, such a wicked bargain. A *real* lady . . .

. . . *Would never find herself in this sort of situation in the first place*, Penelope concluded. As she stepped up on the second-floor landing, she was struck by an ironic realization: she, who had once prided herself on being the last word in refinement, who had been so quick to judge and condemn others for the slightest faux pas, now came up shamefully short when measured against her own pretentious yardstick of acceptability. For not only had she considered the terms of Seth's unseemly proposal; she had agreed to them. Most damning of all, she now found the prospect of fulfilling those terms strangely exciting.

With jimjams dancing a jig in her stomach, she wandered down the long hallway, her lips moving soundlessly as she read the brass numbers posted on the doors. Seth's was the last one on the right. Not wanting to disturb the occupants of the surrounding rooms, she rapped on the door very softly. There was no response.

Pressing her ear against the walnut-stained door, she listened for sounds of stirring within. Silence.

"Seth?" She knocked again, this time more insistently.

Still no reply.

With a frustrated snort, she jerked open her reticule and shifted through the catchall contents. After pushing aside several rumpled receipts, clumsily dropping her tin of lip balm and pricking her finger on the end of a broken hat pin, she found the room key stuck to the gooey underside of a half-eaten bonbon.

Sucking on her wounded finger, she fitted the chocolate-and-maple-cream-smeared key into the keyhole and tried to turn it.

It wouldn't budge.

As Penelope wrestled with the lock, she heard the sound of footsteps accompanied by labored grunts and the slosh of water. Peering around her bonnet rim, she spied a porter hauling two steaming buckets heading in her direction at an alarming pace.

Blast! Undoubtedly the man had noticed her trouble with the lock and was about to offer his assistance. With her luck he was probably a regular patron of the variety hall and would recognize her on the spot.

Desperate now, she gave the key a forceful shove to the right. With a loud *click!* the safety lock released. In the twinkling of an eye, she slipped into the darkened room and closed the door behind her, shutting out not only the prying eyes of the passing porter, but the hall light as well.

Relieved at her narrow escape, she closed her eyes and sagged against the door, trembling as she listened to the frantic drumming of her heart. When her pulse had returned to normal, she opened her eyes and squinted into the gloom-filled room.

Shafts of hazy sunshine filtered through the filmy lace sub-curtains and around the edges of the carelessly drawn drape panels, scattering faint, weblike patterns of light across the shadowy landscape of furniture. From the murky depth of the bed, which was little more than an inky silhou-

ette against the charcoal background of the room, came the
sound of soft snoring.

"Seth?" Penelope whispered, her eyes straining as she focused on the spectral contours of his prone figure.

His only reply was another snore.

As disoriented as an explorer lost in an uncharted cave,
Penelope stumbled through the dark, embarking on a light-
seeking mission to open the draperies. As she shuffled toward the windows, her hands blindly groping the space
before her, her boot heel caught on something. She teetered
back and forth twice, then tumbled to her knees ... right
into a mound of pillowing softness.

Thanking her lucky stars for whatever had broken her fall,
she flopped back into a sitting position and wrestled whatever had tripped her from her heel. Like a sightless person
reading braille, she ran her fingers over the foot-trussing
culprit, noting the silky fineness of the fabric. By the shape
and feel of it, it appeared to be a pair of Seth's trousers.

Dropping the garment to the floor, she reached out and curiously prodded the knee-saving heap in front of her. She'd
have bet her lucky ribbon *and* her best mother-of-pearl hair
comb that it was the rest of the clothes he'd worn the night
before. Apparently Seth wasn't jesting when he said he
needed a valet.

Without further mishap, Penelope reached the windows
and flung open the draperies. In a blinding flash of white-
gold brilliance, sunlight flooded the room, painting the
night-grayed interior with bold strokes of color and drawing
the once indistinguishable furniture shapes into focus.

After securing the olive plush drapes with their gold tie-
backs, she turned to wake Seth. What she saw left her
breathless.

Bathed in the warm morning light, his sun-kissed skin
gilded to a priceless gold, Seth lay sprawled across the bed
in all his naked glory. He was magnificent in his nudity, all
long, lean lines and hard, sculpted muscles.

Ignoring her conscience, which was sternly lecturing her
on the unseemliness of spying on an unclothed man, she
moved nearer to the bed. When he didn't stir at her approach, she paused to let her admiring gaze sweep his elegant form.

He looked so handsome, so utterly tempting that it took
all her willpower not to reach out and run her hand down the

length of his powerful back. Lying on his belly as he was, with his arm cradling his head and his gold-stubbled cheek resting against the back of his open hand, he reminded her of a painting she had once seen of Apollo asleep in a flowery glen.

Like the beautiful sun god, Seth's features were a striking composite of rugged planes and refined angles, giving him an appearance that was at once aristocratic and savagely earthy. His eyelashes, which were surprisingly dark compared to his hair, lay in spiky crescents against his tanned cheeks. Not for the first time, Penelope caught herself envying their length.

For a very long time she stood there, wistfully etching every feature of his peaceful face into her memory. How many times during the past two and a half years had she imagined Seth lying by her side looking exactly the way he did now?

In response to something in his dream, Seth groaned and restively tossed his head, sending a long tendril of hair tumbling across his forehead.

Smiling with tenderness, she reached down and gently brushed it back, letting her hand linger on the ripe wheat profusion spilling across his pillow and down his back. How she loved the untamed splendor of his mane. Loved the way it felt, so smooth and soft; loved the way it looked cascading wildly over the impressive breadth of his bare shoulders.

With brazen impulse outstripping demure caution, she lightly raked her fingers through the tangled length, marveling anew at the silky texture. As her hand glided from root to end, her fingertips inadvertently grazed the back of his neck, softly caressing him from nape to shoulder.

He whimpered and arched back against her hand, his mouth curving into a smile that could best be described as sultry.

The sizzling impact of that smile hit Penelope with a force that turned her knees to jelly. Even asleep, Seth Tyler oozed a mesmerizing sensuality that made her yearn to surrender the last vestiges of her pride and beg him to love her again.

Aching need blossomed low in her belly as she imagined herself naked and in his arms again. How she longed to feel his body moving against hers, his skin wet with passion-spawned sweat as he drove his masculine hardness into her soft, feminine flesh. She hungered to taste his lips as they claimed hers, to eagerly swallow his sobs of pleasure as he plunged his manhood deeper and deeper into the molten core of her womanhood. And as they climaxed, their bodies convulsing in harmonic ecstasy, she craved to hear him moan his declaration of love, just as in the past.

Penelope's breath strangled in her throat as the liquid evidence of her need dampened her drawers. As if psychically sharing her thoughts, and her desire, Seth released a choked groan and undulated his pelvis against the mattress.

With a groan that echoed his, Penelope's well-bred restraint lapsed. Guided by primal instinct, she lightly skimmed her fingertips down his spine, her breath quickening with his as she rounded the curve of his muscular buttock.

Over and over again she stroked him, trembling with the force of her own desire as he unconsciously thrashed and moaned beneath her hand. He'd always been so responsive to her touch, so shamelessly unbridled in the expression of his pleasure. Once upon a magical time, she had thrilled at her easy mastery over his body, empowered by the knowledge that he not only willingly surrendered his flesh to her, but his heart as well.

Suddenly he whispered, and her hand froze mid-stroke, her gaze darting guiltily from his flexing backside to his face. Expecting him to open his eyes and denounce her for the brazen hussy she was at that moment, she simply stood there, too paralyzed with embarrassment to move.

Except for a moan, he remained silent . . . and sound asleep. Sagging with relief, she struggled to compose herself, determined to stop behaving like a lovesick strumpet.

She almost succeeded. Just as her pulse rate returned to normal, he whispered again, this time clearly, "Penelope."

His voice was filled with such longing, such heartfelt tenderness, that her senses were electrified all over again.

"Penelope," he sighed yet again. Like a cat satiated by a bowl of cream, he released a contented purr and slowly ran the pink tip of his tongue over the sleek lining of his parted lips.

Her own lips burned and tingled in response, his provocative motion reminding her of the times he'd traced the sensitive inner region of her mouth in much the same manner. Staring hungrily at his lips, she remembered every nuance of his unforgettable kisses; the way his mouth had felt against hers, so delectably warm and mobile; the seductiveness with which he'd parted her lips with his tongue and the thrill of his penetration as he leisurely explored the contours of her yielding mouth.

Overwhelmed with the urge to touch his lips, to see if they were as smooth and pliant as she remembered, Penelope reached down and lightly followed the path of his tongue with her finger.

With a strangled moan he opened his mouth wider, and when he sighed, she felt the rush of his breath hot against her hand.

Yet, he didn't wake.

Emboldened by the depth of his slumber, Penelope again caressed his mouth, this time lingering to stroke his full lower lip. His response sent her pulse drumming into triple time.

With a sound halfway between a sob and groan, Seth sucked her marauding finger into his mouth, just as he'd done a hundred times before when she'd lovingly traced his lips with her thumb while expressing her admiration for their elegant shape.

Filled with bittersweet longing, Penelope raised her free hand and lifted a lock of his hair from his cheek. Tenderly she tucked it behind his ear, pausing to trace the shell-like rim with her fingertip . . . another intimate habit from happier days. He'd always loved having his ears touched like this, groaning how the sensual tickling maddened him with lust.

Apparently some things hadn't changed. Expelling an explosive whimper, his body arched up, quivering uncontrollably. Smiling, she snaked her finger down from his ear to trace the strong angle of his jaw. Once, as they had pondered what their children would look like, she'd asked him from whose side of the family he'd inherited that wonderful jaw. As with all her questions concerning himself, he'd somehow managed to avoid answering it by diverting her attention and changing the subject.

Her hand stilled as it suddenly dawned on her what an enigma Seth was. Though she had known him half her life, there was much she didn't know about him, so much she hadn't thought to ask.

Shame washed over her as she realized just how selfish she had been in her dealings with him. During their short courtship and even shorter engagement, she had been so pre-

occupied with her success on the stage that she'd been unable to speak of anything else. Vainly she had centered every
conversation on herself, never once bothering to ask Seth
about himself or his interests.

Not that he'd seemed to mind. In truth, he encouraged her
self-adulation by lavishly praising her talents and by showing a single-minded fascination with everything she said or
did. In her conceit, she'd viewed his attentiveness as gratify-
ing proof of his love for her. Now she wondered if it had
simply been a ploy to avoid discussing himself. But why?

Granted, she knew that his upbringing had been less than
privileged, though the details were sketchy at best. She
frowned suddenly. Could it be that all the adolescent scorn
she'd heaped on him years ago, the way she'd mocked his
once-poor grammar and reproached him for using the wrong
fork at dinner, had cut him deeper than she'd thought?

She stared into space for a moment, sickened to the core
of her very soul as she recalled the terrible way she'd treated
him when her brother first started inviting him to the house.
She'd been cruel in her taunts, spiteful in her youthful prej-
udice.

If the truth were to be told, it wasn't until five years ago
that she had finally seen him for the intelligent man he was
and the cultured gentleman he'd become. It wasn't until this
very moment that she realized how truly remarkable he was
to have bettered himself in such a spectacular manner.

A stab of guilt impaled Penelope's heart. Had she ever
bothered to tell Seth how much she admired him? How
much he thrilled and impressed her? Had she ever thanked
him for so graciously forgiving her the injustices she'd done
him?

Had she ever once said she was sorry for anything?

She sighed, thoroughly disgusted with herself. Sadly
enough, the answer to all those questions was no. Yet, despite her appalling selfishness, Seth had loved her. She
hadn't deserved such a gift; she knew that now. But like the
princess for whom she was nicknamed, she'd accepted his
adoration as her due, thoughtlessly taking it for granted as
she had everything else in her once-charmed life.

Oh! What she wouldn't give for a second chance! Things
would be so different ... better. She would be better.

Closing her eyes, Penelope made a silent vow: should a
miracle occur and she were to regain Seth's love, she'd treat

him with the respect he commanded. She would find out where he was from and what he wanted in the future. She'd learn what gave him pleasure and share his deepest fears. No matter how reluctant he might be at first, she'd coax every last detail of his life out of him. And regardless of how unsavory those details might prove to be, she'd accept them for what they were: a part of the past that had shaped him into the extraordinary man he was today. Most important of all, she'd never again take his love for granted. She would cherish it like the priceless rarity it was, and nurture it like a well-loved child. She would be worthy of him.

Beset with painful longing, Penelope opened her eyes and wistfully glanced down at Seth's sleeping face. She was stunned by his expression, so taut and filled with unslaked lust ... almost as stunned as she was to discover that she'd been the unwitting cause of it. While her thoughts had been virtuously repentant, her hands had been moving by their own lascivious volition, with her right one fondling his backside while the left tickled the long line of his spine. Mortified, she snatched her hands away.

Lord have mercy! Just look at what she'd done to the poor man! As instinctively as if it were something she did every day, she'd whipped him into a sexual frenzy that would have done one of Goldie's girls proud. She stared down at Seth's undulating body with alarm. Perhaps she wasn't *acting* like a wanton due to a temporary lapse of propriety; perhaps she *was* a wanton.

As if to present proof of her licentious tendencies and abilities, Seth growled her name and rolled onto his back, revealing the full extent of his arousal.

Penelope's jaw sagged with shock. Jutting from the nest of tawny curls at his groin, Seth's impressive sex was fully erect and throbbing visibly with need. Without thinking, she bent down for a closer look. She couldn't recall him ever being quite so ... inflamed. Not that she'd ever actually examined that part of him closely enough to know for sure. The three times they'd made love, she'd been too shy to do more than give it a few tentative caresses. Besides, it had been dark. In deference to her modesty, Seth had turned down the gaslights, thus precluding her from taking a really good look at his nude body.

But she was certainly getting an eyeful this morning, and what an eyeful it was! Desire, hot and vaporous, rose within

her as she continued to contemplate her titillating handiwork. As she stared, his hand, which lay spasmodically
clenching and unclenching on his taut belly, snaked downward in the direction of his need. Down it glided, until it
hovered close to his straining hardness. With an agonized
groan, he touched himself.

"Please, sweetheart," he begged hoarsely, then dropped
his hand from his erection to clasp at the sheet bunched up
beneath his hips. Lost in the throes of his lustful dream, his
pelvis thrust upward. Penelope felt her most private place
become slick with desire as she imagined being impaled by
him. Her knees suddenly weak, she sank down upon the bed
next to him.

They lay like that for a long while; she, lulled by the
earthy maleness of his scent; he, softly muttering her name
over and over again. Seduced by the thrilling familiarity of
his nearness, Penelope closed her eyes and drifted on the sea
of gentle memories. Once, not so very long ago, they had
lain in this very position playfully building castles in the air.

Such glorious plans they made! They would ice-skate in
St. Petersburg in the winter and kiss beneath the bridges of
Venice in spring. Come summer, they would frolic on the
warm beaches of Greece. And in the fall, they would float
down the Nile River on a barge fit for Cleopatra, eating
dried figs they had purchased at the marketplace in Cairo.

As they took turns spinning dreams and soaring on outrageous flights of fancy, their conversation had drifted from
the innocuous adventures of their days to the voluptuous
ones of their nights. In his seductive manner Seth had described in smoldering detail all the ways he intended to pleasure her.

Just remembering the images those softly purred words
had evoked was enough to ignite the volatile fires of Penelope's passions all over again. Suddenly mindless of everything but her desire to relive that wonderful time, she melted
against Seth, impulsively rubbing the length of her body
against his.

With a hoarse cry, Seth grabbed her and crushed her into
his embrace, roughly grinding his arousal against her belly.
The feel of him, rock-hard and ramming insistently against
her rucked up skirts was enough to jolt her back to her
senses . . . and to the realization that she was in a shamefully
compromising position.

Flushing at her predicament and guiltily aware that she'd brought it on herself, she tried to pull away. But he tightened his hold, easily immobilizing her.

Her throat clogged by panic, Penelope's wide-eyed gaze flew to his face.

He was awake.

Chapter 14

He was still asleep. Thank God, he was still asleep. A smile of relief tugged at Seth's lips. Obviously he'd only dreamed of being awakened, for Penelope was still in his arms exactly as his imagination had left her. Granted, a moment ago she'd been gloriously naked, not dressed in an ugly wrapper with some sort of absurd headgear dangling around her neck. And her expression had been one of carnal invitation, not the one of shocked dismay she now wore.

He gave a mental shrug. Ah, well. Such was the perverse nature of dreams. No doubt his wicked imagination had some mighty interesting plans for this blushing scullery maid version of Penelope. Hopefully she'd take up where the other Penelope had left off. The other had been a master of erotica.

With a groan Seth closed his eyes and undulated his pelvis, urging her to resume her pleasurable activities.

She shrieked and struggled against him.

His eyes flew open. For a moment he simply lay staring at her, too groggy and confused to form a rational thought.

Penelope's thoughts, on the other hand, had just emerged from the mind-numbing fog of her shock. She wanted to die! To roll back her eyes, turn up her toes and fatally succumb to her mortification. Tearing herself from his slackening grasp, she flung herself from the bed and put several feet between them.

Too humiliated to look at him, she stared down at the floral-patterned carpet. She had to say something, give some sort of explanation for being in his bed.

But what? Wishing that the floor would open up and swallow her, she nervously traced a woven leaf with the scuffed toe of her boot. The truth was out of the question, of course. She could just imagine his reaction if she were to confess to teasing him into his present condition. Knowing Seth, he'd probably invite her to finish what she'd begun. And the way just looking at his magnificent body made her tingle all over, it was dangerously possible that she might accept.

So what should she do? She stole a glance at him. He was staring at her, his expression every bit as bewildered as she knew her own must be.

"Penelope?" he murmured hoarsely, his gaze questioning.

She said the first thing that sprang to her lips, "You attacked me!"

To her astonishment, he blushed. It was that blush that sparked an idea. Praying she didn't look as guilty as she felt, she mustered up her best impersonation of an outraged maiden and berated, "How dare you drag me into your bed like I was one of your—your—doxies!"

"I did that?" He looked appalled.

It was all Penelope could do to stifle her grin as she nodded. "Yes! You were moaning and thrashing and muttering all sorts of lewd suggestions in your sleep. When I tried to wake you, you grabbed me."

Seth felt his flush deepen as he imagined exactly what she must have seen when she walked into the room. He must have looked and sounded like a licentious satyr. Hell, he certainly felt like one. Stunned and shamed, he dropped his gaze from her face.

God! Whatever had possessed him? He, who had always prided himself on his finesse in sexual matters, had never done anything as gauche as force a woman into bed with him . . . awake or asleep. He released a soft groan. Apparently his desire for Penelope was going to be a lot harder to control than he'd anticipated. But that was a problem he was going to have to address later. Right now he needed to smooth over the humiliating predicament at hand.

His first words would have to be an apology, that much was clear. Then he'd have to think of a way to explain his behavior without admitting to his unrelenting lust for her. But how?

He thought for a moment. It wasn't as if Penelope was unaware of his sensual nature . . . unless she'd forgotten the raptures of their lovemaking. Wounded by that possibility, he shot her a disgruntled look from beneath his eyelashes.

She was wearing an expression that was a little bit relieved and a lot triumphant. Gone was the affronted ingenue, and in her place stood a composed woman who looked as though she'd just gotten away with stealing the crown jewels.

Or, he amended with dawning understanding, gotten away with handling his jewels without compromising her dignity. His gaze sharpened as it homed in on her smug little smile. Thinking back, she hadn't looked so much outraged as she had guilty when he'd awakened to find her in his embrace.

Could it be that she'd done something to provoke him into behaving as he had? Seth turned the question over in his mind. It was certainly a possibility, one that bore further investigation. And investigate it he would. Ignoring the fact that his arousal was waving in the air like a flag in a brisk breeze, he folded his arms behind his head and yawned. "I attacked you? Hmm."

The indignant virgin was back in a flash. "Yes, you did! And after the disgraceful way you behaved, I'd think you would have the decency to cover your"—she pointed accusingly at his rigid sex—"your—thing!—and apologize."

Oh, she was good. He'd give her that. Stifling his urge to chuckle at her performance, he followed the line of her pointing finger to stare down at himself. "It's called a penis. Of course, considering its rather inflated state, the more correct name would be erection." Aching with frustrated need and determined to teach her a lesson for working him into such a state, he brazenly lifted the anatomy in question to allow her a better view.

"The other night you seemed inordinately concerned about me being plagued by the pox." With his free hand he ran his fingers down his rigid length, smoothing the skin of his sheath to fully display his unblemished male flesh. "Take a good look, Princess. As you can see for yourself, I'm in the pink of good health. Why, I'm positively bursting with vigor."

There was nothing maidenly or outraged about Penelope's expression as she watched his fingers glide down his shaft. She was wearing that dazed, unfocused look she had worn when he'd made love to her. Seeing her like that gave Seth an almost irresistible urge to wrestle her back into his bed and kiss her until the only word left in her vocabulary was a breathless *yes*.

Cursing beneath his breath, he dropped his sex back to his belly. With a mere look, Penelope had turned the tables on him, and it was he, not she, who was squirming. Irritated by his own lamentable lack of control, he added in a stinging tone, "Of course, seeing as how you've been doing God knows what to my body while I was asleep, you know all about my vigor."

That snapped her out of her calf-eyed stupor. Gasping with genuine affront, she practically spat, "You're an incorrigible bastard, do you know that?"

"Yes. And you're late for your duties." He nodded at the clock on the table next to the bed. "It's seven-twenty."

"I'll have you know that I was here promptly at seven. It's not my fault if you refused to wake up."

"Seven sharp you say?" Seth pushed himself into a sitting position. Folding his arms across his chest, he inquired, "What exactly have you been doing for the last twenty minutes?"

Penelope looked so guilty that he was left with little doubt as to exactly what she'd been doing. So he was right, she had in some way provoked his attack.

Looking as if she wanted to run and hide, she said, "I told you. I was trying to wake you."

"And may I say that you've done a splendid job of it? If you do the rest of your duties with such èlan, I might be tempted to fire Roper and hire you as his permanent replacement."

Penelope bit her tongue to check her barbed retort. No, she wouldn't rise to his bait. If she did, she'd probably be here all day while the blasted man rated her skills on the Roper scale of domestic excellence. And she'd be damned before she'd remain in the same room with him a second longer than absolutely necessary.

Determined to expedite her duties, she pointedly ignored his last remark and asked, "What does Roper do after he wakes you?"

"He fetches me a dressing gown. You'll find several hanging in the wardrobe. Then he summons one of the maids to bring me my coffee. I take it black and strong, and I like it served with ginger biscuits. But you don't have to worry about that. The hotel kitchen sends me up a tray every morning at seven-thirty."

Penelope nodded. "Fine. What else?"

Seth tucked a coil of hair behind his ear as he considered her question. "He lays out my shaving implements—you'll find them in the top dressing table drawer—then runs my bath. Since the civilized luxury of running water has yet to make an appearance in Denver, I've asked to have a tub and water brought to my room along with my coffee."

"You bathe here?" Penelope asked, disturbed at the prospect of spending yet more time with Seth in his current state of undress. To her discomfiture, she found that the sight of all that smooth golden skin did strange things to her. In fact, looking at him now made her palms tingle to touch him again.

"Where else would I bathe?" he inquired.

Slapping her hands against her skirts in an attempt to rid herself of the confounding sensation, she stalked over to the wardrobe. "The advertisement for this hotel claims that there's a bathroom on every floor," she said, flinging open the doors.

"The advertisement is correct," he assured her.

Penelope pulled a burgundy and sapphire paisley print silk dressing gown from its hanger. "Then, wouldn't it be easier to take your bath there?" It would certainly be easier on her.

"Probably. But I like to soak, which is impossible with the other guests pounding on the door and shouting at me to hurry."

Penelope almost groaned aloud. He liked to soak. Wonderful. She could just imagine what the sight of all those sleek muscles glistening with soap and water was going to do to her senses.

Before she could fully contemplate the disturbing effect, there was a pounding at the door. "Porter, sir!"

"It's a valet's job to direct the lower servants," Seth said.

Penelope swung around, gaping at him in speechless panic while he covered the lower half of his body with the rumpled green, gold, and maroon striped damask coverlet. She'd hoped that if she lurked at the side of the tall wardrobe and remained silent, she might escape the porter's notice. But if Seth expected her to instruct the man in his duties . . .

". . . I can't," she blurted out.

"Sure you can. All you have to do is open the door and tell the porter where to put the tub. He'll do the rest."

"It's not that. It's just that if Adele finds out that I was here this morning, she'll—" Penelope shut her mouth abruptly.

"Adele will what?" Seth asked softly. He hadn't miss her obvious terror of her employer's disapproval.

"N-nothing," she stammered, examining the dressing gown in her hands with sudden fascination. "S-she'll scold me, that's all. She demands a high degree of decorum from her performers."

Seth made a derogatory noise. "If Miles is a shining example of her idea of decorum, I doubt she'll so much as bat an eyelash at the news of you being in my room."

"Miles is her son. The rules don't apply to him," she admitted miserably. "Besides, he's a man. As you well know, society is much more tolerant of men's indiscretions."

Again there was a flurry of knocks, accompanied by the impatience-tinged announcement, "Porter, Mr. Tyler!"

"I'll be right there," Seth hollered back, not taking his gaze off Penelope's face. She looked on the verge of tears. Feeling like an ogre for having caused her distress, he beckoned her to his side.

Looking as if she were going to her death, she complied.

He reached over and tugged the dressing gown from her arms. "I'll get the door. You select something for me to wear."

The radiance of her answering smile made Seth's heart contract with longing. It was a real smile, the kind she'd given him during their courtship and engagement. The impact of it was like a powerful blow to his midsection, leaving him breathless and aching inside. Uttering her name in a strangled whisper, he impulsively seized her arm and drew her nearer.

"Seth?" she murmured.

Desperately clutching at the threadbare strings of his composure, he reached out and drew her red calico monstrosity of a bonnet back up on her head. "Your hat," he said, giving silent thanks for the counterfeit calm of his voice.

As he tugged the wide brim around her face, his fingertips accidently grazed the line of her high cheekbone. Her skin was every bit as warm and satiny-smooth as he remembered, and he was unable to fight the urge to cup her cheek in his palm.

Apparently Penelope felt the magic of their closeness as well, for she sighed and nuzzled her cheek against his hand. It was an act of such heartbreaking tenderness that it took the final strand of Seth's willpower not to draw her into his embrace and promise to love her forever.

But, of course, for them there could be no forever.

Wracked with a wrenching sense of loss, Seth drew his now trembling hand from her face and pointed to the wardrobe. 'Go," he commanded in a voice that was little more than a croak.

After gracing him with another of her soul-searing smiles, Penelope hurried across the room to do his bidding. Grappling to regain his emotional equilibrium, Seth slipped from the bed and shrugged on his dressing gown. With his raw backside smarting like the stings from a hundred bees, he limped to the door.

As he grasped the polished brass knob, he paused to glance over to where Penelope stood rummaging through his clothes. Even garbed in a shapeless wrapper, her figure was too alluring by far. A beleaguered groan escaped his lips. Apparently there were some curves no amount of fabric could conceal.

Scowling, he hissed, "Stoop!"

She looked at him as if he'd completely lost his mind.

Bowing at the waist, he repeated, "Stoop!"

Her expression mystified, she did what looked like an imitation of a hunchback.

"Perfect. Now stay that way." With that edict Seth opened the door. "Sorry to keep you waiting, gentlemen," he apologized, stepping to one side as he ushered the porter and his entourage into the room. "Please put the tub over there." He indicated a place at the end of the room opposite from where Penelope stood.

Grunting under the weight of their burden, the porter and a bellboy lugged the sizable tin bathtub over to the designated spot, closely followed by three men-of-all-work hauling buckets of steaming water. Bringing up the rear of the procession was a waiter bearing a tray with Seth's coffee and ginger biscuits.

After setting the food on a small table by the window, the waiter lingered until the bellboy had finished positioning the tub. Then the two men departed the room together.

Under the crisp direction of the porter, the remaining men prepared Seth's bath. Unfortunately the activity didn't prevent them from noticing Penelope, and they spent as much time gawking in her direction as they did tending to their duties.

Deciding it best to nip the men's curiosity in the bud, Seth casually asked, "I assume you all know Mrs. Grubber?"

The porter straightened up. "Can't say I do." He nodded courteously at the figure by the wardrobe. "Pleasure, ma'am."

Seth saw Penelope stiffen, but before she could respond, he said, "Oh, she can't hear you. She's almost completely deaf. You have to get right up to her and shout if you want to talk to her." He shrugged. "Sometimes she hears you."

"So what's she doin' here?" ventured a young man with spiky black hair and a missing front tooth.

"S-sh," hissed the porter, fixing the man with a reproving glare. "It's not your place to question the guests."

"It's all right," Seth reassured him. "Mrs. Grubber will be working for me while I'm in town, so it's just as well that I explain her presence to you."

"Work?" A blond man with a bristly orange mustache scratched his head. "What good is a deaf female?"

Seth glanced over at Penelope, who had pulled out one of his shirts and was studying it with the intensity of a student cramming for a midterm exam. Inclining his head in her direction, he lied, "The woman works absolute magic with starch and an iron. My shirts have never looked so good. My trousers are always perfectly pressed, and she never leaves so much as a speck of lint on my coats. She's also handy with a razor on those mornings when I'm too lazy or too hungover to shave myself."

"Oh, I get it," chortled the fourth man, rubbing the top of his bald pate as if forming a thought made it ache. "She's sorta like a gentleman's gentleman, only she's a lady. Right?"

Seth winked. "Exactly."

The man with the orange mustache looked unconvinced. "Her being deaf and all, how do you give her orders?"

"She doesn't need direction when it comes to seeing to a man's needs. She's been married for thirty-six years and has raised nine sons," Seth explained. "In truth, she takes such good care of me that I'm beginning view her as a second mother."

The four men nodded their understanding as they collected the now empty buckets.

"However," Seth continued. "For all her motherly good intentions, she can be a bit dangerous."

The porter looked up. "Dangerous, sir?"

"Yes. Being deaf has made the poor dear a bit—uh—

high-strung. She always carries a loaded pistol in her pocket and has developed a rather dangerous habit of shooting anyone or anything that happens to sneak up on her. Since she can't hear much, she's real easy to startle."

The man with the orange mustache made a gobbling sound, while the other two workers exchanged worried glances. Clearing his throat, the porter inquired, "So what should we do?"

Bending down to test the water temperature with his finger, Seth advised, "Stay out of her way. You shouldn't have any problem avoiding her. She arrives every morning at seven sharp and comes straight up to my room. Just make sure you let everyone else know that she's not to be stopped or in any way accosted."

"But how will they know who she is?" asked the man with the missing front tooth.

Seth straightened back up to his full height, all six feet two inches of it, to take a long look at Penelope. After considering a moment, he replied, "Tell everyone that she always wears a red bonnet that completely hides her face. She's got a tattoo on her cheek, and she's touchy about people staring at it."

"Tattoo?" choked the orange-mustached man.

"She was captured by the Indians when she was young, and they gave it to her, but we'll save that story for another day."

Casting a look of mock concern at Penelope's heaving shoulders, Seth intoned, "Looks like Mrs. Grubber is getting kind of nervous. Maybe you gentlemen ought to leave now."

That observation was enough to send the four men sidling toward the door. Just as they piled out into the hallway, Seth stopped them. "Gentlemen?"

They froze.

"I'll have Mrs. Grubber ring the bell three times before she leaves my room in the morning. If you wait a few minutes, it should be safe to retrieve the tub. Just don't come up unless you hear the three rings, or unless I direct you otherwise."

Bobbing their heads like loosely stuffed scarecrows in a tornado, the men hurried from the room.

As the door closed behind them, Penelope spun around to face Seth, her whole body convulsing with laughter. "A tattoo? Deaf? Really, Seth! However do you come up with those tales?"

Seth grinned his cockeyed grin. "Just talented, I guess."

She rolled her eyes toward the heavens. "Outrageous is more like it. You made me sound so dangerous that those poor men will run for cover every time they catch sight of a red bonnet." It was then that comprehension of what he'd done hit home. "Why, Seth Tyler! You spun that wicked story to protect me! You did it to insure my anonymity."

Seth merely shrugged and tested the bathwater again. "Will you bring me my soap from the dressing table?"

Penelope found herself smiling as she hastened to do his bidding. For all that he was obviously trying to deny it, it was apparent that his heart was softening toward her. Why else would he have done what he just did? As for her own heart, well, as much as she'd been desperately trying to ignore it, it had been telling her that Seth Tyler was the only man for her.

Her smile faded as she stared down at the clutter of ebony-backed brushes and masculine grooming articles scattered across the marble tabletop before her. Seth may be the man for her, but he'd made it abundantly clear that she wasn't the woman for him. He no longer viewed her as anything but a friend.

Or did he? Her hand froze in the act of picking up his bar of soap. Surely a man didn't dream sensual dreams about a woman who was just a friend? He didn't cry her name in his sleep in a voice thick with desire. And he certainly wouldn't look at a mere friend with passion blazing in his eyes the way Seth had done just now as he'd cradled her cheek in his hand.

Just remembering the smoldering topaz fire in Seth's eyes was enough to fill Penelope with a sunlike glow of warmth. He still wanted her, that much was apparent.

Want. Her inner glow dimmed a fraction. He wanted her, yes. But wanting a woman was a far cry from loving her.

But want is a start in the right direction, she reminded herself with halfhearted optimism.

Behind her, there was the splash of water, followed by a low groan as Seth lowered himself into the bathtub. With faint embers of hope stirring in her breast, Penelope scooped the soap from its dish with one hand, while pushing the unflattering bonnet from her head with the other, then turned to face the man whose love she was now determined to regain.

He wanted her. Perhaps with a little coaxing the seeds of his physical desire might be nurtured to grow into something deeper, more lasting. Perhaps someday his feelings would mature into love. Whatever the outcome, she was going to do everything in her power to cultivate his more tender emotions.

With that vow, she approached Seth. He sat huddled in the tub with his knees drawn up to his chin, his every muscle rigid with tension. Beneath the tangled veil of his hair, she could see that his eyes were screwed closed and that his face was as contorted as if he were enthroned on a bed of hot coals.

Which was exactly how the steaming water felt against Seth's raw backside, like red-hot coals. If Penelope hadn't been in the room, he'd have bolted from the tub and foregone his bath in favor of a thorough sponging at the washbasin. But, of course, he wasn't about to relinquish his manly pride in her presence.

Penelope dropped to her knees next to the tub. "Seth? What's wrong?" she asked, gently tucking his hair behind his ears.

By now the stinging was beginning to subsided enough for him to honestly croak, "I'm fine. Just sore from riding."

Her face flamed the vermillion of a prairie sunset. "Uh . . . I'm sure it h-hurts." She stared at the soap in her hands.

Seth smiled, thinking how charming she looked in her embarrassment. "Yes, but I'll live to ride another day."

When she remained silent, fretfully stabbing at his soap with her thumbnail, he joked, "Unless, of course, I shrivel into a prune waiting for you to give me my soap."

Her head flew up and her cheeks deepened to a particularly flattering shade of ruby. "Oh, sorry." She hastily deposited the bar into his outstretched palm. Looking everywhere but at him, she rose, asking, "I was wondering what you had planned today. I mean, what kind of clothing will you need? Will you be riding—"

"Not riding," Seth groaned. "I'll be walking over to the saloon and spending the day there going over accounts." There was a swish of water, then, "How about you? What are your plans?"

Penelope remained silent, grappling for an answer. It was

her son's second birthday, and she planned to spend the afternoon with him. Miles was to meet her at the Shakespeare at eleven to take her to wherever the Skolfields were hiding the baby.

"Pen?"

She glanced back at Seth. Big mistake. As soon as her gaze touched his body, she was captivated. He was every bit as glorious as she'd imagined he'd be with his tawny skin glistening with soap and water. Just looking at him made her ache to glide her palms across the slick, sculpted plane of his chest and down the muscular contours of his flat belly.

Fighting for composure and stalling for time, she mumbled, "Is that your question for the day?"

Grinning, he lifted one long leg and began to lather his calf. "Why not? It's as good as any question, I suppose."

Distracted by the sight of his foamy hands sliding from his well-formed calf up to his strong thigh, she inadvertently spilled the truth, "I'm going to see the Skolfields." She could have bitten off her tongue the moment the words were out.

"The Skolfields?" His hand paused on his thigh.

Damn. Damn. Damn! Now what?

What choice did she have but to brazen it out? Putting on a casual mien, she explained, "Sam and Minerva Skolfield. They're acquaintances of Adele's. They've invited Miles and me to have dinner with them." Well, it wasn't a complete lie. The Skolfields were acquaintances of Adele's, and Minerva would feed them.

"And where do the Skolfields live?" Seth had resumed washing and was now scrubbing his groin.

Penelope stifled a moan and looked away. She had to gather her wits before she said something completely disastrous. With that mission foremost in her mind, she stalked back to the wardrobe and stared at the clothing within.

"Where do the Skolfields live?" Seth repeated, this time more forcefully.

Penelope pulled out a beautifully tailored coat in a rich shade of claret and pretended to study it. "Not far. Just north of town," she lied.

When he didn't comment, she began to relax. Apparently he was going to let the matter of the Skolfields drop. With her poise slowly trickling back, she selected a pair of gray, black, and claret striped trousers to go with the coat. As she began to thumb through his rainbow-hued collection of waistcoats, he said, "About your proposed visit with the Skolfields."

Penelope's heart plunged to the pit of her stomach. He was going to forbid her to go, or worse, insist on accompanying her. When she refused, he would see to it that she stayed in town and she would miss her darling son's birthday. Her throat tight with dread, she croaked, "What about the Skolfields?"

There was a splash, as if he'd dropped the soap into the water. "Just make sure you're back in town before dark."

Penelope almost keeled over with relief. "Yes."

"Good" was all he said before the sounds of his bathing resumed. After a moment he began to sing ... the quintet from act one of *The Magic Flute* to be exact. In German. All five parts.

In a comic falsetto he sang the two soprano roles of the Night Queen's ladies, dropping a wobbly octave when it came time to screech out the part of the mezzo-soprano third lady. While he did well enough as the tenor Tamino, his baritone Papageno bore an uncanny resemblance to a foghorn. What he lacked in voice quality, however, he more than made up for in enthusiasm.

As he bellowed out the final stanza, he rose from the bathwater, flailing his arms for dramatic effect.

Clapping with delight, Penelope turned from the wardrobe, cheering, "Bravo, Seth! Oh, bravo! Well done!"

Seth grinned and sketched an extravagant bow, completely disregarding the fact that he was buck naked and standing calf-deep in water. It was the naked part that made Penelope flush and turn back to the wardrobe.

All to conscious of Seth's unclothed state and eager to remedy the situation, she made quick work of assembling the rest of his garments. As she pulled the final article of his attire from the shelf, a silky-soft pair of linen drawers, she heard him hobble to the dressing table behind her. There was a scraping sound, followed by a heavy sigh. Then silence.

Her arms laden with clothes, Penelope turned. The sight that met her eyes almost made her drop her soft burden. Seth was bent over the table, awkwardly trying to rub the salve he'd purchased from the pharmacy on his backside.

Her heart went out to him when she saw the open blisters dotting the chafed flesh of his inner thighs and lower buttocks. Poor man. No wonder he was so miserable. How could she have been so blind as to not have noticed his damaged state earlier?

With tenderness outstripping prudence, she dropped the clothing into a nearby chair and went to him. "Whatever have you been doing, Seth? You're horribly raw back here," she murmured standing directly behind him.

He tossed her a sheepish look over his shoulder. "I was up at Silver Plume last week looking at a new invention, a power drill. Stupid me, I let myself be talked into riding back to Denver instead of taking the stagecoach." Pulling a wry face, he mimicked, "Purtiest scenery this side of heaven, Mr. Tyler. Mile-high aspen trees everywhere, and rivers as clear as diamonds." His voice resumed its normal tone. "The guide didn't tell me that it took three days of hard riding to get down the mountain."

"By the look of those blisters, that ride must have been positively grueling," Penelope commiserated.

"If you think it looks awful, you should try how it feels."

"I'll pass," she replied, edging forward for a closer look. Grimacing with sympathy, she pointed out, "You should keep the area covered with salve. Otherwise, it might get infected."

"I'm trying. But I can't reach back there." He gave her a look forlorn enough to melt a heart of stone.

It worked like a charm. Before Penelope could think, she heard herself saying, "Poor man. Of course you can't apply the salve by yourself. Here. Let me help you."

"Would you?" He looked as pathetic as a lost puppy.

She sighed. What could she say to such a pitiful appeal but, "Hand me the jar."

He did. Working as fast as she could without causing him further discomfort, she spread a thick layer of the greasy blue unguent over the affected areas. Aside from wincing once when she tended the chafed underside of his masculine sac, he remained stoically motionless.

When her nursing duty was completed to her satisfaction, she handed him the linen drawers. "Here. These are soft. They will protect your skin from your wool trousers."

Smiling his thanks, he quickly donned the garment. She released a heavy sigh and tossed him his trousers. Leave it to Seth to look as alluring in his unmentionables as he did nude.

Pinning her gaze on his face while he slipped on his pants, she asked, "Do you want me to shave you now?"

Seth rubbed his fingertips over his gold-speckled cheeks as if considering her offer, then shook his head. "I think I'll skip the shave today. I doubt if anyone at the Shakespeare will faint at the sight of a few whiskers."

After that neither spoke beyond a few monosyllabic questions and commands. Article by article Penelope handed Seth his clothes, her pounding heart resuming its normal cadence as his beautiful body was gradually covered by stark white linen and fine worsted wool. By the time he was fully dressed with his fair hair brushed, she had regained her full composure.

With a reminder to ring the bell three times before she left, Seth swept a thick sheaf of papers from the desk and departed.

Alone now, Penelope tidied up the room. A neat man, Seth wasn't. As she paused at the tub to fish his bar of soap from the still-warm water, she was reminded that she had yet to take her own bath. She made a face as she contemplated the backbreaking work of hauling and heating bucketfuls of water. That prospect was enough to make her view Seth's tub with new eyes.

Why not take a bath before she left? The water was still clean and warm. And she wasn't likely to be disturbed. Seth had seen to that.

Why not indeed? she asked herself, reaching back to unbutton her smock.

It seemed she'd just found the silver lining of the dark cloud of being Seth's valet.

Chapter 15

It was a beautiful day, one made perfect by the autumn-kissed wind's soft tempering of the incalescent midday sun. Not a cloud marred the azure splendor of the sky, and the violet-gray vapor that had draped the horizon earlier had lifted, revealing the splendor of Longs Peak and her sister summits with breathtaking clarity. The air was fresh, sweet with the aromatic balm of sagebrush, as invigorating as Colorado itself. It was a day custom-made by God in honor of the joyous occasion at hand.

Penelope's heart soared like the magpie overhead; her spirits were buoyed with euphoria. She'd soon be reunited with Tommy, and together they would celebrate his second birthday.

Smiling gently with maternal adoration, she envisioned the pleasure on her son's face when she presented him with his gifts: a rattle to replace the one lost in a move two months earlier, and a cuddly gray plush toy rabbit, both purchased from a peddlar's wagon in Cheyenne. True, the rattle had cost her almost a full week's pay, but the moment she'd set eyes on it, she'd known her son would love it and had gladly paid the exorbitant price.

Of heavy silver, the rattle was an exquisite creation fancifully wrought to resemble a storybook court jester. He was a droll little fellow, that jester, with a cheery smile and a comically bulbous nose. Around his neck he wore a collar of six golden bells, which tinkled in gay accompaniment to the rolling clatter of the pellets within his roly-poly belly. His pointed hat doubled as a whistle, and he was perched on his tiptoes atop a smooth coral handle that doubled as a teething stick.

Not that Tommy could actually grasp the handle. Penelope's smile faltered a bit as she guided her mare, courtesy of the Summers and Dorsett Livery Stable, across the planked

Platte River bridge. Her poor darling couldn't hold anything, and according to that quack in Philadelphia, he never would.

"We'll stop here," grumbled Miles, who'd remained silent since they had left the Shakespeare a half hour earlier. By his unkempt clothes and surly disposition, it was obvious that he was suffering from one of his frequent hangovers.

Without bothering to reply, Penelope reined her horse to a standstill and dismounted. She knew the routine by heart. First Miles would exchange her mare's bridle for the halter he carried in his saddlebag; then he'd secure a lead rope from the halter to the saddle horn of his sturdy chestnut gelding. That task completed, they would double-mount the gelding, at which point she would be blindfolded. With her practically sitting on his lap, they would ride the rest of the distance to the Skolfields'. It was an elaborate subterfuge, but one insisted on by Adele.

When Penelope had once suggested that she and Miles ride the entire distance on one horse, thus eliminating the time-consuming switch, Adele had coolly pointed out the questionableness of two competent adults riding double like a couple of Georgia crackers. As the woman was quick to remind her, suspicions must remain unaroused at all costs. And so their charade continued.

While Miles coaxed the well-worn halter over the mare's head, cursing darkly when the skittish animal whinnied and balked in protest, Penelope mentally marked their location.

On either side of her, as far as the eye could see, were freshly harvested fields dotted with sheaves of sun-ripened wheat. A quarter mile behind her was the cottonwood-edged Platte River, and before her reared the irregular pyramid of Longs Peak. It appeared they were headed west, but, of course, Miles would probably change directions once she was blindfolded.

"You know, I could fix it so you could see your brat any-time you wanted," Miles said, pausing from his task to squint at her with drink-reddened eyes.

Please Lord. Not this conversation again, Penelope prayed, gazing toward the heavens in beleaguered appeal.

Apparently God was busy elsewhere. "I don't see why you won't marry me," Miles whined for the hundredth time. "I've already promised to get your baby back for you if you do." He shot her a crafty look over the lead rope he was hitching to the halter. "And we all know that you'll do anything to protect him."

He was right; she would do anything to protect Tommy. She'd even have married him, sorry excuse for a man that he was, if she truly believed that by doing so she would secure her son's safety. But she knew better, even if Miles didn't.

While Miles chose to ignore his mother's treacherous nature, blindly viewing her as a benevolent cross between Clara Barton and Queen Victoria, Penelope saw her clearly for the venomous she-devil she was. Knowing Adele, she would probably murder her own son rather than relinquish her primary source of income. And Penelope had enough guilt on her conscience without adding the responsibility for Miles's death to the dispiriting list.

Knowing that to voice her misgivings would be an exercise in futility, she settled on what had become her stock reply: "You're already married. Besides, I don't love you." Then she buried her fingers into the time-softened folds of her split skirt and braced herself for his predictable rebuttal: a heated pledge to secure a divorce, followed by an impassioned vow to win her love.

For the first time since she'd begun her western odyssey, he surprised her. "It's because of Seth Tyler, isn't it?" he demanded, his tone growing sullen. "You're in love with him."

"In love? With Seth Tyler?" Penelope echoed, shaken by his uncharacteristically sharp perception. Good heavens! Were her feelings for Seth really that transparent? Or . . .

Sudden fear clutched at her belly as another, more ominous possibility assailed her thoughts. Had he somehow found out about her early-morning visit to Seth's hotel room?

Dreading the answer, yet knowing that she'd go mad if she didn't ask, she forced herself to say lightly, "Me and Seth Tyler? Really, Miles! Wherever did you get such an absurd notion?"

He gave her a long, knowing look, one that spoke eloquently of an intellect far greater than he normally displayed. That look completely unnerved her.

"You know, Lorelei, you'll never be a truly great actress."

"Oh?" she intoned, struggling to hide her uneasiness. This wasn't the way their dialogue was supposed to go.

With deliberate leisure Miles tied the rope to the saddle

horn, leaving her question dangling in the air while he checked his knot not once, but thrice.

Just when Penelope was about to lose her patience and demand an explanation, he replied, "You'll never be a great actress, because you can't control your face. Everything you think or feel is right there for the whole world to see. Take last night, for example. You were eyeing Tyler like a bitch in heat. I half expected you to rip off his trousers and jump on his cock for a quick ride."

Penelope gasped, too outraged by his crudity to do more than stammer, "H-how dare you s-say such a vulgar thing!"

Miles released a nasty, high-pitched laugh. "Oh, come on, Lorelei. Do you think I can't see what a hot-blooded little slut you are beneath that frigid, I'm-too-good-for-the-rest-of-the-world act of yours? Why, I'd bet my American Horologe watch that when you take your snooty nose out of the air and stick it"—he let his hand slide suggestively to his groin—"someplace useful, that you're no more of a lady than Hell-cat Helga."

Penelope's cheeks stung as if he'd struck her. Everyone knew Hell-cat Helga. She was the coarsest whore in Denver. Of late she'd taken to standing in front of the Shakespeare, hollering obscenities and grabbing the crotches of passing men.

Miles laughed again, this time in a lower, more fiendish timber, which sounded chillingly like that of his mother. "I'd also wager my new enameled watch fob that that Tyler bastard knows a thing or two about your secret talents."

Wanting nothing more than to slap his filth-spewing mouth, but unwilling to jeopardize her visit with Tommy, Penelope forced down her ire and coolly announced, "Then, you'd lose. Mr. Tyler is a friend of my older brother. I've known him forever."

Miles made a nasty snickering noise. "Some friend. I wonder if your brother would still call him 'friend' if he knew that he'd knocked up his baby sister." His smirk broadened at the sound of her gasp. Folding his arms over his chest, he pondered in a menacing tone, "More interesting yet, I wonder what Mother would do if she knew that your brat's father was Seth Tyler?"

Penelope's stomach roiled with terror at the threat behind his words. Dear God! What *would* Adele do if she found out that Seth was Tommy's father? Would she do something drastic out of fear that Penelope might confide in him and finger her for the blackmailing kidnapper she was? The sickening sensation deepened. Tommy was everything to her. If anything happened to him . . .

No! Nothing would happen to him! She wouldn't let it. She'd come up with the money One-eyed Caleb was demanding to track and rescue him, even if she had to steal it. Until then, she had to plant enough doubt in Miles's mind to keep him from voicing his suspicions to his mother.

But what if she couldn't convince him?

She fought down another swell of panic by reminding herself that Miles was merely speculating about Seth's paternity to Tommy, and that Adele was far too shrewd to pay his rambling much heed. And even if he did manage to pique her suspicions, she wasn't bound to do anything hasty. Not when it meant letting a thousand dollars or more a week slip through her grasping claws.

Feeling somewhat reassured by that rationale, Penelope gave a forced laugh and said, "Seth Tyler, Tommy's father? I had no idea you had such an imagination, Miles. Perhaps you should try your hand at writing melodrama."

Miles's normally handsome face contorted into a mask of petulant ugliness. "Don't treat me like an idiot. I've seen your brat enough times to know that he looks exactly like Tyler."

Penelope cocked her head to one side as if considering his charge. "Do you really think so?

Miles grunted. "I know so."

She smiled with feigned delight. "What a kind thing to say! It's wonderful to know that someone besides myself thinks that my son is an exceptionally handsome baby."

"It was an observation, not a compliment," he snarled.

"But how else am I to take such an observation? Mr. Tyler is acknowledged far and wide as being an extremely attractive man . . . as is Tommy's father, Byron Garrett."

Byron Garrett was a devilishly handsome British opera singer with whom she'd sung on several occasions, the last being in Boston during which time Thomas was conceived. When Adele had demanded to know the identity of the baby's father, Byron's name was fresh in her mind, and she'd uttered it for no other reason than that it was too painful to speak of Seth. Besides, she knew that Byron had returned to

England the day after they closed in Boston, thus making it impossible for Adele to learn the truth.

"B-Byron Garrett fathered your b-brat?" Miles stammered, obviously flabbergasted by the news.

"Your mother didn't tell you?" Penelope frowned and shook her head. "She's known since before Tommy's birth."

His astonishment hardened into sullen resentment. "Mother doesn't tell me anything, especially about you. All I know is that she helped you birth your baby and that she's holding him until you've finished paying her for her trouble."

"Paying her for her trouble?" Penelope emitted a derisive snort. "And exactly how much does she figure I owe her?"

His expression went blank, as it always did when he was asked to contemplate his mother's villainy. "Uh . . . plenty, I guess, considering what a saint she's been to you."

"Well, I've already paid her plenty," Penelope snapped. "By my calculations, your saintly mother has robbed me of close to forty thousand dollars in the past year and a half."

Miles's cheeks flushed a hectic red beneath the day-old stubble of his beard. "How dare you imply that Mother is a cheat! Why, if she hadn't nursed you through your fever, you'd have died three days after your precious brat was born. That's worth forty thousand dollars easy, I'd say."

It was on the tip of Penelope's tongue to inform him that she probably wouldn't have caught the fever in the first place if Adele had hired a real doctor instead of a drunken slattern with gin-induced delusions of being a midwife. But before she could voice her dissonant thoughts, Miles continued:

"Don't forget that you owe room and board for the five months prior to your lying-in, plus the additional four months it took for you to recover from the fever. Then there's the cost of keeping your brat, your personal living expenses, and the charges for my escort and the hiring of horses for these trips out to the Skolfields. Add it all up, and it totals a pretty penny."

"Well, at least according to your mother's skewed mathematics," she muttered bitterly.

Miles's face went blank again.

Sighing her ever-present frustration, Penelope chalked the debate up as a lost cause. Like all her efforts to make Miles see his mother's extortion for the conscienceless crime it was, this was proving to be a waste of time ... precious time that could be better spent celebrating her son's birthday.

Checking that her unfashionably wide but functionally protective straw hat was securely tied beneath her chin, she said, "Since I'm being charged for this trip, and plenty I suspect, I want to get on my way."

"Suit yourself." Miles waved toward the horse in a motion exaggerated enough to have been seen from the back row of any theater in America. Spooked by his broadly flourishing arm, the beast nickered and danced away.

Ignorantly muttering a threat to castrate the already gelded horse, Miles seized the nervous animal's bridle and roughly forced it to remain still while Penelope mounted. Then he swung up behind her. Once he'd snuggled his groin indecently close to her backside, he pulled a rumpled length of black cloth from his coat pocket and blindfolded her. That formality completed, he kicked the horse to a canter, and they were off.

This was the part of the journey Penelope dreaded most. Not because she was blindfolded, though not being able to see made her nauseatingly sensitive to the horse's motion and threw her equilibrium so off balance that she usually rode clinging to the edge of the pommel. No. Far worse than those discomforts was the humiliating molestation she often suffered as she sat in unseeing helplessness between Miles's thighs.

With revolting familiarity he would let his free right hand roam intimately over her body, emitting obscene slobbering noises as he ground his arousal rhythmically against her backside.

Today, however, Miles was not in an amorous mood, and after they had ridden a couple of miles in brooding silence, Penelope began to relax. As she always did on these blessed occasions when he left her in peace, she tried to discern their direction by attuning her senses to her surroundings.

By the motion of the horse, the way it slowed and weaved at intervals as if skirting jutting rocks or bushes, they seemed to be climbing the slopes toward the forest. The impression deepened when she smelled the resiny freshness of coniferous trees on the breeze, and felt a subtle cooling of the air against her cheeks, both sure signs that they were moving into the mountain-shadowed upper foothills.

They continued on for a long while, splashing through

streams and trotting past rustling groves of trees. After what Penelope estimated to be about two hours, they came to a stop.

"We're here," Miles announced, fumbling with the knotted cloth at the back of her head. After pulling out what felt like half of her hair, the blindfold fell away.

Penelope's spine stiffened with outrage as she viewed the ramshackle structure before her. How dare Adele expect Tommy to live in such primitive conditions! Why, the dwelling was little better than a hovel ... hardly an appropriate place for a young child, much less one with her son's fragile health.

Set in a copse of autumn-blazed aspen trees, the haphazardly built log cabin was a wretched affair with mudchinked walls and a roof of earth and thatch, which undoubtedly leaked during even the gentlest of rains. Just imagining wintering in such a place was enough to give Penelope a phantom chill. In truth, she wouldn't have been a bit surprised to learn that the former occupants had frozen to death within its flimsy walls during the first hard freeze. Not a comforting thought in light of the fact that this was her son's new home.

But not for long, she vowed, her resolve strengthened a hundredfold by the sight of the tumbledown shack. No matter what it took, she'd have her darling back in San Francisco and safely ensconced in the luxurious nursery at her brother's house before the first snowflake fell.

As Miles helped her from the horse, Minerva Skolfield stepped out of the open front door and waved her welcome. After returning the woman's greeting, Penelope snatched a cloth-wrapped bundle from the saddlebag and started toward the cabin.

Before she had advanced more than a couple of feet, Miles grabbed her arm and shoved his watch close to her face. "You've got two hours. Not a second more."

Giving a curt nod, she jerked her arm from his grasp and hurried to where Minerva waited.

Garbed in a once fine but now much mended tartan poplin day dress with her gray-streaked black hair gathered at the nape of her neck in a smooth chignon, Minerva was the very picture of genteel shabbiness. At Penelope's approach she smiled and graciously extended her hand.

Taking the proffered hand in hers, Penelope stared anxiously into the older woman's careworn face. "How's Tommy? Adele said he's ill." She released Minerva's hand to reach into the bundle and withdraw the expectorant she'd purchased at the pharmacy. "I brought him some medicine."

Minerva took the bottle and peered at the extravagant claims listed on the label. Looking skeptical, she tugged out the cork stopper, saying, "We'll try this next time Tomkins gets the croup. He's completely recovered now." She paused to sniff the contents of the bottle. With her face perfectly expressing her distaste, she jammed the cork back into place and banished the medicine into her pocket.

Looping her arm through Penelope's, she escorted her into the cabin, saying, "The poor mite did have a bad time of it for a few days, but you know what a fighter he is." She winked at Penelope. "Gets his grit from his mama, I fancy. Anyway, as you can see for yourself, he's right as rain now." She nodded toward a cot against the opposite wall.

Penelope almost flew across the room in her eagerness to get to her son. Clad only in a white linen diaper and a pair of crocheted socks, he lay safely cradled in a cozy hollow formed by a pile of buffalo pelts and quilts. Feeling as if her heart would burst with joy at the sight of him, she dropped to her knees next to the makeshift crib and hungrily drank in every detail of his beloved face and body.

He was such a handsome boy, her Tommy. With his silky golden curls and angelic smile, he was the perfect image of a Raphael cherub. At least in her eyes. To her, he was the most beautiful child in the world.

Yet, she was painfully aware that hers was a view not likely to be shared by many. Hard experience had stripped away the last vestiges of her naïveté, and she was now all too aware of the cruelty that lay within the hearts of her fellow man.

Instead of admiring the beauty of Tommy's face, as she did, she knew that most people would see only his stunted growth and pathetically twisted limbs. Instead of having the wisdom to love him for his special qualities—his gentle soul and sweet disposition—they would ignorantly hate him for his physical and mental limitations. Though the rest of the world might view him as an abomination to be locked away in shame, to her he was a priceless treasure to be shown off with pride. And once they were back in San Francisco, she intended to do just that.

Imagining her son dressed like a prince and holding court from an elaborate cane baby carriage, she dropped a kiss on his soft cheek, whispering, "Everything will be perfect, darling. Just you wait and see."

As if sensitive to his mother's pensive mood, he cooed and smiled in a way that never failed to lift her spirits.

"I was just getting ready to change his diaper when I heard you ride up," Minerva said, setting a basketful of infant supplies on the cot. Leaning over and lightly tickling the baby's bare midsection, she crooned, "We're as wet as a flag in a rainstorm aren't we, Tomkins?"

He giggled, and for a fleeting instant Penelope saw the ghost of Seth's heartbreaking smile in that of their son.

Bobbing her head back and forth in a manner that made the baby's giggles escalate into squeals of laughter, the older woman continued, "Well, we'll have you dry in a twinkling, and then you can have a nice visit with your mama. I have a hunch that she's got a surprise for you in that bundle of hers."

Minerva's genuine tenderness toward Tommy warmed Penelope to the depths of her soul, and not for the first time she selfishly thanked God for allowing the Skolfields to fall victim to Adele's blackmail. For without Sam and Minerva's loving care, it was doubtful that the baby would have survived his first precarious months of life. Then, as now, they were a gift from heaven.

Ashamed but unrepentant of her self-serving prayers, she reached up and gave the older woman's arm a fond squeeze. "You work so hard all the time, Minerva. Why don't you rest for a while? I'll take care of Tommy."

"I don't know about resting, but I do need to finish fixing supper," she replied, understanding shining in her brown eyes.

Penelope smiled her gratitude. As usual, the woman was sensitive to her need for time alone with her son.

Lingering long enough to pull back the baby's diaper and point to the patchy red skin on his groin, she said, "I've been treating Tomkins' rash with zinc powder. You'll find a box of it in the basket along with clean napkins. The rest of his clothes are in the chest under the cot." After giving the baby's belly one last tickle, she went to the table at the far end of the cabin and began chopping vegetables.

Left alone, Penelope undertook the painstaking task of

changing Tommy's diaper. No larger than an infant of seven or eight months, her frail son's legs were unyieldingly rigid and locked in a closed, almost scissorlike configuration that made the changing process into what most people would view as a trying ordeal. But not for Penelope. She cherished the few precious moments she spent caring for him. So much so, that she promised herself that once they were safely back home, she would forego the services of a nanny and tend to his needs herself.

Singing snatches of a lullaby remembered from her own childhood, she cleaned and diapered him, then turned her attention to finding something special for him to wear.

From the chest beneath the cot she pulled out a woolen binder, followed in quick succession by a hand-knitted undervest and two flannel petticoats. After a moment's deliberation, she drew out an elaborately tucked and embroidered white muslin gown she'd purchased in Chicago. A soft linen day cap, a pale blue knitted outdoor bonnet lavishly trimmed with darker blue satin ribbon, and several warm shawls completed her selections.

As with changing his napkins, dressing Tommy was a task that required the patience of Job. Like his legs, his upper extremities were stiff and pulled into unnatural positions. His wrists were twisted back at awkward, inflexible angles, terminating in hands that were forever clenched into fists. His arms, reed-thin and as delicate as those of a Dresden doll, were fixed at the elbow in a crooked position reminiscent of a gentleman offering a lady his escort.

Though Penelope knew that most people would find his deformed limbs repulsive, she accepted them with as much love as she would if they were strong and straight. In truth, she loved him more because of his infirmities, for he needed her as no fit child ever could.

When she'd finished tying, buttoning, and hooking him into his garments, she stuffed the bundle of birthday gifts beneath her arm and then swung him into her embrace. With him tucked securely in her arms, she marched around the tiny one-room cabin singing a rousing chorus of "For He's a Jolly Good Fellow!"

After several turns, she waltzed him to the table where Minerva sat and, leaning sideways, let the bundle drop from beneath her arm to the tabletop. Ducking her head forward to cover her son's smiling face with kisses, she murmured, "Would you like to see your presents now, darling?"

He gurgled in sunny response.

Settling in the rickety chair opposite Minerva, with Tommy propped comfortably against her body, she began to unwrap his gifts. As she launched into another round of "For He's a Jolly Good Fellow!" Minerva put down her knife and joined in. With her monotone alto sounding much the worse in contrast to Penelope's well-trained soprano, she wiped her hands on a ragged bit of toweling and came around the table to share in the fun.

The first thing to fall under Penelope's hand was the plush rabbit. Holding the toy of the scruff of its neck, she pulled it from the burlap bundle just enough so that its head and floppy ears were visible. Wagging its head back and forth, she said in what she hoped was a bunnylike voice, "Happy birthday, Tommy!" Then she made it leap the rest of the way from its wrappings and pretend-hop across the table toward the fascinated baby.

"Will you look at the pretty bunny, Tomkins!" Minerva crowed as Penelope gently butted the toy's cross-stitched nose against her son's button one in a bunny kiss. "Why, it looks just like the furry little darlings we see on our walks." Meeting the younger woman's gaze, she explained, "Our Tomkins seems to have a special fondness for rabbits. Every time we see one in the woods, he giggles and follows it with his eyes until it's out of sight."

As if to validate the woman's words, Tommy laughed and batted at the toy with one tiny fist.

Tucking the velvety rabbit into his arms, Penelope promised, "Later I'll tell you a story about a wise bunny who outwitted a greedy fox set on having rabbit stew for supper. But first, I have something else for you. A special gift for my special boy."

"Two presents in one day!" cried Minerva in mock amazement. "Aren't we a spoiled boy!"

If Penelope had had her way, he'd have had a hundred gifts instead of just two. But, of course, the rabbit and the rattle were the best she could afford with her limited funds.

Firmly pushing aside her monetary woes, she drew the rattle from the bundle and presented it with a clattering flourish. Both Tommy and Minerva gasped aloud.

Kneeling next to the chair to put herself at eye level with

the baby, Minerva crooned, "Isn't that just the fanciest rattle you've ever seen? I swear it's fine enough for a prince."

Tommy stared wide-eyed at the shiny toy, as if mesmerized.

Lifting the silver jester to her lips, Penelope lightly blew into his whistle-hat, tooting out a series of shrill notes.

The baby's mouth opened and closed several times in rapid succession before he let out a hiccuping squeak.

"And see here, Tomkins!" Minerva ran her index finger across the gold bells, which twinkled softly beneath her touch. "A rattle, a whistle, and *bells*. Why, you can be a one-man band!"

Smiling as the older woman chattered on about a one-man band she'd once seen in Boston, Penelope drew a length of royal blue ribbon from the now almost flat bundle and began to tie the toy to Tommy's wrist. When the handle was secured, she gently wiggled his arm to demonstrate the sound-producing motion. After several such demonstrations, he gave a tentative jerk on his own. Laughing with pleasure at the discordant results, he repeated the action. And then again. Within the space of a minute, he was shaking the rattle in earnest.

"There goes the peace and quiet," Minerva said, chuckling.

Penelope shot the woman an apologetic look. "How terribly thoughtless of me. I didn't stop to consider the noise when I got the idea to tie the rattle to his arm." Glancing wistfully down at her son's rapturous face, she admitted, "All I wanted was for Tommy to be able to enjoy his new toy."

"Which he's doing," Minerva observed as she rose to her feet. Giving the younger woman's shoulder a warm squeeze, she reassured her, "Now, don't you go bothering yourself any about the racket. It does my heart good to hear it. You know how it worries me the way our Tomkins is so quiet all the time."

It worried Penelope, too. Chronically ill since birth, her son had spent most of his short life lying listlessly on his blanket, his frail body often wracked by terrifying seizures. While most two-year-olds ran rather than walked and echoed every word they heard like precocious parrots, Tommy never so much as lifted his head or uttered a sound other than the most rudimentary expressions of pleasure or distress.

Sighing at her troubling thoughts, Penelope lifted a corner of her son's blue woolen shawl, and wiped a trail of drool from his chin. Then she glanced back up at Minerva, who was dropping the chopped vegetables into a pot cooking over the hearth fire.

"Where's Sam?" she asked.

"Last time I looked out the window, I saw him and Miles headed up into the woods. Sam had his gun, so I'd guess they've gone hunting."

"Sam's become quite a hunter in the last year and a half," Penelope commented, remembering Minerva's hilarious accounts of the man's first few rather comical attempts at procuring game.

"Yes, he has," Minerva agreed, her voice touched with pride. "In fact, he killed a deer yesterday morning, so we've got fresh venison for supper." She stabbed at the contents of the pot with the blunt end of a wooden spoon. "Unfortunately, fresh is the best I can say for this meat. It's as tough as cheap shoe leather. Between you and me, I suspect that the animal was ready to keel over of old age when it was shot." Grimacing, she placed a lid on the pot and turned from the fire. "Oh, well. I guess the Lord wanted us to be thankful for our teeth this Sabbath."

"Speaking of food . . ." Minerva's discourse reminded Penelope of her final surprise for Tommy. "I brought the baby some baked custard as a special birthday treat. It's soft, so he shouldn't have trouble swallowing it." She crossed her fingers. Like everything else in his difficult life, eating was a trial for her son, and he more often choked on his food than swallowed it.

The older woman nodded her approval at the muslin-wrapped parcel Penelope had pulled from the now flat bundle. "You'll be happy to hear that he's been doing much better with his eating of late. Why, he only choked on his pap twice this morning."

"You've done a wonderful job with him," Penelope commended sincerely. "Perhaps when this is all over, I can find some way to repay you for your kindness."

Minerva shook her head as she crossed the room and sat in the chair at Penelope's left. "Like you, I'm just doing what I must to protect my own son from Adele. Besides, Tommy is a joy."

"He is sweet, isn't he?" Penelope acknowledged, smiling

down at her baby with maternal pride. "And what about your son? Have you heard anything from him?"

"One of his letters caught up with us a couple of weeks ago. He's doing well in the town council and says that his fellow council members are prompting him to run for mayor." She rubbed her temples wearily. "He also wants to know when Sam and I are going to stop traipsing around the West and come home to Boston to see our new granddaughter."

"A granddaughter," Penelope echoed softly. "How lovely. Congratulations."

Minerva heaved a frustrated sigh. "I hate not having been there when she was born. She's my first grandchild, you know. What I wouldn't give to hold her."

"You might get your chance soon," Penelope said, crossing her fingers that her plan to regain Tommy would succeed.

The other woman snorted. "If you believe that, then you've got a lot to learn about Adele du Charme. The woman is a vampire. She doesn't release anyone—man, woman, or child—until she's sucked every last bit of usefulness out of them."

"Well, in that case, I guess we're about sucked dry," Penelope declared. "According to Miles, Adele plans to quit the West within the next few months and settle in Boston. Apparently she's scheming to catch a rich husband ... you know, one of those Beacon Hill types whose wives become instant social aristocracy the second they say 'I do.' With those ambitions, I doubt she'll want to be associated with a third-rate theatrical company."

"Perhaps she'll no longer need the company, but I can't see her dismissing me and Sam. Not while our son is a member of the town council and a possible mayoral candidate." Minerva shook her head, her expression troubled. "If she starts demanding favors from the council, well, then I'll have no choice but to tell Alex the truth."

The truth was that the Skolfields' son, Alexander, was not only a bastard, but one-eighth black as well. And Adele had the papers to prove it. By way of explanation for her and Sam's participation in Tommy's kidnapping, Minerva had told Penelope the whole story.

Like her mother before her, Minerva, the quadroon offspring of a wealthy Creole planter and his mulatto mistress, had been groomed from birth to be *placée* with the right rich man. With that goal in mind, she'd been presented at the Quadroon Balls held at the infamous Salle d'Orléans in New Orleans.

It was there that she met handsome Samuel Skolfield. By his father's decree, he had recently wed the ill-tempered daughter of one of New Orleans's finest families. As a way of reparation for forcing his son into an unhappy marriage, the elder Mr. Skolfield had offered to set him up with the mistress of his choice.

And Sam had selected Minerva. As protector and placée, they had expected to be fond of each other, but neither anticipated falling in love. But fall in love they did, passionately so, and the result of that love was their son, Alexander.

All too aware of the stigma of being colored, and unable to bear the idea of his blue-eyed son being denied opportunity and social position because of the hue of his great-grandmother's skin, Sam persuaded Minerva to flee north with him. Abandoning everything, including Sam's shrewish wife and the sizable yearly stipend he received from his father, they migrated to Boston, where they passed themselves off as man and wife.

As the years went by, they prospered, with Sam fighting his way up from the lowly position of clerk to that of full partner at the respected accounting firm of Grossman and Shepard. The only shadow over their otherwise bright life was Sam's estranged wife's refusal to grant him a divorce.

As disturbing as living in adultery was to Sam and Minerva, their real problems didn't start until fifteen years after leaving New Orleans. That trouble came in the form of a maid named Dorcas Grace Butler.

At first she was everything they could wish in an employee: reliable, even-tempered, and hardworking. But all that changed with the flick of a feather duster. While cleaning the study one day, or so she claimed, she came across and stole the correspondence between Sam and his wife's lawyer. Those papers gave Dorcas Butler, now Adele du Charme, the leverage she needed to blackmail the Skolfields. For not only did they damn Sam and Minerva as adulterers, they branded Alexander a bastard of color.

At first the woman's demands for silence were small, a hundred dollars here, fifty dollars there. But over the years her demands grew, taking the Skolfields to the brink of bankruptcy.

Yet, no matter how devastating the price, Sam and Minerva always paid. They were willing to do anything to keep Adele from destroying their son's future . . . even be party to kidnapping.

After hearing the story, Penelope had tried to hate the Skolfields, for weren't they using her son to insure their own son's future? Yet, try as she might, she couldn't find it in her heart to condemn them. After all, who was she to fault parents for loving and wanting to protect their child? If their situations were reversed, wouldn't she do the same for Tommy?

Guilt stabbed at Penelope's conscience as she looked down at her baby, who was still preoccupied with his new rattle. What would happen to the Skolfields when One-eyed Caleb stole Tommy from their care? Would Adele be infuriated enough to ruin Alexander's life as she had threatened?

It was a possibility that Penelope found unsettling. After all, Sam and Minerva had not only looked after Tommy, they had taken him into their hearts and nursed him through his frequent illnesses as tenderly as if he'd been their own. Didn't she owe them some consideration for that?

Torn apart by conflicting emotions, yet knowing that she must remain resolved for Tommy's sake, she let her gaze stray to where Minerva sat lost in her own thoughts. She'd become fond of the Skolfields. They were good people who, like herself, were simply trying to make the best of a terrible situation.

They were also creditors to whom she owed a debt of gratitude. But tragically, the price of repayment was one she couldn't afford. Not when the price might cost her son his life.

Surrender, My Heart

Ah, yes, there is no defying,
A love beyond denying—
For love must have its way!

—*Don Giovanni*

Chapter 16

Penelope was full. Corset-busting, I-couldn't-swallow-another-crumb-if-my-life-depended-on-it full. The kind of full she hadn't been since she was six and had eaten an entire pan of gingerbread she'd found cooling on the kitchen windowsill.

Groaning, she erased the heartburning incident from her mind. Recalling it now only deepened her overstuffed misery.

Unfortunately clearing her mind left it free to dwell on other matters, namely her corset. She gave the binding undergarment a surreptitious tug through her bodice. The blasted stays were poking into her distended belly with a vengeance that made her feel like a harpooned whale.

Certain she'd belch if she didn't relieve the pressure at once, she cautiously eased back until she leaned half reclining against a cottonwood tree. Mercifully her new position did much to ease the potentially disastrous constriction. Too relieved to care that she was crushing her bustle, she lay in glutted languor marveling anew that she had been allowed to come on this picnic.

Earlier that day, Seth had complained to Adele that Penelope was looking peaked and had demanded that she be allowed some leisure, namely a picnic. After a rather heated discussion during which Seth slyly pointed out that the company would be ruined and thus useless in repaying Miles's debt if Penelope should fall ill, the woman had grudgingly agreed.

Sighing her contentment, Penelope drowsily admired her surroundings. The site Seth had selected for their hard-won picnic was unrivaled in beauty by any place she'd ever dined. It was like a little piece of heaven on earth.

As far as the eye could see, the arms of the Platte River sparkled between islands and banks edged with copses of

autumn-flamed foliage. The small grove of cottonwoods
where they dined was carpeted with leaves in vivid shades
of orange, gold, and scarlet, hues that were echoed in the
canopy of branches overhead. Enhancing nature's ambiance
were the gurgling serenade of the river and the smoky aroma
of fall.

Seth, who sat beside her on the faded crazy quilt, his long
legs crossed Indian style before him, seemed less enamored
with his surroundings than with the food. Right now he was
practically inhaling the last of the Saratoga potatoes. When
he noticed her watching him, he picked up a cranberry tart
and waved it temptingly beneath her nose. "Last one. Want
it?"

Just the sight of the buttery pastry oozing with syrupy red
fruit almost made her gag. Motioning it away with the same
aversion she'd have shown a plate of the infamous lamb
fries, she groaned, "I can't eat another bite. I'm stuffed."
She was about to add that she doubted if she'd be able to eat
for the next year when an obstreperous belch slipped out.

Mortified, she slapped her hand over her mouth, her face
burning with shame. She'd wanted so badly to impress Seth,
to advance in her stratagem to recapture his heart, and here
she was making noises reminiscent of a barnyard scuffle.

Seth merely chuckled and plopped the rejected tart down
on his own plate. Grinning good-naturedly, he teased, "I always say that there's nothing more enticing than a woman
with a healthy appreciation for food. Especially one who
knows how to express it with such eloquence."

Despite her humiliation, Penelope smiled. Leave it to Seth
to make light of what most men would view as an unpardon-
able act of vulgarity. *But then,* she reminded herself as she
watched him make short work of the remaining tart, *he isn't
like most men.*

Unlike the other men she knew, Seth had never felt it necessary to adhere to the rigid dictates of society. Instead he
viewed them only as loose guidelines to be bent, broken, or
eliminated to suit his own purposes. As her sister-in-law had
pointed out more than once, Seth Tyler was a charming ren-
egade, always refreshingly candid and delightfully witty.

Oddly enough, his flaunting of convention hadn't made
him an outcast, as one would expect. It had endeared him to
hostesses, and gained him the respect of powerful men who

openly admired his daring. In truth, he was more received than anyone else she knew.

Right now, society's darling was licking his fingers with gusto. Smiling at his expression of gastronomic ecstasy, she teased, "It's a wonder you're not as big as a barn the way you eat."

He laughed at that. "Never fear, Princess. I'm hardly in danger of becoming one of those men who's bigger around than he is tall. In truth, if I didn't eat as much as I did, I'd be as skinny as an over-whittled broomstick."

She eyed his muscular physique dubiously. "You? Skinny?"

"As a string bean," he confirmed blithely. "You should have seen me when I was a youth. I was all gangly arms and legs with a bony backside and ribs to match."

Penelope stared at Seth, trying to visualize him as a spindly boy. Odd, but she'd never stopped to wonder what kind of child, or even youth, he'd been. In truth, she'd never considered the fact that he'd ever been anything other than what he was now: a strong, fiercely independent man who had the world by its tail. And since he'd never brought up the subject of his childhood, or willingly volunteered information about his life prior to his partnership with her brother, it had never seemed important.

But suddenly it seemed very important indeed. His waving that tidbit of information in front of her was like waving a meaty bone in front of a dog's nose: it made her crave more.

She watched in silence as he finished the tart. The question was, how should she broach the subject of his past? Even when their relationship had been at its closest, he'd been an intensely private person.

Granted, he'd told her the little, superficial things about himself. Like that his favorite color was red, his favorite food was pineapple ice-cream pudding, and that he particularly enjoyed naughty stories. Yet what did she really know about him?

She searched her mind for an answer. She knew that he was born in New York and had spent his childhood in Massachusetts; a childhood that, if his unpolished manners and poor grammar when she'd first met him were any indicator, appeared to have been less than privileged. But of his family she knew nothing.

The single time she'd asked him about them, he'd turned as taciturn as a Southerner on the topic of the War Between the States, so she'd assumed they were dead and had never asked again.

But what of the other details? The seemingly unimportant ones that would give her a picture of who he'd been? Like who was his boyhood best friend, what games had he liked best, and had he had a pet? Those were things she'd either never bothered to ask, or that he'd avoided telling her by guiding every conversation to the subject nearest and dearest to her heart . . . herself.

She grimaced at the remembrance of her own selfishness. How had he stood her? Looking back, it was a wonder that she'd been able to tolerate herself.

She eyed him speculatively as he set aside the plate and lay back upon the quilt with a satiated grunt. The early afternoon sun speckled through the barren gaps left by the fallen leaves, burnishing his outspread hair until it gleamed like fire-lit gold. His eyes were closed, and he looked supremely contented as he bathed his face in a ray of sunshine.

Suddenly determined to learn more about the enigmatic man before her, she asked, "Tell me about your childhood."

He lay very still, and for an instant she wondered if he slept. But then he opened his eyes and looked at her. "Why?"

She shrugged as casually as she could manage. "It's just that we agreed to be friends, and, well, friends share information about themselves."

"Do they?" His gaze bore into hers. "I haven't noticed you being any too eager to share information with me lately."

She plucked at the ruche trimming on her skirt, unnerved by the intensity of his stare. "That's because you already know everything about me. As you might recall, I was never shy about talking about myself during our courtship. In fact, I distinctly remember myself as being a conceited little chatterbox. I don't know how you stood me." Her voice rang with self-condemnation.

A tiny smile danced on his lips. "I enjoyed your chattering. I thought it charming. You were so full of enthusiasm, so excited about your career on the stage, and rightfully so, I might add."

She shook her head ruefully. "That gave me no right to be

so selfish. I should have paid more attention to you and your desires. I should have been thoughtful enough to ask you what was happening in your life and what it had been like before we met. We were engaged, for pity's sake. I should have at least known that my husband-to-be was a skinny youth."

At that last remark his gaze slid from hers. She followed it until it came to rest on an object that she recognized as his cigar case. Strange, she'd been so intent on making her clumsy apology, that she hadn't even seen him pull it from his pocket.

Caressing the gleaming silver case in a way that made Penelope envy it, he murmured, "Perhaps you never found out because I didn't want you to know. Perhaps . . ." His voice faltered. When, after taking a deep breath, he continued, it carried a note of uncertainty she'd never before heard. "Perhaps I was afraid that you wouldn't marry me if you knew about me."

"Your being skinny wouldn't have made any difference," she scolded him lightly. "Nor would anything else you could have told me. I loved you for the man you are, not for who you once were. To me, you were the most perfect man in the world. Perhaps I should have told you so more often."

He lifted the cigar case to examine it closer. "You could have complimented me a hundred times a day; it wouldn't have made any difference. I still wouldn't have felt worthy of you. You were so intelligent, beautiful, talented, and despite your protests to the contrary, loving, that I was ashamed to tell you about myself." By the strain in his voice, it was apparent that that confession had cost him a great deal.

Aching to touch him, to tell him that she would love him no matter how sordid his past, yet sensing that he'd see her gesture as unwelcome pity, she suggested, "Then, why don't you tell me now? Since we're no longer engaged, you have nothing to lose."

"Nothing except your respect," he rejoined quietly.

His admission sent an odd thrill racing down her spine. That he cared what she thought of him was unexpected, yet welcome, news. Giving him her warmest smile, she hastened to reassure him, "There's no one in this world I respect more than you, and there's nothing you can tell me that will change my mind."

He smiled back, gently and with a sweetness that sent her pulse racing. "In that case, I'll tell you anything you want to know. But"—he rolled over and sat up—"not now. I promised Adele I'd help you rehearse the new play for tonight, and unless you want our circus tickets to go to waste, we'd best get started."

"Circus tickets!" Penelope threw herself at him to give him a delighted hug. "Why, you darling—darling!— wonderful man! I saw the cavalcade come through town this morning, and I wanted to see the show so badly, I thought I'd die. I never imagined . . ." She broke off to give him another squeeze.

Seth returned her hug, chuckling. "You made the circus sound so exciting the other day, that I decided I should see it for myself. And who better to show me the wonders than you?"

She drew back to stare at him in surprise. "This will be your first circus? Your parents never took you?"

His smile faded. "Yes and no, respectively. And I won't be going this time, either, if we don't rehearse your lines." With that curt reminder, he pulled the script from the picnic hamper and handed it to her. "Here. Show me where you want to start."

She thumbed through the pages until she came to the scene where her character, Talutah, a lovelorn Indian maiden, has wandered to the edge of the camp, mooning over Roscoe, her frontiersman lover. It was, in effect, the balcony scene from Romeo and Juliet minus the balcony. It was the scene she hated most, for it required her to kiss Miles several times.

She stole a glance at Seth from beneath her lowered lashes. With Seth acting out the role of Roscoe, the scene might easily prove to be her favorite. All the kissing might also provide her with the chance she needed to rekindle the sparks she'd seen smoldering in his eyes when he thought she wasn't looking.

Biting her lower lip to suppress her smile, she handed him the script. "Except for page thirty-two, I pretty much know the play by heart. I still get confused on a couple of the lines."

"Fine, then we'll go over the lines that are troubling you." He gave the dialogue a cursory glance. "From the top?"

She nodded. "That will be fine."

"You start. You say, 'Don't swear your love . . .' "

" ' . . . By the silvery moon, lest it prove to be as inconsistent as her shape,' " Penelope finished.

" 'Then, what should I swear by?' " he intoned.

" 'Don't swear, show me your love. Demonstrate with your lips.' " Penelope's heart pounded like a tom-tom as she breathlessly awaited Seth's response. This was where he was supposed to sweep her into his embrace and kiss her.

When he finally looked up, the rhythm in her chest quickened into triple time. A sensual half smile curved his lips, and his eyes were ablaze with topaz fire.

Looking at her in a way that made her hotter than if she were staked out in the desert in 110-degree weather, he murmured, "It says I'm supposed to kiss you now."

She ducked her head in an attempt to hide her burning cheeks. "Miles was complaining about my stage kiss this morning, so I guess we had better practice it."

He laughed in a low, throaty way that sent rivulets of liquid fire shooting through her belly. "Well, I did promise the company that I'd see to it that your performance was rehearsed to perfection if they excused you for the afternoon. And seeing as I'm a man of my word . . ." In one fluid motion he tossed down the script and pulled her onto his lap. Holding her in a half-reclining position with her back cradled against his left arm, he covered her mouth with his.

His kiss was gentle, almost impersonal, with his cool lips barely caressing hers. Yet, for Penelope, just being in Seth's arms again and feeling the warmth of his breath washing over her cheeks was enough to send a shiver of excitement up her spine.

How many nights had she lain awake, her body taut and aching with unfilled desire, wishing for a moment such as this? How many times had she hungered for his taste, ravenous to feel his tongue burning against hers as she feasted upon his passion?

Suddenly frustrated with their chaste kiss and impatient to deepen it into one more satisfying, she coiled her arms around his neck and parted her lips.

"Penelope!" he groaned, dragging his mouth from hers.

She tightened her grip on his neck and pulled his head back down until his face was just inches from hers. "You promised to help me perfect my kissing skills. Remember?"

"They're perfect. Trust me," he muttered, looking everywhere but in her eyes.

She shook her head. "Not according to Miles. He said I need to . . . *hmm,* what did he say?" She creased her brow as if baffled, though she clearly remembered and looked forward to following the actor's directions with Seth. After slowly counting to five, she released a soft, breathy laugh. "Oh, yes. He said I'm supposed to press my body against Roscoe's and cling to his shoulders."

"I don't think . . ." Seth began, but his words were cut off by his own moan as she shifted to straddle his lap.

With her skirts immodestly rucked up to her thighs and her knees pressing into either side of his hips, Penelope molded her torso to his, crushing her breasts against his chest until they swelled in tempting mounds above her square neckline. "How is this?" she asked, nodding at her enticing display. "Do you suppose I'm close enough?"

Seth looked down and released a ragged sob. Even through the wadded layers of her skirt, she felt the already pronounced bulge in his trousers thicken and harden against her buttocks.

Feigning oblivion to his aroused state, she mused, "Perhaps the embrace would look better onstage if I were to position my body so." She squirmed a fraction to the right, deliberately grinding against his erection as she moved.

His body jerked as if jolted by an electrical shock.

She stared into his contorted face, her features schooled into an expression of bemused innocence. "Not right? Oh, dear." Biting her lip to keep from smiling at his groaning, inarticulate response, she ventured, "Would you prefer it if I cheated more to the left . . . like this?"

He let out a yelp as her pelvis undulated against his groin. "Dear God . . . Pen . . ." he whimpered, shutting his eyes and gasping as if suffocated by his passion. "You . . ."

"Need to close my eyes like you're doing," she finished, bringing her mouth so close to his that their lips brushed as she spoke. "What an inspired touch! But then, I knew you'd be a good teacher, Seth. Your lessons in love have always been most"—she boldly nipped his lower lip—"edifying."

Emitting a sound, half sob, half growl, Seth crushed her into his embrace and roughly claimed her mouth with his. She returned his kiss with reckless abandon, the savage fire of her desire burning hotter with every intimate brush and nip.

Never had his kisses been so urgent, never had she craved them more. Every fiber of her being was alive and tingling with pleasure, heat danced beneath her skin. And when his tongue parted her lips, an aching need exploded low in her belly.

Moaning in a way that resonated through her soul, Seth slowly reclined back upon the quilt, never once pausing in his sensual assault as he dragged her down on top of him.

His tongue was hot, wet, insistent, like steel sheathed in moist velvet, as it plundered the sensitive recesses of her mouth. Sighing her pleasure, she melted against him, drowning in a delicious tide of sensation. His kisses were everything she remembered and more. Much more. They kindled within her fierce womanly desires, which had been but restless, girlish stirrings during their courtship.

As if in reply to the beckoning of her newly awakened body, Seth clasped her buttocks and pinned her pelvis against his groin. Releasing a quivering groan, he arched up and slammed his arousal hard against her belly. Over and over again he repeated his inflamed motion, shuddering and jerking with every thrust.

With her own desire pooling like molten lava in her secret place, Penelope wantonly rubbed her woman's mound against his pummeling manhood. How she wanted him! She longed to see him lying naked before her, his sex erect and visibly throbbing with need. She ached to feel him moving inside her and to gift him with the special kind of rapture that only a woman in love can give a man. For love Seth she did, with every breath in her body, with every beat of her heart. And there was nothing in the world she wanted more at that moment than to show him how she felt.

Driven by passion, one more compelling than she'd ever dreamed possible, Penelope slipped her hand between their bodies and brazenly crushed her palm against his wool-encased erection.

His whole body stiffened. "Dear God, Princess! I . . . I . . ." Panting harshly, he pushed her off him and rolled away. As he struggled to his knees, clutching at his belly as if in terrible agony, he moaned, "I . . . can't." The utterance sounded as if it were torn from the bottom of his soul.

Penelope whimpered, shamed by, but not sorry for her immodest behavior. The only thing she regretted was Seth's gentlemanly ·withdrawal from their pleasurable little tête-à-tête.

Sighing her disappointment, she sat up. Perhaps Miles was right, maybe she was no more of a lady than Hell-cat Helga. Yet if being a lady meant denying her passion for the man she loved, then she wanted no part of that frigid sisterhood. She intended to show Seth her feelings every chance she got, and continue showing them until she won him back. The poor man didn't have a chance. She smiled and shot her quarry a covetous glance.

He still knelt a couple of feet away, his features cloaked by his hair and his breath coming out in great, sobbing gasps. Suddenly, as if rocked by intense pain, his body began to convulse and when he buried his face against his fists, she saw that they were clenched so tightly that the veins stood out.

"What's wrong, Seth?" she cried, alarmed that he was suffering some sort of dangerous seizure. She latched on to his arms, her anxiety escalating as she noted the quivering tension of his muscles. Had he contracted some awful disease during the time they were apart? Could that ailment be the reason for his almost panicked retreat just moments earlier?

As abruptly as his shaking began, it ceased. And beneath her clutching hands, she felt his muscles begin to relax. After a minute more, he dropped his fists to his knees.

Her hands trembling with tenderness, Penelope reached up and tucked his hair behind his ears. Gently cupping his chin in her palm, she tipped his face up. His eyes were screwed closed and his skin was as ashen as if he'd been gutpunched. All in all, he had the look of a man who was suffering terribly.

Aching with compassion, she stroked his cheek, imploring, "Please, Seth. Tell me what's wrong. I want to help if I can."

He remained silent a brief while longer, shaking his head now and then as if engaged in an inner debate. Then he drew in a deep breath and lifted the spiky shield of his eyelashes.

Once again his eyes were the cool, greenish-brown of a mossy forest pond, and as his gaze met hers, it was as dispassionate as if they'd spent the last few minutes discussing the local flora and fauna. Pulling his chin from her hand, he said with a dismissive shrug, "I'm all right."

"I'm not blind!" she exclaimed indignantly. "I can see that there's obviously something terribly wrong with you."

He laughed and picked up the abandoned script. "You've spent way too much time with that sister-in-law of yours. You're beginning to sound just like her."

"Well, one can't live in the same house as a doctor and not learn anything. You'd be surprised at the sorts of things I know."

"Then, perhaps you're familiar with a condition commonly known as blue balls?"

Penelope ducked her head to hide the heat of embarrassment rising in her cheeks. She knew about blue balls, all right. It was Miles's favorite malady, one which, according to his whining, afflicted him with astonishing regularity. Why hadn't she realized that that was Seth's problem as well? It wasn't as if she hadn't been aware of his intense arousal.

"I can see that you know exactly what I'm talking about," he observed, closing the slim volume in his hand. "Now, unless you're set on further aggravating my condition, I suggest we end rehearsal and go on to the circus. I spoke with the circus owner this morning, and he mentioned he has a sideshow with all sorts of exotic spectacles. If we leave now, we'll have time to see it before the main show begins."

As it turned out, the sideshow was every bit as fascinating as the circus owner claimed. There was a sword swallower, an armless woman who drew portraits with her feet, an incombustible man with an appetite for burning coals, as well as the usual assortment of midgets, freaks, and daredevil acts.

It wasn't these marvels, however, as wondrous as they were, that captivated Penelope. It was Seth. That glorious afternoon he was the irrepressible, uninhibited Seth of old; the Seth she knew best who laughed easily and frolicked with a joyous abandon that bordered on hedonism. Now as then, his gaiety was contagious, and she was quickly infected with his merriment.

Though she'd been to dozens of circuses over the years, Seth made this one feel as fresh and exciting as her first. From the moment they arrived at the tent-and-wagon-strewn circus grounds, he took a childlike delight in the colorful sights and sounds around him. He was almost frantic in his eagerness to see, do, and taste everything. He ate taffy, licorice, and popcorn, drank what looked like a gallon of lemonade, and bought trinkets until they were so burdened down that she begged him to stop.

Once in the red, white, and blue tent, settled in their front row, dress circle seats, his high spirits soared until they verged on silliness. Just watching him enjoy the show filled her with pleasure. In fact, she smiled so much that her face ached.

With unbridled enthusiasm he cheered the equestrians, traded jokes with the clowns, and daringly volunteered to have an apple shot from the top of his head, à la William Tell. By the time the performance was over, he'd charmed both audience and performers.

The highlight of the day, however, came after the show was over. Munching on a caramel and carrying a bag full of peanuts, Seth led her around to the back of the tent, where he introduced her to Kongo, the mighty African elephant, and his keeper, Josh. While she got acquainted with Kongo, crooning what a handsome fellow he was while feeding him Seth's peanuts, Seth mysteriously disappeared. When he returned a quarter of an hour later, he was accompanied by another man carrying photographic equipment. Before she quite knew what was happening, she found herself perched on top of Kongo with Seth, having her picture taken. It was one of the most magical moments of her life.

All too soon it came time to bid Kongo and the circus farewell. Yet even then the marvelous afternoon didn't end. As they drove back to the Shakespeare, Seth hilariously reenacted several of the acts, making their short trip almost as entertaining as the circus had been. And by the time they pulled up to the saloon's deserted back entrance, Penelope was helplessly doubled over with laughter.

She was still giggling when Seth came around and lifted her from the buggy. "I can't remember the last time I had such a wonderful day!" she enthused.

"I enjoyed it, too," he replied, plucking a peanut shell from her hair. "It was kind of you to show me the circus."

"Me show you?" Her smile broadened at that notion. "You showed me. You made me see everything in a whole new way."

"And you, Princess, made me see a whole new side of you," he murmured, cupping her chin in his palm to lift her face to his. Without another word, he covered her lips with his.

Stunned and delighted, she returned the unexpected kiss, once again thrilling at the feel of his mouth claiming hers. Like their day together, the kiss was over all too soon.

"W-what was that f-for?" she stammered as he pulled away.

Grinning, he reached under the buggy seat and produced her script. "That was the final rehearsal of page thirty-two."

Chapter 17

"**D**amn that bastard!" Adele hissed beneath her breath, her eyes narrowing into infuriated slits as she watched Seth Tyler kiss her star performer. She'd had a hunch the man was going to be trouble, and as usual her intuition proved correct.

Angered and more than a little disturbed by the couple's affectionate display, she began to tap her bare foot against the wooden floor. In the shadowed alley beneath the second-floor Shakespeare window where she stood, Seth and Lorelei lingered in a cozy tête-à-tête, laughing and clutching at each other's arms in a way that was far too intimate for her comfort.

When Seth swept Lorelei into his arms to kiss her again, this time with leisurely thoroughness, Adele's hands curled into fists so tight that she crushed the edge of the yellow damask curtain she held. Tyler was a quick worker, she'd give him that. He'd been in Denver for a week, and he already had the most sought-after, not to mention the most unattainable, woman in town falling into his arms.

Not that that surprised her. He was just the sort of man to turn the head of a weak-willed ninny like Lorelei; he was rich, handsome, and virile. He was also shrewd, powerful, and honorable. It was that last quality that made him so dangerous. Adele twisted her handful of damask, as if it were Tyler's noble neck. She had to nip their romance in the bud, that much was for certain, and in a way that would assure that it never bloomed. The only question was: how?

Her mind devised and discarded several plans in quick succession. She needed something different from her usual threats and fines. Something unexpected. Something so brutally shocking that just the thought of disobeying her again would make Lorelei swoon with fear. She needed . . .

Inspiration curved her lips as she shifted her gaze from

the laughing girl to the tall man holding her. She needed to make an example of Seth Tyler; a grisly and deadly example. She almost clapped her hands in childlike glee at her own ingenuity. Murdering the handsome saloon owner was the perfect solution, brilliant really. Not only would Tyler's demise remove his potentially dangerous presence; his savagely butchered corpse would demonstrate to Lorelei the lethal sincerity of her threats.

Adele's smile broadened as she imagined telling Lorelei detail by bloody detail of the man's agonizing death. She couldn't wait to hear the girl's hysterical cries and see her too beautiful face contort with pain and guilt when she learned that she, with her waywardness, had caused her lover's death. It would be a cold day in hell before the stupid chit crossed her again.

Feeling almost grateful to the actress for giving her a reason to kill Seth Tyler, she turned her mind to the practical matter of plotting his death. She needed someone to do the deed for her. Someone unscrupulous, yet discreet. Someone easily manipulated, but with enough mind to think on his feet.

And she knew exactly who that someone was going to be.

With a flick of her long saffron hair, she shot a cunning glance at Harley Frye, who lounged naked on the bed across the room, a lit cheroot dangling from his lips. God knows she hadn't been bedding the gambler for the pleasure of his lovemaking.

The swarthy man caught her looking at him and patted the rumpled sheets beside him, his grin wide beneath his droopy black mustache. Carelessly tossing aside the cheroot, he drawled in a voice that bespoke the South. "Come on back to bed now, honey. Me and General Beauregard here"—he reached down and wiggled his flaccid sex—"are gettin' lonesome lyin' here all by ourselves."

Adele dropped the curtain back into place and turned, taking care to display her figure to its best advantage. Letting a delicate shudder convulse her body, she brokenly choked, "I-I don't feel like it," all the while squeezing out several well-rehearsed crocodile tears.

As with all men, her feminine ploy worked on Harley. "What's wrong, sugar?" he asked, springing from the bed to hurry to her side. "Old Harley didn't do somethin' to upset you, did he?"

She made a whimpering sound and shook her head.

"Good," he murmured, his features stamped with relief as he swept her into his embrace. "It'd break my heart if I thought I'd done somethin' to make my sweet little gal cry." Tightening his arms around her in a breath-stealing hug, he kissed the top of her head. "Now then, honey. Why don't you stop that sobbin' and tell your Harley what's got you all weepy-eyed?"

"I-It's the new saloon owner, Seth Tyler. He ... he ..." She let her voice fade away as if too overwrought to continue.

"He what?" Harley demanded, his drawling voice hardening into sharp-edged steel. Grasping Adele's shoulders, he pulled her away and held her at arm's length, glowering down into her tearstained face. "That bastard hasn't made advances, has he?"

She released a quivering sob and looked away, as if too distressed to meet his gaze.

"Damn it, Adele. Look at me!"

She did as commanded, her face arranged into the expression of tragic desolation she'd perfected through hours of practice in front of the mirror. It worked like a charm.

"That's it, isn't it?" Harley hissed, murderous rage contorting his features. "He tried to force his attentions on you, didn't he?"

Adele buried her face into her hands as if the humiliation of her fictional molestation was too much to bear. Her voice quivering, she lied, "He didn't just try ... he s-succeeded. He attacked me and had his way with me l-last Tuesday night."

A savage growl ripped from Harley's throat, and his grip turned bruising. "I'll castrate the bastard," he snarled, inadvertently shaking her in his rage. "I'll castrate him and bring you his balls as a trophy."

Adele could barely suppress her smile. Now, there was a provocative idea, one with definite possibilities. She could just imagine the willful Lorelei's anguish at seeing the virile Mr. Tyler mutilated in such an ignominious way, not to mention her horror when she found his severed parts in her cosmetic box that very evening. The girl would be her slave forever.

Looking up at Harley with feigned surprise, she asked in an appropriately meek voice, "You would do that for me?"

"I *will* do it for you," he corrected, his dark eyes burning like hot coals. "You're my woman, and I take care of what's mine. Tyler'll pay, and pay dearly for what he's done."

"But however will you manage?" She wrung her hands in a distracted manner. "Tyler is a big, strong, *dangerous* man. He's not going to just lay down and spread his legs for you."

Harley's craggy features contorted into an ugly scowl. "You don't think I can lick him in a fight?"

Adele could have slapped herself for her stupidity. Harley Frye had more overblown masculine conceit than any man she'd ever met. To him, questioning his fighting skills was akin to belittling his sexual prowess. Set on soothing his ruffled pride, she wrapped her arms around his affront-stiffened torso and lay her head on his shoulder, reassuring him,

"Anyone can see just by looking at you that you're the better man. Why, you'd beat him in a second in a fair fight. But I've heard tell that Tyler fights dirty, that he'd as soon stab a man in the back as look at him. And, well . . ." She let her voice catch. "I-I just can't bear the thought of you being hurt. Whatever would I do without my Harley and his general?" The last sentence was uttered in a series of sobs. Burying her face against his neck, she pretended to weep in earnest.

The angry tension eased from Harley's body. "Aw, come on now, darlin'. Don't carry on like this," he crooned, stroking her back. "Nothin's gonna happen to Harley and the general."

She made an articulate noise and shook her head.

He paused in the act of patting her between her shoulder blades. "Do you really care about me that much?" There was a note of hopeful wonder in his voice.

Her face still against his neck, she nodded, smirking her satisfaction. The fool was falling neatly into her trap.

"Tell you what," he said, finger combing her hair. "So as you won't be worryin' that pretty head of yours, I'll get Bub Willard, Duane Sweeney, and Russ Knox to help me. Tyler kicked 'em out of the saloon for cheatin' last week, so I'm sure they'll be glad to repay the favor"—he chuckled—"with interest."

Arranging her features in a facsimile of a concerned lover, Adele lifted her head to look up at him. "I'm still worried. Tyler isn't the sort of man who's going to crawl away and hide after you maim him in such a humiliating manner. He's ruthless. If you don't kill him, he'll hunt you down and re-turn the deed."

Harley laughed at that, in the cold, humorless grate Adele always found more stimulating than his sweet talk. "Never fear, honey. I don't intend to be gentle or neat when I hand out my justice. And his balls aren't the only things he's gonna be missin' when I'm done. If he doesn't die of shock from the cuttin', he'll bleed to death afterward. We'll do it out of town, where no one'll find him until it's too late."

"When?" she asked, thrilled by his vicious tone.

He pondered a moment. "With your help, maybe next Fri-day."

"How can I help?" Adele reached between their bodies to fondle the general, who suddenly seemed a very tempting fellow.

Harley groaned and clamped his hand around her stroking one to increase the pressure. Rolling his hips to intensify the sensation, he explained between panting breaths, "While I was playin' faro yesterday, I heard some of the saloon gals beggin' Tyler for Friday off so they can go to the bonnet race Mrs. Vanderlyn and some of the other goody-good biddies are holdin' to raise money for the orphanage."

"What's a bonnet race?" Adele asked, impatiently pulling his hand from her now steadily pumping one and guiding it to the lust-slickened flesh between her legs. She quivered with pleasure as he began to tease the hardened bud of her desire.

"God, honey," Harley whimpered, plunging his fingers deep inside her. "You're so hot, so . . . wet." A shudder con-vulsed his body as she deliberately tightened around his fin-gers. "How about givin' General Beauregard a taste of your sugar?"

She writhed against his hand slowly, seductively, emitting throaty moans as she moved. Petting the top of the general's scarlet head with her thumb, she purred, "There will be no sugar until you tell me about your plans for Tyler."

"Aw, come on. Don't torture the poor general like this."

"The general will have a better time for the waiting," she promised, never once pausing from her inflammatory minis-trations.

Gasping harshly with need, Harley hastened to do as in-structed. "There's posters all over Denver announcin' the race. I'm surprised you haven't seen 'em."

"I haven't paid any attention. What do they say?"

Harley huffed out between panting breathes, "The Ladies Social Reform Coalition want all the unmarried men and women to take part in the race. They want the women to lend their bonnets, which"—he paused to release a quivering moan—"which'll be hung on stakes a half mile from the startin' line. For a five-buck entry fee, a man 'll have the chance to race for the hat belongin' to the lady of his choice. If he manages to bring it back to the startin' line, he gets to accompany her to a ball bein' held at Louisa Vanderlyn's big house that night."

"So? What does the race have to do with your plan?" Adele demanded, pressing her naked body against his to temptingly rub his inflamed sex against her slippery woman's flesh.

He arched up aggressively, trying to shove inside her. She released a husky laugh and pulled away. Shaking her finger at the general, she chided, "Oh, no, Beau. No charging allowed until after Colonel Harley finishes briefing me on his plan of attack."

Thus forced into unwilling retreat, Harley continued grudgingly, "The race is bein' held on the Vanderlyn Brewery property, about a mile west of Denver. If we can get Tyler to race, me and the boys might be able to ambush him on his way back into town. That's where you come on. I need you to find out which gal he fancies and convince her to participate in the race."

"That would be Lorelei, and she'll participate," reassured Adele, satisfied enough by his strategy to saunter over to the bed. "I'll appeal to her sense of ... charity." Seductively tossing her thick fall of hair over one shoulder, she swiveled at the waist and beckoned to Harley. Then she lay down and opened her legs, wantonly surrendering to the general's carnal siege.

Soon, very soon, her enemy would be vanquished.

Chapter 18

The water was still warm. Penelope reclined against the bathtub backrest, heaving a weary sigh as the moist heat enveloped her body. She was so tired that it was a miracle she'd managed to get out of bed and be here at Seth's hotel by seven.

Her darling, *messy* Seth. Yawning, she stared bleary-eyed at the wet towels and the red velvet dressing gown littering the floor around the tub. It was all his fault she was so exhausted.

A smile tugged at her lips as she wondered what Seth would say to that accusation, especially after the pains he'd taken to ensure that she got enough rest. Upon taking possession of the saloon, he'd mandated that the cast be allowed leisure time from three to six every afternoon, and had made certain that she was at her boardinghouse every night no later than twelve-thirty.

Generally those measures afforded her plenty of rest. Last night, however, Seth had inadvertently thwarted his own altruistic efforts by informing her that he planned to race for her bonnet and win the privilege of escorting her to the dance.

As giddy as a debutante the night before her debut, she'd tossed and turned till dawn, planning what she'd wear right down to the placement of the silk violets in her hair. She'd imagined thrilling scenes where she so charmed Seth that he waltzed her right off the dance floor and into a dark corner to steal a kiss.

Penelope hugged herself with delight. What made the notion of the dance even more perfect was that she'd be attending with Adele's blessing. In truth, the woman had practically ordered her to participate in the race, claiming that seeing the ladylike Lorelei Leroux at the Vanderlyn house would lure men to the Shakespeare who were normally disinclined to frequent variety halls. It was all almost too good to be true.

Once again picturing herself in Seth's arms, resplendently attired in her ivory crepe de chine ball gown with its numerous violet satin bows and silk flowers, she fished Seth's bar of sandalwood soap from beneath her feet.

The frock she intended to wear had been ordered with Seth in mind just two days before their broken engagement. Unable to bear the sight of it for all the heartbreaking memories it evoked, she hadn't so much as peeked at it when it was delivered from the dressmaker's shop two weeks later. And so the costly creation had languished, unworn, at the bottom of her trunk for almost three years. In fact, she'd forgotten just how exquisite it was until she and Effie had unwrapped it from its tissue cocoon last night.

Just the thought of wearing the wonderful gown made Penelope feel like the princess Seth called her. A satisfied smile touched her lips. Tonight she would look worthy of her title.

Imagining Seth's stunned look when he saw her, Penelope sank deeper into the water. Unlike most mornings when she was too fearful of discovery to do more than take a quick dip, today she felt brave enough to luxuriate. Humming a bawdy ditty she'd heard at the saloon, she rubbed the soap between her palms, delighting in the spicy fragrance of the lather.

Always the considerate boss, Seth was closing the saloon at noon so his employees could participate in the race. As he'd mentioned just yesterday, this was probably the only chance most of the saloon girls would ever have to attend a proper dance, and it was only fair that they be given the opportunity. Though Penelope had attended enough balls to last her a lifetime, she was just as ecstatic as the saloon girls over the early closing, for it gave her her first full day off in a long while.

Languidly trailing her foamy hands down one leg, and then up the other, she tried to decide what to do with the rest of her morning. Perhaps she would splurge on a small bottle of the lilac cologne Seth so loved, and then treat herself to a lemon ice. Or maybe she'd start reading the romantic novel Effie had bought her for her birthday last month. The options spread before her as delicious and tempting as a box of her favorite maple nut candy.

Yawning, she idly contemplated the bar of soak in her hands. Whatever she decided to do, she needed to stop lounging in the tub and get at it. It must be almost eight-thirty, and she needed to get back to the boardinghouse before Effie started to worry.

For the hundredth time in the last two weeks, Penelope thanked her mercurial lucky star for her friend's gullibility. When the woman had questioned her absence the first morning she'd gone to Seth's hotel, she'd claimed that it was part of a new scientific health regimen she was on. She said that the plan required that she rise no later than six and walk briskly for no less than two hours, breathing deeply of the fresh air as she went. It was just the sort of nonsense to which Effie subscribed, and she'd never again mentioned her friend's dawn forays.

Penelope began to grin at her own ingenuity, but another yawn slipped out instead. What she really ought to do was take a nap before the race. She yawned again. Yes. She'd do just that.

Yet, for all her good intentions, she continued to lie there. It seemed like forever since she'd had the luxury of lounging in the bathtub, and today she sorely felt the need for some indulgence. Besides, there was really no reason why she couldn't linger a short while longer. Seth wouldn't be back until after noon, if he returned at all before the race, and she didn't have rehearsal. So why not let herself enjoy her bath just this once?

Five minutes, she told herself firmly. *She'd allow herself five more minutes of relaxation and then be on her way.* With that resolution, Penelope closed her eyes and dreamed of Seth.

Once again she strolled with him in the park, thrilling to his charming banter. They dined by candlelight at Delmonico's, and danced the night away at the German Winter Garden, as secure in their love as they were in each other's arms.

As he tipped his head forward to kiss her, whispering passionately of his everlasting devotion, her wistful imaginings deepened and she slipped blissfully into the world of slumber.

Seth took the hotel stairs two at a time, cursing himself for his forgetfulness. He'd been in such a hurry to meet his solicitor that he'd rushed from his room without his ledgers.

TOMORROW'S DREAMS   221

In one impatient bound he leaped up the last three steps to the second-floor landing. He still had a full day's work to squeeze in before the race began at two, and the last thing he needed was this inconvenience of returning for the books.

The race. Just the thought of the race and what winning it meant sent a rush of chaotic emotion rioting through him. Attending tonight's post-race dance was just the opportunity he'd been hoping for. For not only would it give him the chance to observe Louisa Vanderlyn up close, it would permit him a glimpse of her home, something that would tell him far more about her than a thousand Pinkerton reports.

As he paused to unlock his room door, he wondered if Louisa would notice him among the crush of people sure to be in attendance tonight. If she did, would she mark his uncanny resemblance to her father and approach him? Or would she let her gaze pass coolly over him, denying the Van Cortlandt stamp as easily as she would have denied him his life? Grimly pondering, he shoved the door open.

The sight that met his eyes stopped him in his tracks. The room was a terrible mess. Perplexed, he stepped inside, shutting the door quietly behind him.

Unlike every other morning during the past two weeks, Penelope had left without setting his room in order. His shaving implements were still scattered willy-nilly across the dressing table along with a damp towel, of which several more were strewn across the floor in a white linen trail leading to the chair where Penelope had shaved him. There was a half-eaten ginger biscuit on the desk where he'd paused to attach his watch to his fob, and his nightshirt was still tossed over the top of the dressing screen shielding the bathtub.

The screen, like the nightshirt, had been hastily acquired the afternoon following his first discomforting session with Penelope acting as his valet. Though he'd never have admitted it out loud, both items had been procured as much for the protection of his sensibilities as for hers.

Oh, it wasn't that some latent case of modesty had suddenly reared its prudish head and he'd become self-conscious about his nudity. Quite the contrary. He liked the way Penelope looked at his naked body and from the desire he'd seen blazing in her beautiful eyes, it was obvious that she liked looking at it.

Problem was, he liked it too much. Especially when he'd caught her stealing peeks at him as he'd dried himself after

his bath. To his mortification, he'd hardened instantly and
with a groin-wrenching rampancy that had made him sure
he'd burst with need. It was that shameful lack of control
and the resulting discomfort that had prompted his request
for the screen.

And so since that first morning, he'd bathed and dressed
behind the screen, taking care that he was covered with
enough fabric to mask the telltale signs of what was beginning to feel like his perpetual arousal. It was to that end that
he'd purchased the voluminous nightshirt.

To insure that he didn't repeat his disgraceful performance
of that first morning, when she'd come upon him in the
throes of an erotic dream, he now made sure that he was
modestly garbed in both the nightshirt and a dressing gown
when she arrived.

Seth chuckled. Penelope had looked almost disappointed
when she'd arrived that second morning to find him not only
awake, but dressed like an invalid with lung weakness and
imbibing in his now six-forty-five cup of coffee.

He was about to move to the desk and collect his ledgers
when a daub of cardinal red caught his eye. There, hanging
from the corner of the screen, was Penelope's bonnet.

That she would leave without her identity-masking bonnet
was as confounding as her leaving the room in such disorder.
He was about to pluck the bedraggled hat from its perch,
when he caught sight of something else. Something more interesting.

There on the floor, next to yet another soggy towel, was
a black stocking. A long, slender woman's one. The kind
that looked so fetching when topped by a shapely white
thigh. And no one had shapelier thighs than Penelope, to
whom it undoubtedly belonged.

Seth almost groaned aloud at the picture that thought
evoked. Firmly he pushed the tempting vision from his mind
and forced his attention back to the mystery at hand. So
what had prompted Penelope to leave her bonnet in his
room? More befuddling yet, why had she removed her
stocking?

As if in answer to his questions, there was a faint splash
of water. Not pausing to think, he peered around the screen.

There, fast asleep in the bathtub, was Penelope.

Seth hardly dared to breathe, for fear that the stunning vision would vanish. Since their parting, he'd often escaped

from the grim reality of his life by indulging in fantasies about Penelope. His favorite, one which had never failed to erase the pain from his mind, was that of making love to her in her bath.

Erase the pain? Seth thought sardonically. Transfer it was more correct, and to a part of his anatomy he was beginning to think had a mind of its own. A part that was beginning to make its throbbing presence known at that very moment.

As he hungrily surveyed the woman before him, the throbbing mushroomed into an aching heaviness low in his belly. The times they had made love, she'd modestly insisted that he turn down the gaslights before they disrobed. Because he'd assumed he'd have a lifetime to admire her body, he'd indulged her in her maidenly reticence and had satisfied himself feeling what he couldn't see.

Oh, he'd guessed that she had a beautiful body. The voluptuous curves he'd glimpsed outlined in the shadows had told him that much. So provocative was that silhouette that on nights when he was too troubled to sleep, he often diverted his thoughts by enhancing those dark contours with imaginary color and detail. More times than not, he added endowments so fine that he'd wryly reminded himself that no woman could possibly be so perfect.

But he'd been wrong. His fantasy Penelope was nowhere near as exquisite as the real one. Utterly captivated, he drew nearer.

Dear God, she was beautiful! Just the sight of her choked him to the point where he could barely breathe. Her skin was smooth and pale, like the bisque of an expensive French fashion doll, blushed in all the right places in shades ranging from delicate pink to dusty rose.

Through the still water he could clearly see every detail of her luscious body. Her breasts were full and round, just as he'd visualized as he'd lain beside her in the dark, shaping them with his hands. Her nipples, peeking just over the waterline, were a shade of peony pink that echoed the hue of her sleep-parted lips.

Though her legs were bent at the knees and propped up against the side of the tub in a way that twisted her torso away from him, the distortion of her line was unable to mask the slenderness of her waist or the feminine flare of her hips.

Groaning, Seth sank to his knees beside the tub. If ever a woman epitomized the word *female,* it was Penelope Parrish.

And if ever a man suffered the agonies of temptation, it was he.

God help him! Give him the strength in his lust-weakened knees to rise and run away before he did something he'd regret. Bless him with the wisdom and willpower to keep himself from these dangerous situations in the future. And please! Help him banish his hopeless desire for Penelope.

Yet, even as he prayed, his trembling hand lifted and he lightly ran his fingertips down the sloping plane of her breast. Her skin felt exactly as he remembered, delicate and velvety smooth, like the petals of a newly opened rose.

With desire robbing him of reason, as it always did when he was near Penelope, he dipped his thumb below the waterline to caress her nipple. It hardened instantly. Driven by a need too long denied, he stroked the other one. It, too, responded. As he leaned nearer to examine his handiwork, an explosive gasp erupted from Penelope.

With a violence that sent a tidal wave of bathwater washing over the edge of the tub, she bolted upright, slamming her breasts into his face. He would have tumbled headfirst into the tub had he not flung his arms around her torso to brace himself.

"Seth!" she expelled, her tone aghast.

Chapter 19

Seth yanked his chin from where it had landed between Penelope's breasts and stumbled back on his haunches. He hadn't been this humiliated since he was a boy and had been caught spying on an older girl trying on corsets at the general store. Unlike at ten, however, his depravity at thirty-six wasn't likely to be dismissed as youthful curiosity.

Too ashamed to meet Penelope's gaze, he stared down at his soaked waistcoat, grappling for something to say. He had to make an excuse, fabricate a story, do something . . . anything! . . . to break the tense silence. But for once his glib tongue was tied.

It wasn't that he, with his vivid imagination, couldn't come up with a defense. He could, a dozen of them, and believable ones at that. What he couldn't do was force the words past his lips.

Mutely, Seth cursed himself for a weak-willed fool. Once again his heart was overruling his head, and the damn thing was refusing to let him pass this episode off as a strange accident. Worse yet, it was urging him to tell the truth, to confess the tender feelings that had induced him to act as he did.

But, of course, he couldn't allow himself to do that, no matter how he was tempted. He'd seen the way Penelope looked at him of late, so soft and full of yearning, and he refused to hurt her again by giving her false hope for their future together.

As he stared bleakly at his sodden trousers, wondering what the hell he was going to do, he heard the sound of flesh moving through water and then a hand appeared before his face.

"Would you help me up?" Penelope asked, her voice as matter-of-fact as if she were requesting that he fetch her a shawl. "I'm stiff from sleeping in the tub and doubt I can rise by myself."

Seth glanced at her composed face, stunned. He'd expected her to heap recriminations on his head, or at the very least shield her breasts with her arms and stare at him as if he were a rowdy set on ravishing her.

Instead she sat as unperturbed as if being naked in his presence was an everyday event, casually requesting assistance; assistance that invited him to touch her delectable body. He sucked in a hissing breath between his teeth. He'd have preferred the recriminations. A couple of indignant shrieks and a few shaming rebukes would have done wonders to diminish his obstinate lust, which, despite his mortification, still seared his loins.

"Please?" She leaned forward and held out her arms in a way that displayed her breasts in all their tantalizing glory.

Seth mumbled something, he wasn't sure what, and forced his gaze up to her face. That move didn't do a thing to ease the suddenly too tight fit of his trousers. Though her expression was sweetly pleading, her eyes were luminous with desire.

"The water's terribly cold. I'm afraid I'll take a chill if I sit here much longer. Look"—she nodded down at her chest, an area he was diligently trying to ignore—"I've got gooseflesh."

He'd already behaved like a lecher, and he wasn't about to add insult to injury by acting like a cad. And he would be a cad if he denied her help. Resigning himself to torment worse than the fires of hell, Seth clamped his hands around her upper arms and helped her up. The process went smoothly, with Seth avoiding coming in contact with anything more stimulating than her arms.

Just as she lifted her leg to step from the tub, she slipped and he was forced to whip his arms around her torso to keep her from falling. With a startled cry, she grabbed on to his shoulders and clung to him as if for dear life.

The feel of her body, naked and yielding, crushed against his was almost more than Seth could bear. Groaning, he pushed her away to hold her at arm's length.

Gluing his gaze to the floor, he murmured hoarsely, "I've got you. You can step out now." As soon as her feet entered his line of vision, he released her and poised himself for a hasty retreat. As he turned to flee, she exclaimed, "Oh, dear!"

Her voice was so full of distress that he instinctively glanced back to see what was wrong. He could have kicked himself.

He had thought Penelope's figure stunning when he'd gawked at it in the tub, but seeing it now, upright and fully displayed to its best advantage, he saw that it was better than stunning. It was flawless, perfect in both shape and symmetry.

Her legs were long without being coltish, her rounded hips in perfect proportion with her generous bosom. Add those attributes to her wasp waist and you got a natural hourglass shape that most women had to pad and lace themselves to achieve.

Swallowing hard, he pried his gaze away from the alluring sight and somehow choked out, "What's wrong now?"

"I don't have a dry towel. I left the stack by the washstand when I poured the water for your shave."

As fast as he could, considering his aching groin and constricting trousers, Seth hobbled from behind the screen, muttering, "I'll fetch them," all the while sending up thanks for his long overdue deliverance. Wanting nothing more than to sit down and gather what was left of his composure, he grabbed a handful of towels and hastily dumped them over the top of the screen.

"Thank you, Seth," Penelope called out in a dulcet tone.

He grunted and collapsed in the chair before his desk.

From behind the screen drifted the sounds of humming interspersed with the soft rasp of crisp linen being rubbed against flesh. Smiling at Penelope's musical selection, a bawdy drinking song called "Nellie's Naughty Night on the Town," Seth opened the bottom drawer and removed his ledgers.

Abruptly the humming ceased. "Seth?"

"Hmm?"

"Have you been riding too much again?"

He glanced toward the screen, perplexed. "No. Why?"

"I noticed you were walking funny when you went to fetch the towels. Kind of like when your backside was blistered."

Something in her voice piqued Seth's suspicion. She sounded almost amused, as if she'd noticed his disgraceful condition and was now baiting him about it. He let out a snort of disgust. Of course she'd noticed. She'd have had to have been blind not to, what with the snug fit of men's trousers these days.

So why the coy inquiry when the answer had been so apparent? His wariness deepened. After her blushing response to his reference to blue balls last Saturday, he knew for a fact that she understood about male arousal.

She was obviously up to something. Intrigued to find out what that something was, he replied in like coin, "Remember the condition we talked about after I kissed you last week?"

She peered around the screen at him, her expression as angelic as if she were quizzing her Sunday schoolteacher about the colors of Joseph's coat. "How can that be? We didn't kiss."

"Believe me, Princess. We didn't have to kiss."

She stared at him for a long moment, as if absorbing the news, then shook her head. "You poor man. It must be very inconvenient to get in that condition for no reason at all."

"No reason?" he echoed. "A beautiful woman parades naked in front of me, and you say I have no reason to get aroused?"

"I didn't parade," she retorted, almost flirtatiously.

"It isn't the parading part I find stimulating."

"Then, I can't imagine what worked you into such a state." She reached up and toyed with one of the long red ties dangling from her bonnet. "I'm certain it wasn't the sight of my naked body. As you pointed out to me in regard to your own body, it's not as if you're not familiar with it."

"Just because I've seen your body in the shadows and touched you a few times doesn't mean that I no longer desire you. Good God! If anything, those memories make me want you more."

Seth could have bitten off his tongue. He'd opened his mouth to issue playful flattery, not admit his feelings. Damnation! He should have known better than to have taken Penelope's intriguing bait. Now he was really on the hook. His squirming discomfort didn't ease any as he noted the blazing joy on her face.

Dropping the now twisted bonnet string, she clutched at the edge of the screen with both hands and softly exclaimed, "That's exactly how I felt the first morning I came to your room. You looked so handsome lying there naked, I wanted to touch you."

She flushed pink and ducked her head. "In truth, I did touch you. That's why you awoke in the state you were in." She peered up at him earnestly. "Do you think I'm terribly wicked?"

"No. I think you're terribly charming and beautiful," he murmured, more thrilled than he had a right to be by her halting confession. "And I'm flattered that you find my body tempting enough to steal a caress. Any man would be."

"But I've never been tempted to touch another man. Regardless of what you choose to believe about that incident in New York, there's never been anyone for me but you. I'm beginning to think there never will be."

Seth opened his mouth to head off the conversation, to refuse to discuss Julian or New York, but then her gaze touched his and he was unable to utter the words. For there, reflected in depths of her brilliant eyes were the scars of her wounded soul; wounds inflicted by his cowardice and selfish pride.

Never in his life had Seth hated himself more than he did at that moment. How could he have been so cruel? So wrong? What kind of a man was he to so brutally hurt the woman he loved?

The answers were ones he knew too well: he hadn't been a man at all. He'd been the lowest of God's creatures, the most loathsome of life-forms. He'd been a spineless bastard willing to do anything, hurt anyone to save his own worthless pride.

Something inside him snapped, discharging a powerful stream of resolution through his chest. Well, he would be a man now. He would tell her the long overdue truth about New York, no matter how painful or how humiliating it was. He wouldn't hurt her again by rejecting her pleas of innocence with lies and refusals.

Drawing in a deep breath, Seth said what he should have said two and a half years earlier, "I know there was nothing between you and Julian. I always knew."

She looked as stunned as if he'd struck her. "But . . . then why?" She made a helpless little hand gesture.

Dreading what he was about to do, yet at the same time oddly liberated by it, he walked over to a chair and patted its back in invitation. "Sit down, Princess, and I'll explain as best I can."

She remained stock-still, her hands clutching the edge of the screen. "I can't come out. I'm not dressed."

It was on the tip of Seth's tongue to remind her that she didn't have anything he hadn't seen before, but she looked so utterly miserable that he hadn't the heart. Instead he said, "I seem to remember leaving my dressing gown by the tub this morning. Why don't you put it on and come out. I'd prefer that we both be seated when I tell you what I have to say."

"Is it really that terrible?" 'Her voice was every bit as desolate as her expression.

He nodded somberly. "Worse."

She bobbed her head in return and disappeared behind the screen. After what felt like an eternity, she reappeared.

Despite the dread lying heavy on his heart, Seth smiled. Even with her small form swallowed up by the folds of his robe and her hair in untidy braids atop her head, Penelope somehow managed to look elegant.

When she'd settled in the chair, he pulled the matching ottoman directly in front of her and sat down. He was silent for several tense moments, looking everywhere but in her eyes, searching for a way to begin. At last Penelope took the lead.

"Why Seth?" she whispered, her voice raw with emotion. "Why did you do and say what you did? Was it because you no longer loved me and wanted to be rid of me? I know I was selfish—"

"No!" he interjected, appalled at her assumption that she was somehow responsible for his behavior. "Dear God, no. None of what happened was your fault. You were never anything but wonderful, and there was nothing I wanted more than to marry you."

"I don't understand."

Seth's gaze touched her troubled face briefly before he lowered his head to stare at his hands. Nervously scraping at his calloused palm with his thumbnail, he replied "No, but you will. And I suspect you'll hate me when you learn the truth."

He heard Penelope shift in her chair, then felt her push his hair from his face and tuck it behind his ears. Cupping his cheek in her hand, she murmured, "I doubt if I could ever hate you, Seth. I've tried and failed so many times during the last two and a half years, that I'm beginning to think it impossible."

"You haven't heard my story yet."

"No. But I know you well enough to realize that you probably had a good reason for doing what you did, especially if you loved me as much as you profess," she murmured, her gaze capturing his.

In that instant as Seth stared into Penelope's soft green eyes he saw not just the charming, spirited girl he so loved, but the warm, compassionate woman she'd become. It was that new maturity that gave him the courage to continue.

Gently drawing her hand from his cheek to clasp it in his, he quizzed, "Do you remember the last night we spent together? How I had to rise at dawn for an early-morning engagement?"

"Yes. It was a breakfast meeting, as I recall." She smiled. "I remember you liked to conduct business over meals because everyone remained cordial so as not to risk indigestion. I also remember that you always saved your dinner appointments for me."

"You could have had my breakfast and lunch appointments, too, if you'd but asked," he replied, caressing her thumb with his.

Penelope's dimples peeked out at that declaration. "I was selfish, not stupid. I knew you had to attend to business during the day. I wanted to share your life, not run it."

"Which proves my point that you were never selfish. A selfish woman would have demanded all my time."

Her smile faded. "Then, why did you break our engagement?"

"Because of the news I received at my meeting that morning." He paused to squeeze her hand, as much for his own reassurance as for hers. "My appointment that morning wasn't with a business associate, but with a Pinkerton agent. I'd hired the agency to try and find information about my parents."

"Your parents?" Her brow furrowed. "I always assumed they were dead. You never spoke of them and whenever I mentioned them, you were as obtuse as a captured traitor."

"I never spoke of them because I didn't know who they were."

She looked positively baffled by that notion. "How could you not know who your parents were?"

If Seth hadn't been so tense, he probably would have smiled at her naïveté. For all her education and recent experience, Penelope was still an innocent in many ways. Measuring his words carefully, he replied, "I was found abandoned in the foyer of St. John's Chapel when I was just a few days old. I was wrapped in an old blanket with a handkerchief tied around a gash on my arm. I have a scar on the underside of my right arm from that wound."

"How awful!" she exclaimed, her eyes wide and full of sympathy. "Why didn't you ever tell me this before?"

"Because I was ashamed. You already knew that I was little better than white trash, what with my crude speech and manners when your brother first started inviting me to your house. I thought that stigma damning enough without adding that I was abandoned at birth and most probably a bastard."

"None of that would of have mattered to me," she protested. "By the time we were engaged, I loved you so much that you could have told me you were the man in the moon, and I still would have said 'I do.' You should have had enough faith in my love to trust me to understand about your past."

Seth shifted his gaze from her face to stare down at their clasped hands, aching at the hurt in her eyes. "I know that now, but I was a cowardly fool. I felt unworthy of you and was afraid you might judge me unsuitable to be your husband if you learned the truth. I didn't want to risk losing you."

There was a brief silence, as if she were considering his words. Finally she replied, "I know you asked my brother's blessing before you proposed. Did he know of your past?"

"Everything," Seth conceded.

"And yet he was thrilled at the prospect of our coming marriage. In fact, he wrote to me telling me that he was glad I'd finally come to my senses and was marrying the only man he considered worthy of me. If he thought you were good enough, what in the world made you assume that I'd think any differently?"

"I didn't think, which his one of the more troublesome aspects of being a fool," he admitted, his self-abhorrence clearly echoed in his voice. "At any rate, it was my feelings of inadequacy that led me to contact the Pinkerton Agency.

I hoped that they might turn up something to redeem me in my own eyes."

"But they only confirmed your fears, didn't they?" There was a rising note of anger in her voice. When Seth looked up, startled at her sudden change in tone, he found her staring at him with a soul-scalding mixture of scorn and pain.

"Well? Am I right?" she demanded.

"Yes. But what you have to understand—"

"Oh, I understand perfectly," she spat, jerking her hand from his. "You couldn't deal with your feelings of inferiority from learning that you're a bastard, so you used my friendship with Julian to trump up false charges of infidelity to break our engagement. You put me through two and a half years of hell because of you weren't man enough to face your feelings and tell me the truth. You really are a bastard, and I don't mean the kind born out of wedlock." With that stinging but well-earned set-down, she stood up. "Now, if you'll excuse me, Mr. Tyler—"

"No!" Seth jumped up and grabbed her arms to prevent her from moving away.

"Damn it! Let me go," she snarled, trying to pull away.

He tightened his hold, easily immobilizing her. He knew he deserved her contempt, and if she chose never to speak to him again after he'd said his piece, then he'd honor her wishes by staying out of her life, no matter how much it tore him up inside. But he intended to make her hear the whole truth first.

"Just listen to me for a few minutes," he begged. "Let me finish explaining."

She stabbed him with her infuriated glare. "Why? So you can tell me more lies to justify your vile behavior?"

"No. So I can tell you the truth." His gaze locked into hers, mutely pleading. "Just give me five minutes to explain. Then I'll do anything you ask. Anything."

Penelope froze in his arms as if mulling over his proposal, then nodded stiffly. Looking pointedly at the clock beside the bed, she snapped, "Five minutes."

Seth exhaled with relief. "Thank you." Relaxing his grip, he nodded at the chair. "Would you mind if we sat? You still haven't heard the worst part of my story."

"It gets worse?" She drew back, eyeing him uncertainly. "I'm not so sure I want to hear the rest."

He gave her a brittle smile. "Worse for me, not you. What I have to say might even make you feel better."

She emitted a snort that clearly expressed her skepticism, but sat down nonetheless. He returned to his perch on the edge of the ottoman. Staring down at his clenched fists lying on his knees, he began without preamble, "You were correct when you accused me of using your friendship with Julian to break our engagement, but you were wrong about the reason."

He glanced up briefly to nod. "Oh, you were right about the part of me being a bastard, both kinds, but that wasn't the reason I did what I did. I'd already decided on the way to my meeting with the agent that if I learned I was indeed the bastard of a scrubwoman or prostitute, that I'd tell you the truth and let you decide for yourself if you still wanted to marry me. But what I learned"—he broke off, shaking his head hopelessly.

"Was what, Seth?" The question was asked quietly, without a trace of impatience or enmity.

Not daring to look up for fear of seeing a hostility that belied the gentleness of her tone, he thrust the words past his pain-constricted throat. "I learned that my birth was the result of an incestuous rape. My father was a maniac who raped his own sister in a fit of madness."

"Dear God, no! Are you certain? Couldn't the agency have made some sort of mistake?"

"There was no mistake. The proof is irrefutable." He drew in a shuddering breath and forced himself to look at her face. It was as pale as ashes, with shock tainting every elegant line. Staring into her wide eyes, he added softly, "Don't you see? I couldn't marry you or anyone else, knowing of my birth. Between the taint of incest and my father's madness, it's possible that I'll end up in an asylum for the insane someday."

"You poor man!" she expelled, laying both her hands over his clenched ones. "You must have felt like your world was ending!"

His fists slowly relaxed beneath her touch. "It had. It came to an end the moment I lost you."

"I wish you had come to me. Perhaps I could have eased your pain some."

"There was nothing I wanted more than to lie in your embrace and tell you everything," he admitted, lacing his fingers through hers and clutching her hands as if they possessed miraculous healing powers. But I couldn't. I was . . . afraid."

"Afraid? Of what?" she asked, visibly taken aback. "Surely you didn't think that I'd become repulsed and order you from my sight over something that clearly wasn't your fault?"

"At first, yes," he confessed shamefacedly. "But then I starting thinking about how strong, stubborn, and loyal you are, and I was worried that you might insist on marrying me despite the overwhelming odds against our future happiness."

"You were right. I still would've wanted to marry you. I'd have begged you to take me to the altar, where I'd have promised to love, cherish, and keep the madness from you."

Seth smiled gently and lifted her left hand to his lips to kiss her ring finger. "And I wouldn't have had the strength to say no. I could never deny you anything, which is why I didn't dare tell you the truth."

"But would it really have been so terrible for us to have married? There is always a chance that you won't go insane."

"And an even bigger one that I will."

She shook her head. "Even so, we could have had years of happiness together. That would have been enough for me. All I ever wanted was the chance to love you."

"And all I ever wanted was to love you in return. But I couldn't bear the thought of you watching me go insane or the possibility that I might somehow injure you while in the throes of my madness. Most of all, I hated the idea of you wasting your life being tied to a lunatic. You're so wonderful, you deserve a man who can promise you forever. One who can give you a stable home and a brood of children as special as you are."

"But we could have had all that," she declared, her eyes aglow with a strange light. "The home . . . the children."

Seth stared at her, appalled. "Do you know what you're saying?" he demanded. "Have you stopped to consider what sort of children I might father? God only knows the hideous ways my cursed blood might mark them."

Her face blanched as white as if every drop of blood had been drained away. "Marked? Dear God," she whispered.

"Yes, marked," he echoed, relieved that she was finally

beginning to understand the dangers of his curse. "I saw a doctor right after I spoke with the agent, one who specializes in disorders of the mind. Though he couldn't offer me any help, he did advise me of the threat to my offspring."

Penelope opened her mouth as if to speak, then closed it again. After a moment she licked her lips and murmured, "What would you have done if I'd conceived? I mean, we did make love."

Seth exhaled as sharply as if the air had been slugged from him. "Well, let's just give thanks that you didn't."

"But if I had?" she persisted.

"Then, I would have married you, despite the dangers, and prayed that our child would be spared the curse of my blood."

Her slender fingers tightened suddenly to clench his with a strength he found surprising. "And if he or she were born marked, like that doctor predicted, would you have still loved him?"

Seth stared at Penelope's grave face, shocked that she found it necessary to ask such a question. "Of course I would. I'd have adored our baby every bit as much as I would if it were perfect."

Something about her answering smile sent a trickle of uneasiness down his spine. Strange, but she looked relieved, almost as if she'd just received a favorable response to an urgently important question. The only conceivable reason for her expression shook him to the very core of his being.

Riveting her with a probing stare, he demanded, "What makes you ask such a question?"

She shrugged in an offhanded manner. "Just curious. As you might have noticed, I've become inquisitive in my old age." The breezy nonchalance of both her reply and demeanor did much to put his wariness to rest. With a smile that charmed him right out of his remaining misgivings, she nodded toward the clock, adding, "In case you're curious as well and are wondering about the time, it's nine-twelve. Your five minutes are up."

Seth glanced at the timepiece. "If I'm not mistaken, my time was up three minutes ago." He gave her hands a warm squeeze, then released them. "Thank you for listening to me."

"I'm glad I did." She rose, tightening the dressing-gown sash as she straightened up. "Although I still think you were a bastard to behave as you did in New York, I understand that you thought you were doing it for my own good. I can't hate you for trying to protect me, no matter how misguided your methods."

"Does that mean we can still be friends?"

Her gaze still on the sash, she replied, "Of course. And if you still want to try for my bonnet at the race, I'd be pleased to accompany you to the dance tonight."

"How could I not want to go with the cleanest girl in town?" he teased, more relieved by her reply than words could express.

She flushed a pretty shade of geranium pink at his good-natured reference to her clandestine bath. "I'm sorry. I hope you're not upset with me. I have to haul and heat my own bathwater at the boardinghouse. It's such hard work that I couldn't resist taking a soak in your already filled tub."

"I'm only upset that you didn't tell me, so I could order an extra bucket of hot water for you." Standing up, he added, "I want you to promise to let me know if there's anything you ever need in the future. Friends look after each other, you know."

She gave the robe tie a tug that looked suspiciously like a fidget. "Actually . . . uh . . . there is something I do need."

"Ask away," he directed. When she hesitated, he reminded her, "I promised to do anything you asked if you listened to me for five minutes. You upheld your end of the bargain, and I'm perfectly willing to uphold mine."

"I'll ask only if you promise not to question my request."

Mystified, Seth agreed. "All right, then. No questions."

Twisting the sash into a fat, velvet ringlet, she murmured, "I need to borrow $385. It's just a loan. I'll pay you back when I get to San Francisco."

A request for money was the last thing Seth had expected. So taken aback was he, that he almost slipped and asked her why she needed it. Fortunately he came to his senses in time to stop himself. Giving her shoulder a reassuring squeeze, he said, "It's yours. Come to my office tomorrow after rehearsal."

"Thank you, Seth." Dropping the coiled sash, Penelope stood on her tiptoes and planted a firm but brief kiss on his lips.

Resisting his fierce urge to clamp her into his embrace and steal a real kiss, Seth stepped back, almost tumbling over the ottoman in the process. Flustered as much from Penelope's casual kiss as from his near fall, he muttered, "Now, if you'll excuse me, I have business I need to attend to before the race."

As he moved toward the desk to retrieve the ledgers, he was stopped by Penelope's soft voice. "Seth?"

He glanced back over his shoulder to where she still stood by the chair. She was smiling in a way that displayed her dimples to their most irresistible advantage. "I'll keep my fingers crossed that you win my bonnet this afternoon."

Slowly and deliberately he let his gaze work its way from her bare toes to her prettily flushed face, taking in every delectable detail in between. "Never fear, Princess," he purred. "I won't lose when the prize is so worth winning."

Chapter 20

For the first time in what felt like a decade, luck was on Penelope's side. Not only had she resolved her differences with Seth, he'd promised to lend her the $385 she lacked to regain her baby, *and* he'd won her bonnet in the race that afternoon.

Smiling dreamily she fingered a crushed silk daisy, the only remaining flower on her previously floral straw hat, reliving the moment when Seth had dashed over the finish line.

Never had he looked more handsome than when he'd galloped up to her, waving her bonnet in the air like a trophy of conquest. At that moment, as she'd stared up into his triumphant face, there was nothing she wanted more than to tangle her hands in his tousled mane and bestow upon him a well-deserved victory kiss.

As if sensing or perhaps sharing her thoughts, Seth had leaned low over the pommel and playfully dropped the ruined hat atop her head. "You, my glorious prize," he murmured, his mouth curving into a wicked grin, "I shall claim at nine o'clock." His gaze full of promise, he wheeled his horse around and joined the throng of winners clamoring to claim their vouchers to the dance.

Barely able to contain her excitement for the evening ahead, Penelope hugged herself. Nine o'clock. The magic hour; the hour that would herald in a promising new chapter of her life.

As she sat clutching her tattered bonnet, dreaming of a future where she, Seth, and Tommy lived as a happy family, the tolling of the parlor clock drifted up through the floorboards. Half past eight. Cinderella time was only thirty minutes away.

Laying the hat on the dressing table at which she sat, Penelope turned her attention to the mirror before her. She

wanted to be stunning tonight, to see Seth's eyes glow with
admiration and desire every time he looked at her. With that
end in mind, she'd spent the last two hours primping and
fussing.

Frowning at her reflection, she reached up and pulled a
ringlet over her bare shoulder, critically eyeing the effect in
the wavering lamplight. With Effie's help she'd copied a
coiffure from *Godey's Lady's Book,* an elegant, sophisticated
arrangement consisting of a chignon of cascading long curls.

Giving the fashion plate in the mirror a grudging nod of
approval, she picked up a pearl-drop earring and slipped the
thin wire through her pierced left ear. Though most of her
jewelry had been given to Adele to pay for Tommy's up-
keep, she'd managed to retain these earrings and the matching necklace. Her brother had given her the set the night of
her debut, and it held far too many memories to wind up in
the grimy window of a pawnbroker's shop.

Yet just yesterday afternoon as she'd counted her meager
savings, she'd decided that she had no choice but to sell the
precious set. There were only three weeks left before she
and Seth were to return to San Francisco, and she was desperate for money to pay for her son's rescue.

Penelope smiled as she picked up her right earring. Now,
thanks to Seth's loan, the sacrifice would be unnecessary.

A thrill of excitement quivered up her spine at the thought
of the money and what it meant. Perhaps as early as tomorrow night her darling Tommy would be safe in her arms.
Then she'd go straight to Seth and explain everything. With
the baby out of Adele's harmful way, she could freely confess the events of the last two and a half years without fear.

At least without fear of repercussions against her son. She
paused in hooking her earring to stare soberly at her reflection. When Adele discovered what she'd done, she would
take desperate, perhaps even deadly measures to prevent her
from taking her tale to the authorities. And when the woman
found out that she'd confided in Seth, his life, too, would be
at risk.

With fingers made clumsy by fear, Penelope finished securing the earring. As much as she hated imperiling Seth,
she knew that he, and only he, could protect her and Tommy
from Adele's wrath.

Her mood dampened, she latched the pearl and gold-
filigree pendant around her neck. Finishing her toilet with a

dab of newly purchased lilac perfume, she drew on her gloves and slipped the handle of her beaded reticule over her wrist. After picking up a painted sandalwood fan, one Seth had brought her from London three years earlier, she stood up to survey herself.

Without conceit, she admitted that she'd never looked better. Her spirits rising a bit, she looped her train up over her arm and draped a lacy shawl across her shoulders. As she turned from the mirror, the clock chimed a quarter of nine.

A smile touched her lips. For the first time in their history together, Seth wouldn't have to wait while she finished primping. Grinning at the prospect of seeing his stunned expression when she herself opened the door at his knock, she headed downstairs to await his arrival in the parlor.

As Penelope reached the foot of the stairs, the sound of voices drifting from the porch arrested her. Thinking that Seth had arrived early and was outside exchanging pleasantries with one of her fellow boarders, she moved across the foyer to the door. She froze, hand on knob, when she recognized the voices.

It was Adele and Miles. Mystified, for Adele roomed at the saloon and seldom deigned to visit her son at the boardinghouse, she strained to hear their words.

"Are you sure, Mother?" Miles whined, his high-pitched voice easily piercing the thick wooden door panels.

"Of course, darling" came Adele's lower, yet equally audible, response. "Harley promised that he'd take care of Tyler this afternoon. The bastard is either dead or dying as we speak." She laughed. "I hope kissing Lorelei was worth the price."

Seth, dead? Penelope felt the blood drain from her face.

There was a squealing chortle from Miles. "Wish I could've been the one to slice off his balls. I would've liked to make him scream after the way he's been trying to steal Lorelei from me."

It was all Penelope could do not to scream herself at the hideous vision of Seth mutilated in such an unspeakable manner. Shaking her head in horrified disbelief, she backed away. Her numbness melting into panic, she pivoted soundlessly on the balls of her feet and rushed toward the side kitchen door, taking care not to pound her high heels against the wooden floor as she went.

Holding her skirts above her knees, she slipped around to

the back of the house, breaking into a run as she raced across the neighbors' backyards. When she reached the end of the block, she stopped long enough to suck air into her burning lungs before dashing in the direction of the hotel. If by some miracle Seth had escaped Harley's attack alive, he was probably there.

And if he wasn't in his room? Stubbornly she pushed the ominous thought from her mind. He would be there. He had to be.

The storefronts and passersby were blurs of color as Penelope whizzed past. Once, in front of a seedy Blake Street saloon, a pair of drunks tried to detain her, but she jostled them aside with a strength that amazed even herself. After running what felt like miles, she reached Seth's hotel room.

The door was locked. Winded and panting, she rifled through the contents of her reticule, frantically searching for the key. Of course it wasn't there. There had been no reason to transfer it from her everyday bag into her evening one.

Too panicked by now to care if she made a spectacle of herself, she pounded on the door, breathlessly sobbing Seth's name. As she reached a frenzied peak, the door swung open and she was swept into a strong embrace. She didn't need to see his face or hear his voice to know that it was Seth who held her.

Sagging against him in relief, she pressed her tear-slicked cheek against his bare chest, blubbering, "Seth! Oh, thank God!"

"I'm here, sweetheart. Everything's all right," he crooned. Without easing his grasp on her trembling form, he drew her from the threshold, kicking the door closed behind him. Patting her back in much the same manner she used to soothe Tommy when he cried, he murmured, "Easy now, Pen. Hush. I've got you."

"Oh, Seth! I was so afraid," she blurted out between sobs.

"You're safe now," he assured her, moving his hand up her back to lightly massage her tense neck. "I'll protect you."

She shook her head. "I wasn't afraid for myself. I was worried about you. I thought ... I thought you were ... were dead!" She practically wailed the last word.

"Dead?" His kneading hand stilled. "Whatever gave you that idea?" An odd, almost wary note shaded his voice.

Penelope could have bitten off her tongue. As much as

she ached to tell Seth what she'd overheard, to warn him of
Adele's treachery, she didn't dare. At least not until Tommy
was safe.

Yet she had to say something. Urgently she searched her
mind for an answer, anything to make him watch his back
until such a time as she could reveal the truth. As she struggled to concoct a believable tale, she stole a glance at his
face, trying to gauge his mood. The sight that met her eyes
made her gasp aloud.

Seth hadn't escaped a brush with Harley and his band of
cutthroats. Quite the opposite. From the looks of his battered
face and blood-streaked hair, it was apparent that the men
had come terrifyingly close in succeeding with their murderous deed.

"Oh, Seth!" Penelope wailed, flinging her arms around his
lean torso in a possessive hug.

He let out a mighty yelp. "Ouch! Jesus, Penelope! Be
careful. I think my rib is broken."

"S-sorry. Sorry," she murmured, lightly rubbing her hands
over his rib cage in a helpless attempt to ease his pain. "I
didn't mean to hurt you."

"I know that, and any other time I would have enjoyed
your ferocious hug." He gave her a crooked grin, one made
all the more endearing by the effort it took, what with his cut
upper lip.

Penelope reached up and gently touched his damaged
mouth. He winced, but didn't draw away. "What happened,
Seth?"

He began to shake his head, but then stopped abruptly,
grimacing as if the motion pained him. "Four men attacked
me on my way back into town this evening."

"This evening? But the race was over hours ago."

"The manager of Vanderlyn's invited the winners into the
brewery for a few victory rounds. By the time all thirty-two
of us had finished toasting our ladies, it was seven o'clock."

Staring at a wicked-looking gash on his shoulder, she
asked hopefully, "Do you know who did this to you?"

He shrugged his undamaged shoulder. "No. They were
wearing black hoods, like a vigilante group. It was all I
could do to fight them off. I didn't have a chance to unmask
any of them."

Penelope's hope died as quickly as it was born. If Seth
had been able to identify just one man, Harley and his co-

horts might have fled town to escape retribution. With their anonymity still intact, they would undoubtedly try to kill him again.

Frowning, she gently ran her fingertips over his bruised ribs. She had to do something. She couldn't leave the man she loved vulnerable to another attack. But how?

As she turned the problem over in her mind, Seth cupped her chin in his palm and tilted her face up. "Do you know something about all this, Princess?"

She recoiled backward, pointing at her chest with her index finger. "Me? What makes you think I know anything?"

"It could have something to do with the way you came charging in here, sobbing about me being dead," he replied dryly.

Penelope dropped her guilty gaze from his probing one, certain that the truth was visible in her eyes. Staring down at her shawl, which she'd dropped during her impetuous hug, she improvised, "While I was waiting for you in the parlor this evening, I overheard two metallic casket salesmen discussing a murder that took place just outside of town this afternoon. They were at the undertakers when the body was brought in, and described the victim as a tall man with blond hair. Since you were outside the city this afternoon and fit the description, I was terrified that it was you." She crossed her fingers in the folds of her skirt, praying that he'd believe her story.

There was a long silence during which Penelope was sure she could feel Seth's gaze burning through her skull and right into her brain. Finally he sighed. "Apparently someone has it in either for me, or for a man who fits my description."

Wishing she could wrap him in cotton and tuck him in her pocket, as she'd done with her favorite dollhouse china doll when she was a girl, Penelope pleaded, "Promise me you'll be careful." She grasped his arms and gave him a shake, well, as much of one as she could considering his greater size. "Promise me!"

Seth gently disengaged her hands from his arms to lace his fingers between hers. "Don't worry, sweetheart. I can take care of myself. I've managed to keep myself alive thus far."

Penelope shook her head. "Promise me that you'll take

extra precautions. I couldn't bear it if anything happened to you."

Seth tilted his head to one side, staring down into her face with wonder. "After the terrible way I've wronged you, do you still care for me that much?"

"Care?" She let out an hysteria-edged laugh. "Care? I love you! Fool that I am, I've never stopped loving you."

"Then, God help us both," he whispered, his face contorting as if he were in unbearable pain. "For I love you, too."

Penelope almost hugged herself in her joy. Seth loved her! That being the case, he'd surely insist on marrying her when she introduced him to his son. Breathless with delight, she stood on her tiptoes and covered his battered face with soft kisses, declaring, "You don't know how I've longed to hear you say that."

With a groan of pure misery, he pulled his hands from hers. "Don't! Don't love me. It will only bring you pain."

She shook her head and smiled, desperate to assuage the torment shadowing his eyes. "Not being able to love you will hurt me worse." Careful to avoid his injured ribs, she drew his tense form into her embrace, pleading, "I don't care about the future. I just want to be with you for however long fate grants us."

"I can't let you throw your life away," he growled, trying to back out of her arms. "Damn it! I refuse to allow it!"

Penelope held firm, clinging to him as if he were the last solid tree in a raging hurricane. "And I refuse to let you go."

"And when I become mad?" he demanded. "What then? Have you considered the shame and stigma you'll suffer when it becomes apparent that your husband is a madman?"

Penelope looked up, only to find his face inches from hers. Meeting his desolate gaze with her reassuring one, she pledged, "I swear on our love to be your anchor to this world and to keep the madness from you." She rose to her tiptoes to kiss him, taking care not to hurt his cut lip. "Well, except for the madness of desire. I intend to drive you crazy with wanting me."

He groaned. "I'm already crazy with wanting you. It's getting positively embarrassing the way my body insists on responding every time you get within a mile of it."

She slanted him a wicked look. "Your male 'thing' has been rather insistent on making its presence known of late."

One corner of his mouth curved up slightly and to Penelope's amusement, he blushed as red as her old calico bonnet.

Pleased to see him smile, even faintly, she continued, "Aside from staying away from me, which, of course, is not an option, I see only two ways out of your all-too-obvious dilemma."

He raised one eyebrow in question. "Oh?"

She nodded solemnly. "You can either buy unfashionably baggy trousers so your condition doesn't show, or you can let me relieve you on a regular basis, which I assume will banish the problem altogether. Personally I prefer the latter remedy. Your body is much too fine to be hidden by loose trousers." She drew back to stare pointedly at the prominent bulge at his groin.

He let out a strangled sound that was halfway between a laugh and a moan. "Only you, sweetheart, could manage to arouse a man who's been beaten within an inch of his life."

"Oh! How thoughtless of me to keep you standing," she exclaimed, stricken with sudden guilt at his words. "Here"— she looped her arm around his waist—"let me help you to the bed."

"Actually I was about to take a bath. I can't attend the dance covered with dirt and blood."

She stared up at him, appalled. "You can't seriously be thinking of going tonight? Dear God, Seth! You should be in bed."

"What? And miss escorting the prettiest girl in town to the social event of the season?" Letting his appreciative gaze sweep her length, he added, "By the way. You look beautiful tonight."

Penelope scowled, not a bit diverted by his flattery. "And you look awful. Your hair is all bloody, and your face is a mess."

"I daresay I'll look better once I've washed up a bit." Gently disengaging himself from her arm, he said, "Now, if you'll excuse me, I'll go do that now."

"No. I won't excuse you," she retorted, stubbornly wrapping her arm around his waist again. "If you insist on taking a bath, I'm going to help you. With all the blows you've obviously taken to that thick head of yours, you could become dizzy and drown."

As if sensing the futility of arguing, Seth merely sighed. Lecturing him about mutton-brained fools who hadn't the sense to know what was good for them, Penelope escorted him behind the screen. The fact that he was limping and winced with every step only increased the fervor of her discourse.

"Really, Seth," she chided as she tested the temperature of the bathwater poured earlier by the porter. "You should at least have a doctor examine you to make certain that you aren't hurt inside. I remember Hallie telling me a story about a man who fell from a horse, and nobody even suspected that he was hurt until he died from internal injuries two days later."

There was a low chuckle from Seth. "I've noticed that your sister-in-law is inordinately fond of her hidden-injuries-turned-fatal tales. She never fails to recount at least one every time your brother and I engage in a few friendly rounds of boxing."

"Well, in this instance I think you'd do well to heed her warning," Penelope cautioned, pouring a steaming bucket of water into the tub. "There's a lot of blood in your hair, and Hallie says that head wounds are particularly dangerous."

"Apparently her word has spread far and wide, because the porter took one look at me and insisted on sending for a doctor. He should be here soon."

"Then, you'd best stop dawdling and take your bath." Deeming the water temperature comfortable, she turned back to Seth.

He was standing rather unsteadily a couple of feet away, struggling to unfasten his trousers with one hand while bracing his damaged rib with his other. By his pale drawn face, it was apparent that he was in a great deal of pain.

Aching with compassion, she went to him and laid her fingers over his clumsily fumbling ones. "Here. Let me help you."

Nodding, he dropped his hand from the buttons. With calm efficiency she unfastened his dusty trousers and eased them off. Remaining on her knees only long enough to ascertain that the damage to his lower body was limited to a few bruises and minor abrasions, she rose and helped him into the tub.

When he sat huddled in the water, his knees drawn up to his chin and his eyes closed, Penelope picked up the bar of soap and began to lather away the evidence of his ordeal. He remained stoically still beneath her ministrations, not so much as wincing when she swabbed out his gaping shoulder wound.

When she'd cleansed all the areas she could reach with him sitting the way he was, she dropped a kiss on his cheek and whispered, "You need to recline back now, so I can wash your chest and torso. Then I'll tend to your face and hair."

He opened his eyes, smiling faintly. "If I'd known how pleasurable it is to be bathed by you, I'd never have bartered away the privilege for a mere question a day."

"And if I'd guessed how much I'd enjoy bathing you, I never would have taken the questions," she countered honestly, though in truth his queries had proved surprisingly simple to answer. Never once had he pried into her relationship with Adele or asked any of the other questions she'd been expecting and dreading.

Raking his hair from the side of his face to tuck it behind his ear, she added, "Speaking of baths, we need to finish yours. Can you lie back by yourself, or do you need me to help you?"

"I can manage. I don't want to spoil that magnificent gown with water spots." With that, he reclined backward, visibly favoring his left side. As he settled against the high backrest, he teased, "Too bad I didn't get myself beaten up sooner. We could have renegotiated the terms of the bargain to include baths, and spared me the trouble of thinking up questions for you."

Penelope was about to suggest that they agree on that particular deal when there was a banging at the door.

"Sir? It's me, Sydney, the porter. Doc Larson's with me."

Seth shot her a reassuring look. "You can wait back here while the doctor examines me. I'll hurry him along."

It was on the tip of her tongue to agree, but then she looked into his bruised face and shook her head. How could she make him face the doctor alone when he so clearly needed her love and support? Besides, it was doubtful that word of her presence here tonight would reach Adele's ears before Tommy's rescue, so there was really no reason for her to cower behind the screen.

Laying her palm against his cheek, she shook her head. "By the looks of that shoulder wound and the blood in your hair, you'll probably need to be stitched. Perhaps it won't hurt so bad if I hold your hand and talk to you while the doctor does it."

Seth laid his hand over hers on his cheek. "Are you sure?"

She nodded and planted a quick kiss on his lips.

"Mr. Tyler? Are you alive?" came a frantic call.

"And kicking," Seth hollered back. "I'm taking a bath. Use your passkey to let the doctor in. I'll be out in a minute."

As the porter followed instructions, Penelope finished bathing Seth. When he was thoroughly washed, except for his hair, which she deemed futile to clean until after his scalp was stitched, she dried him off and helped him into a dressing gown. Then she escorted him around the screen.

"Thank you for coming, Dr. Larson," Seth said, extending his hand to the physician, who stood at the desk rummaging through a shabby black bag.

The doctor, a slight man with a thick mane of silver hair and a mustache to match, moved forward to give his hand a cordial pump. "Glad to be of assistance, Mr. Tyler."

"Seth," Seth corrected as he drew Penelope forward. "And this is my lovely bride, Ettalee."

Penelope bit her lip to keep from giggling as she presented the doctor with her hand. Ettalee was the name of the girl in Seth's favorite naughty rhyme.

The man squeezed her hand and murmured a pleasantry, then turned back to his patient. "The hotel fella said you had a run-in with some rowdies. Looks like they did a job on you."

"He has a deep cut on his shoulder and another on his scalp," Penelope told him. "They're bleeding an awful lot."

The doctor peered up at Seth's matted hair and frowned. "Sit down and let me have a look, son," he urged, thumping the back of the desk chair with his palm.

As the man shifted through Seth's hair, pausing now and then to take a closer look at his scalp, he shot off questions in a rapid-fire barrage. Was Seth dizzy? Did he see shooting lights or was his vision blurred? Seth answered each query negatively.

"Amazing," the doctor said at last. "By the looks of the laceration and bump on the left side of your head, you should be either unconscious or in bed with a brutal headache."

Seth winced violently as the man prodded the area. "Except for your poking, I feel fine."

"Be that as it may, the injury is still worrisome." As the doctor fished his instruments from his bag, he continued, this time speaking to Penelope as if Seth were a very young child and she were his mother. "I'm going to stitch the wound, Mrs. Tyler. Then I want you to put your husband to bed with an ice pack on the area. Make sure he stays there until the swelling goes down."

From beneath his eyelashes, Seth slanted her a look that told her quite succinctly that it would take the combined efforts of both God and man to make him stay in bed this evening.

Ignoring his subtle show of defiance, Penelope reassured the doctor, "I'll see that he behaves." Kneeling before Seth, she asked, "Would you like to see his shoulder now? By the looks of it, it could use a few stitches, too."

At his nod, she loosened Seth's dressing gown and slipped it off his shoulders. When he sat bared to the waist, she added, "You need to check his ribs, too. They're paining him terribly."

After the doctor pronounced one of the ribs fractured and the shoulder in need of suturing, he set to work. To Seth's credit, he didn't cry out once, not even when the doctor began to stitch the bruised and swollen flesh on his scalp.

As Penelope kneeled before him, clutching his hands as if it were she, instead of he, who was enduring the stitching, tears of guilt and regret streamed down her cheeks. Her poor, poor love! It was all her fault he was hurt. She should have guessed that Adele would harm him, what with the way he'd flaunted his interest in her. She should have done something to discourage his attention. Before she could repress it, a sniffling sob escaped.

"What's this?" Seth murmured, disengaging his hands from hers to tip her face up. Staring tenderly into her tear-drenched eyes, he teased, "Seems to me that I should be the one crying."

His brave attempt at humor served only to suck Penelope deeper into her vortex of remorse. Though his words were uttered in jest, the truth of them tore at her conscience. She should be soothing him, not vice versa.

"I'm sorry to behave like such a ninny," she whispered brokenly. "It's just that I can't bear to see you hurt."

His smile was warm as he brushed away a newly fallen tear with his thumb. "You're not a ninny and don't apologize for caring. Your tender heart is what I love best about you."

Penelope shook her head ruefully. "But I feel so useless. Surely there's something I can do to make you more comfortable."

"You could stop crying. This little bump on my head isn't enough to warrant your tears. Why, I've taken worse thrashings from your brother during our friendly boxing matches."

"The doctor doesn't seem to think that bump such a small matter," she pointed out, nodding up at Doc Larson.

Seth made a droll face. "This bump might present a problem for some men, but as you yourself have pointed out on numerous occasions, I've got an inordinately hard head."

"Hard head or no, son," the doctor interjected, snipping the catgut after his final stitch, "you'll need to take it easy for a few days. You can't be too careful with head wounds." With that cryptic warning, he began to clean and repack his instruments.

As he worked, he recounted several Hallie-like hidden-injury-turned-fatal tales, each after which Penelope mouthed to Seth, "I told you so." To which he rolled his eyes and hardened his jaw into a more stubborn line.

When the doctor's cleanup was complete and his fee paid, he gave Seth one last admonishment to rest, then left. As soon as the door closed behind him, Penelope strode to the bed.

"You heard the doctor," she said. "We'll get you tucked all cozy into bed, then I'll ring for some ice. Hallie taught me how to make a proper pack for the head."

"We're going to the dance."

"Oh, for pity's sake. Don't be a mule," she exclaimed. "You're in no condition to go anywhere, much less dancing."

"I'm all right," he protested, rising to his feet with a care that belied his words.

"All right? Ha! Just look at you! You're teetering like a drunken bar hound." She braced her hands on her hips and scowled at him. "How do you expect to dance when you can barely stand?"

He shrugged his uninjured shoulder. "Maybe I'll just sit and watch you." His most beguiling smile appeared. "Have I ever told you how much I love to watch you dance?"

She emitted a snort of exasperation.

"No? Well, I do. There's nothing I like more than to see your cheeks flushed pink and your eyes gleaming with pleasure as you float across the dance floor. I've never seen anyone who enjoys dancing as much as you."

Penelope's eyes widened with sudden understanding. "Are you worried that I'll be disappointed at having to miss the dance? Is that what all this nonsense is about?" She advanced toward him, shaking her head. "For God's sake, Seth. Staying here and making sure that you're all right is far more important to me than some silly dance." As she came to a stop before him, she added, "In fact, I want to take care of you."

"And there's nothing I want more than to lie in bed and let you fawn over me. But I can't. And not just because I'm worried about disappointing you. I know you well enough to know that you'd never put your own enjoyment ahead of my well-being."

"Then, why?" she wailed, growing more bewildered by the second. "What's so important about this dance?"

"My mother."

Though he'd whispered the words, Penelope was as taken aback as if he shouted them. "Your . . . mother?"

Seth's gaze touched hers then, his eyes dark with turbulent emotion. "I lied when I said I'd come to Denver out of a fascination for the West. My sole reason for coming was to find my mother. The Pinkerton Agency traced her here. I happen to know that she'll be at the dance tonight, and I want to see her."

"You've been here all this time and haven't approached her?"

He looked away, but not before she saw the crushing ache in his eyes. "I didn't know what to say."

Penelope's heart bled at the raw pain in his voice, prompting her to wrap her arms around his waist and pull him into her embrace. Tilting her head back in an attempt to glimpse his downcast face, she said, "An introduction is a good start."

Seth shook his head, his expression lost in the shadows of his hair. "It would be easier for me to meet her anonymously at first, preferably in a social setting. After I've studied her awhile, I'll be better able to determine how to approach her."

"And the dance tonight is your first opportunity to do that." The utterance was a statement, not a question.

He nodded. "I don't know when or if I'll ever get another chance quite as perfect as this one."

Convinced more by the quiet desperation in his voice than by his words, she declared, "Well, then I guess we'd better get busy. It's going to take me a while to tame that mane of yours."

Seth raised his head, smiling his thanks. The tender gratitude of that smile went straight to Penelope's heart, warming her from the top of her well-coiffed head to the tips of her satin-clad toes. Basking in the satisfying glow, she led him to the dressing table, where she bid him to sit. After fetching a basin of fresh water and several clean towels, she began the painstaking task of setting his hair in order.

In preoccupied silence she worked, section by snarled section, sponging and combing his hair. When she came to the area around the wound, she paused to glance doubtfully at his reflection in the mirror. He seemed perfectly relaxed, sitting with his eyes closed and a faint smile curving his lips.

"Seth?"

"Hmm?" He slit open one eye.

"I need to tend the area around the wound now."

He opened both eyes then, meeting her anxious gaze in the mirror. "After all the years I've spent tugging tangles from this overgrown rat's nest, my scalp isn't overly tender. Do what needs to be done. I'll be fine."

As Penelope separated the blood-caked strands, carefully scrubbing at the dark streaks with a wet, soapy towel, she muttered, "It's no wonder you've developed such a tough scalp. I've never seen anyone with so much hair."

He looked at her with inquiry. "Think I should cut it into a proper, gentlemanly style?" Damn if he didn't look serious.

"Don't you dare!" she exclaimed, laying a possessive hand over the tawny length. "I love your hair! It's beautiful and unique, like you. Besides, I doubt I'd recognize you without it."

"After twenty years of living beneath it, I doubt I'd recognize myself," he countered, smiling.

"Twenty years? Goodness! Has it been long that many years?"

"As ancient as it makes me feel to admit it, yes." He fingered a damp lock thoughtfully. "When I was a child, I worked at a mill where they'd line us boys up every month and crop our hair to the scalp. After ten years of having it clipped, I vowed never to wear it short again."

Penelope did some quick calculations in her head. "Why, that means you started working when you were only—"

"Six," Seth supplied casually.

"Six! Dear God, Seth! I knew children worked at those places, but I never realized that some of them were so young."

"Most aren't. But I was tall and smart for my age, so no one at the orphanage bothered to point out my tender age."

"But you were just a baby! How could anyone be so inhuman?" she wailed, her heart weeping for the ill-used child he'd been.

"The orphanage was overcrowded, and they were glad to get rid of what children they could."

"How terrible that must have been for you!"

Seth shrugged. "No worse than the orphanage. My first job was that of bobbin doffer. Since I didn't have to watch the machine constantly, I was allowed to play with the other doffers during those idle periods. The hard work came later."

"It's a wonder you're so strong and healthy," Penelope declared, dropping her hands from his now clean and smoothed hair. "I've read the most dreadful things about those mills, accounts of children being beaten by heartless overseers and of workers dying in terrible accidents or of lung rot."

"Most children learned early on to avoid the whipping room," Seth replied. "One trip was certainly enough to break me of any thoughts of mischief. As for accidents, well, those happened, and a few of the workers did develop bad lungs." He shrugged. "But enough of this gloomy talk. We have a dance to attend."

She nodded and moved to the desk to retrieve her reticule. Pausing a moment to rummage through it, she produced a crumpled length of pink ribbon. "Here. I want you to carry this with you tonight . . . to bring you luck with your mother."

Seth grinned. "Is that your infamous lucky ribbon? The one you're always threatening to wager?"

"One and the same."

"And what makes it so lucky?"

"It was tied around the volume of poetry you gave me the first time you told me you loved me," she replied with a saucy grin. "In my book, that was the luckiest day of my life."

Chapter 21

It was just after eleven when Seth reined the buggy horse to a stop in front of the Vanderlyn house. By the sights and sounds that greeted him, it was apparent the dance was in full swing.

Laughter, drifting on strains of gay music, spilled from the imposing brick structure, flooding the dark street with a warmth rivaled only by that of the hundred blazing lights. Men, smoking and speaking of things not fit for feminine ears, congregated in tight clusters on the spacious front yard, while women in wildflower-hued gowns relaxed on the sweeping veranda, passing gossip behind their fans.

To most people the scene would be pleasant, even welcoming. But to Seth it was like a spoiled apple: deceptively tempting on the outside, repulsively corrupt on the inside; the rotten core of which was Louisa Vanderlyn and all her false goodness.

After paying a youth to watch the hired horse and buggy, he led Penelope up the long brick walkway, conscious of the admiring looks they drew from the onlookers. He smiled wryly when he caught a feminine whisper describing him as a dazzling dream of a man. What man wouldn't look dazzling with a beauty like Penelope on his arm? Still smiling, he handed his dance tickets to the maid at the door, then stepped into the well-appointed foyer.

By the looks of the entry hall, with its richly paneled walls and gracefully curving staircase, it was obvious that Louisa had done well for herself. Not that Seth needed to see all this elegance to know that. He knew the Vanderlyns' every profit and, of late, every loss, right down to the penny.

Perhaps when they were forced to sell this house, and that time was almost upon them, he'd buy it and burn it to the ground. A bonfire to his broken hopes and dreams—an inferno of hate.

Yet for all his knowledge that vengeance would soon be his, Seth felt no sense of pleasure or vindication. He felt oddly lost, afraid. And as he paused at the ballroom door to hand his top hat and evening cape to a starchily uniformed maid, that fright sharpened into a piercing shard of pure panic.

Stop being a shrinking coward, he commanded himself, disgusted by his own spineless quailing. Wasn't this the moment he'd dreamed of? The one he'd plotted so cunningly to bring about? He should feel exhilarated, vitalized by the heady thrill of at last realizing that dream. Yet here he was paralyzed by fear, terrified to face the woman who was his mother.

"Do you see her?" Penelope asked.

Seth stared at her blankly.

"Your mother. Is she here?" She nodded at the milling throng before them. While he'd been busy mollycoddling his cowardice, they'd somehow made their way into the over-crowded ballroom and now stood on the far side.

"Well?"

At her third query, he reluctantly swept his gaze over the colorful assembly, systematically examining and eliminating every fair-haired woman present. At last he shook his head, oddly more anxious than relieved by his temporary reprieve.

"Are you absolutely certain she's going to be here?"

"I'd stake my life on it."

She considered the matter for a moment. "Perhaps she's in the ladies' retiring room. If you tell me who she is, I'll check for you." Her beautiful eyes, made all the more striking by the tenderness glowing in their emerald depths, begged him to take her into his confidence. To prove that he truly trusted her.

Aching with regret, Seth shook his head. "I can't. Not until after I've spoken with her. Alone."

She turned away, but not before he saw her look of pained disappointment. Feeling like the world's biggest bastard, not an unusual sensation for him of late, he sought to assuage her hurt.

"It's not that I don't trust you, sweetheart. I do, wholeheartedly. And if it were only me involved in this, I'd tell you in a second. However, since there is someone else's feelings and reputation to consider, it's only fair that I con-

sult her in private before making any possibly damaging dis-
closures."

Not that he cared a whit for Louisa Vanderlyn's feelings,
or for her reputation for that matter. By the time he was finished with her, the former would be thoroughly shattered
and the latter nonexistent. It was just that he didn't want Penelope present for what was sure to be an ugly showdown
between Louisa and himself.

Apparently she wasn't buying his excuse any more than
he was, for her shoulders remained rigid, her head turned
away.

"Miss Leroux?" A rather homely young man with slicked-
back hair and a spanking new set of clothes stood before
them, a nervous tick working in his cheek as he stared long-
ingly at Penelope. "I was wunderin' if you might be persuaded to take a turn on the dance floor with me?" He shot
a flustered glance in Seth's direction. "Uh, with yer permission, of course, sir."

Seth gave Penelope's would-be suitor an impatient frown.
"Later. Miss Leroux and I are having a discussion right
now."

The man ducked his head in abashed assent and turned to
leave, only to be stopped by Penelope in the next instant.

"Wait!"

When he looked back, she smiled sweetly and extended
her hand. "I believe I would like to dance, sir. Thank you."

The man hesitated, glancing uncertainly at Seth. Grudgingly he nodded his consent.

Seth stood there for a long while, watching Penelope and
her partner romp through the Virginia reel, stalling his
search for Louisa by convincing himself that he needed to
make things right with Penelope before he progressed. But
when the reel lines broke and she was immediately swept up
by a new partner in a schottische, he knew he could procras-
tinate no longer. By the covetous looks being cast at Penelope by the scores of unattached men—all race losers who'd
paid ten dollars to attend the dance—he'd be waiting all
night for a word with her.

With a fresh rise of dread gripping at his belly and an
ache gathering in his head, he skirted the chattering mob and
slipped into the hall. It was cooler out here, with the crisp
night breeze reaching from the open front door to caress his
hot cheeks. As he paused to decide his best course of action,

he reached up and massaged his throbbing head. Perhaps there was some truth to those hidden-injuries-turned-fatal stories after all.

Pushing the morbid thought from his mind, he steered back toward the front door. Like a proper hostess, Louisa might be out on the porch circulating among her guests.

But she wasn't there, nor was she on the front lawn or in the garden out back. With his frustration exceeded only by his growing tension, Seth returned to the house. As he stood at the foot of the staircase in the now deserted foyer, contemplating searching the hall on the side of the house opposite the ballroom, he was startled from his thoughts by a strong but distinctly young female voice behind him.

"Are you looking for the necessary room, sir?"

Seth swung around so fast that his head spun, and he had to grab onto the carved pineapple newel post finial to keep from toppling over. Within a span of seconds, a vision-blurring pain exploded behind his eyes, accompanied by an almost incapacitating swell of nausea. Mercifully the pain receded as quickly as it came on, and his eyes focused on the owner of the voice.

Sitting on the stairs, peering curiously at him over the top of a magazine through thick-lensed spectacles, was a girl of sixteen or seventeen. It was no wonder he hadn't noticed her. Her deep green gown blended with the homogenous hue of the carpet runner beneath her, while her chestnut hair seemed one with the richly stained woodwork against which she leaned.

Here, Seth thought, *sits the epitome of a wallflower.* Poor creature. She'd probably been relegated to reading on the stairs by her lack of dancing partners. That thought tugged at his heartstrings. Hoping to lift what he was sure were her low spirits, he flashed her his most charming smile.

The girl sighed, looking more impatient than impressed by the grin that had never before failed to beguile its recipient. Laying the open magazine across her knees, she pointed toward the hallway from which he'd come. "The necessary room is three doors up from the ballroom. The last time I went past, there was a long line. So if you're desperate to relieve yourself, I'd suggest you go out back and find a likely bush." With an air of dismissal, she picked up the magazine and turned the page.

Seth gaped at the cheeky baggage, at first taken aback and

then amused by her unladylike address. Perhaps it wasn't her appearance, but her tongue that put the young pups off. The longer he looked at her, the more certain he was that that was the case. If he didn't miss his guess, and he seldom did where women were concerned, there was a tearing beauty lurking behind those spectacles.

After several moments she lifted her gaze from the page and fixed it on him. Her spectacles slipped down her nose a fraction. "What are you staring at?"

"You."

"I ascertained as much," she replied dryly. "Why? Haven't you ever seen a woman read before?"

"The *Home Journal,* yes. The *National Police Gazette,* no."

She shrugged, a gesture that sent her glasses inching closer to the end of her nose. "I have no interest in learning how to make infant pap or in reading about the fancy doings of society."

"But you are interested in crime and mayhem?" Seth teased.

"Not so much in the mayhem as in the solving of the crimes and the workings of the criminal mind. I intend to be a detective someday, maybe even work for the Pinkerton Agency." She glared at him over the top of her spectacles; her back stiffened visibly with defiance, as if she expected him to laugh.

Moving from the newel post to sit on the stair two steps below hers, Seth mused, "A detective, you say?" He peered up at her stubbornly set face for a moment and then nodded. "Yes, I believe you will make a fine detective."

Her mouth gaped open. "You do?"

He nodded again. "You have a fine mind and a bold manner, both desirable attributes for a detective. Add that to your interest in the subject matter, and I'd say you're almost there."

"But I'm a female," she blurted out, as if the fact had somehow escaped his notice.

He chuckled, thoroughly enjoying himself . . . well, at least as much as his aching head would allow. "You most definitely are a female. And by all appearances, a remarkable one."

She flushed at that, her defensive demeanor instantly softening. "Do you know that you're the first gentleman who's ever believed me . . . about being a detective, I mean? Most laugh and tell me that females can't be detectives."

"I believe a woman can be or do anything she wants. Just like a man," he informed her honestly. "In fact, my best friend's wife is living testimony to that belief. She's a doctor."

"A doctor? Really?" She looked intrigued by that notion.

He gave his head an affirmative jerk, a move that rewarded him with an intensified throbbing in his temples. He must have looked as bad as he felt, for the girl observed:

"You look as if you could use that lady doctor's services." She leaned forward to peer at his face, her glasses slipping until they dangled precariously from the end of her small nose. "What happened? Did you get caught in a brawl at one of those Blake Street saloons?"

"Nothing as mundane or with as good of odds as that," he replied, his hand itching to push her spectacles into a more secure position. One more move and they'd be in her lap. "I was set upon by a band of masked men whose motives baffle me."

Her almond-shaped gray eyes brightened with fascination, and to Seth's relief, she shoved the straying glasses back to a safe perch on the bridge of her nose. "Masked men? Unknown motive?" Her voice was breathless with excitement. "Now, there's a mystery worth solving." Meeting his gaze with a look that was eager yet uncertain, rather like a puppy who wants to be petted but half expects to be rebuffed, she said, "If you tell me about the attack and give me the details, I might be able to figure out who did this to you and why."

Seth stared into her wide eyes, magnified to look even wider by the thick lenses covering them, wanting to deny her request. How could he, in good conscience, allow this charming child to pry into what could easily turn out to be dangerous business?

Yet how could he not? For more potentially tragic than the results of her meddling would be the crushing of her dreams. And by denying faith in her and her abilities now, no matter how well intended that denial, he would be doing just that.

Eyeing her anxious face solemnly, he mused, "Perhaps you're just the detective to solve this mystery, at that." By the luminosity of her responding smile, he knew that he'd made the correct decision.

Settling back against the turned baluster, he proceeded with his tale, selectively recounting those details he deemed suitable for a young lady's ears. He'd just gotten to the part where he'd dragged himself down the road to find his horse placidly grazing in a field, when Louisa emerged from the unexplored hallway.

Without pausing from his story, Seth marked her progress. She was headed their way, drawing nearer as the seconds ticked by. When she was almost to the stairs, he averted his face, expecting her to pass. To his surprise, her footsteps faltered and then halted, as did his speech.

"I see you've made a new friend, Lisbet," she commented, her voice surprisingly warm and sweet.

"Oh, Mama!" The excited girl bound to her feet, sending the forgotten magazine on her lap tumbling down the stairs. "This gentleman was set upon by a band of masked men just a half mile from our brewery, and he's consented to let me be the detective on the case. He was just giving me the details."

Mama? Our brewery? Seth stared up at the girl, who was beaming down at him as if he were some sort of hero, too stunned to speak. *This lovely, intelligent, and thoroughly delightful chit was his sister?* His next thought made him as sick as his dizziness had a quarter of an hour earlier.

When he finally destroyed Louisa's life, he'd also wreck Lisbet's. All her hopes and dreams, her youthful exuberance for life would be quashed, perhaps forever, beneath the grinding despair of shame, poverty, and ruin.

"And does your client have a name?" Louisa prompted.

Lisbet's smile faded, and she flushed a shade of pink that perfectly matched the sunset sky in the still-life hanging behind her head. His little sister was a regular chameleon.

"Oh! I'm so sorry," the girl exclaimed. "Where are my manners? I never even bothered to introduce myself."

"My fault entirely," Seth reassured her, hating to see the light of her pleasure dimmed by her distress. Miserably aware that that vital flame would probably be snuffed out forever when he exacted his revenge, and fiercely determined to make it burn as brightly as possible, for as long as was feasible, he continued, "As a gentleman, I should have undertaken the duty of introductions. Allow me to remedy the situation now."

With his face still averted from Louisa, Seth rose to his

feet. Once again dizziness engulfed him, this time with a vengeance that almost brought him to his knees. Emitting an involuntary moan, he grabbed at the handrail, wavering like a sapling in an autumn wind as he waited for the spell to pass.

Unlike his first disconcerting bout of dizziness, however, his equilibrium didn't return immediately. And as he stood clinging to the handrail, battling as much to hold on to the contents of his stomach as to regain his balance, he felt a strong arm wrap around his waist. Through the crashing pain in his head, he heard Louisa command Lisbet to support him on his other side and then felt himself being urged away from the rail, securely braced between the two women.

"Sir? Do you want to sit down on the stairs, or do you think you can make it to the front parlor?" The worry in Louisa's voice was unmistakable. "You can lie down in the parlor."

For the first time since his mother had come upon him talking with Lisbet, Seth raised his head and looked straight at her. Even through the fog of his hazy vision, he saw her expression change from one of sympathetic concern to one of baffled recognition. Then, as if chasing away a troubling thought, she shook her head and her face cleared.

If Seth hadn't been so wretched, he probably would have chuckled. He'd have bet his entire fortune *and* Penelope's lucky ribbon that he could guess exactly what that thought was. Instead he muttered, "I think I can make it to the parlor."

She nodded and smiled. "Good. It's best that you lie down for a while."

Clucking like a couple of mother hens over a newly hatched chick, the two women led him to a spacious parlor pleasantly decorated in shades of salmon, blue, and ivory.

The pain in Seth's head was excruciating now, almost unbearable, and as the women eased him down onto the firmly stuffed salmon brocade sofa, the pain exploded behind his eyes. Then everything went black.

Slowly Seth emerged from the peaceful darkness, drawn by the feel of something cool and wet against his face.

What the hell? he wondered, groggily moving through the shadow lands of unconsciousness toward the light of lucidity.

Music? He heard music and the sound of distant voices. Dully he fought to raise the leaden weight of his eyelids, struggling to recall time and place.

A concert? No ... a ball, he amended as he recognized the lively piece as a mazurka. *But where?*

Louisa! He bolted upright, his eyes ripping open as the evening's events came flashing back. Wildly he stared at the woman by his side, a gaze that she returned with a serene smile. She'd dragged one of the dozen rosewood rail chairs lined up against the far wall to a position next to the sofa, and with the wet towel dangling from her hand, had been bathing his face.

Laying a firm but reassuring hand on his shoulder, she pushed him back down again, murmuring, "Rest. You fainted."

Fainted? Then he remembered his crippling pain. Gingerly he touched his temple. Odd. When he'd sat up just now, he hadn't felt even the slightest bit dizzy, and aside from the understandable soreness from the stitches, his head didn't hurt at all.

"How long was I unconscious?" he finally asked.

"Just a few minutes. Lisbet has gone to send a servant for the doctor. By the looks of your face, you need one."

Seth shook his head. Again, no pain. "She needn't bother. Dr. Larson examined me earlier this evening. I'm fine."

Frowning, Louisa laid her hand on his forehead as if checking for fever. "Men who are fine don't faint."

Her motherly gesture touched something deep inside him, drawing a response so fierce and elemental that his enmity cringed beneath its humbling force. With an impulse so strong as to be almost undeniable, his troublesome heart urged him to lay his head on her lap and beg her to stroke his hair the way he'd seen mothers do as they calmed their crying children. He longed to hear her croon all sorts of soothing silliness, to feel special as she fussed over his comfort. He wanted to experience the tenderness a treasured son received from his loving mother.

But you're not her treasured son, and she's never been your loving mother, his head challenged his heart. One by one the dismal visions of his childhood rose from his memory. And for the first time in a long while, his mind defeated his emotions.

Bitterness, blistered with rage and scorching with disappointment, seared his desperate yearnings, charring them to ashes of hate. For all her benevolence and saintly posturings, Louisa Vanderlyn was nothing but a conniving, murderous bitch.

And his reason for coming here tonight was to confront her with that fact. Once again focused on his purpose, Seth jerked his head away from her hand and sat up.

Apparently his expression reflected his mood, for she flinched away, eyeing him with sudden trepidation. For a moment they simply stared at each other; he, with a lifetime full of fury and resentment; she, with a look that wavered between apprehension and bewilderment.

Slowly a chilled smile twisted his lips. "Louisa Van Cortlandt," he intoned at last, sharply enunciating each syllable like a judge announcing a death sentence.

Her eyes narrowed. "Do I know you, sir?"

He leaned into the lamplight to fully illuminate his features. "Do you?" he countered, cryptically.

Her brow furrowed as if she ferreted the farthest reaches of her mind. "Your face is familiar, though your name and acquaintance elude me."

"Our acquaintance *eludes* you?" He let out a harsh grate of laughter. "My guess is that you've *chosen* to forget it."

"It's those whom I would most like to forget who I make a point of remembering best," she replied with admirable aplomb. "Especially if I suspect that they bear me ill will, which by your tone you obviously do."

"Oh? And are there many such persons?" he purred, his trap baited and ready to spring.

She shrugged. "A few. But none of consequence."

"Most people find my wrath of great consequence. Downright ruinous, in fact." He leaned back, chuckling humorlessly. "By the way, how are your fortunes of late?"

Louisa stiffened visibly, her eyes now little more than glittering slits. "Just by the asking of that question, sir, it's apparent that you already know the answer."

"You're a very perceptive woman, Mrs. Vanderlyn. But then, such keenness is a Van Cortlandt family trait, as are intelligence, ruthlessness . . . and insanity.

She took the bait. "Just who are you?"

The trap snapped shut. "Most people call me Seth Tyler." He paused for a significant beat. "You may call me son."

"S-son?" The blood drained from her face, and for a moment Seth was certain she would faint. Instead she surprised him by leaning forward and almost reverently touching his trademark Van Cortlandt jaw. "Oh ... how could I have been so blind? There is so much of your father about you."

Seth yanked his face away, as infuriated by the tender longing in her voice as by her touch. Bent on ripping away her glowing mask of heartfelt welcome and exposing the malevolent face he knew lay beneath, he gritted out, "How that resemblance must pain you. Or is a cold-blooded killer like you capable of feeling such emotions as pain, shame, and remorse?"

"Killer!" she gasped, looking as taken aback as if he'd declared that he was Christ Almighty and had just risen from his tomb. "I-I don't understand."

She was good, he'd give her that. So good that if he weren't familiar with her evil nature, he might have been fooled into believing her seemingly guileless protest of ignorance.

Unfortunately for her, he knew exactly what kind of monster she was. "Don't play coy with me—Mother," he hissed, spitting out the maternal appellation as if it were a mouthful of poisoned wine. "I know all about you and how in your selfishness you ordered me, your unwanted bastard son, murdered at birth."

To Seth's satisfaction, she turned a shade more ashen. "I—I never ordered you killed." Her voice quavered with emotion. "That was my father's doing. He didn't want anything to ruin his plans to wed me to our neighbor. I didn't find out about his treachery until seventeen years later."

She slipped from her chair to kneel at his knees. Reaching forward to grasp his arms in her trembling hands, she declared fervently, "I loved you from the very instant you were born. So much so that when I was told you had died several hours later, I went almost mad with grief. You were everything to me."

Hating her all the more for saying what he'd once so desperately yearned to hear, and knowing that she lied, Seth roughly shook her hands away. "Keep your lies for someone who will believe them. They're not going to save you. I know the truth, and that truth gives me the right to destroy you."

"But you don't know the truth!" she protested, latching on

to his arms again as if in doing so she could also connect with his mind. "If you'll just listen—"

"I didn't come here tonight to listen to your false tales of motherly woe," he interjected brutally. "No matter how creative and entertaining they may be. So save your breath."

"Then, why did you come?" Her hands dropped back to her sides, as if in defeat.

"Because I wanted you to know who I am and why I'm ruining you. More importantly, I wanted to warn you that there will be no clemency granted on your loan. In one week's time, unless you can come up with thirty-seven thousand dollars plus interest, I will foreclose on the brewery. And you, dear Mother, will lose everything."

Trembling now with barely contained fury, Seth reached into his waistcoat pocket to retrieve his cigar case, only to pull it out again, empty. In his rush to get to the dance, he'd forgotten his talisman of calm. Expelling a crude oath, he pushed himself to his feet, unrepentant when his abrupt move sent Louisa sprawling backward onto her gray-silk-clad backside.

Staring coolly down at the woman at his feet, he bit out, "Now, if you'll excuse me, I have a dance to attend." With that, he sketched an elegant bow and then turned on his heels to leave.

"I really did love you," she said quietly, stopping him at the door. "And despite everything, I love you still."

Seth paused, his back to her.

"Perhaps someday when you're no longer blinded by your lust for vengeance, you'll remember that and seek me out to learn the real truth. I hope so. I want my son back."

Her voice was filled with such yearning, her words so compelling, that for one mad moment he was tempted to succumb to her siren's song. But then he reminded himself that this was a desperate ruse to save her own skin, and his sanity returned.

Emitting a strangled noise of disbelief, he stalked from the room and made his way back to the foyer. He had to get away from this house, away from *her* before he let down his guard and did something stupid.

"Seth! I've been looking everywhere for you." It was Penelope. She stood by the staircase, her cheeks pink and her anger at him obviously cooled from dancing. Moving forward to take his arm, she whispered eagerly, "Did you find her?"

"Yes."

"And?"

"We're leaving."

"But—" she began.

"You!" he barked rudely at a passing maid bearing a fresh bowl of punch. "Where will I find our wraps?"

"I'll have Daisy help you, sir," the harried woman replied.

"Forget Daisy," he ground out, feeling more and more trapped as the seconds ticked by. "Just tell me where they are, and I'll get them myself."

She sighed and shifted the heavy bowl a fraction to point at a door beneath the stairs. "In there."

Without bothering to so much as nod his thanks, Seth strode to the closet and made quick work of finding their garments. Not pausing to allow Penelope to wrap her shawl around her shoulders, he grabbed her arm and all but dragged her out the front door.

"Seth! Will you slow down and tell me what happened!" Penelope implored, almost running in an effort to keep pace with his long, angry stride.

Too choked up by his warring emotions to reply, Seth scooped her up and practically tossed her into the waiting buggy. The second his own backside touched the seat beside her, they were off. Whipped to a furious gallop the horse tore down the hard-packed dirt street, pulling the light buggy with a speed that made it sail over the ruts and bumps.

Turning a deaf ear to Penelope's shrieked prophecies of broken necks and cracked heads, Seth continued his mad flight until they were well out of sight of the house. Only then did he slow the horse to a fast trot.

"Damn it, Seth! Were you trying to get us killed?" Penelope exploded. "Have you completely lost your mind?"

Seth snorted at her choice of words but didn't deign to reply. All he wanted right now was to curl up with a bottle of whiskey and forget his disturbing encounter with his mother. He definitely wasn't in the mood to listen to Penelope's haranguing.

Unfortunately for him, she was just gearing up to her tirade. "You owe me an explanation, Mr. Tyler, and an apology as well. Why, you practically dragged me out of the Vanderlyn house, and in full view of half the town. I've never been so humiliated in my life! I can just imagine what everyone must be thinking!"

"I don't give a damn what they're thinking," he muttered, peering at the address on a building. Damn! Six more blocks to the boardinghouse. He urged the horse back up to a safe gallop.

"That's because you don't have to go out on that stage every single night and face those same people you disgraced me in front of," she pointed out with a sniff. "I don't know how I'll ever be able to bear the embarrassment, what with knowing that they'll be looking at me and remembering me being hauled down the sidewalk like a felon caught in the act of a heinous crime. Whatever possessed you to behave in such an ill-bred manner?"

When he didn't reply, she persisted, "Well? What do you have to say for yourself?"

He slanted her a jaundiced look. "Your yammering is giving me a headache, and I need to relieve myself so badly that my bladder will probably burst if we hit another bump."

"That isn't at all what I meant, and you know it!"

He shrugged his undamaged shoulder. "Well, it's all I have to say for myself." Two more blocks to peace and quiet.

To his relief, she remained silent for the next block.

When she continued, it was in a different vein. A more discomforting one. "Was the meeting with your mother really so awful?"

Keeping his tone light, he replied evasively, "Let's just say that your lucky ribbon didn't live up to its reputation."

"What happened?"

"It's not worth discussing."

"You meet your mother for the very first time and come away practically foaming at the mouth and gnashing your teeth, and you say the event is not worth discussing?" She sounded incredulous. "I'd say it's something that very much needs to be discussed."

He reined the horse to a stop in front of the boardinghouse. "Perhaps I didn't phrase my reply quite right. I don't wish to discuss what happened."

"Of course not. You never wish to discuss anything with me. You've never given me credit for having a lick of sense." She eyed him with exasperation. "I don't know why I bother with you."

"I don't know why you bother, either," he replied, ready to break from the tension of the evening's events. "Now, let me walk you to the door. I wasn't joking about my need to relieve myself." With that curt rejoinder, he slipped to the street and moved around the buggy to help her down.

Penelope, however, remained firmly rooted to her seat, ignoring his outstretched hands of assistance. "As infuriating as you are at times, I bother with you because I love you. And because I love you, I'm not going to leave you alone while you're in such terrible distress." She folded her arms across her chest, glaring down at him defiantly. "Now, if you truly need to relieve yourself as badly as you claim, you'd better start talking. I'm not budging until you tell me what's got you so upset."

With a snort of irritation, Seth reached up and hoisted her from the vehicle, ignoring the stabbing pain in his shoulder and ribs, and her squawk of protest. "Look sweetheart," he said brusquely, pulling her resisting form through the open gate and down the walkway. "I don't wish to discuss my mother with anyone, so stop taking all this so personally."

"But it is personal," she contradicted, jerking her arm from his grip at the foot of the front steps. "Anything that affects you affects me as well. If you hurt, I hurt. If you're upset, then so am I. That's an inescapable part of being in love."

Something deep inside of Seth snapped as he recognized the dangerous truth of her words. Grasping her arms and giving her a shake, as if in doing so he could jolt some sense into her, he snarled, "I told you not to love me. Damn it, Penelope! I don't *want* you to love me!"

Ready to weep both at the grievous hurt in her eyes and that in his heart, he pushed her away and stalked back to the buggy.

It was all for her own good, wasn't it?

Chapter 22

Not love him? Ha! Penelope fumed as she climbed the shadowy back staircase of the Shakespeare saloon. Did the blasted man really think that she could shut off her love as easily as if it were water flowing from a faucet?

Did he truly want her to?

Of course not! she scolded herself, remembering his agonized declaration of love earlier that evening. The foolish man was simply indulging in more of his misguided gallantry, the same heroic nonsense he'd pulled in New York. Well, she'd be damned if she was going to let him get away with it this time, especially when it was so obvious from the ache in his eyes that he was hurting badly inside. Why, she'd never in her life seen a man more in need of loving, and she intended to do just that, despite his pigheaded efforts to push her away.

That is, if she could find him. Penelope's brow furrowed with bafflement as she stepped onto the second-floor landing.

Incensed at his martyrization of their love and determined to tell him exactly what she thought of his asinine sacrifice, she'd stormed to his hotel room, heedless of the dangers of walking the streets alone a night. Luckily for her, her furious muttering coupled with her murderous glower proved an effective deterrent of unwanted attention, and she'd navigated the sidewalks with no more harassment than a lewd catcall or two.

Unfortunately her luck hadn't extended to finding Seth, for his hotel room was deserted. And so with her wrath tempered by mounting anxiety—what if he'd been attacked again?—she'd come to the saloon, the only other place she could think to look.

And if he wasn't here? Stubbornly she pushed the troubling thought from her mind and started down the gloom-shrouded hallway toward Seth's office. Except for the faint rustling of her skirts, quiet reigned supreme. Apparently the saloon girls and gamblers who roomed at the Shakespeare were still at the dance.

As Penelope came within sight of the office, her heartbeat quickened with hope. Light spilled out from around the ajar door, casting warm halos upon the scarlet drugget floor covering, bearing glowing testimony to life within. Crossing her fingers that it was Seth and not Monty inside, she peeked into the room.

Her luck had returned. Sitting at the enormous mahogany desk, trimming a cigar, was Seth, He'd discarded his jacket, collar, and tie, and now sat with his shirt open at the throat and his sleeves rolled up to his muscular forearms. At his elbow were a three-quarter full bottle of whiskey and a box of cigars, to his right a small dish full of butts.

She stared for a moment, taken aback by the sight. Seth Tyler smoking? Why, the man hated everything about tobacco. Oh, she knew he always carried a cigar case, but she'd assumed the cigars were used as gentlemanly offerings to his acquaintances.

Hovering uncertainly at the door, she watched while Seth jammed the cigar into his mouth and struck a match. Tipping his head forward, he touched the flame to the stubby brown end and took a deep drag. There was an explosive cough followed by a smothered curse. Hacking as though he were choking to death, he yanked the cigar from his lips and snubbed it out in the dish.

To Penelope's bewilderment, he immediately pulled a fresh cigar from the box and repeated the whole process. It wasn't until he'd snubbed it out unsmoked and began on yet another, that she began to understand what was happening. Where she fidgeted or chewed her nails when she was distressed, he apparently trimmed and lit cigars. And by the mounting pile of butts in the dish, it was clear that he was as miserable as she'd suspected.

With her confidence returning in a bolstering flood, she pushed the door the rest of the way open and stepped inside, her determination to soothe him strengthening by the second.

He glanced up sharply, a cigar dangling from the corner of his mouth, a lit match in hand. When he saw who it was, he scowled. "Come to harp at me some more?" he muttered.

Chalking up his surly greeting as more of his principled stupidity, she smiled sweetly and approached the desk. "I'd rather have a civil conversation than harp at you."

"We don't have"—a graphic oath and the cigar flew from his lips as the flame of the now burned-down match licked his fingertip. With a furious wave of his hand, he extinguished the flame, then shoved his singed finger into his mouth.

Leaning over the cluttered landscape of papers, whiskey bottle, and cigars, Penelope gently pulled his hand away from his lips and drew it to her own to kiss the tip of his damaged index finger. "My poor darling. You've had a rough day, haven't you?"

Seth made an impatient noise and snatched his hand away. "What do you want? I'm sure you didn't come to kiss my wounds."

Turning a deaf ear to his querulous tone, she sauntered around to his side of the desk, stopping only when she stood next to his chair. Tenderly stroking his bruised cheek, she said, "That's exactly why I've come. You've been beaten up both inside and out this evening, and as the woman who loves you, it's my duty to kiss away your hurts."

He jerked his head away from her caressing touch and glared up at her. "Damn it, Penelope! I told you not to love me!"

"Since when have I done what you told me?"

He grunted.

Undeterred, she translated his grunt. "That's right. Never. And I'm not about to start now, especially when your orders are so contrary to both our best interests."

Emitting an incredulous snort, he swiveled his revolving desk chair around until his back was to her. "Oh, and since when is it in a woman's best interest to shackle herself to a madman?" he growled, pulling yet another cigar from the box. "Seems to me that that's a sure way for her to waste her life."

It was Penelope's turn to snort. Enough was enough. And she'd had enough of Seth Tyler's mule-brained postulating! Not certain whether she intended to kiss him or slap him, she grasped the back of his chair and spun him back around to face her. Before he could protest, she sat on his lap straddling his knees and pulled the cigar from his lips. Bracing her hands on either side of his head to force him to look at her, she exclaimed:

"Now, see here, Seth. You're going to listen, and listen good. I love you, and by your own admission you love me, too. It seems to me that if we can love each other after all the hurtful things we've said and done, then we're destined to be together."

Making a noise that perfectly articulated his skepticism, Seth tried to look away, but she refused to let him. "Stop being a fool! Love like ours isn't something you can sweep under the carpet and pretend doesn't exist. It only gets stronger with time, more insistent with denial."

"Penelope—" he began.

She laid a finger over his lips, silencing him. "No. I know what you're going to say. You're going to tell me that you won't allow me to waste my life loving a madman." She shook her head. "But don't you see? I can't help loving you. And by denying me the fulfillment of expressing that love, my life is nothing but an accumulation of empty, fruitless hours spent yearning for you. It will never be anything more. Not as long as we're apart."

Seth moaned and closed his eyes, but not before Penelope saw the conflicting emotion warring in their pain-darkened depths.

Determined to turn the tide of his inner battle to her advantage and thus win their war of wills, she twined her arms around his neck, pleading softly, "Please, Seth. Don't make me waste another moment. Let me fill my hours with the satisfaction of loving you. Let me fill yours with the warmth and security of being cherished. It's not too late for us. We can still make a wonderful life together."

"Please," he implored, the emotional texture of his hoarse voice a heartbreaking weave of torment, grief, and longing. "Please don't do this to me. I can't bear it."

Relentless now, for in her heart she knew this might be her last chance, Penelope gambled on a desperate hunch. "Then, look me in the eye and tell me that you don't want me." She pressed her face so close to his that their now rapid breath collided and mingled. "Say you no longer care for me. Do that, and I'll never again bother you with my feelings."

For what seemed like forever, he sat motionless. Then his lashes lifted, revealing eyes as empty as those of a dead man. His expression not betraying even a flicker of emotion, he disengaged her arms from his neck and pushed her away. After impassively surveying her from head to toe, he looked her straight in the eye.

Penelope's soul cried out in anguish as she waited for him to utter the words that would destroy their future. She'd been so certain of his feelings for her, so confident that her love could defeat his terrible fears. But it was apparent she was wrong.

Flexing his jaw into a hard line, he began, "I don't want you and"—his mask of composure crumbled then, and he choked.

"Seth?" she whispered, freeing her arms from his slackening grasp to take his face in her hands. He looked awful. Misery so raw and intense contorted his features, that it was all she could do not to weep at the sight of his suffering.

"I can't. God forgive me, I can't say it. I love you," he groaned. "I love you so damn much that I wish I'd hurry up and lose my mind so I can escape this hell of wanting you."

"But what if you don't go mad? You'll have thrown away our happiness for nothing," she argued, her hope reaffirmed by his words. "So why not wager on love instead of doom? I'm willing to gamble on us. Won't you do the same?" Her voice dropped now, becoming soft, beseeching. "Please, Seth. Give our love a chance. You won't lose, no matter what happens. I promise."

"I want to love you . . . more than anything else in the world." His voice was broken, quivering with anguish. "But I . . . I'm . . . afraid." A tear escaped with that confession, followed by another, and yet another. "I . . . I . . ." His speech faltered then, and when he was finally able to continue, his voice was little more than a ragged whisper. "Help me . . . please. Help me find the courage to believe in our dreams."

The sight of Seth, always so strong and self-assured, defeated and crying for help hurt Penelope almost beyond bearing. Yet she knew that as wrenching as this moment was for them both, that it was only through this purging of his fears he could find the peace that would allow him to at last accept her love.

Desperate to give him what little ease she could during the painful process, she leaned forward and pressed a soft kiss to his tear-salted lips. "I'm here, love, and of course I'll

help you. I'll always be here when you need me," she
crooned, wrapping her arms around his trembling torso to
hold him close. Gently, so as not to hurt his scalp wound,
she pulled his head down on her shoulder and began to
stroke his hair. "There now, darling. Go ahead and cry.
You've held it in for too long."

With a choked sound that seemed ripped from the bottom
of his soul, Seth broke completely. Crushing her into his
needy embrace, he buried his face against her neck and released his maelstrom of pent-up emotion.

Great heaving sobs ripped from his chest, eloquently ar-
ticulating the dark hopelessness shadowing his soul. His hot
tears, falling against her bare shoulder like summer rain,
spoke of a torment almost beyond salvation. His convulsive
kneading, his every strangled gasp, told of a despair too
deep for words.

For a long while Penelope simply held him, stroking his
hair while whispering of her dreams for their future, promising him forever. Beneath the caressing comfort of her
hands and voice, the savage fury of his weeping gradually
abated and ceased. Then she, too, fell silent. Lost in the
emotional aftermath of the moment, they sat slumped in
each other's arms; he, physically drained yet spiritually
strengthened; she, sending up prayers of thanks for giving
her this second chance at loving Seth; both feeling as if
they'd come home at last.

They remained like that until Penelope felt Seth's head
move against her shoulder and heard him heave a faint sigh.
"Better, love?" she murmured, kissing the back of his bowed
neck.

He nodded and raised his head, grinning sheepishly as he
rubbed at his red eyes. "Sorry. I didn't mean to carry on like
that. I haven't cried in over thirty years."

Never had he looked more vulnerable; never had he been
dearer to her heart. Smiling her reassurance, Penelope caressed his tear-ravaged cheek. "You should do it more often.
I've found that nothing cleanses the soul better than a good
cry."

He sniffled noisily. "If you'll hold me like this, I just
might do that."

"You've got yourself a bargain, Mr. Tyler. I stand ready to
hold you anytime you need me," she declared, fumbling in
his waistcoat pocket to withdraw his handkerchief.

"The way I've felt lately, I'm probably going to be spending a lot of time in your arms. Are you sure you want to waste your time coddling a blubbering, sorry excuse for a man?"

"It's not a waste of time, and you're not a sorry excuse for a man. In my book, it takes a mighty courageous man to admit and face his fears. And I feel privileged that you're allowing me to help you conquer them." With that, she lifted his handkerchief to his nose and commanded, "Blow." He complied, loudly. "Good." She kissed his forehead and then tossed the now crumpled handkerchief onto the desk. "Now. Do you feel up to talking?"

"Depends."

"On what?"

The gleam in his bloodshot eyes was almost wicked. "On whether or not you'll remain on my lap. I might need to be held again, you know. And I don't want you too far away."

It was all Penelope could do not to wrap her arms around him and give him a fierce hug. Here was the sweet, loving Seth she remembered and adored. However, since she didn't want to hurt his broken rib, she satisfied herself by giving him a quick peck on his lips. "You couldn't make me move even if you wanted to."

"Good. Because I wasn't going to let you go." He tipped his head down and returned her kiss. "Now. What shall we talk about?"

"Us and our future, for starters." She waited breathlessly, expecting to see uncertainty shadow his eyes at the mention of the future. But he merely nodded, his expression untroubled.

Exhaling her relief, she began, "I want us to be together, of course. All the time and in every way." She paused a beat, half expecting him to protest. When he didn't, she continued, "You don't have to marry me if you don't feel comfortable doing so. I'll be perfectly happy living with you as your—"

"Don't even say the word," he interjected sharply. "You'll marry me, and do it in front of all our friends and neighbors. If we're going to gamble on our future, we're going to gamble big."

Penelope stared up at him, too choked with joy to speak.

Raising one eyebrow in query at her silence, Seth asked, "That is, if you'll have me."

"Have you? Of course I will! I love you!" Giddy with excitement, she recklessly threw herself against him and gave
him the hug she'd so scrupulously avoided only moments
earlier.

He smiled, wincing slightly. "If you love me, then kiss
me."

Penelope didn't need any further prompting. Looping her
arms around his neck, she pulled his face close to hers. She
wanted this kiss to be special, to be as tender and memora-
ble as their first one. Not quite certain how to make it so, yet
determined to try, she closed her eyes and drew his mouth to
hers.

Just like the first time, and every time thereafter when
their lips touched, there was a feeling of rightness, a bond-
ing as if each had been created for the specific purpose of
loving the other. As if he, too, felt the draw of destiny and
was overpowered by it, Seth crushed her to his chest, his
mouth moving hungrily against hers. Boldly he thrust his
tongue between her lips, probing and plundering her mouth.
With every responsive move, Penelope's tension from wanting him mounted until she was feverish with anticipation.

Panting harshly, his whole body trembling with the power
of his emotions, Seth at last dragged his lips from hers.
"Dear God," he groaned, staring at her as if he couldn't
quite believe she was real. "I dreamed and wished, but I
never really believed that I'd have you in my arms again.
I'm half-afraid you're some mad delusion and will vanish at
any moment."

"Then, love me and reassure yourself that I'm real," she
murmured, melting against him with a sigh.

Enslaving both her heart and mind with the seductive tenderness in his eyes, he buried his hands into her curls and
pulled out the pins. When her hair fell tumbling down her
back, he gently combed his fingers through its length.

As he twisted the end of one jet ringlet around his finger,
he murmured huskily, "Many a night I lay awake imagining
doing this. Sometimes I get so worked up picturing you naked amid all this tangled glory, that I ache till dawn." He
glanced up from his coiled handiwork, grinning wryly. "It's
a wonder I haven't been driven stark-raving mad by my unrelieved lust."

Thrilled by his confession, yet too embarrassed to tell him
so, Penelope assumed the formidable air of her childhood

nanny and playfully scolded, "Well, you're not to carelessly risk your sanity like that again." She wagged a reproving finger beneath his nose. "The second you feel even the slightest ache, you're to come directly to me and let me take care of it. Understood?"

Seth laughed and kissed her scowling lips. "Perfectly."

Still pretending, she leaned back and fixed the enormous bulge at his groin with a look of mock disapproval. "What is this, young man?" She poked the bulge with an accusing finger, almost giggling when he jumped and gasped in response. "Shouldn't you have brought this problem to my attention sooner?"

He tried to look properly contrite, but a chuckle slipped out, spoiling the whole effect. "I promise I will in the future."

He looked so endearingly roguish with his battered face and crooked grin, that a smile stole to her own lips as she began to unbutton his black brocade waistcoat.

"Since you're in such a desperate state, my boy," nanny Penelope continued, "we'll let your shameful lapse pass. But just this once. Understood?"

"It won't happen again," he promised, his eyes dancing with devilry. "So what do we do now that I'm forgiven?"

"I think the most important matter right now is to get you out of your clothes and get to work on relieving your lust." Giving him an un-nanny-like leer, she removed his waistcoat and tossed it to the floor, then pulled out his diamond shirt studs.

"You know," he murmured as she began yanking his shirt-tail from his trousers. "An important part of this lust-relieving business is that the lustee divest the reliever of her clothes."

Nanny was back. "Patience, young man," she admonished sternly, pulling him forward so she could slide off his shirt. After discarding the garment, she pushed him back in his chair to admire his masculine beauty.

His shoulders were wide and powerful, his chest broad with each muscular contour perfectly delineated by hard, sculpted bulges and deep, shadowed grooves. Though the bandage bracing his ribs covered much of his midsection, it couldn't disguise the spectacular taper of his torso.

Filled with breathless awe, Penelope let her appreciative gaze trace the dramatic curve, down the steeply narrowing line from his expansive chest to the sinewy leanness of his waist, stopping only when she came to the top of his trousers.

Staring hungrily at the black fabric, she gently traced the edge of his waistband with her finger, visualizing the rippling grid of belly muscle she knew lay beneath. When she could bear the anticipation no longer, she reached for his buttons.

With an agonized groan, Seth caught her fingers. He, too, was beyond bearing. So much so, that he knew if she opened his trousers and touched him now, his passion would explode. And he'd dreamed of this moment too long to let it end in such disgrace.

Ignoring her moue of protest, he drew her fingers to his lips to kiss them. "Oh, no, my greedy princess. Not yet. There are certain rules to be observed in this lust-relieving business. One of which is that both lustee and reliever get equal time admiring the other's body. Now, since this is usually done in stages so as not to drive the lustee into a state of premature madness, I suggest that I take a turn and remove your bodice now." Hopefully the tedious task of unfastening all those hooks would give him a chance to regain some of his now almost nonexistent control.

Penelope stared at him through the thick fringe of her lowered lashes as if considering his proposal, then nodded.

Gingerly Seth pulled her against him. Ignoring the way her soft cleavage seemed to burn his chest skin, he pushed her hair aside and began to fumble with the fastenings at the back of her bodice. As he'd hoped, by the time he clumsily wrestled the last hook free, his frustration had pushed his need back to a manageable level.

More in command now, he tilted his head down and gave Penelope's rosy earlobe a soft nip. He felt rather than heard her moan against his chest. "Sweetheart," he whispered. "You need to sit back now so I can remove your bodice."

With a purring sigh, she complied.

Never had she looked more desirable than she did now, wantonly straddling his knees with her bodice sagging off one shoulder and her unbound hair tumbling around her passion-flushed face. She was staring at him with such adoration, such undisguised longing, that Seth had to grasp the edge of his chair to keep from ripping himself from his trousers and taking her where they sat.

As if sensing his precarious state and eager to incite him to action, Penelope removed her bodice herself. Her motions slow and teasing, she slipped one arm out of its tiny puffed sleeve, then the other, holding the bodice in place the whole time so as not to give him the briefest peek at her hidden delights.

When he responded simply by gawking like a lust-besotted fool, which is exactly what he was at that moment, she gave the frilly bodice a tempting wave. "Rules are rules, and you said that it's the lustee's job to disrobe the reliever." She lowered her violet and ivory silk shield a fraction to give him a titillating glimpse of her décolletage. "Unless you haven't the constitution for the task?"

The teasing challenge in her voice snapped Seth out of his moonstruck stupor. Growling in reply, he snatched the bodice from her hands and tossed it aside. His bold growl faded to a whimper of defeat. God help him! How was he supposed to look at such feminine perfection and still maintain himself?

He smiled with sudden inspiration. Perhaps the answer to his problem was as simple as extinguishing the light. In the past they'd always made love in the dark, and the lack of visual stimulation had done much to bridle his runaway passions.

But would it work now that he'd had an eyeful of her gorgeous body? Desperate enough to try anything, Seth reached over Penelope's shoulder to turn down the flame of the desk lamp.

"It's all right," she said, stopping him. "I don't mind if you see me naked."

"Well, I do mind," he growled.

There was short pause and then, "You don't . . . like my body?"

"Not like it?" Seth drew back, staring at her in amazement. "I like it too damn much. Just the sight of it is almost enough to make me lose myself. That's why I need to turn down the lamp."

She returned his stare for a moment, then laughed, a low, husky sound. "A man of the world like yourself losing himself at the sight of a half-naked woman? Really, Seth! How absurd."

"Not so absurd when the half-naked woman happens to be you," he retorted, his urgency almost peaking as she stood up and let her skirts slowly slide to the floor. The fabric of her drawers was so sheer that to Seth's almost ruinous disconcertment, the dark triangle between her legs was clearly visible.

As she posed before him, one hand on her sweetly rounded hip, the other resting on the tantalizing swell of her breasts, something inside him snapped.

Sobbing with the agony of long-repressed need, he lunged forward and grabbed her, raining reckless kisses on her face and breasts as he wrestled her to the plush red carpet. When she lay sprawled beneath him, moaning in kiss-dominated submission, he rose shakily to his elbows to stare down at her flushed face.

"I wasn't joking about your beauty," he croaked. "If I don't turn down the lamp now, I don't think I can hold back long enough to make love to both our satisfaction."

Smiling tenderly, she wrapped her arms around his neck to pull his face close to hers. "Remember my first morning as your valet, how I found you aroused and thrashing with desire in your sleep? Since then, I've dreamed of seeing you like that again, only writhing in response to my touch instead of to a dream."

Pressing her forehead to his to capture his gaze, she implored, "Make my dream come true. I can think of no greater satisfaction than watching your body respond to my touch and seeing the look in your eyes as you find your pleasure."

Inflamed as much by her words as by her nearness, Seth pulled from her embrace to straddle her hips. Knowing that he was probably going to regret his words, yet powerless to resist her sweetly whispered plea, he said, "Very well, my lovely reliever. The lamp stays lit, but only if you agree to let me pleasure you first."

"The lustee wants to bargain does he?" Penelope purred, running her finger across the flesh abutting his waistband.

A gasp exploded from Seth at the resulting shock of erotic sensation. Sucking in a labored breath, he pulled her hand away and pinned it to her side. "It's a lustee's privilege to negotiate the terms of his relieving. Especially if he's in love with his reliever and wants to assure her sexual satisfaction."

"And the terms?"

"Are that you promise not touch me in an inflammatory manner, which includes no rubbing up against my male parts, until after I've given you your woman's pleasure. I will not take my release until I've given you yours first."

She slanted him a seductive look. "And then you'll allow me to do my duty as a reliever?"

He nodded.

"Then, what choice do I have? If I don't agree, you might drive yourself mad by foolishly prolonging your lust. And since I'm not about to allow you to do that"—she stretched her arms above her head in voluptuous surrender—"I give myself over to your sensual ministrations."

Chapter 23

S eth gazed down at the temptress beneath him, uncertain for the first time in his two decades of sexual experience how to proceed. Never had a woman aroused him as Penelope did, never had he been so anxious to please. What if, for all his best efforts, he failed to satisfy her?

Stop it! his heart commanded. *You've never failed before and you're not going to now. Don't you remember the times you loved her? How naturally she responded to your touch? You love her and she you. Let that be your guide, and you won't go wrong.*

Trusting in his heart's wisdom, he leaned down and gently kissed Penelope's slightly parted lips. "Do you know how much I adore you?" he asked, his fingers finding and releasing the fastenings at the front of her corset.

She reached up to stroke the long line of his back. "If it's even half as much as I adore you, then it's a great deal."

He moaned and pushed her arms back to her side. "Don't!"

"Our deal specified that I not touch you in an inflammatory manner, and I'm not," she said, lifting her arms again.

Gently, but firmly, he wrestled them back to the carpet. "Sweetheart, your every touch inflames me. So unless you want to breach our agreement, in which case we turn down the lamp and grope blindly in the dark, I suggest that you just lie still."

It was Penelope's turn to moan. Didn't the blasted man know that she found his body as irresistible as he did hers? That she couldn't help touching him? And the smell of him . . .

She closed her eyes and inhaled as Seth bent near. A heady fusion of heated male flesh and spicy soap assailed her nostrils, robbing her of all awareness but that of wanting him; a sensation that deepened as he finished removing her clothes.

His touch was gentle, almost caressing as he drew off her undergarments; his lips soft and worshipful as he kissed each newly exposed area. So sensual were his ministrations that by the time she lay completely naked, her body was charged with an excitement that was both shocking and pleasurable.

Breathless with expectation, she waited for Seth to transport her to the next level of passion. But to her squirming dismay, he sat back on his haunches and simply looked at her.

Taut seconds stretched like hours as he surveyed her. Just when she was sure she could bear the anticipation no longer, he reached down and lightly trailed one finger down her torso.

Electrified, she arched up, crying her pleasure. Smiling in a way she found indecently thrilling, he slowly retraced his tingling path, meandering upward until he reached the base of her breast. Then his hand stilled.

Aching to be fondled, Penelope begged, "Seth . . . please."

"Please . . . what?" he purred, his tone provocatively baiting.

She rubbed against his hand. "Please . . . touch me."

He chuckled. "What's this? The reliever succumbing to the carnal wiles of her lustee?" As if testing his theory, Seth ran an experimental finger up through the cleft between her breasts.

She whimpered and jerked in positive response.

"Aha! As I suspected." His grin grew very wicked. "There's a penalty for such weakness," he said, drawing rings around one breast, circling nearer and nearer to the hardened peak.

"Penalty?" she managed to grasp, writhing in a desperate attempt to propel his hand to her aching nipple.

Deliberately ignoring her efforts, he stopped just short of the rosy border to explain. "When a reliever falls victim to passion while in the line of duty, she is required to endure whatever amorous punishment the lustee deems appropriate."

"Which is?" she groaned.

He stared at the stiffened crest less than an inch from his finger as he seemed to consider. Finally he replied, "I think it only fitting that a weak-willed reliever be pushed to her libidinous limits, at which point she must beg for mercy. This will show her that she can endure more lust than she suspects, and she might not be so quick to surrender in the future." With that decree, he traced the very edge of her puckered areola.

The resulting sensation was almost more than she could bear. Her breath coming out in sharp, trembling sobs, Penelope did as he demanded. "Please, Seth. I'm begging you."

"Tell me what you want," he coaxed.

Emitting a quivering moan, she seized his hand and pressed his fingers against the throbbing point. "Stroke me here."

"Like this?" he murmured, advancing to the center to capture the crest between his thumb and index finger.

Her breath quickened at the contact, and she was unable to do more than mew her approval.

Alternately stroking and tweaking, he teased her sensitive peaks, rousing her responses until they hit a fevered pitch. When she lay panting and thrashing, he replaced his fingers with his lips. Just when she was certain she would die from pleasure, he pulled away.

"Seth," she moaned, slitting her eyes open to peer imploringly up at him. "Please ... more. I need ..."

"Oh, no, my wayward reliever," he chided in an oddly strangled voice. He, too, was flushed and breathing hard. "It's much too early in your discipline to grant clemency."

"But I ache so badly," she protested, dragging his hand from his side back to her breast.

Sensual fire flared in his eyes at her confession. "You ache do you? Hmm." His hand skated from her breast, moving lower. "Shall I guess where?"

Her only reply was a breathy sob. He was drawing tight, looping lines down her torso now; exciting, tickling manipulations that sent molten spurts of desire rushing through her veins. When he paused to tease her navel, her belly muscles convulsed with a violence that rocked her entire body.

"Let me see, now. Where do you ache?" His hand rounded the contours of her belly, gliding down until it brushed the dark triangle of her intimate hair. "Am I getting warm?"

"Hot," she gasped, a searing ache exploding low in her

belly. He dipped lower. "Very ... h-hot." Her thighs parted instinctively.

Her panting breath now punctuated by moans, Penelope waited for him to reach her core, to stroke the pulsating bud of her need. With maddening leisure he inched nearer and nearer. Then he was at her nether lips. His touch delicate, he outlined the needful swollen edges, occasionally grazing yet not quite touching the moist, burning flesh within.

Sobbing her torment, Penelope strained her legs apart, frantically thrusting her hips in a desperate attempt to guide his fingers to the fiery center.

"Please, Seth," she begged. "I can't stand any more."

"Tell me what you want," he purred.

"Touch me," she moaned. "I'm begging you."

"Where?" His fingers hovered just over her core.

She reached down and crushed his hand against her. "Here. Touch me here ... the way you used to."

Laying on his belly between her legs, he gently separated her passion slickened flesh and blew on her hardened bud.

White-hot sensation streaked up through Penelope, sending another rush of moisture flowing to her already soaked womanhood. Bucking her hips impatiently, she wailed, "Seth ... touch me!"

Ducking his head, he examined her closer. "You're beautiful down here." He briefly touched her inflamed nub.

She shrieked, her body jerking in savage response.

Moving away to stroke her wet folds, he continued, "You're like a newly unfurled rose with your soft pink petals open like this to expose your nectarous center." She whimpered with exquisite shock as he returned his finger to her pulsating core.

Over and over again he caressed her, sometimes with unbearable gentleness, others with a firmness that almost drove her over the edge. Just as she mounted the crest of her rapture, he pulled back, leaving her writhing in heated agony.

For a moment he lay motionless between her legs, watching her feverish twisting, his labored breathing echoing hers. When her frantic gyrations had calmed a fraction, he inched his face nearer to the tormenting source of her need.

Fixing her with a smoldering gaze over her womanly mound, he mused, "I wonder if your nectar, like that of a rose, is sweet to the tongue?" He eyed the object of his speculation thoughtfully. "Shall I sample it to find out?"

Just the suggestion was enough to make Penelope moan. Taking that moan for the yes it was, Seth dipped his tongue into her scalding depths, tasting her deeply and intimately.

Screaming her pleasure, she rocked against him, eager to accept every thrilling motion of his mouth. The sweeping sensation of his private kiss was everything she remembered and much, much more. Repeatedly he drove her to the edge, only to retreat and begin again. When her ache was so intense that she wept with need, he at last released her.

Screaming at the rapturous violence of her climax, she shoved hard against his mouth, the stimulation of his tongue against her core heightening a hundredfold as spasm after powerful spasm jolted through her. Never had her climax been so intense, never had she felt so alive. And by the time the lingering bliss of the last contraction faded, she was certain she'd died and gone to heaven.

As Penelope lay in the aftermath, too glutted with contentment to move, she murmured, "That was . . ." but words failed her. How could she possibly describe what she'd just felt?

Grinning, Seth covered her body with his, drawing her into his embrace. "Learned your lesson, did you?"

She slanted him a wicked look. "For the moment, yes. But I'm certain I'll need frequent refresher courses."

He leered back. "Which I always stand ready to provide."

"So I've noticed." She grasped his taut buttocks and gave the bulge in his trousers a significant rub with her pelvis.

His breath exploded from his chest in a moan. "Don't, sweetheart! I can't—" he choked, frantically trying to squirm away.

She tightened her grip on his backside, stopping him. "A deal is a deal," she reminded him. "I kept my end of the bargain. Now I expect you to do the same."

Without waiting for his reply, Penelope shoved her small body against his powerful one, pushing him until he rolled helplessly over onto his back. On top now, she straddled his hips. Eyeing his magnificent body with lascivious intent, she laid her palm over his erection, scolding,

"Careless man! You're so aroused I can feel you throbbing all the way through your trousers. Now unless you want to further endanger your sanity, I suggest we relieve you immediately."

Seth snatched her hand from his hardness, his pink flushed face darkening to a hectic red. "Not . . . yet. I need . . . just give me a few minutes to"—he sucked in a whistling breath between his gritted teeth—"compose myself."

"Compose yourself? But why? I'm going to relieve you."

He closed his eyes, his face twisting in a way that perfectly conveyed his discomfort. "Because I've yearned for this moment for over two years, and I don't want to ruin it by losing myself the second you open my trousers."

Penelope stared down at him in amazement. "Are you really that close? I mean, I haven't even touched your 'thing' yet."

"You don't have to. It's been so long since I've had sexual relations, that the mere idea of having it fondled is almost enough to drive me over the edge."

"A long time?" She shook her head skeptically. "But what about that saloon girl I found you with your first night here?"

His flush deepened to burgundy. "Nothing happened. I just led you to believe it had. I wanted you to think that I was a heartless bastard and that I no longer cared for you."

"But—"

"Oh, at first I intended to make love to her," he admitted, deaf to her interruption. "I was desperate to spend my lust so I wouldn't get aroused every time I looked at you. But I couldn't do it. All I could think of was you"—he turned his head away, as if ashamed—"and I simply couldn't get excited enough over her to do anything. In truth, I haven't been able to bring myself to have relations since I fell in love with you."

Penelope was speechless. Never had Seth done or said anything that touched or pleased her as much as this softly uttered confession. That he loved her so much as to deprive himself in such a manner was more than she'd ever dared to believe possible. When she finally spoke, her voice was as strangled as his. "You haven't had relations since our last time in New York?"

He nodded, his cheek still pressed against the carpet. "Nor did I have any for almost two years prior to our engagement."

"Two years before?" Her brow furrowed. "I don't understand."

"Remember the ball your brother gave the night before you left for your first musical tour?"

"Of course. How could I forget an occasion like that?"

"It was then that I realized I loved you. From that point on, aside from the three times we were together, I've been celibate. Before our engagement, I forwent relations out of respect for my feelings for you. Afterward it was because no other woman could measure up to you."

Tenderness swelled in Penelope's chest, making it difficult to draw a breath. Never in a million years had she expected to find a man who would love her so completely. Especially not an extraordinary one like Seth Tyler.

Resisting her almost overwhelming urge to take him in her arms and demonstrate the depth of her emotion, she lay her hand against his cheek, murmuring, "No wonder your control is so frayed. It's a miracle you've managed as well as you have."

"After waiting and wishing for so long, I want our love-making to be perfect. I want to hold you and hear your cries of pleasure as we find our release together." He implored her with his eyes. "But I won't be able to last long enough to do that if you don't give me a few minutes to regain my control."

Penelope pressed a kiss to his lips, then crawled off him. "I won't touch you again until you say you're ready."

For a long while they simply lay there sharing dreams for their future; he on his back with his head pillowed on his folded arms; she on her belly beside him, her chin propped up on her hands. As they were deciding how to furnish the still empty mansion he had built for them in San Francisco, Seth announced, "I'm ready to continue now, provided you take it easy on me."

"I won't torment you any worse than you did me," Penelope joked. Grinning at his responding groan, she rose to her knees beside him, her gaze admiring as she scrutinized his supine form.

He was such a beautiful man, both inside and out. And he deserved to be loved in a manner that would bring him the same kind of ecstasy he'd brought her. Her smile slowly faded. But how? What did she know about this pleasuring business?

Admittedly, nothing. She looked helplessly at the man before her. Wherever did she start?

Where had he started? Her gaze skimmed his impressive length as she tried to recall, finally halting at his hair. Remembering the sensual feel of his fingers combing through her own locks, she gently followed suit. He closed his eyes, sighing.

He looked so handsome lying there, his thick golden mane haloing around his head and a peaceful smile curving his lips. Thanking her lucky star, ribbon, and the being above for giving him to her, she leaned down and pressed her lips to his. Moaning, he dragged her into his embrace, deepening the kiss.

"Oh, no," she chided, pulling away. "We'll have no more of your lustee wiles. You'll lie still, as promised, and let me have my way with you."

"Oh, and what is your way?" he inquired, his grin roguish as he obediently returned his arms to his sides.

"This," she murmured, swooping down to reclaim his lips. This time she pinned his hands to the carpet with hers, forcing him to lie submissively while she plundered his mouth.

As she caressed his tongue with hers, he pulled away, gasping, "You . . . promised to take it . . . easy . . . on me."

Smiling down into his passion-flushed face, Penelope lightly ran her thumb across his lower lip, murmuring, "If I take it any easier, I won't be touching you at all."

Seth jerked his face away, an explosive groan ripping from his throat. "I can't—"

"Ssh, love," she soothed, tracing the strong angle of his jaw with her fingertips. "Relax. Let me make this experience everything you dreamed."

Seth tried. God only knows he tried to bear up manfully beneath her caresses. But when she began to tease his ear, at first fondling and then licking the ticklish inner contours, the resulting sensations were so sensual that he was unable to endure the torment. Yanking his head away, he groaned, "I can't do this! I just don't have enough control."

She lay a firm hand on his heaving chest. "Just calm down. I won't let you take your release before you're ready."

Seth slit open one eye to shoot her an incredulous look. He doubted if anything short of an act of God could stop him from spilling himself if she continued her erotic ministrations. When he said as much, she laughingly replied:

"You said that I was able to bear more lust than I knew, and you were right. I suspect you're equally capable." As if to prove her point, she leaned down and began kissing his chest.

Her tongue was warm and moist as she trailed licking kisses from his collarbone to his bandaged ribs, her lips soft yet insistent as she suckled on his nipples. Now and again she paused to nip at his chest hair, her tugging motions blatantly erotic in their gentleness.

Writhing in helpless urgency, Seth again broke. "Please stop. I'm about to . . ." To his everlasting relief, she did.

"All right, love," she agreed, sitting back on her haunches. "I'll stop and let you compose yourself, but only for a moment."

Seth grunted and closed his eyes, too entrenched in his lustful misery to do more. As he lay struggling to subdue his passion, certain his manhood would pop his trouser buttons at any moment, he felt Penelope lay her palm against his bandaged ribs. "No . . . not . . . yet," he gasped, his stomach muscles tightening in involuntary anticipation. "I need a minute longer. I—"

"Ssh. I'm not going to touch you like that yet. I was just wondering if your ribs are all right. Looking at you just now, I realized how careless I've been. All my hugging must have hurt."

He made a strained, raspy sound that was meant to be a chuckle. "When a man is as badly aroused as I am, no pain in the world is severe enough to distract him from his need. Lust is better than morphine, I always say."

Penelope eyed the swathe of white linen beneath her hand thoughtfully. "In that case, I'll have to keep you in constant lust until you're completely healed."

"Unless you kill me with an excess of it first, in which case I won't be feeling anything anyway," he muttered.

She laughed. "Well, since we don't want you coming to an untimely end, I'd better relieve your lust before it reaches a lethal level." With that she swooped down and pressed slow, shiver-inducing kisses to the narrow strip of exposed stomach between the bottom of the bandage and the top of his trousers.

When she'd completed that task with groin-tightening thoroughness, she slipped a finger beneath his waistband and gave it a meaningful tug. "You have one minute. Then these come off."

"Three," he moaned, his pelvis lurching in sizzling response to her knuckles grazing his belly. "Three . . . minutes."

"The lustee wants to bargain, does he?" She slanted him a crafty look. "Hmm. All right, then. What do you intend to trade for the extra two minutes?"

Seth frantically searched his passion-dazed mind for something to offer, something she would find irresistible. Foggily recalling her material weaknesses, he bid, "A five-carat diamond necklace? Your very own pet circus elephant? A shopping trip in London? Anything!" Hell. He was desperate enough right now to give her his favorite silver cigar case if she asked.

Penelope's expression was positively wicked as she considered his proposals. Suddenly she smiled and not in a way he found encouraging. "Two extra minutes to calm yourself in exchange for two minutes of you lying unresisting while I touch you intimately . . . both periods to be timed by your pocket watch, mine starting when you're completely naked."

Seth closed his eyes, groaning aloud. Didn't his lovely little haggler understand that in his inflamed state, enduring even a half minute of intimate fondling would be impossible? Suppressing a shudder at the very idea of suffering two minutes of such torment, he choked out:

"I hear Tiffany's has an emerald and diamond necklace, earrings, and bracelet set that once belonged to Marie Antoinette. Forget the two minutes of touching, and it's yours."

Her jaw dropped at his fabulous offer. Seth mentally chalked it up as a deal, for he knew Penelope to love both emeralds and history.

However, she came back with, "Tempting, but no. The jewels I want are far more precious than anything offered at Tiffany's." She shook her head. "Either you agree to two minutes of touching, or I remove your trousers now. We've argued for at least a minute."

Considering the fact that he was so far gone that he would disgrace himself for sure if she so much as brushed against his sex while undressing him, Seth had little choice but to groan, "All right. You win." Hopefully three minutes would be long enough for him to regain enough control to last during the removal of his trousers. As for the fondling, well . . .

Looking ready to crow her triumph, Penelope crawled over to their discarded clothes and retrieved his watch from his waistcoat pocket. Returning to his side, she dangled the timepiece before his eyes. "You have until one fifty-three to compose yourself; then I remove your trousers."

Minutes flew like seconds as Seth lay silently reciting Tennyson's "The Charge of the Light Brigade," in a wild attempt to distract his mind and nether regions from his over-stimulated state. Just as he mouthed, " 'While horse and hero fell, They that had fought so well,' " Penelope trumpeted, "Time's up!"

With unladylike eagerness she unbuttoned both his trousers and drawers, then moved to his feet to tug off his shoes and stockings. That chore completed, she began to draw off his pants.

Please, God, don't let her touch me yet, Seth prayed, his belly muscles contracting and quivering with jittery expectation. Apparently God was sympathetic to his plight, for she removed them without so much as grazing his male parts.

When he lay completely naked, she crawled back to his side and picked up his watch again. "It's one fifty-eight. I get to have my way with you until two o'clock sharp." She pried open his clenched hand and laid the timepiece in his palm. "Here. You tell me when my two minutes are up." With that, she turned her attention to the jutting flesh at his groin.

Seth squirmed fitfully as she leaned near, tilting her head to one side as she surveyed it. Dear God! Why didn't she just touch it, and let him get the initial shock over with quickly? Couldn't she see that his erotic anticipation was killing him?

After a half minute of scrutiny, according to the watch, her hand strayed to his belly. For several seconds it lay over his navel, motionless. Then it slowly drifted downward, her fingertips lightly tracing the arrow-straight line of hair leading to the object of both their carnal fixation.

Seth's breath strangled in his throat, his stomach muscles heaved as she moved nearer and nearer. By the time she stopped just short of his twitching staff, his pelvis was bucking wildly.

Ignoring his frantic undulations, Penelope idly coiled his intimate hair beneath her finger, musing, "If my feminine parts are a rose in the garden of sensual delights, then your male ones are a tulip." Drawing tight circles in his curls, her finger looped lower. "A very pink, very long-stemmed tulip," she elaborated, spiraling yet closer to his source of need.

Seth sucked in a deep breath, bracing himself for the electrifying jolt of her touch. To his frustration, she veered to the right, completely bypassing him. He exhaled in a hiss. Damnation! At this point, her careful avoidance was far more torturous than any amount of fondling could be.

Penelope's hand rounded his tension-flexed upper thighs to drop between his legs. "You see," she explained, "like a tulip, your 'thing' springs from a bulb." She cupped his masculine sac in her palm to illustrate her point.

A guttural cry ripped from Seth's throat, his back arching up at the resulting shock of exquisite sensation. Dear God! If his body reacted like this to her merely holding his sac, however would he survive her touching his arousal?

Handling him like fine china, she gently squeezed and caressed each taut globe, her every thrilling move wrenching him with an urgency so intense that it took all his self-control not to moan aloud; a control that shattered the moment she pressed her lips to him.

As he lay wracked with deep tremors, certain his groin would burst with her every lick and kiss, she slid her hand upward.

Sensing what she was about to do and too aroused to withstand it, Seth slapped a protective hand over himself, groaning, "No. Please. Don't. I can't take any more!"

"Ssh. Of course you can," she crooned, prying his hand away and replacing it with her own. "There. Is that so terrible?"

He moaned and turned his face away, unable to reply in his struggle to contain himself. Couldn't the woman see how torturous this was for him? How perilously close to the brink he was?

Apparently not, because her fingers encircled his shaft then and pulled it away from his belly. As if measuring his thickness and turgidity, she lightly rubbed up and down the throbbing length, stroking the underside with her thumb as she moved. He groaned and tried to pull away, but she held firm.

"One more move like that, lustee, and you'll forfeit an additional two minutes of fondling," she warned.

His breath coming out in ragged sobs now, Seth snatched up the watch at his side and peered desperately at the time. The big hand was just a hair away from being dead center on twelve. Just a few seconds more ...

Sensation, intense and raw, surged up through his loins as her finger brushed across the delicate flesh of his unsheathed tip. His whole body stiffened with momentary shock; then a hoarse scream tore from his throat, and his hips rocked with uncontrolled violence. At her next caress, he felt a hint of telltale dampness, the warning sign that he was almost to the point of no return. Smothering a curse, he jerked himself from her hand.

"Time's up," he growled, rolling to his side.

She laid her palm against his hip. "Seth—"

"Don't ..." he rasped, squirming away. "I'm ... starting to ... lose myself." This time she did as he asked, sitting quietly by his side while he lay in a quivering heap, squeezing himself hard in a desperate attempt to retard his climax.

After a couple of minutes, he felt Penelope's hand on his hip again. "Seth?"

Feeling in control again, he rolled onto his back. "Hmm?"

She bent down and kissed him. Holding him captive with her lips, she straddled his hips. "Love me," she whispered. "Please love me." Without waiting for a reply, she thrust down and impaled herself on him.

Seth almost screamed his pleasure as he slipped into her embracing flesh. Dear God! She felt so good, so perfect. Clutching her waist in a viselike grip, he arched up and drove himself deeper. She moaned and writhed, rubbing her core against his shaft as he pulled back to drive in again.

"You feel wonderful," she sighed, matching her rhythm to his.

He was about to return the compliment, when a frightening realization dawned; one that made him cease all motion.

"Sweetheart," he murmured, grasping her buttocks to still her as well. "We have to stop for a moment. It's important."

"But why?" she groaned.

"You'll see," he assured her, urging her resisting form off him and crawling to the desk.

She moved to his side as he began rifling through the bottom drawer. "What are you looking for?"

"This." He pulled a small blue paper packet from beneath a dog-eared copy of *Carriage Monthly,* and handed it to her. When she shot him an inquiring look, he urged, "Open it."

She did, her expression even more bewildered as she held up the object inside by its red ribbon ties. "What is it?"

"A condom, of course."

She looked blank.

"A man puts it over his 'thing' during intercourse so as not to impregnate his partner or to contract any nasty diseases. Not," he added, "that I'm worried about you being diseased."

She glanced from the condom to his erection, then smiled mischievously. "Oh, I see. You slide it over your 'thing' like this," she eased it over him. "Then you secure it with the ribbon thus." She tied a perky bow at the underside base of his staff. Leaning back to admire her handiwork, she mused, "You do look rather dashing all tied up like a Christmas present, but doesn't being covered up like that ruin your pleasure?"

Seth stared down at his festooned masculinity thoughtfully. "I don't know. I bought them after I found out about my father, and since I haven't had relations since, I haven't tried them."

"And I see no reason for you to start now," she declared, untying the ribbon. "I want to feel you, not your condom."

He stopped her hands. "You know that's impossible. We can't run the risk of having a child."

"I've already taken precautions," she assured him, pulling her hands from his to tug the condom off.

That bit of news gave him a jolt. "Oh? And what reason have you had to learn of such matters?" he inquired darkly.

She grinned, obviously amused by his jealous tone. "I intended to seduce you after the dance, so I discussed it with one of the saloon girls at the race today. She told me that if I put a sponge soaked in vinegar deep inside me, that I wouldn't conceive. I did so just before I got dressed this evening."

Seth gaped at her in flattered amazement. "You went to all that trouble so you could seduce me?"

"Yes. Now, how about making my trouble worthwhile?"

She didn't have to ask twice. With one wild swipe of his arm, Seth cleared a space on the desk, sending papers, cigars, and the whiskey bottle scattering to the floor. Then he lifted Penelope to the edge. She leaned back and opened her legs in wanton invitation. Again, she didn't have to ask twice.

Hot and primed to take her, Seth thrust inside, convulsively grabbing her thighs, pulling her body hard against his. With a hunger that mirrored his, Penelope tilted her hips up and wrapped her legs around his waist, eagerly accepting every plundering inch of him. Over and over again Seth buried himself inside her, angling his body so that his shaft caressed the bud of her desire with every motion.

Penelope grasped his clenched buttocks and rocked against him, matching him stroke for thrilling stroke, moan for impassioned moan. "Seth! Oh, dear God!" she sobbed, tightening around him in an intimate embrace that almost sent him over the edge. "This is . . . this is . . . oh!"

Seth's thrusts were frenzied now, his moans escalating into hoarse cries of pleasure as they strained and arched against each other, their bodies in perfect harmony as they coaxed each other nearer and nearer to mutual bliss. Then Penelope slammed her pelvis against his, screaming her rapture.

Seth, too, lost control. His climax was like nothing he'd ever felt before: intense, electrifying; a thrilling, pulsating charge that raced up through his sex and exploded in his groin, shooting sparks of glorious sensation throughout his entire body. Strangled with ecstasy, he swept Penelope into his embrace and buried his face against her lilac-scented hair, quivering uncontrollably as he shoved into her depths one last time.

For several delicious moments they remained in that position: she with her legs clenched around his waist, clinging to his torso; he holding her suspended in air, his face pressed against her hair and his sex buried in her.

At last she tilted her head back to look into his face. Smiling the luminous smile of a woman in love, she reached up and tucked his tousled hair behind his ears. "Was it everything you dreamed?" she whispered, staring anxiously into his eyes.

He tipped his forehead against hers. "Everything and more."

Chapter 24

H is luck was about to change; he could feel it in his bones. After a night of losing, his big win was only a card turn away. All he needed was a thousand dollars for ante.

Miles crept down the hallway toward Seth Tyler's office, his body tense as he listened for signs of life behind the closed doors on either side. All was quiet. He smiled. Yes. His luck was definitely improving. None of the saloon girls were up yet, though the sun was rising steadily over the horizon.

As for the other boarders, he hadn't seen his mother since the evening before, and the rest, gamblers all, were downstairs waiting for him to produce his ante for the final poker hand.

Which was exactly what he was doing, producing his ante ... courtesy of Tyler's office safe. Since the bank had been closed the day before in honor of the race, the entire Thursday-night take was in the safe along with the usual saloon cash reserve. From what he'd gleaned eavesdropping on Monty and Tyler yesterday morning, there was over two thousand dollars stashed in there.

Miles's grin turned sly as he stopped at the office door and pulled several oddly bent wires from his pocket. While he knew that most people thought him a complete fool, he was clever at picking locks and adequate at cracking safes, both skills learned from his mother's larcenous lover when he was fifteen. Though he seldom got up the nerve to actually use those skills—much to his mother's displeasure—when he did, he was rarely suspected of the crime, for few people believed him capable of forming a serious thought, much less possessing the cunning for safecracking.

He figured it would be the same here, if anyone even noticed the theft in the confusion that was sure to result when

Tyler's mutilated body was hauled into town, probably sometime this morning. Miles giggled as he fitted a wire into the keyhole. He intended to be at Lorelei's side when she saw Tyler's corpse, so he could tell her who was responsible for his death and why. She was bound to be so terrified that the same fate would befall her brat, that she'd do whatever he told her.

Even bed him. He licked his lips in carnal anticipation as he imagined lying between her sweet thighs and shoving himself into her. Undoubtedly she would be tense with reluctance, which meant she would clutch his cock all the tighter. He felt himself harden as the lock clicked open beneath his probing hands.

Shoving his tools back into his pocket, he opened the door and slipped inside, only to stop short. On the corner of the desk was a lamp ... a lit one. His throat tightened with alarm. Someone had been here, and recently. Was it possible that Tyler had somehow escaped death and ...

Of course not, he chided himself. Mother had promised to kill Seth Tyler, and Mother never broke her promises. No. If someone was here, it was probably Monty. The bartender had been doing the liquor inventory yesterday when he'd overheard Miles talking to Tyler, and it was possible that he'd come in early to finish the task. That being the case, he was probably down in the saloon verifying a count, which meant he might return any moment.

Determined not to be caught with his hands in the till, Miles scrambled toward the safe at the far side of the room. As he rounded the expensive desk, he came to another abrupt stop, this time not from apprehension, but from shock.

There, naked and fast asleep on the floor, were Lorelei and a very alive Seth Tyler. They lay half covered by a black evening cape with his front spooned intimately against her back, their clasped left hands resting on her bare right breast. They were the very picture of satiated lovers.

Miles stood there for a moment, too stunned to do more than gape at the couple. Then his shock erupted into murderous rage. *Lorelei was his! His, damn it!* Snarling his fury, he pulled out his bowie knife, one he always wore concealed in his boot during high-stake card games, and lunged at the sleeping man's exposed back. *Tyler would pay for stealing his woman, and pay big! He'd do exactly what Harley had failed to do, then send the bastard straight to hell where he belonged!*

Seth lurched up with a howl, ripped from his dreams by a sudden burning pain branding his back from shoulder to waist. Desperately he tried to focus his eyes, to see who was shouting half-garbled threats and curses, but his head was spinning with blinding speed and he saw only a shadowy blur swooping down on him.

As if through a tunnel, he heard Penelope scream, "No, Miles! Dear God, no!" then her soft body hurled against his, knocking him back down and covering him as if to shield him.

Which was exactly what she was doing, he realized through the clearing mists of his foggy mind. Protecting him from Miles. Gritting his teeth against his mounting nausea, he concentrated on the wavering form above him, willing his gaze to adjust. Damn it to hell! He should be defending her, not the other way around. She could be hurt or worse shielding him like this.

Mercifully, Miles paused in his physical attack to parry Penelope's verbal one, giving Seth the critically needed time to regain his equilibrium. When his sickening dizziness had slowed to a drunken list, he evaluated the situation at hand.

"You're mine, Lorelei! Mine!" Miles was declaring, his voice shrill with rage. "It's time you realized it!"

"I'm not yours. I never was," she retorted. "I've told you that a thousand times before. Why can't you accept it?"

Miles released a nasty, squealing laugh. "We'll see who accepts what when your lover is carved up like a—uh—Thanksgiving turkey!—and your brat is missing a finger or two. I have a hunch you'll accept whatever I damn well tell you."

She stiffened. "You harm either Seth or my son, and I'll kill you. I swear I will!"

Her son? Seth's gaze swerved from Miles's knife-brandishing form to Penelope's scowling profile. *Son? What the . . . ?*

One by one the pieces began to fall into place: the tension in her voice when she'd posed her seemingly theoretical questions on the consequences of conceiving his child; her wistful expression when she'd wondered if he would have loved their child; and her visible relief when he'd admitted that he would.

Miles grabbed Penelope by the hair and hauled her to him. "Bitch!" he screeched in response to whatever she'd just said. Before Seth could make his slowed reflexes react, the actor dropped the knife and administered a brutal backhanded slap to her face that sent her sprawling hard against the floor, sobbing.

Propelled by the sheer force of his fury, Seth lunged at the other man, knocking him backward. Ignoring the renewed reeling of his head, he wrestled Miles to the ground, shoving the bowie knife out of reach in the process. When the actor lay restrained beneath him, spitting crude curses and threats, Seth stared him in the eye and hissed, "Lesson number one: A gentleman never strikes a lady." With that, he viciously slammed his fist into Miles's face. There was a sickening *crunch!* and a splattering of blood as the actor's nose cracked beneath the impact of the blow.

Miles arched up screeching his agony, his elbow connecting sharply with Seth's damaged rib in the process. Half-blind with dizziness and tears of pain, Seth fell off his thrashing opponent, convulsively clutching his side.

As he lay doubled-over, Penelope screamed, "Seth! Look out!"

He glanced up in time to see Miles swooping down on him, the knife catching the gleam of the early-morning sun as it arched toward his chest. Bracing his injured rib, he rolled away, taking the stabbing blow in his raised upper right arm.

As the razor-sharp blade sliced through his flesh, Penelope jumped on Miles's back and began pummeling his head and shoulders, shrieking, "Help! Please ... somebody stop this!"

"Shut up, slut!" Miles squealed, dropping the knife to drag her fiercely flailing form off him and slam her to the floor. As he viciously jerked her head up by her hair, she screamed and punched him in his broken nose. He wailed and smashed his fist into her face. She fell back upon the carpet, as limp as a loosely stuffed rag doll.

Howling his rage, Seth sprang at Miles, ramming him with a violence that sent him crashing to the floor. Pinning him beneath his greater weight, Seth rained blow after flesh-splitting blow to his face. Through the oblivion of his mindless fury, and Miles's agonized cries, he heard, "Stop that!

Damn it, stop!" Then someone attacked him from behind, slugging him in the kidneys.

Cursing, he rolled off Miles, tackling his new attacker, a blonde in a blue silk night rail, as he moved. It wasn't until he'd completely immobilized the ferociously punching and clawing woman that he identified her. It was Adele du Charme.

"Damn you, Tyler. Let me up," she hissed, baring her teeth like a viper ready to strike.

From the opposite side of the room came a chorus of gasps. Seth glanced toward the sound, still holding Adele firmly to the carpet. Clustered in the door were three saloon girls, their mouths agape and their gazes obviously trained on his nude body; gazes that darted to the woman beneath him the second she wailed:

"Help me! Please help! He's trying to rape me!"

That accusation was enough to send one of the saloon girls scurrying down the hall, babbling something about the deputy being on the third floor with Titania. The two remaining women stood shuffling their feet, looking at each other uncertainly.

As Seth opened his mouth to denounce Adele for the lying bitch she was, he heard Penelope moan, "S-Seth?"

"Here," he cried hoarsely, climbing off Adele to crawl over to where Penelope was woozily sitting up. "I'm here, sweetheart. Everything's fine now." As he tenderly covered her naked form with his cape, he heard a low snarl behind him.

With equilibrium robbing speed, he swung around to see Miles charging at him with the knife. Unable to spring aside for fear of leaving Penelope in direct line of the blade, Seth did the only thing he could do: leap straight at Miles.

Squealing like a wounded pig, Miles flew back beneath the projectile of his adversary's body. In a blur of motion the men tumbled across the floor, thudding against furniture and walls as they wildly grappled for possession of the knife.

At last they came to a crashing stop against the desk.

Not a word passed as the women stared at where a limp Miles lay atop an equally lifeless-looking Seth. From between their bodies seeped a widening pool of blood.

Sobbing her panic, Penelope scrambled over to the men, disregarding her nudity in her desperation to get to Seth. "Seth!" she cried, gently smoothing his hair back from his pale face. The tendrils were sticky with blood, as was the side of his head where the doctor had stitched his scalp the night before. "Please, love. Please don't be dead," she begged. "I need you."

His long lashes fluttered once, then his eyes opened. For several seconds he stared up at her as if disoriented. Then one corner of his mouth curved up. "Princess?"

She went weak with relief. "Yes, love. I'm here."

"Miles!" Adele shrieked abruptly, as if suddenly coming to her senses. Kneeling on the opposite side of the men as Penelope, she began shaking her slack-limbed son as if to wake him, alternately commanding and crooning, "Damn it, Miles! You get up this instant! Come on. Be a good boy and open your eyes now."

When he didn't respond, she glared first at Penelope, then at the pair of silently gawking saloon girls. "Well? Don't just stand there like stupid cows. Help me turn him over."

The saloon girls exchanged an apprehensive look, then glanced at Penelope. She nodded, as anxious as Adele to move Miles so she could see how badly Seth was hurt. With visible reluctance, the saloon girls did as ordered, one crossing herself before joining the others in their grisly task. After much tugging and pushing, they rolled Miles off Seth. As he flopped over onto his back, all four women drew back, gasping in unison.

He was dead. Stabbed through the heart with his own knife.

For several seconds the women stood transfixed: the saloon girls with wide-eyed horror, Adele with what appeared to be grief, if the woman was indeed capable of such an emotion, and Penelope with relief that it was Miles, not Seth, who was stabbed.

Penelope was the first to break free of the macabre trance. Ripping her revulsed gaze from Miles's face, now pummeled beyond recognition and frozen into a mask of demonic hatred, she returned her attention to Seth, who was struggling to sit up.

The binding on his ribs was long gone, as was the bandage on his shoulder, though those stitches had miraculously held. Anxiously, she scanned the rest of his body. Despite the profusion of blood on his torso and face, his only real injuries appeared to be his cut arm and the reopened scalp wound.

Still, Penelope wasn't about to take any chances, so she laid her palm against his chest, urging him back down again.

"You should lie still until after we have the doctor examine you."

He lifted her hand from his chest and kissed it. "I'm fine. Just a little bruised and dazed." He nodded down at himself, as if to prove his point. Then he frowned. "And naked."

"I'll fetch your trousers."

"Cover yourself first," he barked as she moved away.

From down the hall came the pounding of rapidly approaching boots, accompanied by the excited chatter of voices. Hastily Penelope wrapped herself in Seth's cape, then retrieved his trousers. Smiling his thanks, he drew them up over his legs.

As he lifted his hips to pull them the rest of the way up, he flinched violently, expelling, "Jesus!" Clamping his lower lip between his bared teeth, he gingerly shifted his weight to his right hip, tipping up his left one to expose his buttock. It was deeply slashed from his hipbone to the rounded medial curve.

Just then the deputy, wearing only his trousers, boots, and guns, an equally disheveled Titania, and the saloon girl who'd fetched them, erupted through the open door.

Gritting his teeth, Seth shoved his pants the rest of the way up, a gasp escaping him as the woolen fabric scraped over his wounded flank. As Penelope placed a comforting hand on his shoulder, someone grabbed her arm and hauled her from his side.

It was Adele. Her hands and night rail were smeared with Miles's blood; her red eyes glinted with a wild desperation more terrifying than her malice. Digging her sharp nails deep into Penelope's forearm, she dragged her into her embrace, snarling, "If you love your brat, you'll keep your mouth shut and go along with what I say."

Long months of brutal conditioning made Penelope cringe and nod, the woman's words conjuring up the tormenting visions of Tommy's demise, which had been so cruelly planted in her mind.

In three long strides, the deputy covered the distance from the door to Miles's body. He was a tall man, almost as tall as Seth. But where Seth was all lean, sinewy muscles, this man was stocky and soft around the middle. Hunkering down next to the corpse, he bellowed, "What in Sam Hill happened here?"

"He," piped up the saloon girl who'd fetched him, pointing at Seth, "tried to rape her." She shifted her finger to Adele. "Me an' Cleopatra an' Juliet saw him. He wur on top of her an' she wur strugglin' real hard."

Seth made a derogatory noise and stood up. Everyone else began to speak at once.

The deputy jumped to his own feet and drew his gun. Leveling it on Seth's head, he barked, "You, Tyler, stay put! The rest of you, pipe down! I'll hear your piece one by one."

Seth shrugged nonchalantly and sat down on the desk.

Gracing him with a final warning look, the deputy shifted his gaze to Adele. "We'll start with you, ma'am. What happened?"

Adele clutched Penelope tighter, patting her back as if comforting her. "I heard Lorelei, here, screaming, and when I came to investigate, I found Tyler raping her. I tried to stop him, but he turned on me and attempted to do the same. When my son heard the noise and came to my rescue, Tyler"—her voice broke with a pitiful sob—"he stabbed him through the heart!"

Penelope gasped loudly, horrified by Adele's lies.

The woman grabbed the back of her head and shoved her face against her breast, silencing her. "Ssh, dear. I know this is embarrassing for you, but if justice is to be served, we have to tell the deputy everything," she crooned for the benefit of her audience. Then she pressed her lips to Penelope's ear and hissed, "One more sound, and your brat is dead. I mean it."

From fearful habit, Penelope meekly complied, but only for a moment. Then it dawned on her. Adele was in no position to carry out her threats. Not without Miles's help, and she knew it. No wonder she looked so desperate. She realized that if Penelope told the deputy of her kidnapping and blackmail scheme now, that she had no one to get rid of the crime evidence—Tommy—and back up her pleas of innocence.

Once the baby was located, which wouldn't take long when Seth learned Tommy was his son and took charge of the search, this nightmare would end. Adele would be behind bars where she belonged, and Tommy would be safe. The only catch was that she might have to reveal her own sordid actions leading to this mess.

Her stomach twisted with dread at that thought. There were things she might be forced to tell that she'd prayed Seth

would never find out. Things that might make him loath her
as much as he'd once pretended, and with good reason.

But what choice did she have? If she didn't speak out, it
was likely that Seth would be convicted of rape and murder.
And God only knows what would happen to Tommy.

Penelope swallowed hard, though her mouth was suddenly
dry. No. No matter the cost to herself, she wouldn't risk the
lives of the man and child she loved. For once she was going
to do the unselfish thing . . . the right thing. If Seth chose to
hate her when he learned the truth, well, she'd deal with that
later.

Thus resolved, she began to struggle against Adele in earnest. Yet, despite her best efforts to free herself, the older
woman proved stronger and easily kept her in check without
so much as pausing in her diatribe against Seth.

"What is it, Miss Lorelei?" the deputy cut into Adele's tirade, having obviously noticed her writhing.

Penelope tried to lift her head, to brand Adele as the liar
she was, but the woman crushed her face harder against her
breast, almost suffocating her. "The child is hysterical," she
informed him, furtively grasping her captive's hair close to
her scalp. When Penelope let out a squawk of protest, Adele
gave her curls a wicked twist, adding, "Shame, Deputy!
You've made her cry again."

"Sorry, Miss Lorelei." The deputy sounded truly contrite.

Desperate now, Penelope gave her head a mighty jerk, ignoring the pain as Adele's handful of hair ripped from her
scalp. Flinging her now freed head back from the woman's
body, she shouted, "She's lying! She's the criminal, not Seth
Tyler! She kidnapped my baby and has been blackmailing
me with threats to his life."

"As you can see, she's out of her mind with shock,"
Adele countered, fighting to hold onto her thrashing burden.

"No!" Penelope shoved against Adele with all her might,
then bucked back in the same motion, heaving backward out
of the woman's arms. Like a sail in a blustery wind, the
cloak unfurled from her body as she toppled, billowing to
the ground where she fell upon it, naked and with the breath
knocked out of her.

A buzz went up among the steadily swelling crowd at the
door, while Seth rushed to her side. Where he was pale before, he was positively ashen now. Without a word he
rewrapped the cape around her and helped her sit up, keep-

ing his gaze averted from hers the whole time. Penelope, too, remained speechless, at first because she hadn't the breath to speak, and then because she simply didn't know what to say or where to begin.

It was Seth who finally broke their silence. "The child, is it . . . ?" he asked, his hoarse voice breaking as his gaze met hers. His eyes were dark and shadowed with raw emotion: rage, betrayal, and a pain so terrible that it hurt to see it.

As much as she wanted to look away, to escape the soul-piercing sight of his anguish, she couldn't. Not when she knew that she'd caused it; not when she wanted so badly to soothe it.

Gently laying her hand against his face, so white and rigid that it could have been carved from alabaster, she whispered, "Yes, Seth. You have a son. A beautiful, wonderful son."

He closed his eyes then, as if in doing so he could shut out his pain. "Why didn't you tell me? Why?" His voice was as tight and choked as if he'd just been gut-punched.

"I wanted to . . . I was going to," she replied slowly, moving her hand from his cheek to tuck a tendril of hair behind his ear.

He jerked from her touch. "When?" he demanded. His eyes were open now and flickering like twin flames. "You, with all your talk of love and trust . . . when were you going to tell me of our child?"

"I was going to tell you just as soon as he was rescued from Adele. I had a plan. I was going to hire a tracker—"

"A tracker?" he echoed. His growing wrath was truly frightening to see. "You'd rather trust a tracker—a stranger—to rescue our son, than me, his own father? Christ, Penelope! How little you must think of me and my abilities."

"No! It wasn't like that. I wasn't thinking straight," she said in a rush, desperate to explain. "You don't understand—"

"That's because there is nothing to understand," Adele cut in. "She had a baby, that much is true. I helped deliver it. But it died at birth, and she's never been able to accept the loss."

"That's a lie!" Penelope exclaimed, looking wildly from Adele to the deputy. "Our baby is alive."

Adele gave her a patronizing look. "Poor girl. She has these spells where she still believes he's alive. Sometimes she tries to steal another woman's baby, claiming it's hers. Other times she blames me, or whoever happens to be handy, of kidnapping it. Obviously the trauma of the rape has prompted her delusions."

"No!" Penelope glanced frantically from the deputy's frowning face to Adele's falsely solicitous one and finally back at Seth. Aside from a muscle working in his jaw, his face was now completely void of expression. Speaking more to him than the others, she explained softly:

"It's true that Adele helped deliver our baby, but he didn't die . . . though I almost did. It was a hard birth . . . a breech . . . I hemorrhaged badly and, in my weakened state, contracted a fever. While I was delirious, she stole the baby, and she's been using him to blackmail me ever since . . . threatening to do all sorts of horrible things to him if I didn't do her bidding."

She touched Seth's tense jaw then, a jaw so like that of their son, imploring him with her eyes to believe her. "I love my baby, just as I love his father. That love was what pulled me through my fever. Since then, I've done everything Adele has demanded to assure his well-being. I deserted my operatic career to travel the West with her company; I relinquished my money, my freedom, my self-respect; I deceived and lied to those I care for most. All to keep our child safe. All well worth the sacrifice."

She thought she detected a softening in his eyes then, a barely perceptible change that she might have missed had she not known him so well. Lightly caressing his jaw with the thumb of the hand cupping it, she whispered, "At first I didn't confide in you because of the things you said in New York . . . about me and Julian. I was afraid that you wouldn't believe that the baby was yours, that you'd laugh and tell me that I got what I deserved."

His face contorted, as if he were pierced by a savage pain. "Perhaps you were right in thinking me a fool. Perhaps—"

"Perhaps," she cut him off quietly, "we are both fools. I should have confided in you yesterday when you trusted me with the truth about what happened in New York." She shook her head. "But I couldn't. I was ashamed to confess that our son had been kidnapped. I thought that if I had him rescued before I told you, that you might not think me such a complete failure as a mother."

Seth laid his hand over hers on his jaw. "I wouldn't have thought you a failure, not if you'd told me everything exactly like you just did. I'd have thought, like I do now, that you're a wonderful, loving mother. The exact kind I want for my son."

"This is all very touching, but a farce," Adele snapped, effectively shattering the tender moment. "The child is dead, and he wasn't yours anyway, Tyler. He was Byron Garrett's."

Seth's eyes narrowed as he transferred his gaze to Adele. Pulling his face from Penelope's hand, he rose to his feet.

"Seth—" Penelope began to explain, standing as well.

But he cut her off. "Byron Garrett? The actor?"

"The very same. Lorelei, or shall we say"—Adele glanced at Penelope smugly—"Miss Parrish, told me that she had relations with him while performing some opera at the Boston Theater."

"I only said"— Penelope tried to interject.

Again Seth cut her off. "The opera was Wagner's *Tristan and Isolde*. For the record, Miss Parrish was a superb Isolde."

Adele shrugged. "I'm sure, but the opera or her performance is hardly of any importance in this matter."

"Every detail of her stint at the Boston Theater is of extreme importance to me," Seth retorted, coolly. "For it was there, after the closing night curtain, that Miss Parrish agreed to marry me."

Adele snorted. "No doubt she found herself caught and thought to cuckold you into giving Garrett's bastard a name."

"Seth . . . no," Penelope gasped, the cape sliding down her shoulder as she reached out to clutch his arm.

But he ignored her. "You're sure it was Garrett's child?" His eyes were little more than glowing slits now as he studied Adele.

"Oh, it was Garrett's, all right," she asserted, tossing Penelope a triumphant smirk. "It looked just like him."

Seth nodded slowly, as if mulling the idea over. "Then, Garrett is a man of rare skills. Very rare indeed. For Miss Parrish"—he shot Penelope a look of gentlemanly apology—"was a virgin when I first took her . . . just hours before he sailed for England."

She smiled her forgiveness, her heart flip-flopping with joy as his lips crooked up into a faint grin. Everything was going to be fine. How could it not be with Seth on her side?

"Seems to me that the important question isn't who fathered the baby, but whether or not it's alive," interrupted the deputy, who'd been silently following the exchange.

"Which is a separate matter from what happened here." He pointed to Miles's body.

Penelope stepped forward, clutching the cape to her breasts. "If you don't mind, Deputy, I'd like to tell my side of the story now." When he nodded, she told of Miles's obsessive infatuation with her, then recounted the events leading up to his death.

"And so you see, Deputy," she finished, "Mr. Tyler was simply protecting himself when Mr. Prescott was killed."

"It's true, Deputy," Seth confirmed, wrapping his arm around Penelope's waist and kissing the top of her head.

The deputy glanced from the couple before him to the two saloon girls who had yet to speak up. "You," he barked, beckoning the women forward. "What did you see?"

"It's true that Mr. Tyler was on top of Adele, and that it looked like he was roughing her up," replied one woman, a plump redhead with a pretty, freckled face. "But he got right off her and went over to Lorelei when she called him. The way he covered her up and touched her all tender and loverlike, well, it was obvious that things weren't like they looked."

The other girl, a petite brunette, bobbed her head. "Looked to me the way Lorelei said."

The deputy turned back to Adele. "Well, ma'am?"

She shrugged, as cool as if she'd faced this sort of situation a hundred times before, which perhaps she had, given her nefarious activities. "Maybe I misread the situation," she admitted with a snort. "But then, what was I supposed to think when I saw Lorelei lying there naked? I hadn't a clue she was carrying on with Tyler."

She fixed her icy gaze on Penelope then. "As for this nonsense about a baby, all I can do is plead innocent and challenge Lorelei to produce proof of its existence."

The deputy considered for a moment, then nodded. "Seems fair enough to me. Miss Lorelei?"

Penelope looked frantically from Adele's gloating face to the deputy's querying one. She had no proof, and Adele knew it. The woman had taken great pains to see that she had none.

"Sweetheart?" Seth murmured, his arm tightening around her.

"I—she—" Penelope stammered in her urgency to make the deputy understand her position. "She's got him hidden in a cabin in the foothills. I'm not exactly sure where . . . I was blindfolded when we went up there. But if you'll hold her for a few days while I search, I know I can find him."

The deputy shook his head. "Unless you can produce evidence that this baby exists, some sort of paperwork, or even someone who's seen him, I have no grounds to hold Madame du Charme."

"But can't you see?" she cried, her voice now edged with hysteria. "If you let her go, she'll take him away where I'll never find him. Or maybe even kill him. Please—"

"Deputy, do you really want to chance having an innocent child's blood on your hands?" Seth interjected, giving Penelope's waist a reassuring squeeze. "Be warned: if this child comes to harm because of your failure to take action, I'll see that you're stripped of your badge and never hold a decent position again. By the time I'm done, you'll be lucky to find a job digging graves."

The deputy quailed visibly beneath Seth's threat, yet he doggedly insisted, "The law is the law, and I can't be arresting folks without evidence that a crime has been committed. Now, if the lady can show me something to back her claims—"

"I can back her claims," boomed a deep voice from the door.

Penelope's heart seemed to miss a beat as she swiveled her head to identify her savior. It was One-eyed Caleb. He was lounging against the doorjamb with his arm thrown casually around the shoulders of a buxom blond saloon girl. With a grace that was as beautiful as it was predatory, he straightened up and sauntered into the room, coming to a stop opposite Penelope.

"You've seen this child?" the deputy asked, hopefully.

Caleb nodded. "Lorelei, here, came to me a few weeks ago, wantin' to hire me to rescue her kid. She didn't have the money for my fee, but I knew by the look in her eyes that she'd get it somehow, so I went ahead and did the trackin' on faith. I followed her and Prescott to a cabin in the foothills one Sunday, and saw her bring a baby outside to show it a couple of rabbits."

Adele began to protest, but he cut her off. "It was Lorelei's kid. Don't let Madame, here, tell you any different. I heard Prescott and another man talkin' about it out back of the cabin. Seems Madame, here, has been up to some nasty tricks." He fixed Adele with a look of pure loathing. "Never could abide anyone usin' kids like that. Been eatin' at me so bad that I was gonna get Lorelei's kid back for her, free of charge."

Seth stepped forward to offer Caleb his hand. "I'll pay you double your usual tracking fee if you'll take us to that cabin now. I want my baby safe as soon as possible and"—he shot a commanding look at the deputy—"Madame du Charme arrested immediately."

While the two men shook hands, the deputy seized Adele.

"Yes. Hurry after your brat," she taunted with wicked glee. "Who knows? You might even get there in time to find him alive."

Penelope gasped, panic exploding in her chest.

Seth snarled, his hands clenched into fists as he advanced toward the gloating woman. "If you've harmed that baby—"

She laughed, a vicious, ugly sound. "Oh, I haven't done a thing to your little darling. I didn't have to. I got word days ago that he contracted measles from a wagonful of homesteaders who stopped at the cabin for water. Sam says he's real sick." Her eyes glittered with malice as she fixed her gaze on Penelope. "Seems you might get rid of your brat after all, Lorelei, just like you wanted when you came to me whining for an abortion."

Penelope felt the color drain from her cheeks as Seth slowly turned to face her. He looked devastated, more wounded even than when he'd told her of his parentage. "You sought to rid yourself of my child?" he whispered hoarsely.

"Seth," she murmured, shaking her head helplessly as she moved toward him. "I—"

"Is it true?" he demanded, cringing from her touch as if it burned him. "Did you wish to destroy our child?" His anguished gaze bore into hers, ruthlessly seeking the truth, fervently imploring her to tell him that it was all a lie.

After a beat, she opened her mouth to explain, to beg him to understand. But it was too late. He'd turned away.

He'd seen the answer in her eyes.

Chapter 25

No one in the party spoke as they made their way up the foothills toward the cabin where the baby was being held. Caleb, astride a black and white pinto, led the way, followed by Penelope and Doc Larson, with Seth trailing several paces behind.

Penelope had ridden by Seth's side for the first few miles, tearfully trying to explain why she'd sought Adele's services. But he was in no mood to listen, and after ignoring her for what felt like an eternity, she gave up and urged her horse forward to ride with the more congenial Doc Larson.

God, he was tired. So damn exhausted that he couldn't see straight. Seth rubbed his eyes for the hundredth time that morning, then squinted painfully at the rocky horizon. What the hell was wrong with him, anyway? Not only did everything look like a badly focused photograph, but the sunlight, dim as it was through the covering of clouds, hurt his eyes almost unbearably.

And then there was his head. He soundlessly groaned his misery. The throbbing that had plagued him at the dance was back, and becoming alarmingly more intense as the hours went by. So were the dizziness and nausea.

Seth gritted his already clenched teeth tighter and braced himself more firmly in the saddle. It was a miracle he hadn't fallen from his horse, what with his light-headedness. And thank God he hadn't eaten anything since yesterday. He could just see it if he were to fall from his horse and be sick, Penelope would fuss and fawn over him, and show him all the sweet compassion of which he knew she was capable. That would be intolerable . . .

. . . And wonderfully welcome. He grunted his frustration. He was so damn confused about his feeling for Penelope and what she'd done, that he didn't know if he was coming or going.

While half of him understood the desperation that had
driven her to seek Adele's services, the other, perhaps the
unwanted child he'd once been, cried out in protest. That an
innocent babe should pay for his parents' mistakes was an
outrage he found unforgivable.

And yet how could he not forgive her? Especially when it
was he who had driven her to Adele? By the very nature of
his accusations, he'd made it impossible for her to come to
him, leaving her with few options, none of them pleasant.
Perhaps if he were in her shoes, he, too, might have approached Adele.

Seth shuddered. No. He doubted if he could be so cold-
blooded. After all, was tearing a child from the womb really
any more forgivable than killing it after it was born, as his
mother had sought to do? If indeed his mother was guilty of
that crime. Suddenly things were less black and white.

Hadn't he seen by the example of his own son's present
circumstances that a mother was sometimes powerless to
control her child's fate? And knowing that, wasn't it only
fair to consider the possibility that his grandfather had kidnapped him, as Louisa claimed, and that she truly hadn't
found out that he was alive until years later?

That troubling hypothesis simply made his head pound
harder, so he pushed it from his mind. He'd think about Louisa later, when his mind was clearer . . .

. . . *If it cleared,* Seth brooded, the ominous hidden-
injuries-turned-fatal tales springing to the forefront of his
mind. He grunted at his own foolishness. Ridiculous. There
was nothing wrong with him. He was just tired, and with
good reason. He'd spent the entire night making love to Penelope . . .

Like the thoughts of his mother, he instantly banished the
remembrance of their night together. He wouldn't think
about their passion, their sweet rapture. To do so would only
further muddy his judgment, and he had to view the present
situation as objectively as possible. He had to decide what
was best for their son, and then act on that decision.

Not that there was really anything to decide. Marrying Penelope and providing the baby with a home and a name was
the only right choice there was. The real question was: could
he live with Penelope knowing she was capable of being so
heartless?

Could he live without her, loving he as he still did?

He was so preoccupied with his tormenting thoughts, that he almost fell from his horse when it skittered to a dancing halt. With a sharp jerk of his head, he glanced up to see what was wrong, a move that set the world spinning before his eyes. Through the speeding blur of his dizziness, he discerned that the rest of the riders had stopped and were starting to dismount.

In a flash of hunter green, Penelope was off her horse and running toward a ramshackle cabin, shouting, "Sam! Minerva!"

The sagging door opened instantly, and on the threshold appeared a gray-haired man of medium build. When he saw Penelope, he took her arm and escorted her inside. After several seconds, Seth and the doctor followed, leaving Caleb to tend the horses.

While the doctor bustled directly into the cabin, Seth lagged behind, strangely apprehensive. What should he say to his son? Uncomfortably he remembered the scene from the night before, and his own cruel rejection of his mother. What if his own son spurned him as well? How would he bear the hurt?

Then he laughed at his own foolishness. His son was two years old, for God's sake, hardly of an age to notice much less make a value judgment of his father's absence. Undoubtedly after getting over the initial shyness most children displayed around strangers, they would get along splendidly. Suddenly eager to make his son's acquaintance, he hurried through the door.

The cabin was a one-room affair, primitively crafted with an odd assortment of animal pelts nailed to the walls, probably to block out the wind. The floor was packed earth, and there was a crude stone hearth at the far wall.

As rough as the structure was, there were visible signs that someone had tried to make it homey. Colorful autumn leaves and late-blooming fire wheels were arranged in a dented coffeepot atop the scarred dining table. A rag rug, round and rainbow bright, lay next to a bed covered in a quilt gaily patterned with red, white, and blue fans. Over the cot that Penelope, Doc Larson, and two other people hovered, someone had tacked up several etchings portraying rabbits, all obviously torn from magazines and painstakingly tinted by a skilled hand.

In several long strides, Seth covered the short distance be-

tween the threshold and the cot. Like the Red Sea to Moses'
command, the small group parted, making space for him
next to the baby's side. One of the strangers, a woman,
spoke to him, but he was too stunned by the sight of his son
to comprehend her words.

Never had he felt more cursed, never was he more aware
of his tainted blood than at that moment as he looked upon
his son's twisted limbs. Slowly his shock gave way to grief-
stricken guilt, and he sank to his knees, suddenly too weak
to stand.

Dear God! What terrible sin had he committed to evoke
such wrath? And how, in the name of heaven, could a being
touted as infinitely kind, merciful, and fair be so vicious as
to take His fury out on an innocent babe?

As Seth knelt beside his son, alternately raging against
God and cursing himself, he felt a tentative touch on his
arm. "His name is Thomas Albert, after my grandfathers,"
he heard Penelope say.

Too choked with emotion to reply, he merely nodded.

"I know I should have warned you about Tommy's—
afflictions," she continued, stumbling over the word *afflictions,* "but I . . . I didn't know what to say. I hoped that once
you saw him and saw how beautiful he is, that it wouldn't
make any difference."

The pleading note in her voice made him glance at her
sharply. She was watching him anxiously, her eyes mutely
imploring him to forgive their son his shortcomings and to
try to love him in spite of them.

There was something about her silent plea, perhaps its in-
timation that he might think their son unworthy of love because of his deformities, that sent a sudden, fierce sense of
paternal protectiveness hurling through him. That he, or anyone, would shun a child simply because it was different was
a thought almost too monstrous to comprehend.

Yet, sadly, he knew that it happened all too often. While
at the orphanage, he'd seen countless children abandoned
because their parents couldn't accept their imperfections.
Even now he remembered those poor creatures, the way they
were rejected and scorned, addressed only with the cruelest
of taunts. It had broken his heart then; it enraged him now.

And at that moment, as Seth enfolded his son's tiny, awkwardly contorted fist in his hand, he silently swore that no
matter what it took, his child would never suffer for being

different. He'd see that Tommy never knew anything but love and kindness, and that he was cherished as no child before him.

Seth smiled down at his son then, his heart swelling with tenderness. "He's beautiful," he murmured to Penelope.

And he was, Seth realized, releasing the baby's hand so Doc Larson could examine him. Despite the brownish-pink spots marring his skin and the swelling in his face, he was a very handsome boy. But then, how could he not be with Penelope as his mother?

"Seth?" Penelope whispered. She sounded breathless, choked.

"Hmm?" He dragged his gaze away from the baby to glance at her. Her eyes shimmered with tears, but she was smiling sweetly and with a gratitude that made him all the more determined to do right by their son. For Tommy's sake . . . and hers.

"Thank you."

He shook his head and returned her smile with his own gentle one. "No. Thank you for giving me such a perfect son."

"This child is very ill," the doctor announced, though to all present he was merely stating the obvious. "His temperature is 104, and he's dehydrated. I can't tell for certain, but I suspect by his high fever and the convulsions Mrs. Skolfield described that the infection has spread to his brain."

"His brain?" Penelope repeated, her fear reflected in both her face and voice. "But he will be all right, won't he?"

The doctor rose slowly. "I'm going to be blunt with you, Mrs. Tyler," he said, still laboring under the misconception that she and Seth were married. "When the infection spreads to the brain of a healthy child, I'm generally less than optimistic, but hold out enough hope to say that a recovery is possible. However, with a baby already so weak and frail . . ." He shook his head.

She turned so ashen, that Seth was certain she would faint. Wrapping his arm around her waist and drawing her close, he reassured her, "Tommy will be fine. Between the two of us, we'll pull him through." And he meant it. He'd just found his son, and he'd be damned if he'd lose him again. Transferring his gaze to the doctor, he asked, "What can we do to help him?"

Doc Larson shook his head again. "I'm going to leave some drops for you to give him every four hours. Aside from that, all I can suggest is that you get as much nourishment in him as possible and sponge him down with tepid water for the fever."

"Would it be all right to move him into town?" Seth inquired, anxious to provide his son with every possible comfort.

"No. He's much too ill to make the journey." The doctor bent closer to Seth. "You don't look much up to it, either, son," he observed. "Why don't you lie down over there"—he indicated the bed with the fan quilt—"and let me examine you."

Seth started to protest that he was all right, but Penelope cut him off. "Stop arguing, Seth. Your scalp needs to be restitched and that cut on your arm should be cleaned. And don't forget about your hip. I noticed fresh blood on the seat of your trousers when you mounted your horse earlier."

Seth grimaced. As if he could forget about that particular wound. His backside was so damn sore that if his head weren't plaguing him so, he'd have probably found riding unbearable. Still he hesitated, reluctant to leave his son's side.

"Go on," she urged, giving his arm a reassuring squeeze. "There's nothing you can do for Tommy right now, anyway. Minerva and I can—Oh!" She glanced apologetically at the older couple, who'd been standing silently at the foot of the cot, holding hands and exchanging worried glances. "I'm sorry. Seth, this is Sam and Minerva Skolfield. They've been caring for Tommy, but"—she waved dismissively—"I'll tell you all about that later."

Seth stood up and shook hands with the couple, then, at Doc Larson's prompting, followed him to the bed.

"Been fighting again, have you, son?" the doctor asked, setting his bag on the small table next to the bed. When Seth nodded, prompting a mild bout of dizziness, the man shook head in disapproval. "Not a healthy hobby, fighting."

"And certainly not one of my own choosing," Seth muttered, gingerly favoring his injured left buttock as he sat on the bed.

"Didn't think it was." The doctor popped open his black bag and pulled out several items, among which was a bottle of antiseptic that Seth remembered stinging like a son of a bitch. "You're going to need to get out of those clothes so I can see what kind of damage you've done to yourself this time," he continued. "The little woman said something about a cut rump?"

"Knife wound," Seth supplied, shooting a self-conscious glance at the Skolfields. Their backs were turned to him, and they appeared to be absorbed in listening to Penelope, who was tenderly bathing the baby's fevered body as she recounted the details of Adele's arrest. Still, preoccupied or not, he was uncomfortable about removing his clothes.

Apparently his embarrassment showed, because the doctor murmured, "Hell of a place to get stabbed, huh?" When Seth nodded miserably, he added, "Well, since it's not likely to be fatal, I'll tend it last. We'll see if we can't get you some privacy then. Guess I'll start with that head wound."

Which he did, and which proved to be an extremely unpleasant experience. Having his scalp stitched the night before had hurt, but it was nothing compared to having the bits of broken thread plucked out of the reopened wound. As he sat there, manfully stifling his moans, Sam approached.

"Minerva and I have a few things to settle with Adele," he said, grimacing his sympathy as he watched the doctor. "We'll be back tomorrow. Do you need anything from town?"

"How are we set for supplies—food, kerosene, and such?" Seth gritted out from between his clenched teeth.

"You're set for at least a couple of weeks."

Without moving his head, Seth drew a handful of coins from his pocket and gave them to Sam. "Buy a nice cradle, and whatever else you think might make my son more comfortable." He thought for a moment, then added, "I'd also like to send a telegram." At the man's nod, he gave his message and where it was to be sent.

When he'd finished, Sam peered down at the gold in his hand, almost a hundred dollars' worth, and asked, "Anything else?"

Seth started to say no; then his gaze fell on Penelope, who was still sponging their now feebly wailing son, her face the picture of maternal distress. "See if you can find a big box of maple nut candy," he said, remembering how the treat always made her smile. "And ask the store to tie it up with ribbons."

Fifteen minutes later, the Skolfields were off. By then the

doctor was restitching Seth's scalp, quizzing him as to whether he was ... dizzy? ... headachy? ... nauseated? ... and other symptoms to which he would've replied yes if he were being truthful. However, since he was in no mood to endure any more of the doctor's fussing than was absolutely necessary, he said no to everything.

As for Penelope, she sat on the cot at the other side of the cabin, gently rocking and singing to the fretful baby. Now and then she glanced wistfully at Seth, longing to be near him but doubtful if he would welcome her company.

Little did she know that having her by his side, holding his hand and distracting him from his pain as she'd done the night before, was exactly what he craved at that moment. Yet, he figured that after the way he'd treated her this morning, she was probably about as eager for his company as she was for Adele du Charme's. So he sat silently enduring his solitary misery.

He soon discovered, however, that he was not a man who suffered well alone. And by the time the doctor had finished stitching his scalp and was preparing to tend the cut on his arm, he was so desperate to have Penelope near that he was ready to throw himself at her feet and beg her forgiveness.

Well, perhaps I'd better forgo the throwing myself at her feet part, he decided, his head resuming its drunken reeling as he stripped off his shirt. As dizzy as he got every time he moved, he'd probably pass out, or worse, vomit on her boot from his nausea ... both misadventures that would win him lectures and probably more unpleasant poking from Doc Larson.

The begging part, however, he could manage. Prepared to do just that, he called softly, "Penelope?"

She looked up from the baby, stopping mid-lyric of the lullaby she was singing.

"Would you and Tommy sit next to me?" He smiled with all the charm he could muster. "Please?"

To his relief, for in truth his head was pounding way too much for him to beg effectively, she readily complied. As she sat next to him, rocking the mewling baby and crooning soothing, motherly nonsense, Seth studied his son.

There was no doubt that Tommy was his. From the color of his eyes, a striking shade of light hazel, to his square jaw and fair hair, he was every inch a Van Cortlandt. Yet there was much of Penelope in him as well.

Where the Van Cortlandt family had a strong, bold sort of handsomeness, his son was nothing short of beautiful ... a legacy from his mother. As anyone acquainted with the Parrish family could attest, they looked like heaven's fairest angels.

As did Tommy, Seth thought with fatherly pride. Like all the members of the stunning Parrish clan, his son's eyes were distinctly tip-tilted at the outer corners and fringed with impossibly thick lashes. And he was certain he saw evidence of their trademark dimples lurking beneath the measles. He'd also inherited his mother's well-shaped mouth and perfect ringlets.

For a long moment Seth stared at his son's fair curls, wondering if they were as soft as Penelope's ebony ones. Slowly he reached down to touch them, then paused. With his hand hovering just over the baby's head, he glanced uncertainly up at Penelope. She nodded her encouragement.

Trembling with tenderness, he gently stroked his son's hair. Amazing. It was even silkier than Penelope's. Filled with sudden awe at what he'd helped create, he moved his hand from the baby's hair to cradle his tiny fist in his palm. While Tommy's fingers were crooked and contorted at unnatural angles, there were five of them, all with perfectly shaped nails. He was so preoccupied admiring his son, that he forgot about the doctor until he said:

"I need to look at your rump now, son."

Seth glanced down at his injured arm in surprise. It sported a clean white bandage. He hadn't even felt the doctor tend it.

However, he certainly felt his hip wound when he tugged down his trousers. Hours of sitting on horseback had made the fabric stick to the cut, and he almost hit the ceiling howling his pain as wool ripped from flesh.

"Nasty one," Doc Larson observed as Seth stood with his trousers to his knees, convulsively clutching his buttock.

"That's the understatement of the century," Seth muttered, though he doubted if the man could hear him through the baby's squalling. Poor little fellow had been startled by his bellowing. Biting his lower lip to keep from crying out again, he cautiously finished removing his trousers, then lay belly down on the bed.

A few feet away, Penelope paced back and forth, making soothing noises and gently jiggling the wailing baby; a wailing that Seth was half tempted to join in the second the doctor began to clean his wound with the fiery antiseptic.

"Whoa there, son!" the doctor exclaimed as Seth bucked violently beneath his ministrations.

"That hurts!" he spat, jerking his hip away as the man made to dab at it again.

"I'm sure it does, but it'll hurt a lot worse if it gets infected," Doc Larson replied, pressing his hand into the small of Seth's back and flattening him, belly flush, against the mattress. "Now, lie still."

Seth tried his best to comply, honestly he did, but he couldn't help jumping every time the cut was touched.

Finally, after what felt like a century of poking, the doctor announced, "It isn't too deep here." He indicated an area in the center of his buttock. "The rest of it'll need stitching, though. Looks like you got stabbed here"—he touched an area about three inches from Seth's hip, almost making him howl again—"and then had the blade dragged the rest of the way across in the scuffle."

Penelope wandered over to stand next to the doctor, patting the back of her now-hiccuping baby as she peered down at Seth's backside. Seth felt like the main attraction at a sideshow the way they were gawking at him. Shooting them both a disgruntled look, he mumbled, "Skip the commentary and get on with the stitching."

The doctor shrugged and threaded his trusty needle, while Penelope sat at the edge of the bed near Seth's head. Seth reached up and lightly clasped the baby's hand again, then lay quietly staring up at Penelope's face. She returned his gaze steadily, her expression compassionate and her eyes filled with such love, that he felt suddenly shamed by his earlier thoughts. How could he have ever thought her heartless?

While it was true that she'd sought to abort their child, in the end she hadn't gone through with it. She'd risked being shunned by the society she so loved to bear his bastard ... not the act of a pitiless monster by any stretch of the imagination. In all fairness he should have praised her for her final decision, not condemned her for her first desperate impulse.

Well, he'd make amends just as soon as they were alone, he promised himself, gritting his teeth as Doc Larson leaned over his backside. He'd apologize for being a judgmental ass, and then tell her just how brave and truly wonderful she was. After he'd said all that, he would beg her to marry him and not just because of their son. No. He wanted to marry her because he loved her.

He gasped aloud as the doctor began to sew. As his body convulsed reflexively at the next stab of the needle, he hastily released Tommy's hand, afraid he might inadvertently crush the baby's fragile bones in a spasm of pain.

Without her gaze wavering from his, Penelope made one of her soothing noises and slipped her hand into his now empty one. As she laced her fingers between his, she sang in a low voice:

"Sleep, my love, my heart's desire. Let slumber come, gentle and sweet. Close your eyes, drowse soft and deep. And I will sing my song of dreams."

Seth recognized the lullaby as the one she'd been singing earlier. It was a pretty tune, one made beautiful by the sweet perfection of her voice. And as he lay listening to the melodious flow of notes, lulled as much by the tenderness in her eyes as by her song, the stabbing pain in his backside receded.

On and on she sang, of hope, joy, and love. By the time the last note faded away, Seth was astonished to discover Doc Larson applying a dressing to the area. Why, after the initial pain the stitching hadn't hurt at all. And all because of Penelope's song.

Smiling gratefully up at her, he gave her hand a warm squeeze. "That was a splendid song. What was it?"

She returned his smile and hand squeeze. "I call it my "Song of Dreams." I made it up for Tommy shortly after he was born."

"I had no idea you were such a talented songwriter."

She glanced down at their son, fast asleep on her lap. "I'm not. I was only singing what's in my heart."

"There now, that wasn't so bad was it?" boomed the doctor.

"No," Seth replied honestly, then mouthed to Penelope, "Thanks to you."

"Good. Now, I'm leaving some salve, which I want you, Mrs. Tyler, to rub into his arm and rump wounds," the man continued, handing Penelope a jar. "Think you can manage that?"

Penelope slanted Seth a saucy look. "Believe it or not, Doctor, I do have some experience in applying salve."

When the doctor had cleaned his instruments and neatly packed his bag, he took one final peek at Tommy.

Seth started to rise then, but the doctor laid his hand on his shoulder and urged him down again. "Whoa there, son! Not so fast. You're in no shape to be gadding about. You need to rest, sleep if possible. You won't be doing your missus or your baby any good by getting up and making yourself sick."

"He's right, Seth," Penelope concurred with a nod. "Besides, there's no reason for you not to rest awhile. Tommy's asleep, and there's nothing that needs doing that can't wait."

"Except pay the doctor and Caleb," Seth reminded her.

She shook her head. "You stay put. Just tell me where the money is, and I'll make sure everyone gets paid."

He lightly touched one of their son's curls. "He looks so comfortable, it seems a shame to disturb him."

"He'll be even more comfortable lying next to his papa," she declared, carefully laying the baby next to him. Tommy made a feeble mewling noise, but didn't wake.

There was something homey and comfortable about lying next to the baby, a new feeling that Seth found he liked immensely. Propping his head up on his arm to study his son, he said, "All right. You win. Bring me my saddlebag."

After draping a crocheted lap robe over his naked lower body, Penelope did as instructed. When he'd doled out portions of gold for both the doctor and Caleb, he eased onto his side and curled his tall body around his son's diminutive one. Laying his aching head next to the baby's, his cheek resting lightly against his soft curls, he closed his eyes and savored the simple pleasure of feeling his child's heart beating close to his.

He was just drifting off to sleep when he heard Penelope come back into the cabin and kneel by the bed. He cracked his eyes open to look at her, smiling his contentment. She returned his smile, a smile that faded as she touched Tommy's cheek.

"He's so hot," she whispered, her hand drifting upward to feel his forehead. "If only there were more I could do for him. I feel so helpless."

Seth knew exactly how she felt. While he knew almost everything about making money, he was completely ignorant about child care. Except, of course, for the bits of information he'd gleaned from being around Jake and Hallie's brood. He related one of those bits now in hopes of easing Penelope's mind.

"I remember when your niece and nephews had the measles last year. Little Reed was as sick as Tommy is now, and he recovered just fine. Hallie said children are like that, on their deathbed one instant, and whooping it up like Indians on firewater the next. I'm sure it'll be the same with our son."

Penelope shook her head pessimistically. "Tommy has never been able to whoop it up, or do anything else children his age are supposed to do. He's been sickly since the day he was born."

Seth looked at the tiny swollen face so near to his, realizing in a rush of regret just how little he knew of his son's birth and short life. Suddenly anxious to know every detail, he asked, "Would you mind telling me about Tommy?"

"What would you like to know?"

"Everything. Where he was born. What he looked like the first moment you saw him. What makes him smile." He glanced up from the baby then to meet Penelope's gaze. "I'd also like to know how you got involved with Adele du Charme."

She looked away and was silent for so long that Seth was beginning to think she wouldn't reply, when she began.

"Adele du Charme and her services were legendary among the New York theater set. She was the one an actress saw if she wanted to prevent conception; she was the one to take care of the 'problem' should those methods fail. Several women at the Academy of Music had used her services and spoke highly of her skills."

She paused a beat to stare at Tommy's face. "I went to see her because I felt I had no other choice. I was too ashamed to turn to Jake and Hallie . . ." She glanced up at him quickly, shaking her head. "Not because I was afraid they would scold me or treat me like a fallen woman, but because I couldn't bear the thought of disappointing them. They had been so supportive of my career, so proud of my accomplishments, that I just couldn't show up on their doorstep pregnant and in disgrace."

"I wish you'd done just that," Seth interjected quietly. "Your brother would have put an end to my nonsense and dragged us both to the altar. We'd have avoided this whole mess."

"Actually, I was afraid Jake would shoot you if I told him. Or even challenge you to a duel. As much as I hated you, I still couldn't bear the notion of you being hurt or killed."

He reached over and took her hand in his. "I deserved to be at the smoking end of a pistol for what I did to you."

"I would have agreed with you while I was in labor." She grimaced wryly. "I can't recall ever hating anyone as much as I did you while I was in the throes of my birthing pains."

"My poor, brave Princess," he murmured, caressing her thumb with his. "It must have been hell giving birth without the comfort of your family around you. Yet you chose to do so instead of ridding yourself of the baby. Why?"

"I fully intended to go through with the abortion when I went to Adele." Her face became pleading then, her eyes begging for understanding. "You have to realize how terrified I was . . . how shamed and alone."

"I don't condemn you for what you did," Seth murmured, drawing her hand to his lips to kiss it. "Granted, I was shocked and hurt at first, but I've had time to think things over and now understand your desperation. In truth, I blame myself for driving you to Adele. If I hadn't been such a bastard in New York, you could have come to me and we'd have been married on the spot."

She shook her head slowly. "We're both to blame. I should have gone to my brother the moment I knew about the baby."

"Perhaps. But wherever the blame falls, the most important thing is that you didn't have the abortion."

"No, I couldn't. I was lying on an old table, all prepared to go through with it, when it struck me just how much I wanted our child. Despite everything, I still loved you, and our baby was all I had left of you. When I told Adele of my decision, she offered to find someplace where I could give birth in secrecy, and then find someone to foster the baby until I could claim it as my own. It seemed the perfect plan, so I agreed.

"And everything was perfect at first. Adele found me a pleasant house just outside the city, where I stayed from my fourth month of pregnancy on." Her face was pale now, her expression bleak. "But then, a week or so before Tommy was born, I fell ill. My legs swelled terribly, and I was in so much pain that I couldn't move from my bed. I begged Adele to send for a doctor, but she refused. I couldn't understand why, but, of course, I know now. She'd already planned to use the baby to blackmail me and realized that her scheme would be almost foolproof if no one knew I'd given birth. Consequently Tommy was delivered by a midwife with at least three pints of gin in her."

That she'd suffered so much because of his stupidity made Seth loath himself almost beyond bearing. Choking on his remorse, he croaked, "You and Tommy are both lucky to be alive."

"Yes. As I mentioned this morning, he was a breech birth. Unfortunately the midwife didn't realize it until she'd sobered up . . . almost twenty-two hours later." Penelope shuddered as she remembered her agony. "When she did discover the problem, she tore me up so badly trying to turn him that I began to hemorrhage. He came out four hours later, all purple and bruised-looking with the birthing cord wrapped around his neck. The midwife told me he was dead . . . strangled in the womb.

She shook her head. "I lost consciousness after that. All I remember in the hours following Tommy's birth is Adele showing him to me and boasting how she'd brought him back to life."

She paused, her eyes taking on a faraway look. "He was so beautiful. He looked exactly like you. As wretched as I felt, I'd never been happier." Her dreamy expression turned somber. "A day later the birthing fever set in. By the time I regained enough awareness to ask for him again, almost three weeks had elapsed and Adele had already taken him away. It was then, while I lay too weak to even sit up, that she informed me of her scheme."

"If only I had been there . . . I *should* have been there," Seth agonized, torn up with self-reproach. "If I weren't such a—"

"Don't, Seth," she cut in gently. "Don't blame yourself. I don't. I'd rather forget the past and concentrate on our future."

Seth stared into her soft green eyes, his heart so filled with tender emotion that he was certain it would burst. Never had he loved Penelope as much as he did at that moment, never had he felt so loved. That she could so generously forgive him his grievous wrongs was nothing short of miraculous.

"I love you," he groaned, aching to hold her close but reluctant to disturb their son. "Say you'll stay with me forever, that you still want to marry me."

"Of course I do. I love you and so will Tommy." She tilted her head to one side and peered down at their son. "What do you say, Tommy?" she murmured to the sleeping baby. "Do you want to be Thomas Albert Tyler?"

"Van Cortlandt," Seth corrected. With the intimacy of the moment came the impulse to tell her about Louisa.

She looked up in surprise. "Van Cortlandt?"

He nodded. "My mother's maiden name was Van Cortlandt, presently Vanderlyn. Louisa Vanderlyn is my mother."

Penelope couldn't have looked more shocked if he'd told her he'd been hatched from an egg. "The same Louisa Vanderlyn who's building the orphanage? The one who's a staunch advocate for the humane treatment of children, and contributes pieces to the *Rocky Mountain News* lambasting business owners and mining companies for their child labor practices? That Louisa Vanderlyn?"

"The very same."

"Are you certain? I mean, it seems inconceivable that a woman who loves children as much as Mrs. Vanderlyn does could have ever done something as heinous as abandon her own child."

And even more far-fetched that she'd order him killed, Seth admitted silently. Indeed, the more he learned about Louisa the more he doubted her capable of such an act. Yet what about the caretaker's story and the Pinkerton agent's report? Could he disregard them? He looked at Penelope in helpless confusion.

She disengaged her hand from his to lay it against his cheek. "Did you ask your mother about those charges last night?"

He closed his eyes with a sigh. "Yes."

"And?" she prompted firmly.

"She denied them."

"And?"

God, his head hurt. "And nothing. I decided she was lying and left."

"You left? Just like that? You didn't even bother to discuss the matter or let her explain?" There was a rising note of amazement in her voice. "Why?"

He shrugged the shoulder he wasn't lying on. "I guess I was confused. She wasn't at all what I expected. She was warm and kind, and when I told her who I was, she seemed genuinely glad I was there. Hardly the cold-blooded murderess I'd envisioned."

"Murderess?!" she echoed, drawing her hand from his cheek.

"Yes. Murderess." He slitted his eyes open to peer at her, gauging her reaction. She was sitting back on her heels, her expression positively dumbfounded.

"I don't understand," she finally whispered.

"No, I'm sure you don't," he admitted with a heavy sigh. "But if you're willing to listen to a long story, I'll explain."

At her nod, he spilled everything. He told of his visit to Van Cortlandt Hall and the caretaker's tale, then went on to detail his vengeance against the Vanderlyn family. By the time he'd given a full account of his confrontation with Louisa, her eyes were the size of saucers. He finally finished: "I don't know what to do. I want to believe my mother's innocence, yet it's hard to erase two years of hatred." He met her gaze then, his eyes mutely pleading. "Please help me. Tell me what to do. I'm so afraid of making the wrong decision."

Without hesitation, Penelope advised, "Talk to her. Give her a chance to explain. I think it possible that she had nothing to do with your abandonment." She gestured to their son. "I mean, just look at my situation. If Adele had abandoned Tommy at an insane asylum like she was always threatening to do, I would have been thrust into a position much like your mother's." She shook her head. "Talk to her, for your sake and Tommy's. It's only fair that he have a real name and perhaps even a doting grandma."

Seth stared down at the baby, who was twitching restively in his sleep. "All right. As soon as Tommy is better, I'll tuck my tail between my legs and go see my mother."

"Good," she said, feeling their son's forehead. Frowning, she fetched a basin of water and began sponging the baby's body. As she worked, she asked, "Where did you get the name Tyler?"

Looking at his son, Seth replied, "Remember me mentioning an old fellow who liked peanuts and reminded me of an elephant?"

Penelope nodded.

"That man was Wilbur Tyler. I met him in Virginia City when I was nineteen. I had just drifted into town looking for work, and he was at a saloon where I stopped for a drink. For some reason he took a liking to me and offered me a job helping him work his claim. Over the course of the next couple of years, he not only taught me the mining business, but became the father I'd never had. We became so close that one night when we were sitting by the campfire getting drunk, he pointed out that I had no last name. He said he'd be honored if I'd be his son and offered me his own. Of course I accepted. When he died a year later, he left me the mine. It was that mine that eventually made me wealthy."

"He sounds like a wonderful old character. I would have liked to meet him," Penelope commented with a smile.

"He would have loved you. He always had an eye for a pretty lady," Seth replied, rubbing at his temples. His head was pounding so hard, it felt ready to explode.

Penelope paused from bathing the baby to lay her hand on his forehead. "Does your head ache?"

Her palm was cool and soft. It felt wonderful. Closing his eyes, he admitted, "It does hurt. I guess I'm overtired."

Making one of her soothing little noises, she laid a damp towel on his forehead. "There, love. Now, try and get some sleep."

Lulled by the gentle sounds of splashing water and Penelope's soft humming, he almost instantly complied.

He didn't wake until early the next morning. Oddly enough, though he'd slept for many hours, he felt even more tired than before. And his head! If anything, it hurt worse than ever. Propping up on his elbow, he squinted at his dimly lit surroundings, bleary-eyed and disorientated. When he finally remembered where he was and why, he reached out to touch his son. The baby was gone.

Irrationally panicked, he bolted up calling Penelope's name, only to sink back down again, clutching his wildly reeling head.

"Over here," he heard her call softly. Through the spinning blur, he located her. She'd pulled the rocker in front of the fire, and now sat in it with the baby. He sagged with relief.

When the dizziness had subsided to a less debilitating degree, he rose shakily to his feet and slowly moved toward her. "How is he?" Seth asked, his voice hoarse from sleep.

"Much better. He's cooler now."

Sinking to his knees next to the rocker, he peered down at his son. He lay motionless in Penelope's arms, snugly wrapped in a blue shawl with a plush toy rabbit tucked in beside him. He was the picture of peaceful slumber with his lips slightly parted and his head lolling against Penelope's breast. Gently, so as not to disturb him, Seth touched his cheek. He was cool.

Very cool. An alarm going off in his head, he dropped his fingers to the side for the baby's neck. For several breathless moments, he tried to find a pulse. Nothing. Frantically he ripped the shawl away from his son's chest.

"Seth! You're going to wake him!" Penelope protested.

Barely hearing her in his terror, he pressed his ear to Tommy's chest, praying to hear a faint murmur. As happened all too often, his prayers went unanswered.

"Seth?"

Slowly he lifted his head to meet Penelope's oddly flat gaze with his anguished one. "Our son is dead."

Chapter 26

Seth watched with helpless anguish as Penelope retucked the shawl around the baby and resumed rocking. In a harsh monotone so different from her usual melodious vocal flow, she started to sing, " 'Hush-a-bye, my precious babe; let lovely dreams—' "

"Sweetheart—" Seth choked out.

" '—In showers fall. Lullaby, sleep through the night and—' "

"Please, love. Listen to me," he begged, standing up and grasping her shoulders to stop her frenzied rocking.

Her voice rose a decibel, drowning him out. " 'Be my cheerful morning light. Close your eyes, my bonny one. And—' "

Brittle with grief and guilt, Seth snapped. "He's dead!" he shouted, grabbing her chin and forcing her to look at him in a desperate attempt to be heard. Her eyes were completely blank. "Our son is dead," he repeated more gently this time.

" '—Listen to my song of dreams." She almost shrieked the words. "I wish you everlasting joy. And—' " Her voice broke then.

Slowly Seth sank to his knees in front of her, his hands sliding from her shoulders, down until he grasped her upper arms. "I'm sorry, sweetheart ... so sorry," he whispered, searching her eyes for a dawning of comprehension. There was none. She stared straight through him, unblinking and unseeing. "Just look at me, love. Please," he implored. "You—"

"It's my fault," she interrupted with unnatural calm.

"No! You're not to blame. You did everything—"

She cut him off as if he hadn't spoken. "God's punishing me for not wanting my baby."

"Of course you wanted him! You loved him! Anyone could see that," Seth denied vehemently.

She looked at him then, not in acknowledgment of who he was, but curiously, rather like the way one views an intriguing stranger. "I didn't want him at first. I resented him terribly while I carried him. I blamed him for ruining my life." She tipped her head to one side, peering at him in a way that reminded him of a sparrow begging for a crumb. "Sometimes when I read of the success of another singer performing a role that should have been mine, I actually hated him."

"Don't . . . please . . ." Seth entreated, her every word ripping at his heart.

But she continued anyway. "I'd think of all I was missing . . . the applause, my fawning admirers, the parties held in my honor, and I'd beg God to take him from me, to make me miscarry so I could reclaim my life." A tear rolled down her cheek then. "I never knew how much I would adore him . . . what my darling Tommy would mean to me. Making me love him was God's punishment."

"No." Seth shook his head, dying a little inside. "Love is a gift, not a punishment."

She nodded, her expressionless face incongruently streaked with tears. "Love . . . yes . . . that is a gift. But to inspire and deepen that love, only to snatch it away . . . ah, now, that is punishment of the cruelest sort. Punishment that I deserve." She shifted her gaze abruptly to the baby's lifeless form. "My poor darling. There, there, now," she crooned, patting his back and making soft, motherly little coos as if he were alive and crying.

It was all too terrible to watch, to hear. Too tragic to bear. Feeling as if he'd go as mad with grief as Penelope if it continued, Seth gently tried to pry the baby from her embrace. She clutched the tiny body tighter, glaring at him as fiercely as a mother wolf protecting her pup from a hunter. "Please, love," he coaxed softly. "Let me hold my son."

She shook her head. "No. I just got him to sleep."

A sob tore at Seth's chest, but he managed to reassure her. "I won't wake him, I promise. I just want to wrap him in something warm so we can take him into town to see the doctor."

She crushed the baby tighter against her breast as she glanced out the window, her face contorted with such intense sorrow that Seth wondered how someone could be so badly hurt inside and still live. "Snow," she whispered, hopelessness woven throughout her voice. "I promised I'd have Tommy home before the first snowflake fell."

She looked back at the motionless bundle in her arms. "I'm sorry, darling," she murmured. "So sorry for failing you. I—" She crumpled forward then, Tommy clutched protectively to her breast. Seth caught her and swept her into his embrace.

For a long while he sat holding her, their dead son cradled between them, rocking them all back and forth, weeping soundlessly. When his tears at last ran dry, he pressed a kiss to Penelope's head and murmured, "Sweetheart?"

She didn't move a muscle. He drew back a fraction to peer at her face. Her eyes were fixed and staring, as if in a trance. "Penelope?" He shook her slightly. Not so much of a flicker. Over and over again he called her, alternately coaxing and demanding, then tearfully begging for a response. There was none.

Falling silent himself, Seth stared down at Penelope's pale, vacant face, panic bubbling up inside him. Though she still breathed, she was as dead to him as his son.

No! he protested fiercely, his every fiber rebelling against the loss of the woman he loved. His son was beyond helping, but she wasn't . . . she couldn't be! He wouldn't let her be! He had to do something to help her.

His mind worked furiously, searching for an answer. Perhaps a doctor? As he stared at her blank face, considering, a single tear escaped the corner of her eye. It was as if she were trapped inside by her grief, her tear a mute plea for release.

How? he wanted to scream. *How can I help you?* But, of course, he knew it would do him no good, just as he knew that hiring a million doctors would be futile. No medicine in the world could cure what ailed her. What he needed was to find someone who'd loved a child against all odds and lost it. Who had suffered what Penelope was now suffering and could tell him how to help her. He needed—

His mother? If she'd indeed loved and lost him as she claimed, wouldn't she understand Penelope's paralyzing sorrow? Wasn't it possible that she might hold the key to release her from her inner prison of pain? Would she help him?

He had to ask her . . . he would ask her . . . for Penelope's sake. He'd crawl to her on his hands and knees, and kiss her feet if necessary. Anything to regain the woman he loved.

As he rose and carefully set Penelope back in the rocker, his reeling head reminded him, as it had earlier, that he was in no condition to prostrate himself at anyone's feet.

Impossibly dizzy, his head aching almost beyond bearing, Seth pulled on his clothes, then bundled Penelope up in several quilts for the ride into town. She was strangely biddable to his commands, responding automatically like the subject of a hypnotism experiment. Not once, not even when he took the baby from her arms, did she display so much as a hint of awareness.

A half hour later they headed for town. Penelope, as limp as a rag doll, rode braced against his chest, while her hired horse bearing the baby trotted placidly behind on a lead rope.

For Seth, the long, cold trip seemed interminable. Never had he felt so wretched, never had he exerted more willpower than during those hours as he struggled to stay in the saddle. Several times as they slowly wound their way down the snowy foothills, his vision grew so fuzzy, his dizziness so intense that he came dangerously close to fainting. Twice his nausea forced him from his horse to the ground, where he lay retching dryly, excruciating pain radiating from his broken rib with every heave. Just when he was certain he could go no farther, they came to the Platte River bridge. Mercifully the Vanderlyn house was only a mile away.

It was just past noon when they reached their destination. The place looked deserted. Not a thread of lamplight spilled through the drawn curtains; not a wisp of smoke curled from the chimneys. The doors of the carriage house, just visible through the scraggly trees, were thrown open, revealing the emptiness inside. Panic slugged at Seth's gut. Where could Louisa have gone in this weather? The answer that sprang to his overwrought mind merely heightened his anxiety.

Could it be that she was indeed guilty of her crimes against him and had fled from his retribution? That possibility made him long to weep. Yet what other explanation could there be? It was Sunday, so she wasn't likely to be at the brewery, or—

Sunday! If Seth hadn't been so weak with his sudden rush of relief, he'd have probably slapped himself. Of course! How stupid of him! From the Pinkerton reports he knew that

Louisa faithfully attended church—one of the Lutheran ones, if he remembered correctly. He pulled out his watch and checked the time. Twelve forty-eight. She could be back anytime now.

As he shoved his watch back into his pocket, a freezing wind blasted from the west. Instinctively he drew Penelope's shivering form against his chest, shielding her from the cold. He had to get her to shelter before she took a chill.

He glanced back at the house speculatively. Perhaps there was a servant inside who would let them wait in the foyer. If not, they would sit on the veranda. At least the building would break the wind and offer a small measure of protection.

With that mission in mind, he dismounted. After waiting a moment for his dizziness to pass, he lifted Penelope from the saddle. He was so weak and shaky that it was only through a sheer force of will that he managed to maneuver her safely to the ground. He was tying the horses to the hitching post when a vehicle came clipping down the street.

It slowed as it approached, and when it pulled to a stop next to him, he recognized it as Lousia's buggy. Squinting painfully against the glare from the falling snow, he looked up from the black and red wheel to the woman within. She looked back; her face was as white as the fur trimming her black paletot-mantle.

For a heartbeat in time, mother and son stared at each other; her gaze uncertain yet yearning; his mutely appealing. Lisbet, who sat beside Lousia clutching a beaver muff, looked back and forth between the parties, visibly baffled.

It was Seth who finally broke the silence. "I need to talk to you. Please . . ." he begged, his voice hoarse with emotion.

She bit her lip and looked away.

Frantic, he hurled into her line of vision. The violent motion set his head spinning with a savagery that brought him to his knees. As he fell, he lifted his trembling hand to her in desperate entreat. "Please . . ." he whispered. Then everything went black. For the second time in as many meetings, Seth fainted at his mother's feet.

" '*Slaap, kindje, slaap,*' " sang a low voice.

Penelope, Seth thought hazily, struggling to open his eyes. But his heavy lids refused to budge.

" *'Daar buiten loopt een schaap,'* " the singing continued, this time accompanied by a faint splash of water.

No, not Penelope. Her voice was higher ... clearer ... sweeter. Then who? With concentrated effort, he managed to slit open one lid. Light, brutal and glaring, pierced right through his eye into his throbbing brain. Mouthing a soundless groan, he clamped it shut again.

" *'Eeen schaap met witte voetjes.'* " A wet cloth moved over his chest in spiraling motions. It felt cool ... wonderful. He opened his mouth to say so, but no words issued from his dry throat.

" *'Drinkt er de melk zo zoetjes.'* " The cloth was drawn away. There was a splash; then it returned, this time gliding down his midsection and over his belly.

Again he tried to speak. This time he succeeded. "Feels good," he muttered, his voice cracking and breaking like that of a youth making the transition into manhood.

The cloth paused on his belly, then was pulled away. After a beat, he felt a work-roughened hand cup his cheek, just as Penelope always did. *No. Not Penelope,* he reminded himself. *Her hands were soft ... silky, like the skin of a newborn lamb.* His brow furrowed. Where was Penelope, anyway? It seemed as if there was something he ought to be remembering about her.

"Can you hear me?" a vaguely familiar voice inquired.

Curious to match the face to the voice, Seth slitted open his eye again. Again he clamped it shut, this time moaning, "Light ... hurts."

She made a soothing little clucking noise and patted his cheek. Something about that noise tugged at his memory. "The doctor warned me that your eyes might be sensitive to the light at first. He said it's normal after what you've been through."

After what he'd been through ... doctor? None of it made the slightest bit of sense. The hand left his cheek, and he felt the bed move as the owner of the voice stood up. He heard her move away, then a-*swish!* and a-*clink!* followed by the sound of muffled footsteps approaching the bed again.

"There. I've drawn the drapes and dimmed the lamp a bit," she said. "Why don't you try to open your eyes again?"

He did, experimentally peeping out of one eye. No pain, just an infusion of soft lamplight. Sighing, he opened the other one. Everything was a blur. He blinked several times in rapid succession trying to clear his vision. Gradually the colors and shadows merged into the shape of a tall, willowy woman; a woman who was older, yet beautiful; one who looked distinctly worried.

Recognition niggled at Seth's brain as he stared up at her face. Though shadows obscured the color of her eyes, there was something familiar about the variegated shadings of her wheat-shot honey hair. And her jaw ... it was unusually strong for a female, square and stubborn, like—

Then memory assailed him. *Louisa ... Tommy ... death ...*

"Penelope!" he screamed, bolting up. Instantly he crumpled back down again, crippling pain lancing through the side of his skull. "Jesus," he muttered, reaching up to press his hand to the throbbing area. His fingers met with what felt like a thick swathe of gauze.

Louisa made a soothing sound and patted his shoulder. "She's fine," she crooned. "She's sleeping right now."

"The ... baby?"

"At the undertakers, poor little dear," she informed him, raising his head a bit to hold a glass of water to his lips. "For a while there we were afraid you might join him."

Seth obediently took a sip. It tasted good. Suddenly thirstier than he'd ever been in his life, he tried to take a bigger gulp, but she pulled the glass away. "Slowly," she instructed, returning it to his lips. "We don't want it coming right back up again."

When Seth had drunk as much as Louisa would allow and was once again lying down, he asked, "What happened?"

"Do you remember fainting?"

He started to nod, but then thought better of it. "Yes."

"Doc Larson said it was due to the swelling of your brain; the result, he believes, of some blows you took to your head a day or so earlier." She gently touched the bandage. "When you didn't regain consciousness after eight hours, he told me quite frankly that there would be little or no chance for your recovery unless he opened your skull and released the pressure."

Her fingers glided downward to cup his cheek again. "As terrifying as I found the operation, I saw no choice but to let him do it. I wanted you to have every possible chance." She bent nearer, and he could see tears shimmering in her eyes. "I simply couldn't bear to lose you again."

Seth laid his hand over hers on his cheek, the genuine tenderness in her expression and voice erasing the last of his
doubts. "You're never going to lose me again," he promised.
"I intend to be your son whether you want me or not."

The joy on her face was so radiant, it was like watching
the sun rise in her eyes. "Of course I want you. I wanted and
loved you from the first second I looked at your wrinkly little face," she declared fiercely.

Seth chuckled. "Wrinkled was I?"

"And red and skinny with the baldest head I'd ever seen."
She reached down and lifted his right arm to reveal the scar
on the underside. "You also had a nasty cut on your arm."
She gently caressed the mark. "The midwife mistakenly
grasped your arm with her forceps during your delivery and
tore your flesh. As tired as I was from giving birth, I insisted
on tending the wound myself."

She smiled suddenly, her eyes misting over. "I'll never
forget how you looked lying naked and squalling on my lap.
You were so beautiful. I'd never seen a newborn before, and
I found every finger, toe, even your tiny sex, fascinating. I
bandaged your arm with my finest cambric handkerchief." A
sob caught her voice. "It was the first and last thing I ever
did for you."

"No, not the last," Seth said in a hushed voice. "How can
you say such a thing after all you've done for me these past
few days? Without your care, I'd probably be dead now." He
shook his head gingerly and took her hand in his. "No . . .
Mother. With God's grace the last will come many years
from now."

"Mother. How I've longed to hear you call me that." The
look she gave him was almost shy. "Do you know what else
I've wished?" At his encouraging smile, she replied, "To
hold you again as I did the day you were born. Though
you've grown to remarkable"—she eyed his long form—
"and splendid proportions since that day, I'd like to hold you
again if you'll let me."

Seth held out his arms, too choked with raw emotion to
tell her that being held was exactly what he wanted at that
moment. With a strength he found surprising, she swept him
into her embrace, hugging him fiercely while alternately
crooning loving nonsense and covering his face with kisses.

Peace such as he'd never known before engulfed Seth as
he laid his head on her shoulder. Sighing his contentment, he

closed his eyes, cozy and safe in the shelter of his mother's arms.

It was a long while later when Louisa eased him back down to his pillows. Then she sat by his side practically devouring him with her gaze. It was as if she was trying to memorize every detail. "Your beautiful hair ... I'm sorry," she murmured, touching the bandage. "What the doctor didn't shave, he cropped."

For some odd reason, Seth didn't feel more than a passing twinge at the loss. What was the sacrifice of a little hair when compared to the gains of a family and his life? He said as much.

She chuckled at his philosophical reply. "You sound just like your father when you talk like that. He was the most levelheaded man I ever met. That's part of why I loved him so."

Seth stared at his mother as if she'd lost her mind as well. Mad Pieter Van Cortlandt, levelheaded?

As if reading his thoughts, she said, "Oh, no, my darling son. I haven't turned lunatic on you. And I know what you're thinking. I saw the Pinkerton reports when I transferred your belongings here from the American House." She shook her head. "My poor, poor dear. How awful it must have been for you these last couple of years thinking that Pieter was your father."

Seth's chest tightened with wary hope at her words. "Pieter wasn't my father?"

She shook her head again. "Oh, no. Your father was Martin Vanderlyn, the finest man in the world."

"Then, I'm not in danger of going mad?" he asked cautiously, afraid to believe in fate's sudden, merciful twist.

"Heavens, no!" she exclaimed. "You don't have a drop of tainted blood in you, and neither do I. Pieter inherited his madness from my father's first wife, Lucy Decker. She hanged herself shortly after he was born. My mother was Sarah De Vries, father's second wife, and a more soundminded woman never lived."

If Seth had had the strength, he'd have jumped up and down shouting his joy. Instead he settled for a weak whoop and a wide grin. But it was enough. He had the rest of his life to celebrate his good fortune. *He had the rest of his life.* He let out another whoop at that exhilarating truth.

"Calm down ... ssh ... lie still," Louisa urged, pushing

him back down on the pillows as he tried to rise. "The doctor said under no circumstances are you to become overexcited."

Too eager for details to heed her admonishments, he struggled up on his elbows and shot off in a barrage, "Why was I told that Pieter is my father, and how did I end up at St. John's Chapel? And why did the caretaker tell me that you ordered me killed at birth? And what about—"

"Later," she interrupted in a firm voice, forcing him to lie down again. "Right now I'm going to finish bathing you; then you're going to sleep." At his mulish scowl, she chided, "It won't do you any good to jerk your chin at me. Don't forget that you're not the first stubborn Vanderlyn I've dealt with."

He slanted her a sly look from beneath his eyelashes. Ah. But she hadn't dealt with this particular Vanderlyn before. Relaxing his frown into a good-natured grin, he bargained, "I'll make you a deal. I'll close my eyes and lie completely still while you bathe me, if you'll answer my questions while you work. Afterward, I'll go straight to sleep. I promise."

She laughed as she poured fresh water into the basin on the bedside table. "Now you really sound like your father. If ever there was a man with a flair for bargaining, it was Martin."

"I wish I'd known him," Seth murmured regretfully.

"I wish you had, too. He'd have been proud to call you son. You look like him, you know."

Seth stared at her, puzzled. "How can that be? I've seen the portrait of your father, and I'm the mirror image of him."

She looked up from the towel in her hands to study his face, then shook her head. "You've got the Van Cortlandt features, true. But those aren't what I see when I look at you. I see the gentleness of your smile and the warm intelligence in your eyes. I see things that have nothing to do with your skin and bones, things that show me what kind of man you are. What I see are all the marvelous qualities I'd hoped you'd inherit from Martin."

"Will you tell me about him, and about yourself?" Seth looked up at her imploringly. "Do we have a deal?"

"That will take far longer than it takes to bathe you," she said, arranging the bedcovers around his waist.

"Then, tell me what you can. Tell me how you met my father and about my birth. Please?"

"All right," she agreed, dipping a clean towel in the water. "But if I notice you becoming even the slightest bit agitated, I'll stop talking."

"Fine."

"Fine," she echoed. "Then, close your eyes."

When he did, she resumed bathing him, starting over again with his face. "Hmm. Now, where should I begin?"

He opened one eye. "The beginning is always a good place."

"A smart aleck?" She heaved an exaggerated sigh. "Another family trait I'm afraid, one of the more unfortunate ones."

"One of my father's?"

"No. Mine," she retorted, grasping his ear and swabbing it as if he were a two-year-old. "Now, close your eyes and be quiet."

He made a face and obeyed.

"All right, from the beginning, then. Our branch of the Van Cortlandt family are direct descendants of the mighty Wouter Van Cortlandt. We, along with the Van Rensselaers and the Livingstons, were one of the few families to successfully cultivate and perpetuate the old system of partroonship." She mopped down his neck. "Are you familiar with a patroonship?"

"No."

"It was an oppressive system, much like the feudal system of the Middle Ages. My father's land tenants were bound by a perpetual lease taken out, in many instances, by their ancestors two hundred years earlier. The terms of the lease were despotic, stating that the manor lord be entitled to a tribute of one-tenth of everything grown, raised, or manufactured on the manor land, plus an annual rent of $300. As if that weren't enough, each tenant was also required to contribute labor toward the upkeep of the buildings and roads; cut, split, and deliver six feet of firewood for the manor hearths; and give the manor lord three days' service with his horses and wagon."

Seth shifted his arm to allow her to wash the underside. "Why didn't the tenants just leave?"

She shook her head. "Most couldn't afford to. The system kept them so poor that they were never able to save enough money to start anew. Besides, their families had lived there for generations, and they viewed the manor as their home. The Vanderlyns were one such family."

"They were farmers?"

"No, brewers. And fine ones at that. Their beer was in demand from the very beginning. So much so, that by the time Martin was born in 1810, the Vanderlyns would have been wealthy had it not been for the heavy tariffs levied by the patroonship on all goods sold outside the manor."

"Surely such tariffs were illegal by then?"

"Most of the tenants thought so," she replied, her touch gentle as she bathed the bruised flesh over his broken rib. "As a result, they organized a farmers' alliance with a common objective of abolishing the patroonship."

She paused to rewet the towel, resuming her story as she washed his belly. "The alliance, however, was split on how to attain their goal. Half thought it best to discredit the Van Cortlandt land grant titles in court, thus dissolving the partroonship, while the rest felt that stronger measures were needed. Those advocating stronger measures soon went their own way. Their first act was to burn an effigy of my father on the throne where he sat to collect his annual tributes."

Louisa pulled the blankets to his knees and draped a towel over his loins in one efficient movement. "When my father retaliated by evicting the farmers his spies said were responsible for the act, things turned violent. From then on, we couldn't leave the manor without having our carriage stoned or being confronted by alliance members. It was as a result of one of those confrontations that I met your father."

Seth cracked open one eye to peer at her. "My father subscribed to the stronger measures?"

She shook her head vigorously. "He just happened along. I was returning from spending a fortnight with a schoolmate when my carriage was set upon by a mob of alliance members. Both my guards were overpowered and pulled from their saddles, and my driver was knocked from his perch by a flying stone. The horses, panicked by the chaos, pulled the driverless vehicle a mile or so down the road before it finally flipped over."

"It's a miracle you weren't killed," Seth commented.

The wet towel swept the length of his thigh. "Even more miraculous still that I wasn't hurt, though I was terrified out of my wits. You can imagine my relief when your handsome father came along and insisted on taking me back to the manor house. He was so courteous and charming that by the time he delivered me to my father's door, I was completely smitten. So much so, that I took to contriving 'accidental' encounters so I could see him."

She moved to his other thigh. "Until my conversations with Martin, I didn't fully understand the patroon system or see how wrong it was. I wasn't even quite sure why my carriage had been attacked. He opened my eyes quickly enough."

The cloth glided over his knee to his calf. "Before long we fell in love and took to meeting in an abandoned farmhouse a couple of miles from the manor. I don't have to tell you what we did during our trysts. Naturally I kept our romance a secret from my father. He harbored hopes of me marrying our elderly, widowed neighbor, Cornelius De Windt, and would have evicted the Vanderlyns if he had so much as suspected my feelings for Martin."

"I was conceived at the farmhouse?"

"Yes. Though your father didn't find out until many years later." She began to scrub his foot. "Not that I deliberately kept the news from him. The morning of the day I intended to tell him, I was called to my father's study. He—"

"Tickles," Seth interrupted, jerking his foot away.

Louisa laughed and tossed the washing cloth into the basin. "Your father had ticklish feet, too," she said, pulling the blankets back up to his waist.

He smiled at that bit of information. "So what happened?"

She rose and went to the highboy across the room. "My maid had noticed my morning illness. Correctly guessing the cause, she took her suspicions to my father," she replied, opening the top drawer. "When I arrived at his study, I found him waiting with the manor midwife. Without giving me a chance to confirm or deny my maid's allegations, he ordered me examined right then and there." She held up a snowy nightshirt for inspection.

Apparently judging it suitable, she tossed it over her arm and brought it back to the bed. "I thought he'd kill me when the midwife confirmed my pregnancy. Only the day before he'd promised my hand in marriage to Cornelius in exchange for a bordering parcel of land he'd coveted for years. Of course he demanded that I name your father. Knowing that he'd have Martin killed if I told the truth, I accused my mad brother, Pieter, of raping me." She looked up from the nightshirt placket she was unbuttoning. "What do you know about Pieter?"

Seth shrugged one shoulder. "The manor caretaker told me that he was mad and forced himself on several of the housemaids."

Louisa nodded slowly. "I'd overheard the servants gossiping about the matter only a week earlier and thought—I—" Her voice failed then, her words strangled by a sob.

"Mother—" Seth began, laying a comforting hand on her arm.

Her face twisting with terrible anguish, she dropped the nightshirt to her lap and grasped his hand, staring into his eyes with desperate appeal. "I know that accusing Pieter was an awful thing to do," she said, her voice vibrating with raw emotion, "but please believe me when I tell you that I thought it the only way to safeguard both you and Martin. I was young and foolish. . . . I never imagined the tragic consequences of my lies or that it would be you, the babe I sought to protect, who would suffer the worst. I—" She broke again, tears raining down her cheeks.

Seth laced his fingers through hers and gave her hand a reassuring squeeze. "Ssh. Don't. You don't have to explain. I understand. I, too, have lied to protect a loved one, and with equally tragic results." He smiled gently at her stricken face. "It seems we've discovered another trait I inherited from you: we both think with our hearts instead of our heads."

At her faint answering smile, he added, "If you don't feel up to telling the rest of the story just now, I'll understand."

She wiped the dampness from her cheeks with the back of her hand. "No. I want to tell you."

"You're sure?" He looked at her dubiously. When she nodded, he said, "I know from the Pinkerton reports that Pieter was confined to an asylum shortly thereafter, and according to the caretaker you disappeared as well. As I remember, your father told everyone that you'd gone to Paris to buy a trousseau."

She nodded. "He wasn't about to let my pregnancy stand between him and his precious land, so he locked me and my shameful condition in the attic of the old patroon house, an abandoned cottage about a half mile from the manor. The

trousseau story was his way of explaining my absence and
stalling the wedding until after you were born."

"I'm surprised your father didn't insist on a hasty marriage so he could fob me off as De Windt's."

"He was worried that you might inherit Pieter's madness
and was afraid that people would think that it was the Van
Cortlandt, not the Decker, blood that was tainted."

"So he planned to wait until I was born and then dispose
of me like an unwanted kitten," Seth stated flatly, chilled
that any human, much less his own grandfather, could be so
cruel.

"I didn't know of his plan, truly I didn't!" she swore, releasing his hand to pick up the nightshirt again. "He told me
that you were to be fostered with a good family. I agreed
only because I was certain that Martin would doubt the stories of my Paris trip and find a way to rescue me before you
were born."

Seth raised up a fraction to help her slip the nightshirt
over his head. "But he never came, did he?" he inquired
gently, sliding his arms through the sleeves.

"No. He thought I'd decided against an uncertain future
with him in favor of a secure one with Cornelius, and left
the county shortly thereafter." She drew back the covers to
pull the hem of the gown over his hips and down to his
calves. "So for the next seven months, I remained a prisoner.
Except for the attendance of my jailer, the midwife, and an
occasional visit from my father, I was left completely alone.
I passed the days talking to you and making plans for your
future. By the time you were born I loved you so much, I
thought I'd die of it. I almost did die of grief when I was
told a few hours later that you had died."

She shook her head, her expression pensive as she tucked
the blankets around his shoulders. "It wasn't until my father
lay dying seventeen years later that he confessed to having
ordered you killed and told me that his manservant had instead abandoned you at St. John's Chapel. I tried to find you
then, but to no avail." She seemed about to add something,
but instead kissed his forehead. "And that, my boy, is the
whole tale."

"Not quite," he contradicted, smiling at her maternal kiss.
"I know that you were widowed in '51, shortly before your
father died, and that you married Martin in '52. But I don't

know how you two were reunited or why you came to Denver."

She nodded. "Martin's father died about the same time as mine, and he returned to the county to sell what was by then his parents' land. As fate would have it, we met on the road where he'd rescued me eighteen years earlier. It turned out that he, too, was widowed. When I told him about you and my father's betrayal, we reconciled. We were married a month later. You know from your reports that Corenlius and I never had a child, so all his property went to his sons from his first marriage. What was left of the Van Cortlandt fortune was put in trust for Pieter's care. Since there was nothing to hold us to the county, we decided to come West and start anew. Except for always wondering about your fate, we lived happily until Martin's death two years ago."

"And that truly is the end of the tale," she declared. "Now, unless you're up to eating some broth, I expect you to honor your part of the deal and take a nap."

Seth made a face at the thought of food. "I'll take a nap."

After giving his cheek a fond pat, she rose. "I'll be nearby if you need anything." As she gathered up the damp towels and basin of water, she began to sing the same song she'd been singing when he'd awakened.

"That's pretty," he murmured. "What is it?"

"It's a Dutch lullaby my mother sang to me when I was a child. I used to sing it to you when you were in my womb." She chuckled. "You were an active baby, and it stilled your kicking."

The mention of lullabies and babies brought forth the memory of Penelope singing her "Song of Dreams" to Tommy. His voice catching on his heartbreak, Seth asked, "Penelope . . . is she well?"

Louisa set the towels and basin on the washstand with a sigh. "She spends most of her time sleeping, though she is talking now. She told me about your son . . . I'm truly sorry. I know how painful it is not having the chance to know and love your own child."

"I've been too ill to feel much grief," he admitted, guilt stabbing at his chest. While he'd been lying here in sweet oblivion, Penelope had undoubtedly been suffering the torments of hell. Wanting nothing more than to hold her, comfort her, and promise her the forever he was now free to pledge, he asked, "Can I see her? I mean, after I take my nap?"

When Louisa didn't immediately respond, he rolled onto his side to look at her. Her face was turned away from him, but there was something about the set of her shoulders that sent a shiver of uneasiness tingling up his spine. "What is it, Mother?" he demanded, dreading the answer.

She turned around then and faced him, her expression an unsettling combination of misery and compassion. "She refuses to see you. She—"

"Blames me for the death of our son," he finished for her.

"No . . . no!" she exclaimed, shaking her head as she rushed across the room to the bed. "It's not like that. She blames herself for the baby's death and for almost causing yours as well. She thinks that she's cursed by God. She fears that if she comes near you, you'll come to more harm."

"That's ridiculous," he snapped, laboring to sit up, determined to somehow go to Penelope and talk some sense into her. "None of what happened was her fault."

Louisa easily wrestled him back down to his pillows. "I've told her that, but she won't listen. She won't listen to you, either. She's too full of grief to see logic."

"But I have to do something to help her!" he protested, frustrated by his invalid state. That Penelope was suffering and he was unable to comfort her was beyond bearing.

Louisa shook her head and braced both hands on his shoulders, pinning him to the bed as he tried to rise again. "She'll simply be all the more convinced that she's a curse if you get up too soon and have a relapse. Give her time. She'll come around. I promise."

A sob ripped from Seth's chest as he stared helplessly up into his mother's sympathetic face. "I love her so much. There has to be something I can do to help her."

"I think you already have," she said, stroking his cheek with loving hands. "Some friends of yours, the Skolfields, came by. Apparently you left them a note informing them of your whereabouts and your baby's death. Anyway, they expressed their condolences and brought a reply to the telegraph you had them send. I took the liberty of opening it."

"Penelope's brother is coming, I assume?" he asked, though he never doubted it for a moment.

"Yes. He and his wife will be here on the fifteenth. That's the day after tomorrow."

Seth frowned. The fifteenth? That meant he'd been uncon-scious for . . . "I've been here four days?" he asked, aghast.

"Yes. And according to the doctor, you'll be here for a great while longer. Not," she added, giving his shoulder a squeeze, "that I'm complaining. I'm looking forward to pampering you."

He smiled faintly at that prospect.

"As for your young lady," she continued, "I think that seeing her brother and most especially her sister-in-law will do her a world of good. She said that her sister-in-law is a doctor, and she seems to put a great deal of stock in her skills. Perhap's the woman can disabuse this notion of a curse."

Hallie. Seth felt a weak rush of hope. If anyone could make Penelope see logic, it was her no-nonsense sister-in-law.

As he'd seen Penelope do a thousand times before, Seth crossed his fingers and wished upon his lucky star.

Chapter 27

They picnicked on her favorite bluff by the ocean. Like the weather and her company, the scene was perfect. Billowy white clouds paraded across the cerulean sky, each in the unmistakable shape of a circus animal. The air, scented with lilac and clover, was sweeter than the perfume of Eden; the breeze carried the warm kiss of spring. Below them, smooth and gleaming like an endless spill of liquid jade, stretched the sea. All around them bloomed flowers of every color and genus. There were rabbits everywhere.

Seth had laid a jewel-toned Persian carpet on the grass upon which they now lay arm in arm, watching the delighted Tommy scamper from rabbit to rabbit, feeding them gingerbread and nuzzling his rosy cheek against their fur.

He was such a bright, curious boy, their Tommy. So tall and straight and healthy, like his father. He continually ran to and fro, forever in motion, forever into mischief. "A real handful," as his nanny would say, a fond smile wreathing her lips.

"Look, Mama," he piped, his childish voice shrill with excitement. "I found a lucky bunny!" He ran toward her carrying a gray rabbit with a frayed pink ribbon tied around its neck.

Penelope pressed a kiss to Seth's smiling lips, then sat up, her heart soaring with perfect bliss as she held out her arms to welcome her son into her embrace. On and on Tommy ran, his sturdy legs pumping furiously. Yet he drew no nearer. It was if he were frozen in time and space, forever a heartbeat away.

Then she saw it, a dark, formless horror shadowing his steps. "Tommy!" she screamed, frantically trying to rise to her feet. Her legs were like rubber, weak and boneless, unable to support her. Calling his name over and over again, she tried to crawl to him, to save him from the nightmare swooping down upon him. But like her legs, her arms, too, failed her, and she fell, clawing helplessly at the ground. "Tommy . . ."

Then the blackness engulfed him, swallowing him until all that was left was the faraway echo of his voice as he cried for her one last time.

"Oh, please, no," she sobbed. "Please . . ." Slowly her surroundings faded, leaving her alone and shattered in endless nothingness. "Tommy . . ."

"Shh. It's all right, dear," said a soothing voice in the dark. There was something familiar about the voice, something kind and safe that was as comforting as a loving embrace. Someone grasped her shoulders then and gave her a gentle shake. "Open your eyes and look at me, Pen. Come on. It's time to wake up."

With herculean effort, Penelope obeyed. Still foggy from sleep, she blinked up at the figure bending over her. She didn't have to wait for her hazy vision to clear to know who it was; she'd know that copper-penny bright hair anywhere. "Hallie!" she exclaimed, throwing herself into her sister-in-law's arms. "Is it really you?"

"In the flesh," Hallie assured her, returning her hug.

"But how . . . when?" She pulled back to stare at the other woman's face, not quite daring to believe she was really there.

"Jake received a telegram from Seth asking us to come. The bartender at the Shakespeare told us you were here."

Penelope groped anxiously at Hallie's arm. "Have you seen Seth yet?"

"Poor man. He's had an awful time of it," Hallie clucked. "We spoke with him when we first arrived. Jake's still with him."

"But he is all right now, isn't he?" If anything happened to Seth . . .

"He seems on the mend, but I'll know for sure after I've examined him. He asked me to speak to you first . . . alone." She cupped Penelope's cheek in her cool palm then. "He told us about the baby. I'm so sorry. I wish there was something I could do."

Penelope swallowed hard and pulled away, too ashamed to meet Hallie's compassionate gaze. Staring at the gray plush rabbit ears poking out from beneath the tangled blankets by her side, she murmured, "You must think I'm awful."

"Awful?" She sounded genuinely surprised. "Of course not. Whatever makes you think that?"

Penelope bowed her head, too crushed beneath her guilt and sorrow to hold it up a second longer. "Because I killed my son and almost got Seth killed as well."

There was a long pause, then Hallie sighed. "Look at me, Penelope." When she didn't immediately obey, Hallie grasped her chin and raised it for her. "I want you to look at me so I can be certain that you understand what I'm about to say to you."

Reluctantly Penelope raised her lashes to meet her sister-in-law's gaze. Hallie's golden-brown eyes were soft and warm, inviting trust. "None of what happened is your fault," she said, enunciating each word with emphasis. "As tragic as it is, children die from the measles every day."

"But it was my fault," Penelope insisted, pulling her chin away. "Tommy was weak . . . sickly. He needed and should have had proper medical attention from the moment he was born. Because of my selfish mistakes, he wasn't attended by a real doctor until the very end. By then it was too late."

"You didn't deny him care," Hallie countered firmly. "Seth told us that that was the du Charme woman's doing."

Penelope glanced back down at the rabbit ears. "If I'd swallowed my pride and come home to San Francisco when I found myself pregnant, he never would have fallen into Adele's hands in the first place. Then none of this would have happened." She reached down and ran her finger down the velvety length of one ear. "He'd be alive today."

"If you'd come home to San Francisco to have your baby, and I don't deny that that would have been the sensible thing to do, it's possible that he might have died of the measles there. A terrible epidemic of the disease swept the city last year and a great many children were lost. We almost lost our Reed."

The rest of what she said faded away as Penelope slipped Tommy's bunny from beneath the blankets. Convulsively clutching it by the scruff of its neck, she slowly raised it before her. The sight of its cross-stitched nose and shiny glass eyes pitched her back to the day of her son's second birthday. As she recalled his delight in the toy, the fragile sound of his laughter, the feeble squirming excitement of his body, she thought she caught a glimpse his face reflected in the depths of the rabbit's eyes. He looked so happy . . . so very beautiful . . . like an angel.

"Oh, Tommy," she whimpered, crushing the toy to her breast. "My darling. I'm so sorry. Please . . . please forgive me. I love you. I didn't mean to kill you . . . I . . ."

"For heaven's sake, Pen! Listen to me!" Hallie commanded, grasping her shoulders to give her a hard shake.

Penelope jerked away, hugging the rabbit tighter. "No, you listen to me," she countered her words, coming out in a rasping whisper. "God took my baby because I'm selfish and wicked, because I'm undeserving of love. He tried to take Seth for the same reason."

Hallie shook her head. "That's nonsense. God didn't take your baby to punish you, and you had nothing to do with what happened to Seth. He said that his injury came from being set upon outside of town."

Penelope fixed her with a bleak stare. "Seth was attacked because of me. Adele sent those men to castrate and then kill him because he loved me." She shuddered violently, as she always did when she thought of what the outcome of that episode might have been. "Don't you see? God is punishing me by taking everyone I love. He's cursed me."

"No. I don't see," Hallie retorted stoutly. "Seth is very much alive and nobody, not even God, can ever take away your baby or the special love you shared."

Penelope's nails dug into the rabbit's back. "How can you say that?" she demanded, hysteria rising in her voice. "He did take him! Tommy is dead!"

Hallie smiled gently. "No. Not dead. He's very much alive . . . here," she touched the place over Penelope's heart, "and he'll live there forever, growing in the love you share with Seth. He'll live and thrive through your memories."

"Those memories are my torment . . . my punishment," she choked out, drawing the rabbit up to her face to rest her cheek against it. "They remind me every second of the day what I've lost . . . and why. They make me ache with a longing so terrible that I want to die to escape the pain."

"Penelope—" Hallie murmured, reaching out to draw her into her embrace again.

Penelope hurled away to the other side of the bed, crouching over the rabbit as if it were her son and she was shielding him from death. Peering wildly through her ropy tangles of hair, she demanded, "Do you know about Tommy's afflictions?"

Hallie nodded. "Seth told us."

Penelope returned her nod. "I understand now that they were part of my curse."

"Curses have nothing whatsoever to do with your son's infirmities," Hallie countered in a no-nonsense tone. "There's a perfectly logical reason—"

"Oh, at first I didn't question why he was born different or really even care. I just loved him," Penelope cut in as if the other woman hadn't spoken. "Then Seth told me about his tainted blood." Her eyes narrowed as she met Hallie's troubled gaze. "I assume you know about that?" She paused just long enough for Hallie to nod before continuing.

"When he explained how that taint could mark his offspring, I began to think about Tommy and was certain his afflictions were a consequence of Seth's cursed blood. But then, two days ago, Mrs. Vanderlyn told me the real story of Seth's birth, and I saw the truth: it wasn't his curse that marked our baby, but mine."

"You are not cursed." Hallie practically shouted to be heard above Penelope's rising voice. "I know for a fact that Tommy's infirmities were caused by a birth accident."

But Penelope was too deeply rooted in her guilt-ridden misery to listen to logic. "My poor baby," she keened. "He was forced to suffer because of my wickedness . . . because I swore at God and told him I hated him when I found myself pregnant—"

"Damn it! You will listen to me!" Hallie exclaimed, flinging herself at Penelope to wrestle her onto her back and force her to look up at her.

Penelope whimpered and tried to roll away, but Hallie refused to let her. Pinning her firmly beneath her taller, stronger form, she pressed her face close to Penelope's, forcing her to meet her determined amber gaze.

"You are not cursed, Penelope," she declared. "There is no such thing as a curse. Tommy's afflictions were due to a birth accident, nothing more."

Penelope shook her head, tears streaming from the corners of her eyes. She was suddenly tired, so very tired. She didn't want to talk about Tommy, or Seth, or her curse anymore. She wanted Hallie to go away and leave her alone so she could sleep, so she could curl up with the rabbit and dream of Tommy, so she could escape the pain.

But Hallie wouldn't go away. "It's true! It was an accident," she persisted, giving Penelope a shake that made her teeth chatter. "Seth told me about Tommy's difficult birth, how he was born with the birthing cord around his neck and was strangled. I've seen that happen before and seen the results. Those babies, if they don't die immediately, usually end up with infirmities such as those Seth described Tommy suffering. There's a name for what afflicted Tommy: it's called Little's disease."

"But if he'd had medicine ... a doctor ..." Penelope sobbed, not yet ready to let go of her guilt.

Hallie shook her head. "The only medicine for what ailed your Tommy was love, and you gave him plenty of that. The fact that he lived as long as he did is testimony to how potent it was. So you see? You aren't cursed at all."

"I've tried so hard to make sense of all this, to find logic in his death. But I can't! All I can think is that I must be cursed for something so terrible to happen to me ... and to Tommy."

Hallie rolled off her and drew her into her arms, patting her back as she held her close. "Terrible things happen everyday to all sorts of people. I've had terrible things happen to me. So has your brother, so has everyone else in the world. Does that mean we're all cursed? If so, then you have nothing to fear in visiting Seth or being around those you love, because we're all doomed anyway."

She drew back a fraction to look at Penelope's face. Smiling gently, she added, "Bad things happen to everyone. But so do good ones ... wonderful ones! ... like Tommy and Seth. And I've always found that the good things outweigh the bad a hundred to one."

Penelope lay very still, thinking about her words. Hallie was right, of course. Bad things happened to everyone. But then, so did good ones. And Tommy had been a good thing ... the best. If given the choice, she'd rather suffer the pain of losing him than never having had the chance to love him at all.

"Perhaps you're right," she finally choked out. "While losing Tommy feels like a curse, having him was a blessing, the greatest blessing I can imagine."

"And that blessing will go on forever, long after the terrible pain of your grief has faded," Hallie assured her.

"Will it fade? And the emptiness, too?" Penelope asked, wondering if her arms would ever stop aching to hold her baby.

"I'm not going to lie and tell you that it will go away completely, that your life will be the same as before. It won't." Hallie shook her head. "There will be times when you'll feel a shadow of emptiness, times when you'll even cry. But in the years to come you'll see your tears as a good thing, because they'll mean you're remembering Tommy. And remembering means that a part of him is alive within you."

She reached out and gently lifted a snarled tendril of hair from Penelope's wet cheek. "What I can promise is that someday his memory will make you smile instead of cry."

Penelope sniffled, desperately wanting to believe her promise, desperately wishing that the day she spoke of was now. "But how do I go on living until then? My whole life has been Tommy. Everything I've done has been for him. I don't know what to do with myself, I feel so lost."

"There's always Seth. He loves you and wants to fill your life. He's been in torment not being able to comfort you."

Penelope sighed. "Poor Seth. I've been so stupid and selfish in my grief."

"No. No more self-recriminations," Hallie chided softly. "Your behavior was perfectly normal, and we all, including Seth, understand. You need to accept that, as well as the fact that nobody is perfect and that we all make mistakes. You also need to give thought to what you want to do now."

"I know I want to take Tommy home to San Francisco," she replied, almost breaking again at the thought of Tommy, so tiny and dear, left to lie alone in Denver, the city that held so much sorrow for her. "But that's all I know right now."

"And what about Seth?" Hallie quizzed gently. "He wants to marry you, you know."

"Seth." She sighed. "I . . . I don't know. I love him, but we've been through so much together, so much sorrow. I'm afraid the pain will always be between us and shadow our future happiness."

"It might also create a stronger bond between you," Hallie pointed out. "Before you decide, you should speak with him. He's terribly anxious to see you. When I left the men, he was trying to cajole your brother into helping him out of bed so he could come to you."

"You're right ... as usual," Penelope admitted with a wan smile. "I do need to talk to Seth."

"Good." Hallie sat up and ineffectually smoothed her now crushed amber silk skirts. "Now, I know Jake is eager to see you. And no," she added as if reading her mind. "He's not going to scold you. He simply wants to hug you and make sure you're all right." Pressing a kiss to Penelope's forehead, she stood up. "May I tell Seth that you'll visit him later this afternoon?"

Penelope nodded as she sat up.

Nodding briefly in return, Hallie started for the door, only to pause with her hand on the knob. "Pen?"

Penelope looked up.

"You won't always feel the way you do now. The hurt will ease in time, I promise. Remember that when you speak with Seth."

"It looks like you'll be back to your irrepressible old self in no time," Penelope heard Hallie say as she approached the open door to Seth's room. Picking nervously at her black crepe skirt, she paused on the threshold to peer at the pleasant scene within.

Seth, colorfully garbed in his favorite red velvet dressing gown, sat in an overstuffed chair by the fire while Hallie tended his scalp and Louisa tucked a striped lap robe over his propped-up legs. Completing the cozy tableau were her brother, who lounged against the mantel, filling Seth in on their latest business venture, a sugar refinery, and Lisbet, who sat Indian-style on the floor, staring worshipfully up at Jake.

Penelope smiled faintly. She'd be rich if she had a dollar for every woman she'd seen look at her handsome brother like that. She surveyed her brother critically for a moment, then shifted her gaze back to the man in the chair. As much as she loved Jake and as undeniably handsome as he was, in her eyes he couldn't hold a candle to Seth. Not even with Seth in his present, admittedly diminished state.

Her heart ached at the sight of him. Her poor love. His face was thin, all sharp planes and sunken hollows, his golden skin bleached to the ashen pallor of one who'd been gravely ill. The flesh around his closed eyes was dark, almost bruised-looking, shadowing a purplish hue that perfectly matched the cheek and lip contusions left by Harley and his gang several days earlier.

Hallie had removed his cap of bandages to examine his surgical wound, exposing a head shaved smooth on one side with spikes of unevenly cropped hair on the other. The jagged line of neat black stitches bisecting his shaved left side bore grisly testimony to just how close to death he'd come.

A sob escaped Penelope as she stared at the evidence of his suffering, suffering that she in her foolishness had caused.

Louisa looked up from her fussing at the sound. "Penelope. Come in, dear," she invited cordially, while Hallie gave her an approving nod, and Lisbet and Jake voiced effusive greetings.

Seth didn't say a word. He didn't have to. The way he looked at her as she stepped into the room, so warm and loving, expressed his welcome far more eloquently than mere words.

As she approached him, Hallie gave his shoulder a fond squeeze and said, "I was just telling Seth how remarkably well his recovery is going. He'll be back on his feet in no time."

Penelope nodded, feeling suddenly awkward. Not quite certain what to say or do, she stopped next to his chair and resumed fidgeting with her skirt, only half listening as Jake launched into a description of a new refining process he'd recently seen demonstrated. As she stood fretfully unraveling a piece of jet braid trim, uncomfortably aware of the speculative glances being shot in her direction, Hallie interrupted Jake, exclaiming:

"Oh Lord! Will you look at this? I'm all out of boric acid." She waved an empty green bottle in the air. "I can't finish tending Seth's scalp until I get more." She shifted her gaze meaningfully from Seth to Penelope, then to her husband. "Jake, darling. Will you run out and buy me a new bottle?"

Jake lifted one dark brow in acknowledgment to her transparent ploy and nodded. "I'll be glad to, provided Lisbet will be kind enough to show me the way to the nearest pharmacy." He smiled and held out his arm to the girl on the floor.

Lisbet jumped up so fast that Penelope wondered if she

had springs instead of legs beneath her skirt. As Jake escorted the young girl from the room, Louisa gathered up the pile of soiled gauze strips from the dressing table, inquiring, "Would you like me to help you tear some fresh bandages, Dr. Parrish?" At Hallie's reply in the affirmative they, too, left, leaving Penelope alone with Seth.

For a long moment neither spoke. Finally Seth murmured, "I know I look awful, sweetheart, but you won't turn to stone if you look at me."

Though the words were uttered lightly, they were shaded with pained self-consciousness that made her long to pull him into her embrace and comfort him the way she had the night he'd cried in her arms. It was remembering that night and her pledge to marry him, a pledge she now knew she must break, that stopped her.

Pasting a reassuring smile on her lips, she looked up from the now shredded braid to meet his gaze. "You don't look a bit awful," she declared, reaching over to stroke his cropped hair. "You could never look anything but handsome."

He shuddered and caught her wrist, stopping her before she could touch his head. Drawing her hand to his lips to kiss it, he said, "I appreciate the vote of confidence, but I've seen myself in the mirror. I know I look like a dog half gone with mange." He gave her one of his crooked grins. "As much as I hate having you see me like this, I had to assure myself that you're all right."

That he, who'd been beaten within an inch of his life and almost died because of her deceit, was unselfishly concerned for her well-being shattered the hastily erected dam of her emotions. As her pent-up guilt, remorse, and sorrow spurted forth in a gut-wrenching rush, she slowly crumpled to her knees before him. "Oh, Seth," she choked out brokenly, clutching at his lap robe. "I'm so sorry. I-I've made such a mess of everything."

"Shh, Princess. Don't," he soothed, leaning forward to wipe a stray tear from her cheek. "What happened was as much my fault as yours."

She shook her head. "You were just trying to protect me."

"And you were trying to protect your son. So you can't be blamed, either." He cupped her chin in his palm and tipped her head up to stare at her face. His eyes soft with tenderness, he said, "We were both simply doing what we thought best. I think it's time we forgive ourselves for our mistakes and get on with living the rest of our lives."

She smiled faintly. "Your mother told me that Martin Vanderlyn was your father. You truly do have the rest of your life to live as you choose."

"And I choose to live it with you, if you still want me." His eyes sparkling with the topaz heat she knew so well, he begged, "Marry me, Penelope. We'll have a good life together, one filled with love and joy. We'll do everything we planned . . . we'll make tomorrow's dreams come true."

She opened her mouth to tell him that all their dreams would be impossible now, but he cut her off before she could speak. "I can offer you a real name now, a proud one to give to the houseful of children we'll have. Not," he added, his voice growing gentle, "that those children will ever replace Tommy. He'll always be a cherished part of our lives, I promise. And though it's true that I never really knew him, I expect you to acquaint me with him through your shared memories."

He leaned nearer until his lips were scant inches from hers. "Please say yes, sweetheart. Say you'll be Mrs. Seth Vanderlyn."

Penelope pulled away, her already broken heart splintering into a million excruciating slivers. "I can't," she whispered. "I'm sorry . . . but I can't marry you."

He looked as stunned as if she'd punched him in the belly.

"Can't you see, Seth?" She tugged desperately at his lap robe, wanting to weep at the hurt in his eyes. "Our marriage would never work. Not now. Though I love you as much as ever . . . more even . . . there's too much pain and sorrow between us for us to ever find peace together. We'd just destroy each other."

"You were once willing to gamble on our love, and against much greater odds," Seth whispered hoarsely. "You dared to believe then; can't you do the same now?"

She stared down at the gold, blue, and white wool blanket pleated between her fingers, tears blurring her vision as she shook her head. "Believing then meant having faith in you. And I did so willingly. I knew that even if madness tried to take you, you would find some way to overcome it so you could remain with me. But this"—she shook her head again—"this means believing in myself. Believing that I can

look at you and not think of Tommy . . . not be reminded of
my failures, my regrets."

She released the lap robe to sit back on her heels, forcing
herself to meet his bleak gaze. "Please forgive me, Seth. But
I can't believe. I haven't the strength."

He reached up to massage his temples with a sigh. If ever
a man looked beaten by life, it was Seth Vanderlyn. "You
feel that way now," he murmured, closing his eyes as if it
hurt to look at her, "but in time you might change your
mind. Perhaps you should wait a few months before giving
me an answer."

"And if the answer is still no?"

"All I've ever wanted was to make you happy, Penelope.
But if you decide that my love can't do that, then I won't
press you." He dropped his hand to his lap and slowly
opened his eyes. "Would you do me a favor and make one
last bargain with me? I'll never ask you for another."

She smiled in spite of the heaviness crushing her heart.
"Name it, Mr. Tyler . . . uh . . . Vanderlyn."

He smiled faintly at her use of his new name. "My mother
and I have decided to merge Vanderlyn Brewery with Queen
City. By my calculations, the whole transaction should take
about six months. Afterward I'll return to San Francisco. If
at that time you've changed your mind, I want you to ask me
to marry you and I'll do so immediately. Otherwise, I'll
know the answer is still no and never bring up the subject
again." He held out his hand. "Deal?"

As they shook on their bargain, Penelope prayed, *Please,
Lord. Please give me the wisdom to make the right decision.*
Then she pressed her free left hand into the folds of her skirt
and crossed her fingers.

Dare to Believe

❧

Sleep soft and safe, my darling one,
And seek tomorrow's dreams.
Laughter gay
Shall light your way
If you follow your heart.

—Penelope Parrish
"Song of Dreams"

Chapter 28

"What is it, Jake?" Hallie asked, looking up from wiping oatmeal from their one-year-old son, Teddy's, face. "Not bad news, I hope?"

Jake shook his head. "Seth is back in town. He's paying us a visit this afternoon."

Penelope didn't miss the way both Hallie and Jake glanced in her direction at the news, visibly gauging her reaction. Nor was she blind to their exchanged frowns when she merely smiled and continued tying a napkin over the elegant silk gown of the fashion doll her five-year-old niece, Ariel, was pretending to feed poached eggs.

In truth, Jake's announcement was no surprise to her. She'd seen the servants unloading Seth's distinctive scarlet and gold trunks from his equally distinctive black and gold carriage when she'd driven past his Rincon Hill mansion the previous morning.

Driving past the sixty-five room Italianate showpiece, their House of Dreams as they had dubbed it when he'd commissioned it built during their ill-fated engagement, had become part of her daily routine since returning to San Francisco. On mornings when the street was deserted, she'd pull her parasol-top basket phaeton to a stop in front of the house, pretending that it was her home and that Seth and Tommy awaited her arrival beneath its stylish mansard roof. She'd sit there lost in her daydreams until the clattering of another vehicle drew her back to her own hollow reality, at which point she'd resume her daily trek out to Laurel Hill Cemetery to lay fresh flowers on Tommy's grave.

Tommy. She smiled as she sat the now properly bibbed doll next to Ariel's plate. Hallie had been right. She now more often smiled than cried when she remembered her

son's gentle sweetness. Though she still felt an emptiness
when she thought of him, his memory was no longer unbearably painful. Even the sight of his bunny, which she had lovingly tucked away in a memory box along with his silver
rattle, his birthday gown, and other belongings that Seth had
so thoughtfully sent to San Francisco, no longer evoked terrible feelings of guilt and failure.

Her smile faltered a bit at the thought of Seth. True to
their bargain, he'd never once mentioned marriage or in any
way pressed the issue by hinting at his feelings in his unfail-
ingly amusing correspondence. And for that she was eter-
nally grateful.

But now the time had come for her to keep her end of
their bargain and answer his proposal, an answer she didn't
have despite months of contemplation.

It wasn't that she didn't love him. The way her heart
ached every time she looked at the photograph of them
perched atop the circus elephant told her she did, as did the
crushing loneliness she suffered every night as she lay
awake yearning to feel the satiny warmth of his body
wrapped around hers.

But was love enough to make their marriage work? Was
it enduring enough to weather the bouts of darkness that still
plagued her? Was it strong enough to withstand the attending bitterness? Could she look at Seth every day for the
rest of her life and not feel a constant renewal of the grief
that was just now starting to ease? Was she brave enough to
risk failing another person she loved? She had so many
questions she couldn't answer, so many fears she couldn't
assuage.

Curling a corner of the napkin on her lap between her
thumb and index fingers, she wondered for the millionth
time what to say to him. Perhaps if she explained her feelings and asked him for more time . . . ?

She heaved a frustrated sigh. Where was the use in that?
Even if he gave her the rest of their lives, she doubted she'd
ever be sure enough either way to decide.

"He'll be here at one," Jake added, his pointed tone piercing her meditation.

A wave of relief washed through Penelope. She'd promised to fill in for Alberta Filer at the Mission School for
Special Children this afternoon, and therefore wouldn't be

home when Seth called. That meant she'd have a reprieve from making a decision, at least for a few hours.

Slowly and with exacting deliberation, she retied the ribbons on one of the fashion doll's kid slippers, careful to avoid looking at Jake and Hallie as she said, "I'm afraid I'll have to miss his visit. I'm due at the school at eleven, and probably won't be back until after five. You will give him my best, won't you?"

"I thought Thursday was Alberta's day to teach the class hygiene and etiquette?" Hallie said with a frown in her voice.

Penelope made a show of straightening the lace trim on the doll's petticoat, feigning a nonchalance she didn't feel. "She does," she murmured, not lifting her gaze from her fussing. "But her husband is leaving for business back East today, and she wants to see him off. I promised that I'd help the children practice tying their shoes and buttoning their coats in her absence."

There was a beat of silence, in which she was sure Hallie and Jake exchanged troubled glances. Then Hallie sighed. "I see no reason for us to pretend that we don't know that it's you Seth really wants to see. He's going to be terribly disappointed when—" She was interrupted by a clattering racket, accompanied by a duet of childish shouts.

"Reed! Ross! You stop that this instant and eat your breakfast," Hallie commanded her four-year-old twins. For all their angelic beauty, the boys were regular imps.

With smiles sweet enough to beguile a saint, the twins plunged the spoons they'd been using as swords into their oatmeal and took an obedient bite, exchanging a look that anyone could see prophesied more mischief.

Silently blessing the boys for their interruption, Penelope wadded up her napkin and tossed it next to her untouched breakfast plate. Excusing herself, she headed for the door, anxious to retreat before Hallie resumed her lecture, thus making her feel more guilty about Seth than she already did. She was halfway across the room when her brother's voice stopped her.

"He loves you, Penelope, but he won't wait forever."

She nodded her bowed head without turning, then exited.

A half hour later, she was on her way to the cemetery. For the first time since returning to San Francisco, she circled, rather than cut through, Seth's Rincon Hill neighborhood, though the most convenient route from her brother's South Park home took her right past his mansion. With her luck of late, she'd probably run right into him, and she wasn't about to risk a chance meeting.

She arrived at the cemetery just as the morning fog lifted. Fringed with evergreen oaks and frosted with dew-kissed white lilac, the verdant dell where Tommy lay was like a little piece of heaven on earth. To the right lay a magnificent view of the city, this morning looking almost mythical in its shroud of white haze. To the left was the ocean, an endless, ever-changing study of blues and greens. Warblers, their throats swelled with shrill yet ecstatic song, serenaded her from the drooping boughs above.

Someone—Seth, she was certain—had laid an impressive bouquet of lilies, roses, and irises at the feet of Tommy's white marble angel monument, reminding her anew of her quandary. Tucking a pink rosebud next to the rabbit cradled in the angel's arms, she whispered, "Oh, Tommy. Whatever am I going to do? I love him so much that I can't imagine living without him. Yet, I'm afraid to marry him."

Torn by warring emotions, she sank to her knees before the angel and began to arrange the rest of her roses. As she covered the tiny grave with the flowers, softly singing a lullaby as she worked, a nearby bush began to shake. Out wandered a gray rabbit with three babies. While the mother and two of her offspring placidly nibbled at the grass several feet away, the third hopped bold as brass right up to the angel, its nose twitching frantically as it eyed Seth's flowers.

Penelope held stock-still, barely daring to breath for fear of scaring it away. How Tommy would have delighted in the baby bunny. She smiled then, sudden peace warming her soul as she watched the tiny animal sit up and steal a particularly tender-looking piece of greenery from the bouquet. No. Tommy *was* delighting in the rabbit. She could feel his joy as surely as if he sat on her lap chortling his pleasure. As Hallie had promised, he was very much alive within her.

She was still smiling when she arrived at the school, a smile that broadened as she greeted her class. Ranging from ages four to sixteen, her eleven students were the children no other school would accept and no governess would teach. They were children like Tommy: different, yet wonderful, each blessed with a capacity for love that was nothing short of miraculous. They had renewed her interest in life and given it meaning. They were her salvation. And she adored every last one of them.

Like the other days she spent with "her children," usually teaching them simple songs and reading them stories, this one flew by in a haze of satisfaction. Over and over again she guided clumsy, and in instances like Tommy's, twisted, fingers through the simple acts of buttoning and tying, giving hugs and praise for every effort, successful or not.

She was showing eight-year-old Hattie Lawrence how to direct the button through the hole for the ninth time when thirteen-year-old Emmett Lockwood let out a strangled laugh and began thrashing his hands in the air in frenzied excitement.

"Look, Miz Parr-sh," he chortled, gesturing at his correctly tied shoes and buttoned jacket with spastic jerks.

Penelope returned his gap-toothed smile as she admired his handiwork. "Well done, Emmett! Perfect!" she praised, as pleased as if he'd mastered the principles of algebra. Giving him a congratulatory hug, she pulled him up from the circle of children on the floor and stood him in the place of honor in the center.

Clapping to get the attention of the other students, she exclaimed, "Three cheers for Emmett! He's tied his shoe and buttoned his coat for the first time." She nodded at the boy, who looked ready to burst his properly anchored buttons in his pride as his classmates shouted, "Hip-hip-hooray!" as she'd taught them. "Emmett, dear," she whispered into his malformed ear, "why don't you bow like Miss Filer showed you last week?"

He did so, several times, more than making up for his lack of grace with his enthusiasm. When the applause died, she put her arm around his thin shoulders and announced, "As your reward, you get to choose what game we'll play for the rest of the day."

He grinned and shook his head. "No game. You sing."

The rest of the students bobbed their heads in agreement, several clapping and echoing, "Sing! Sing!"

She returned their eager smiles with one of pure pleasure. Of all the audiences she'd sung for, none had been more appreciative or given her more joy than did her children. "Then, a song it is," she agreed, sitting Indian-style on the floor, not caring that she crushed the crape trimming on her black mourning skirt.

After a moment of deliberation, she began to sing her "Song of Dreams," the first time since Tommy's death she'd sung it. As she sang, her voice soft and filled with tenderness, she saw a bit of Tommy in the delight beaming from every face before her. Truly at peace for the first time in months, she closed her eyes and poured her heart into the song. The children sat in perfect enchantment, not stirring or making a sound.

For several seconds after the last note faded away, there was complete silence. Then someone began to applaud. After a beat everyone else joined in, adding a chorus of "Hip-hip-hooray!"

When she opened her eyes to acknowledge their tribute, she found herself staring at a very fine pair of brown riding boots, which now occupied the previously empty space between Minnie Rinehart and Michael Maloy. Up she looked, past muscular thighs encased in snug gold, olive, and cream checked trousers, up over a gold Chinese silk waistcoat half-covered by a dark olive jacket dandified with cream braid binding. Up right into a pair of sparkling hazel eyes.

"Seth," she exclaimed, holding out her hand to him as she rose to her feet. "It's wonderful to see you." And it was. More wonderful than she'd ever have believed.

As he swept off his hat, his mouth crooking into a grin as he stepped into the circle of children and took her outstretched hand in his, she was struck by the purity of her joy. She'd expected to feel pain at the sight of him, to be stricken anew with the crippling sorrow she'd suffered during the terrible weeks following Tommy's death. But she felt only gladness.

"I know I shouldn't have disturbed your class, but I couldn't wait to see you," he murmured, bending down to kiss her palm.

She smiled at the head bowed over her hand, a head now covered with thick, gloriously shiny hair. It was wavier than she remembered, darker, too, in a shade closer to the deep burnished gold of her great-great-grandmother's wedding bracelet than its previous sun-kissed honey. It was the most beautiful hair she'd ever seen, and she said as much.

He chuckled as he straightened up. "I admit it is looking better, though it does seem odd to see myself looking so conventional." He chuckled again. "Oh, well. At least I no longer scare myself when I look in the mirror."

"Your hair might be cut in a proper, gentlemanly style now, but you'll never be conventional," she teased.

His gaze met hers, his eyes simmering with the topaz heat that had haunted her dreams of late. "You used to say that you loved my unconventionality," he said, his words a sultry whisper.

She wanted to tell him that she still did, that she loved not just his wild spirit but every untamed inch of him. Yet she couldn't bring herself to say the words. She didn't want to give him hope for a future she was still uncertain existed for them.

Hating herself for her cowardice, she looked away and asked, "Speaking of unconventional, how is Lisbet? Her last letter mentioned something about you talking your mother into letting her take a detective correspondence course she saw advertised in the *Police Gazette*."

"She's doing fine, as are her course studies. I don't doubt that she'll make a fine sleuthhound someday." The teasing warmth had fled his voice, leaving it as coolly polite as that of a stranger extending careful, well-bred courtesy at a social event.

"And your mother?" she asked, stealing a glance at him through her eyelashes. Always the master of the moment, he was still smiling. In truth, if she hadn't known him as well as she did, she'd never have guessed how deeply her subtle rejection had cut him. Knowing him as she did, however, she had only to look into his expressive eyes to see how truly devastated he was. The sight of his hurt deepened her loathing for her fears.

"Mother is extremely busy with the newly merged Queen City and Vanderlyn breweries, and loving every moment of her frantic life," he reported, releasing her hand to slip his own into his coat pocket. "Right now we're in the process of converting the Shakespeare into a respectable beer garden, where men can take their wives and sweethearts dancing." He chuckled dryly. "You should have seen the look on Monty's face when I told him that he'd be serving ice cream and lemonade at his bar."

Penelope managed a faint smile as she pictured the lively bartender's indignation. "Effie mentioned your plans in her last letter. She also said that you've asked her and Bert to perform skits during band intermissions. Neither of the actors had anyplace to go after the company disbanded, and they're both terribly grateful to you for your offer."

He shrugged. "It's the least I could do after the way they came forward to testify against Adele on your behalf."

"Adele." She sighed. She was still haunted by nightmares about the awful woman. "Sam and Minerva wrote that she's been transferred to Boston to stand trial for three counts of murder and twenty-two counts of extortion. Apparently she's blackmailed just about every family on Beacon Hill over the course of the last twenty years, and society is all in a froth to see her brought to justice."

She reached out and gave his arm a warm squeeze. "They were also singing your praises. Between the political endorsements you secured and the money you contributed to their son's campaign, Alexander Skolfield is expected to be the next mayor of Boston."

"Sir?" piped up a childish voice. Penelope glanced from Seth's handsome face to see Emmett tugging at his sleeve.

Seth smiled warmly at the boy. "Yes, young man?"

"See!" He pointed excitedly at his coat and shoes.

At Seth's questioning glance, Penelope explained, "Emmett buttoned his coat and tied his shoes for the first time today. We're all extremely proud of him."

"Did he indeed?" Seth intoned, his face serious as he bent down to examine the boy's handiwork. After a moment of intense scrutiny, he praised, "Fine job, Emmett. Well done! I couldn't have done better myself." The boy practically glowed with pride, especially when Seth offered him his hand, which he shook just the way Alberta Filer had taught him.

"Who's him?" asked seven-year-old Minnie, crawling forward to pull at Penelope's hem while staring shyly up at Seth.

Penelope gently hoisted the girl's stunted form to her feet and introduced her to Seth. To Minnie's wide-eyed delight, he bowed and kissed her hand while addressing her with the same courtly charm he often used to ease the jitters of overly shy debutantes. Like those debutantes, Minnie was immediately put at ease. So was the rest of the class.

One by one those children who were able came forward, seeking an introduction. Seth treated each child as if he or she were a visiting member of the peerage, shaking or kissing their hand, and taking the time to ask each a simple, but personal question. He then went to the students who were too physically impaired to come forward and included them in the introductions.

By the time he was finished, every person in the room was completely taken with him. Especially Penelope. Seeing him chattering with and obviously enjoying the children whom most society men would barely look at, much less acknowledge, made her realize anew just how truly special he was.

As he rose from kneeling next to Herbert Brigman's caned wheelchair, where he had been admiring the boy's prized wooden horse, he lauded, "You've got wonderful students, Miss Parrish. You should be very proud of them."

She didn't miss the way the children's faces lit up with pride at his acclaim. Smiling at her own pride in them, she said, "You're welcome to visit us anytime you like. Perhaps you'll come someday and spend time with the boys. Our children learn mostly by example, and our boys have had far too few male examples to follow. Especially excellent ones like yourself."

One corner of Seth's mouth turned up in a wry half smile. "An excellent example, am I?" He slipped his hand back into his pocket and appeared to fidget with something. "I'd be glad to help if I were staying in town, but I've decided to leave for Denver first thing in the morning."

Her heart gave a painful lurch at the news. "So soon? But you just got here."

He shrugged. "I see no reason to stay any longer. Your brother has offered to handle my affairs here, and at this point there's nothing more to keep me."

"But what of ... your house?" She almost blurted out "our House of Dreams," but stopped herself in time. It wasn't "our" house, and it never would be if she didn't dare to believe in their love and ask him to marry her before morning.

The hand in his pocket gave a sharp jerk. "I'm thinking of selling it. I see now that it will never be the home I dreamed of." He looked about to add something else when Marcella Stewart, who taught the girls basic homemaking skills on Friday mornings, came through the door, burdened by two oversize baskets.

"Penelope!" she exclaimed, her dark eyes lighting up with

pleasure at the sight of the other woman. "I didn't expect to see you here today. Where's Alberta?"

As much as Penelope adored Marcella, she could have strangled her for her poor timing. Pasting on a strained smile, she replied. "Alberta had to see her husband off on business this afternoon, and I'm filling in for her. What brings you here?"

Marcella set the baskets by the door, straightening her stylish cherry Gypsy bonnet as she cast Seth an appreciative look. "Mr. Bryerton over at the Delaware House was kind enough to lend me china, silver, and linen for my table-setting lessons tomorrow. I was on my way home from picking it up and saw no reason not to drop it off now." She gave Seth a dazzling smile as she approached him. "You're Mr. Tyler, aren't you? My brother, Freddy Stewart, introduced us at Davinia and Cyrus King's wedding last year."

"Formerly Tyler, now Vanderlyn, and yes, I do remember you, Miss Stewart," Seth replied, taking her proferred hand.

"You used to be Seth Tyler, but are now Seth Vanderlyn?" Marcella quizzed, visibly confused. "How very odd!" She looked at him expectantly, obviously waiting for him to elaborate.

He shrugged one shoulder and gave her a charming smile. "Miss Parrish will have to fill you in on the details. I haven't the time now. I'm leaving town tomorrow morning and still have business to complete. So if you ladies will excuse me?" He kissed Marcella's hand, then turned to Penelope.

"Seth," she whispered brokenly, her regretful gaze seeking his as he lifted her limp hand from her side. "I wish I could believe ... I want to, but ..." She shook her head helplessly.

"Don't," he murmured. "I promised not to press you to marry me, and that promise included your not having to explain should you decide that your answer is no. However, if it eases your mind any, please know that I don't hate you for your refusal and that you may always count me among your friends." His solemn face softened with tenderness as he reached up and cupped her cheek in his palm. "Be happy, sweet princess. That's all I ask of you. Just be happy." With that he kissed her forehead, then turned and headed for the door.

Every fiber of her being cried out in agonized protest as

she watched her dream walk away. And Seth Vanderlyn was her dream; she knew that beyond all doubt. He was her every hope, her desire, her heart and soul. He was her everything. Feeling that way, how could she stand there and simply let him go, when all she had to do to keep him by her side was utter two little words? Why was she so afraid to say them?

True. She knew there would be moments when their lives would be shadowed by their past sorrow. But wouldn't that sorrow be easier to bear if it were shared? And who better to share it with than Seth? Only he truly understood her grief; only he loved her enough to be her light and lead her from her darkness.

Marcella began to chatter on about something, but Penelope was deaf to her words, her heart and mind racing as she watched Seth pause at the door to shake hands with Emmett again, who'd tagged after him like an affectionate puppy.

As for her fear of being reminded of her guilt and failure every time she looked at him . . . ? If that were the case, surely she'd have felt at least a tinge of those emotions in those first few moments when she'd looked up and met his gaze? But she hadn't. All she'd experienced was exquisite pleasure at seeing him again.

So what was she afraid of?

What indeed?

"Seth," she cried so breathlessly that she was certain he hadn't heard her. To her surprise, he glanced up from Emmett.

"I—" She took a couple of steps forward, her mouth working soundlessly as she tried to shove the words past the ball of emotion swelling in her throat.

He straightened up and stuck his hand back into his pocket, his eyes naked with longing as his gaze met hers from across the room. "Yes, Penelope?"

"I . . . I . . . do believe," she finally managed to choke out. "Oh, Seth! I love you!" She rushed across the room, clutched his hand between both of hers, and begged, "Marry me!"

"Do you believe enough to marry me right now? At this very moment?" he asked, pulling her into his embrace.

She twined her arms around his neck to guide his lips down to hers. "I'd marry you this very second if we had a preacher!" she declared as he claimed his mouth with hers.

Thoroughly and with a hunger that left no doubt as to his love for her, he returned her kiss. So lost were they in their passion, that they probably would have continued on like that for a long while had it not been for the giggling chorus of "Hip-hip-hooray! Hip-hip-hooray!" rising around them.

Pulling his lips from hers, Seth grinned first at the cheering children, then at the smiling Marcella, who was leading them in their merriment.

"I hope you don't mind taking the class for the rest of the day, Miss Stewart," he hollered over the revelry. "I intend to marry Miss Parrish before she has a chance to change her mind."

With that announcement, he jammed his hat on his head and held out his arm to Penelope. "If we hurry, we can catch Judge Dorner and secure a special license before he leaves his chambers. We'll be married this very evening, if you don't mind."

"Mind? I insist!" As she looped her arm through his, anxious to begin her life as Mrs. Seth Vanderlyn, her gaze was arrested by something caught on the cuff button of his jacket.

It was a ribbon, a frayed and rumpled black one.

"My lucky ribbon!" she exclaimed, plucking it from his cuff to stare at it in delighted wonder. "Wherever did you find it?"

His smile broadened. "It was in the pocket of my evening jacket. I've been carrying it with me for months now, rubbing it with my crossed fingers, wishing upon my lucky star, and begging lady luck for another chance to love you."

"I told you it was lucky where we were concerned," she declared with a giggle, standing on her tiptoes to plant another kiss on his curved lips. "All we had to do was believe."

Author's Note

Since I couldn't resist the drama of having Penelope sing *Der Fliegende Holländer (The Flying Dutchman)* to Seth, her cursed Dutchman, I took the liberty of manipulating opera history a bit. Though the opera made its debut in Dresden on January 2, 1843, it wasn't performed in this country until over thirty years later. The first American performance took place at the Philadelphia Academy of Music on November 8, 1876, with Eugenia Pappenhiem singing the role of Senta.

█ TOPAZ

SIMMERING DESIRES

☐ **HARVEST OF DREAMS by Jaroldeen Edwards.** A magnificent saga of family threatened both from within and without—and of the love and pride, strength and honor, that would make the difference between tragedy and triumph.
(404742—$4.99)

☐ **BEDEVILED by Bronwyn Williams.** Flame-haired Annie O'Neal and fiercely proud T'maho Hamilton, who chose the path of his Indian forebears rather than his white father, were as different as night and day. T'maho taught Annie the power of desire, and she showed him the meaning of love. But their fire was doused by the wealthy and iron-willed Jackson Snell, who demanded Annie be his bride. Now Annie was torn between the man she loved and the man it was folly to fight.
(404564—$4.99)

☐ **WIND SONG by Margaret Brownley.** When a feisty, red-haired schoolmarm arrives in Colton, Kansas and finds the town burned to the ground, she is forced to live with widower Luke Taylor and his young son, Matthew. Not only is she stealing Matthew's heart, but she is also igniting a desire as dangerous as love in his father's heart.
(405269—$4.99)

☐ **BECAUSE YOU'RE MINE by Nan Ryan.** Golden-haired Sabella Rios vowed she would seduce the handsome Burt Burnett into marrying her and become mistress of the Lindo Vista ranch, which was rightfully hers. Sabella succeeded beyond her dreams, but there was one thing she had not counted on. In Burt's caressing arms, in his bed, her cold calculations turned into flames of passion as she fell deeply in love with this man, this enemy of her family. (405951—$5.50)

*Prices slightly higher in Canada

Buy them at your local bookstore or use this convenient coupon for ordering.

PENGUIN USA
P.O. Box 999 — Dept. #17109
Bergenfield, New Jersey 07621

Please send me the books I have checked above.
I am enclosing $_____ (please add $2.00 to cover postage and handling). Send check or money order (no cash or C.O.D.'s) or charge by Mastercard or VISA (with a $15.00 minimum). Prices and numbers are subject to change without notice.

Card #_____ Exp. Date _____
Signature_____
Name_____
Address_____
City _____ State _____ Zip Code _____

For faster service when ordering by credit card call 1-800-253-6476
Allow a minimum of 4-6 weeks for delivery. This offer is subject to change without notice.

WE NEED YOUR HELP
To continue to bring you quality romance
that meets your personal expectations,
we at TOPAZ books want to hear from you.
Help us by filling out this questionnaire, and in exchange
we will give you a **free gift** as a token of our gratitude.

- Is this the first TOPAZ book you've purchased? (circle one)

    YES   NO

    The title and author of this book is: _____

- If this was not the first TOPAZ book you've purchased, how many have you bought in the past year?

    a: 0 - 5   b 6 - 10   c: more than 10   d: more than 20

- How many romances in total did you buy in the past year?

    a: 0 - 5   b: 6 - 10   c: more than 10   d: more than 20 ____

- How would you rate your overall satisfaction with this book?

    a: Excellent   b: Good   c: Fair   d: Poor

- What was the main reason you bought this book?

    a: It is a TOPAZ novel, and I know that TOPAZ stands
       for quality romance fiction
    b: I liked the cover
    c: The story-line intrigued me
    d: I love this author
    e: I really liked the setting
    f: I love the cover models
    g: Other: _____

- Where did you buy this TOPAZ novel?

    a: Bookstore   b: Airport   c: Warehouse Club
    d: Department Store   e: Supermarket   f: Drugstore
    g: Other: _____

- Did you pay the full cover price for this TOPAZ novel? (circle one)

    YES   NO

    If you did not, what price did you pay? _____

- Who are your favorite TOPAZ authors? (Please list)

- How did you first hear about TOPAZ books?

    a: I saw the books in a bookstore
    b: I saw the TOPAZ Man on TV or at a signing
    c: A friend told me about TOPAZ
    d: I saw an advertisement in _____ magazine
    e: Other: _____

- What type of romance do you generally prefer?

    a: Historical   b: Contemporary
    c: Romantic Suspense   d: Paranormal (time travel,
       futuristic, vampires, ghosts, warlocks, etc.)
    d: Regency   e: Other: _____

- What historical settings do you prefer?

    a: England   b: Regency England   c: Scotland
    e: Ireland   f: America   g: Western Americana
    h: American Indian   i: Other: _____

- What type of story do you prefer?
  - a: Very sexy
  - b: Sweet, less explicit
  - c: Light and humorous
  - d: More emotionally intense
  - e: Dealing with darker issues
  - f: Other

- What kind of covers do you prefer?
  - a: Illustrating both hero and heroine
  - b: Hero alone
  - c: No people (art only)
  - d: Other_____

- What other genres do you like to read (circle all that apply)

  Mystery   Medical Thrillers   Science Fiction
  Suspense   Fantasy   Self-help
  Classics   General Fiction   Legal Thrillers
  Historical Fiction

- Who is your favorite author, and why?_____
  _____

- What magazines do you like to read? (circle all that apply)
  - a: *People*
  - b: *Time/Newsweek*
  - c: *Entertainment Weekly*
  - d: *Romantic Times*
  - e: *Star*
  - f: *National Enquirer*
  - g: *Cosmopolitan*
  - h: *Woman's Day*
  - i: *Ladies' Home Journal*
  - j: *Redbook*
  - k: Other:_____

- In which region of the United States do you reside?
  - a: Northeast
  - b: Midatlantic
  - c: South
  - d: Midwest
  - e: Mountain
  - f: Southwest
  - g: Pacific Coast

- What is your age group/sex?   a: Female   b: Male
  - a: under 18
  - b: 19-25
  - c: 26-30
  - d: 31-35
  - e: 36-40
  - f: 41-45
  - g: 46-50
  - h: 51-55
  - i: 56-60
  - j: Over 60

- What is your marital status?
  - a: Married
  - b: Single
  - c: No longer married

- What is your current level of education?
  - a: High school
  - b: College Degree
  - c: Graduate Degree
  - d: Other:_____

- Do you receive the TOPAZ *Romantic Liaisons* newsletter, a quarterly newsletter with the latest information on Topaz books and authors?

  YES   NO

  If not, would you like to?   YES   NO

  Fill in the address where you would like your free gift to be sent:

  Name: _____

  Address: _____

  City:_____ Zip Code: _____

  You should receive your free gift in 6 to 8 weeks.
  Please send the completed survey to:

Penguin USA•Mass Market
Dept. TS
375 Hudson St.
New York, NY 10014